A DISTANT EPISODE

THE SELECTED STORIES

BOOKS BY PAUL BOWLES

NOVELS

The Sheltering Sky

Let It Come Down

The Spider's House

Up Above the World

NOVELLA

Too Far from Home

SHORT STORIES

The Delicate Prey

*A Hundred Camels in the
    Courtyard*

The Time of Friendship

*Pages from Cold Point and
    Other Stories*

*Things Gone and Things
    Still Here*

A Distant Episode

Midnight Mass and Other Stories

Call at Corazón and Other Stories

Collected Stories, 1939–1976

Unwelcome Words

A Thousand Days for Mokhtar

AUTOBIOGRAPHY

Without Stopping

Days: A Tangier Diary

LETTERS

In Touch: The Letters of Paul Bowles
    (edited by Jeffrey Miller)

POETRY

Two Poems

Scenes

The Thicket of Spring

*Next to Nothing: Collected Poems,
    1926–1977*

NONFICTION, TRAVEL, ESSAYS, MISCELLANEOUS

Yallah! (written by Paul Bowles,
    photographs by Peter W.
    Haeberlinb)

*Their Heads Are Green and Their
    Hands Are Blue*

Points in Time

Paul Bowles: Photographs
    (edited by Simon Bischoff)

A
DISTANT
EPISODE

THE SELECTED STORIES

——PAUL——
BOWLES

ecco

An Imprint of HarperCollinsPublishers

Grateful acknowledgment is made to the following sources for permission to reprint certain of the stories contained herein: Black Sparrow Press, Tombouctou Books, and *The Threepenny Review*.

A paperback edition of this book was published in 1988 by Ecco Press.

HarperCollins books may be purchased for educational, business, or sales promotional use. For information, please e-mail the Special Markets Department at SPsales@harpercollins.com.

First Harper Perennial edition published 2006.

Designed by Kingsley Parker

The Library of Congress has catalogued the Ecco Press paperback edition as follows:
Bowles, Paul.
   A distant episode : the selected stories / Paul Bowles.— 1st ed.
   p. cm.
I. Title.
PS3552.0874D57   1988   813'.54—dc19   88-24553

ISBN 0-88001-501-2

ISBN-10: 0-06-113738-3 (pbk.)
ISBN-13: 978-0-06-113738-9 (pbk.)

23 24 25 26 27 LBC 13 12 11 10 9

CONTENTS

PREFACE

The stories in this volume were written during a period which covers approximately forty years. Many are the result of nostalgia for places left behind; the composition of these began with an evocation of the *ambiance* of the locale, a general atmosphere out of which the protagonists were born. It seems a practical procedure to let the place determine the characters who will inhabit it.

Often the settings used are precise descriptions of actual places: "At Paso Rojo" on a ranch in Guanacaste, Costa Rica, "The Time of Friendship" at a hotel which existed during colonial times in Taghit, Algeria, and "He of the Assembly" is the streets of the Medina of Marrakech. Characters, being determined by the backdrop, are of necessity entirely improvised, as is the action in which they become involved. For me the pleasure of writing stories, as opposed to novels, lies in the freedom to allow protagonists to invent their own personalities as they emerge from the landscape.

As we know, creativity is an eruption of the unconscious. Exposed to the light of reason, this subterranean material ordinarily discovers the uses to which it will be put, and the form it will assume. The author, aware of what he is doing, gives it an argument and a voice. The end product is man-made. Most of the tales in the collection adhere to this formula.

There is, however, another way of treating this basic element, which is to use it "raw," without questioning its sense, allowing it to cool and harden into its own natural shape. Here the author remains ignorant of what he has written, and is not likely to be able to assign a "meaning" to it, inasmuch as that consideration did not occur to him during its composition. "Tapiama" is an example of this approach.

—PAUL BOWLES
Tangier, Morocco
January, 1989

A DISTANT EPISODE

THE SELECTED STORIES

A DISTANT EPISODE

The September sunsets were at their reddest the week the Professor decided to visit Aïn Tadouirt, which is in the warm country. He came down out of the high, flat region in the evening by bus, with two small overnight bags full of maps, sun lotions and medicines. Ten years ago he had been in the village for three days; long enough, however, to establish a fairly firm friendship with a café keeper, who had written him several times during the first year after his visit, if never since. "Hassan Ramani," the Professor said over and over, as the bus bumped downward through ever warmer layers of air. Now facing the flaming sky in the west, and now facing the sharp mountains, the car followed the dusty trail down the canyons into air which began to smell of other things besides the endless ozone of the heights: orange blossoms, pepper, sun-baked excrement, burning olive oil, rotten fruit. He closed his eyes happily and lived for an instant in a purely olfactory world. The distant past returned— what part of it, he could not decide.

The chauffeur, whose seat the Professor shared, spoke to him without taking his eyes from the road. *"Vous êtes géologue?"*

"A geologist? Ah, no! I'm a linguist."

"There are no languages here. Only dialects."

"Exactly. I'm making a survey of variations on Maghrebi."

The chauffeur was scornful. "Keep on going south," he said. "You'll find some languages you never heard of before."

As they drove through the town gate, the usual swarm of urchins rose up out of the dust and ran screaming beside the bus. The Professor folded his dark glasses, put them in his pocket; and as soon as the vehicle had

1

come to a standstill he jumped out, pushing his way through the indignant boys who clutched at his luggage in vain, and walked quickly into the Grand Hotel Saharien. Out of its eight rooms there were two available— one facing the market and the other, a smaller and cheaper one, giving onto a tiny yard full of refuse and barrels, where two gazelles wandered about. He took the smaller room, and pouring the entire pitcher of water into the tin basin, began to wash the grit from his face and ears. The afterglow was nearly gone from the sky, and the pinkness in objects was disappearing, almost as he watched. He lit the carbide lamp and winced at its odor.

After dinner the Professor walked slowly through the streets to Hassan Ramani's café, whose back room hung hazardously out above the river. The entrance was very low, and he had to bend down slightly to get in. A man was tending the fire. There was one guest sipping tea. The *qaouaji* tried to make him take a seat at the other table in the front room, but the Professor walked airily ahead into the back room and sat down. The moon was shining through the reed latticework and there was not a sound outside but the occasional distant bark of a dog. He changed tables so he could see the river. It was dry, but there was a pool here and there that reflected the bright night sky. The *qaouaji* came in and wiped off the table.

"Does this café still belong to Hassan Ramani?" he asked him in the Maghrebi he had taken four years to learn.

The man replied in bad French: "He is deceased."

"Deceased?" repeated the Professor, without noticing the absurdity of the word. "Really? When?"

"I don't know," said the *qaouaji*. "One tea?"

"Yes. But I don't understand . . ."

The man was already out of the room, fanning the fire. The Professor sat still, feeling lonely, and arguing with himself that to do so was ridiculous. Soon the *qaouaji* returned with the tea. He paid him and gave him an enormous tip, for which he received a grave bow.

"Tell me," he said, as the other started away. "Can one still get those little boxes made from camel udders?"

The man looked angry. "Sometimes the Reguibat bring in those things. We do not buy them here." Then insolently, in Arabic: "And why a camel-udder box?"

"Because I like them," retorted the Professor. And then because he was feeling a little exalted, he added, "I like them so much I want to make a collection of them, and I will pay you ten francs for every one you can get me."

"*Khamstache,*" said the *qaouaji,* opening his left hand rapidly three times in succession.

"Never. Ten."

"Not possible. But wait until later and come with me. You can give me what you like. And you will get camel-udder boxes if there are any."

He went out into the front room, leaving the Professor to drink his tea and listen to the growing chorus of dogs that barked and howled as the moon rose higher into the sky. A group of customers came into the front room and sat talking for an hour or so. When they had left, the *qaouaji* put out the fire and stood in the doorway putting on his burnoose. "Come," he said.

Outside in the street there was very little movement. The booths were all closed and the only light came from the moon. An occasional pedestrian passed, and grunted a brief greeting to the *qaouaji.*

"Everyone knows you," said the Professor, to cut the silence between them.

"Yes."

"I wish everyone knew me," said the Professor, before he realized how infantile such a remark must sound.

"*No* one knows you," said his companion gruffly.

They had come to the other side of the town, on the promontory above the desert, and through a great rift in the wall the Professor saw the white endlessness, broken in the foreground by dark spots of oasis. They walked through the opening and followed a winding road between rocks, downward toward the nearest small forest of palms. The Professor thought: "He may cut my throat. But his café—he would surely be found out."

"Is it far?" he asked, casually.

"Are you tired?" countered the *qaouaji.*

"They are expecting me back at the Hotel Saharien," he lied.

"You can't be there and here," said the *qaouaji.*

The Professor laughed. He wondered if it sounded uneasy to the other.

"Have you owned Ramani's café long?"

"I work there for a friend." The reply made the Professor more unhappy than he had imagined it would.

"Oh. Will you work tomorrow?"

"That is impossible to say."

The Professor stumbled on a stone, and fell, scraping his hand. The *qaouaji* said: "Be careful."

The sweet black odor of rotten meat hung in the air suddenly.

"Agh!" said the Professor, choking. "What is it?"

The *qaouaji* had covered his face with his burnoose and did not answer. Soon the stench had been left behind. They were on flat ground. Ahead the path was bordered on each side by a high mud wall. There was no breeze and the palms were quite still, but behind the walls was the sound of running water. Also, the odor of human excrement was almost constant as they walked between the walls.

The Professor waited until he thought it seemed logical for him to ask with a certain degree of annoyance: "But where are we going?"

"Soon," said the guide, pausing to gather some stones in the ditch.

"Pick up some stones," he advised. "Here are bad dogs."

"Where?" asked the Professor, but he stooped and got three large ones with pointed edges.

They continued very quietly. The walls came to an end and the bright desert lay ahead. Nearby was a ruined marabout, with its tiny dome only half standing, and the front wall entirely destroyed. Behind it were clumps of stunted, useless palms. A dog came running crazily toward them on three legs. Not until it got quite close did the Professor hear its steady low growl. The *qaouaji* let fly a large stone at it, striking it square in the muzzle. There was a strange snapping of jaws and the dog ran sideways in another direction, falling blindly against rocks and scrambling haphazardly about like an injured insect.

Turning off the road, they walked across the earth strewn with sharp stones, past the little ruin, through the trees, until they came to a place where the ground dropped abruptly away in front of them.

"It looks like a quarry," said the Professor, resorting to French for the word "quarry," whose Arabic equivalent he could not call to mind at the moment. The *qaouaji* did not answer. Instead he stood still and turned his head, as if listening. And indeed, from somewhere down below, but very far below, came the faint sound of a low flute. The *qaouaji* nodded his head slowly several times. Then he said: "The path begins here. You can see it well all the way. The rock is white and the moon is strong.

So you can see well. I am going back now and sleep. It is late. You can give me what you like."

Standing there at the edge of the abyss which at each moment looked deeper, with the dark face of the *qaouaji* framed in its moonlit burnoose close to his own face, the Professor asked himself exactly what he felt. Indignation, curiosity, fear, perhaps, but most of all relief and the hope that this was not a trick, the hope that the *qaouaji* would really leave him alone and turn back without him.

He stepped back a little from the edge, and fumbled in his pocket for a loose note, because he did not want to show his wallet. Fortunately there was a fifty-franc bill there, which he took out and handed to the man. He knew the *qaouaji* was pleased, and so he paid no attention when he heard him saying: "It is not enough. I have to walk a long way home and there are dogs. . . ."

"Thank you and good-night," said the Professor, sitting down with his legs drawn up under him, and lighting a cigarette. He felt almost happy.

"Give me only one cigarette," pleaded the man.

"Of course," he said, a bit curtly, and he held up the pack.

The *qaouaji* squatted close beside him. His face was not pleasant to see. "What is it?" thought the Professor, terrified again, as he held out his lighted cigarette toward him.

The man's eyes were almost closed. It was the most obvious registering of concentrated scheming the Professor had ever seen. When the second cigarette was burning, he ventured to say to the still-squatting Arab: "What are you thinking about?"

The other drew on his cigarette deliberately, and seemed about to speak. Then his expression changed to one of satisfaction, but he did not speak. A cool wind had risen in the air, and the Professor shivered. The sound of the flute came up from the depths below at intervals, sometimes mingled with the scraping of nearby palm fronds one against the other. "These people are not primitives," the Professor found himself saying in his mind.

"Good," said the *qaouaji*, rising slowly. "Keep your money. Fifty francs is enough. It is an honor." Then he went back into French: "*Ti n'as qu'à discendre, to' droit.*" He spat, chuckled (or was the Professor hysterical?), and strode away quickly.

5

The Professor was in a state of nerves. He lit another cigarette, and found his lips moving automatically. They were saying: "Is this a situation or a predicament? This is ridiculous." He sat very still for several minutes, waiting for a sense of reality to come to him. He stretched out on the hard, cold ground and looked up at the moon. It was almost like looking straight at the sun. If he shifted his gaze a little at a time, he could make a string of weaker moons across the sky. "Incredible," he whispered. Then he sat up quickly and looked about. There was no guarantee that the *qaouaji* really had gone back to town. He got to his feet and looked over the edge of the precipice. In the moonlight the bottom seemed miles away. And there was nothing to give it scale; not a tree, not a house, not a person. . . . He listened for the flute, and heard only the wind going by his ears. A sudden violent desire to run back to the road seized him, and he turned and looked in the direction the *qaouaji* had taken. At the same time he felt softly of his wallet in his breast pocket. Then he spat over the edge of the cliff. Then he made water over it, and listened intently, like a child. This gave him the impetus to start down the path into the abyss. Curiously enough, he was not dizzy. But prudently he kept from peering to his right, over the edge. It was a steady and steep downward climb. The monotony of it put him into a frame of mind not unlike that which had been induced by the bus ride. He was murmuring "Hassan Ramani" again, repeatedly and in rhythm. He stopped, furious with himself for the sinister overtones the name now suggested to him. He decided he was exhausted from the trip. "And the walk," he added.

He was now well down the gigantic cliff, but the moon, being directly overhead, gave as much light as ever. Only the wind was left behind, above, to wander among the trees, to blow through the dusty streets of Aïn Tadouirt, into the hall of the Grand Hotel Saharien, and under the door of his little room.

It occurred to him that he ought to ask himself why he was doing this irrational thing, but he was intelligent enough to know that since he was doing it, it was not so important to probe for explanations at that moment.

Suddenly the earth was flat beneath his feet. He had reached the bottom sooner than he had expected. He stepped ahead distrustfully still, as if he expected another treacherous drop. It was so hard to know in this uniform, dim brightness. Before he knew what had happened the dog was

6

upon him, a heavy mass of fur trying to push him backward, a sharp nail rubbing down his chest, a straining of muscles against him to get the teeth into his neck. The Professor thought: "I refuse to die this way." The dog fell back; it looked like an Eskimo dog. As it sprang again, he called out, very loud: "Ay!" It fell against him, there was a confusion of sensations and a pain somewhere. There was also the sound of voices very near to him, and he could not understand what they were saying. Something cold and metallic was pushed brutally against his spine as the dog still hung for a second by his teeth from a mass of clothing and perhaps flesh. The Professor knew it was a gun, and he raised his hands, shouting in Maghrebi: "Take away the dog!" But the gun merely pushed him forward, and since the dog, once it was back on the ground, did not leap again, he took a step ahead. The gun kept pushing; he kept taking steps. Again he heard voices, but the person directly behind him said nothing. People seemed to be running about; it sounded that way, at least. For his eyes, he discovered, were still shut tight against the dog's attack. He opened them. A group of men was advancing toward him. They were dressed in the black clothes of the Reguibat. "The Reguiba is a cloud across the face of the sun." "When the Reguiba appears the righteous man turns away." In how many shops and marketplaces he had heard these maxims uttered banteringly among friends. Never to a Reguiba, to be sure, for these men do not frequent towns. They send a representative in disguise, to arrange with shady elements there for the disposal of captured goods. "An opportunity," he thought quickly, "of testing the accuracy of such statements." He did not doubt for a moment that the adventure would prove to be a kind of warning against such foolishness on his part—a warning which in retrospect would be half sinister, half farcical.

Two snarling dogs came running from behind the oncoming men and threw themselves at his legs. He was scandalized to note that no one paid any attention to this breach of etiquette. The gun pushed him harder as he tried to sidestep the animals' noisy assault. Again he cried: "The dogs! Take them away!" The gun shoved him forward with great force and he fell, almost at the feet of the crowd of men facing him. The dogs were wrenching at his hands and arms. A boot kicked them aside, yelping, and then with increased vigor it kicked the Professor in the hip. Then came a chorus of kicks from different sides, and he was rolled violently about on the earth for a while. During this time he was conscious of hands reaching into his pockets and removing everything from them. He tried to say: "You have all my money; stop kicking me!" But his bruised facial muscles would not work; he felt himself pouting, and that was all. Someone dealt him a terrific blow on the head, and he thought: "Now at least I shall lose consciousness, thank Heaven." Still he went on being aware of the guttural voices he could not understand, and of being bound tightly about the ankles and chest. Then there was black silence that opened like a wound from time to time, to let in the soft, deep notes of the flute playing the same succession of notes again and again. Suddenly he felt excruciating pain everywhere—pain and cold. "So I have been unconscious, after all," he thought. In spite of that, the present seemed only like a direct continuation of what had gone before.

It was growing faintly light. There were camels near where he was lying; he could hear their gurgling and their heavy breathing. He could not bring himself to attempt opening his eyes, just in case it should turn out to be impossible. However, when he heard someone approaching, he found that he had no difficulty in seeing.

The man looked at him dispassionately in the gray morning light. With one hand he pinched together the Professor's nostrils. When the Professor opened his mouth to breathe, the man swiftly seized his tongue and pulled on it with all his might. The Professor was gagging and catching his breath; he did not see what was happening. He could not distinguish the pain of the brutal yanking from that of the sharp knife. Then there was an endless choking and spitting that went on automatically, as though he were scarcely a part of it. The word "operation" kept going through his mind; it calmed his terror somewhat as he sank back into darkness.

The caravan left sometime toward mid-morning. The Professor, not unconscious, but in a state of utter stupor, still gagging and drooling blood, was dumped doubled-up into a sack and tied at one side of a camel. The lower end of the enormous amphitheatre contained a natural gate in the rocks. The camels, swift *mehara*, were lightly laden on this trip. They passed through single file, and slowly mounted the gentle slope that led up into the beginning of the desert. That night, at a stop behind some low hills, the men took him out, still in a state which permitted no thought, and over the dusty rags that remained of his clothing they fastened a series of curious belts made of the bottoms of tin cans strung together. One after another of these bright girdles was wired about his torso, his arms and legs, even across his face, until he was entirely within a suit of armor that covered him with its circular metal scales. There was a good deal of merriment during this decking-out of the Professor. One man brought out a flute and a younger one did a not ungraceful caricature of an Ouled Naïl executing a cane dance. The Professor was no longer conscious; to be exact, he existed in the middle of the movements made by these other men. When they had finished dressing him the way they wished him to look, they stuffed some food under the tin bangles hanging over his face. Even though he chewed mechanically, most of it eventually fell out onto the ground. They put him back into the sack and left him there.

Two days later they arrived at one of their own encampments. There were women and children here in the tents, and the men had to drive away the snarling dogs they had left there to guard them. When they emptied the Professor out of his sack, there were screams of fright, and it took several hours to convince the last woman that he was harmless, although there had been no doubt from the start that he was a valuable possession. After a few days they began to move on again, taking everything with them, and traveling only at night as the terrain grew warmer.

Even when all his wounds had healed and he felt no more pain, the Professor did not begin to think again; he ate and defecated, and he danced when he was bidden, a senseless hopping up and down that delighted the children, principally because of the wonderful jangling racket it made. And he generally slept through the heat of the day, in among the camels.

Wending its way southeast, the caravan avoided all stationary civilization. In a few weeks they reached a new plateau, wholly wild and with a sparse vegetation. Here they pitched camp and remained, while the *mehara* were turned loose to graze. Everyone was happy here; the weather was cooler and there was a well only a few hours away on a seldom-frequented trail. It was here they conceived the idea of taking the Professor to Fogara and selling him to the Touareg.

It was a full year before they carried out this project. By this time the Professor was much better trained. He could do a handspring, make a series of fearful growling noises which had, nevertheless, a certain element of humor; and when the Reguibat removed the tin from his face they discovered he could grimace admirably while he danced. They also taught him a few basic obscene gestures which never failed to elicit delighted shrieks from the women. He was now brought forth only after especially abundant meals, when there was music and festivity. He easily fell in with their sense of ritual, and evolved an elementary sort of "program" to present when he was called for: dancing, rolling on the ground, imitating certain animals, and finally rushing toward the group in feigned anger, to see the resultant confusion and hilarity.

When three of the men set out for Fogara with him, they took four *mehara* with them, and he rode astride his quite naturally. No precautions were taken to guard him, save that he was kept among them, one man always staying at the rear of the party. They came within sight of the walls at dawn, and they waited among the rocks all day. At dusk the youngest started out, and in three hours he returned with a friend who carried a stout cane. They tried to put the Professor through his routine then and there, but the man from Fogara was in a hurry to get back to town, so they all set out on the *mehara*.

In the town they went directly to the villager's home, where they had coffee in the courtyard sitting among the camels. Here the Professor went into his act again, and this time there was prolonged merriment and much rubbing together of hands. An agreement was reached, a sum of money paid, and the Reguibat withdrew, leaving the Professor in the house of the man with the cane, who did not delay in locking him into a tiny enclosure off the courtyard.

The next day was an important one in the Professor's life, for it was then that pain began to stir again in his being. A group of men came to the house, among whom was a venerable gentleman, better clothed than those others who spent their time flattering him, setting fervent kisses upon his hands and the edges of his garments. This person made a point of going into classical Arabic from time to time, to impress the others, who had not learned a word of the Koran. Thus his conversation would run more or less as follows: "Perhaps at In Salah. The French there are stupid. Celestial vengeance is approaching. Let us not hasten it. Praise the highest and cast thine anathema against idols. With paint on his face. In case the police wish to look close." The others listened and agreed, nodding their heads slowly and solemnly. And the Professor in his stall beside them listened, too. That is, he was *conscious* of the sound of the old man's Arabic. The words penetrated for the first time in many months. Noises, then: "Celestial vengeance is approaching." Then: "It is an honor. Fifty francs is enough. Keep your money. Good." And the *qaouaji* squatting near him at the edge of the precipice. Then "anathema against idols" and more gibberish. He turned over panting on the sand and forgot about it. But the pain had begun. It operated in a kind of delirium, because he had begun to enter into consciousness again. When the man opened the door and prodded him with his cane, he cried out in a rage, and everyone laughed.

They got him onto his feet, but he would not dance. He stood before them, staring at the ground, stubbornly refusing to move. The owner was furious, and so annoyed by the laughter of the others that he felt obliged to send them away, saying that he would await a more propitious time for exhibiting his property, because he dared not show his anger before the elder. However, when they had left he dealt the Professor a violent blow on the shoulder with his cane, called him various obscene things, and went out into the street, slamming the gate behind him. He walked straight to the street of the Ouled Naïl, because he was sure of finding the Reguibat there among the girls, spending the money. And there in a tent he found one of them still abed, while an Ouled Naïl washed the tea glasses. He walked in and almost decapitated the man before the latter had even attempted to sit up. Then he threw his razor on the bed and ran out.

The Ouled Naïl saw the blood, screamed, ran out of her tent into the next, and soon emerged from that with four girls who rushed together into the coffeehouse and told the *qaouaji* who had killed the Reguiba. It was only a matter of an hour before the French military police had caught him at a friend's house, and dragged him off to the barracks. That night the Professor had nothing to eat, and the next afternoon, in the slow sharpening of his consciousness caused by increasing hunger, he walked aimlessly about the courtyard and the rooms that gave onto it. There was no one. In one room a calendar hung on the wall. The Professor watched nervously, like a dog watching a fly in front of its nose. On the white paper were black objects that made sounds in his head. He heard them: "*Grande Épicerie du Sahel. Juin. Lundi, Mardi, Mercredi. . . .*"

The tiny inkmarks of which a symphony consists may have been made long ago, but when they are fulfilled in sound they become imminent and mighty. So a kind of music of feeling began to play in the Professor's head, increasing in volume as he looked at the mud wall, and he had the feeling that he was performing what had been written for him long ago. He felt like weeping; he felt like roaring through the little house, upsetting and smashing the few breakable objects. His emotion got no further than this one overwhelming desire. So, bellowing as loud as he could, he attacked the house and its belongings. Then he attacked the door into the street, which resisted for a while and finally broke. He climbed through the opening made by the boards he had ripped apart, and still bellowing and shaking his arms in the air to make as loud a jangling as possible, he began to gallop along the quiet street toward the gateway of the town. A few people looked at him with great curiosity. As he passed the garage, the last building before the high mud archway that framed the desert beyond, a French soldier saw him. *"Tiens,"* he said to himself, "a holy maniac."

Again it was sunset time. The Professor ran beneath the arched gate, turned his face toward the red sky, and began to trot along the Piste d'In Salah, straight into the setting sun. Behind him, from the garage, the soldier took a potshot at him for good luck. The bullet whistled dangerously near the Professor's head, and his yelling rose into an indignant lament as he waved his arms more wildly, and hopped high into the air at every few steps, in an access of terror.

The soldier watched a while, smiling, as the cavorting figure grew smaller in the oncoming evening darkness, and the rattling of the tin became a part of the great silence out there beyond the gate. The wall of the garage as he leaned against it still gave forth heat, left there by the sun, but even then the lunar chill was growing in the air.

THE ECHO

Aileen pulled out her mirror; the vibration of the plane shook it so rapidly that she was unable to see whether her nose needed powder or not. There were only two other passengers and they were asleep. It was noon; the tropical sun shone violently down upon the wide silver wings and cast sharp reflections on the ceiling. Far below, the uniform green carpet of the jungle moved slowly by. She was sleepy, but she was also excited to be going to a new home. From her handbag she pulled a folded letter which she read again intently, as if to decipher a meaning that did not lie in the sequence of the words. It was in her mother's script:

"Aileen, Sweet—

"I must begin (and finish) this before supper. Prue has gone out for her shower, and that means that by the time she has Luz (the cook) heat the water and can find José (the gardener) to carry it up on the roof to the tank, it will be about an hour. Add to that the time it takes her to do her actual bathing and to dress, and you can see I'll have just about time for a nice chat.

"Perhaps I should begin by saying that Prue and I are sublimely happy here. It is absolute heaven after Washington, as you can pretty well imagine. Prue, of course, never could stand the States, and I felt, after the trouble with your father, that I couldn't face anyone for a while. You know how much importance I have always attached to relaxation. And this is the ideal spot for that.

"Of course I did feel a little guilty about running off down here without seeing you. But I think the trip to Northampton would have sealed my doom. I honestly don't believe I could have stood it. And Prue was nervous about the State Department's passing some new law that would prevent citizens from

13

leaving the U.S. because of the disturbed conditions, and so on. I also felt that the sooner we got down here to Jamonocal the more of a home we could make out of the old place, for you to spend your vacation in. And it *is* going to be beautiful. I won't drag out my reasons for not letting you know beforehand or it will sound apologetic, and I know I never have to apologize to you for anything. So I'll leave that and get on. I'm sure anyway that the eight months passed very quickly up there for you.

"We have had swarms of men working on the house ever since last October. Mr. Forbes happened to be in Barranquilla for a new American project in the interior, and I wanted to be sure of having him supervise the construction of the cantilever in the foundation. That man is really a prince. They don't come much finer. He was up again and again, and gave orders down to the last detail. I felt guilty about making him work so hard, but I honestly think he enjoyed himself with us girls. In any case it seemed silly, when one of the best architects in the U.S. was right here in Colombia and happened to be an old friend, not to use him when I needed him. Anyway, the old house is now the old wing and the new part, which is so exciting I can't wait for you to see it, is built right out over the gorge. I think there's not likely to be another house like it in the world, if I do say it myself. The terrace makes me think of an old cartoon in *The New Yorker* showing two men looking over the edge of the Grand Canyon, and one is saying to the other: 'Did you ever want to spit a mile, Bill? Now's your chance.'

"We are all installed. The weather has been wonderful, and if Luz could only learn a little more about what white people like to eat and how they like it served, the setup would really be perfect. I know you will enjoy being here with Prue. She and you have many things in common, even if you do claim to 'remember not liking her much.' That was in Washington and you were, to put it mildly, at a difficult age. Now, as an adult (because you really are one by now), you'll be more understanding, I'm sure. She loves books, especially on philosophy and psychology and other things your poor mother just doesn't try to follow her in. She has rigged up a kiln and studio in the old guest house which you probably don't remember. She works at her ceramics out there all day, and I have all I can do keeping the house tidy and seeing that the marketing is done. We have a system by which Luz takes the list to her brother every afternoon, and he brings the things from town the following day. It just about keeps him fully busy getting up and down the mountain on his horse. The horse is a lazy old nag that has done nothing but plod back and forth between house and the valley all its life, so it doesn't know the meaning of the word speed. But after all, why hurry, down here?

"I think you will find everything to your liking, and I'm sure you won't require more than five minutes to see that Prue is a dear, and not at all 'peculiar,' as you wrote in your letter. Wire me as soon as you receive this, and let me know just what week you'll be finishing classes. Prue and I will meet you in Barranquilla. I have a list of things I want you to get me in New York. Will wire it to you as soon as I hear. Prue's bath finished. Must close.

Love,
Mother."

Aileen put the letter away, smiling a little, and watched the wings diving in and out of the small thick clouds that lay in the plane's way. There was a slight shock each time they hit one, and the world outside became a blinding whiteness. She fancied jumping out and walking on such solid softness, like a character in an animated cartoon.

Her mother's letter had put her in mind of a much earlier period in her life: the winter she had been taken to visit Jamonocal. All she could recall in the way of incidents was that she had been placed on a mule by one of the natives, and had felt a painful horror that the animal would walk in the wrong direction, away from the house toward the edge of the gorge. She had no memory of the gorge. Probably she had never seen it, although it was only a few paces from the house, through a short but thick stretch of canebrake. However, she had a clear memory of its presence, of the sensation of enormous void beyond and below that side of the house. And she recalled the distant, hollow sound of water falling from a great height, a constant, soft backdrop of sound that slipped into every moment of the day—between the conversations at mealtimes, in the intervals of play in the garden, and at night between dreams. She wondered if really it were possible to remember all that from the time when she had been only five.

In Panama there was a plane change to be made. It was a clear green twilight, and she took a short walk beyond the airport. Parakeets were fighting in the upper branches of the trees; suddenly they became quiet.

She turned back and went inside, where she sat reading until it was time to go aboard.

There was no one there to meet her when she arrived at Barranquilla in the early hours of the morning. She decided to go into town and take a room in the hotel. With her two valises she stepped outside and looked about for a cab. They had all gone to the town with passengers, but a man sitting on a packing case informed her that they would soon be coming back. Then suddenly he said, "You want two ladies?"

"What? No. What do you mean?"

"You want two ladies look for you this night?"

"Where are they?" said Aileen, understanding.

"They want a drink," he answered with an intimate grin.

"Where? Barranquilla?"

"No. Here." He pointed down the dark road.

"Where? Can I walk?"

"Sure. I go you."

"No! No thanks. You stay here. Thank you. I can go all right. Where is it? How far?"

"O.K."

"What is it? A bar? What's the name?"

"They got music. La Gloria. You go. You hear music. You look for two ladies. They drinking."

She went inside again and checked the bags with an airline employee who insisted on accompanying her. They strode in silence along the back road. The walls of vegetation on each side sheltered insects that made an occasional violent, dry noise like a wooden ratchet being whirled. Soon there was the sound of drums and trumpets playing Cuban dance music.

"La Gloria," said her escort triumphantly.

La Gloria was a brilliantly lighted mud hut with a thatch-covered veranda giving onto the road. The jukebox was outside, where a few drunken Negroes sprawled.

"Are they here?" she said out loud, but to herself.

"La Gloria," he answered, pointing.

As they came opposite the front of the building, she caught a glimpse of a woman in blue jeans, and although instantaneously she knew it was Prue, her mind for some reason failed to accept the fact, and she continued to ask herself, "Are they here or not?"

She turned to go toward the veranda. The record had finished playing. The ditch lay in the dark between the road and the porch. She fell forward into it and heard herself cry out. The man behind her said, *"Cuidado!"* She lay there panting with fury and pain, and said, "Oh! My ankle!" There was an exclamation inside the bar. Her mother's voice cried, "That's Aileen!" Then the jukebox began to scratch and roar again. The Negroes remained stationary. Someone helped her up. She was inside the bar in the raw electric glare.

"I'm all right," she said, when she had been eased into a chair.

"But darling, where've you been? We've been waiting for you since eight, and we'd just about given up. Poor Prue's ill."

"Nonsense, I'll recover," said Prue, still seated at the bar. "Been having a touch of the trots, that's all."

"But darling, are you all right? This is absurd, landing here this way." She looked down at Aileen's ankle.

"Is it all right?"

Prue came over from the bar to shake her hand.

"A dramatic entrance, gal," she said.

Aileen sat there and smiled. She had a curious mental habit. As a child she had convinced herself that her head was transparent, that the thoughts there could be perceived immediately by others. Accordingly, when she found herself in uncomfortable situations, rather than risk the danger of being suspected of harboring uncomplimentary or rebellious thoughts, she had developed a system of refraining from thinking at all. For a while during her childhood this fear of having no mental privacy had been extended to anyone; even persons existing at a distance could have access to her mind. Now she felt open only to those present. And so it was that, finding herself face-to-face with Prue, she was conscious of no particular emotion save the familiar vague sense of boredom. There was not a thought in her head, and her face made the fact apparent.

Mornings were hard to believe. The primeval freshness, spilled down out of the jungle above the house, was held close to the earth by the mist. Outside and in, it was damp and smelled like a florist's shop, but the dampness was dispelled each day when the stinging sun burned through the thin cape of moisture that clung to the mountain's back. Living there was like living sideways, with the land stretching up on one side and down on the other at the same angle. Only the gorge gave a feeling of perpendicularity; the vertical walls of rock on the opposite side of the great amphitheatre were a reminder that the center of gravity lay below and not obliquely to one side. Constant vapor rose from the invisible pool at the bottom, and the distant, indeterminate calling of water was like the sound of sleep itself.

For a few days Aileen lay in bed listening to the water and the birds, and to the nearby, unfamiliar, domestic sounds. Her mother and Prue both had breakfast in bed, and generally appeared just before the midday meal for a few minutes of conversation until Concha brought the invalid's lunch tray. In the afternoons she thumbed through old magazines and read at murder mysteries. Usually it began to rain about three; the sound at first would be like an augmentation of the waterfall in the distance, and then as its violence increased it came unmistakably nearer—a great roar all around the house that covered every other sound. The black clouds would close in tightly around the mountain, so that it seemed that night would soon arrive. She would ring a small bell for Concha to come and light the oil lamp on the table by the bed. Lying there looking at the wet banana leaves outside the window, with the rain's din everywhere, she felt completely comfortable for the precarious moment. There was no necessity to question the feeling, no need to think—only the subsiding of the rain, the triumphant emergence of the sun into the steaming twilight and an early dinner to look forward to. Each evening after dinner her mother came for a lengthy chat, usually about the servants. The first three nights Prue had come too, carrying a highball, but after that her mother came alone.

Aileen had asked to be put into the old part of the house, rather than into a more comfortable room in the new wing. Her window looked onto the garden, which was a small square of lawn with young banana trees on either side. At the far end was a fountain; behind it was the disordered terrain of the mountainside with its recently cut underbrush and charred stumps, and still further beyond was the high jungle whose frontier had been sliced in a straight line across the slopes many years ago to make the plantation. Here in her room she felt at least that the earth was somewhere beneath her.

When her ankle ceased to pain her, she began going downstairs for lunch, which was served out on the terrace at a table with a beach umbrella stuck in its center. Prue was regularly late in coming from her studio, and she arrived in her blue jeans, which were caked with clay, with smears of dirt across her face. Because Aileen could not bring herself to think what she really felt, which was that Prue was ungracious, ugly and something of an interloper, she remained emotionally unconscious of Prue's presence, which is to say that she was polite but bored, scarcely present in the mealtime conversations. Then, too, Aileen was definitely uncomfortable on the terrace. The emptiness was too near and the balustrade seemed altogether too low for safety. She liked the meals to be as brief as possible, with no unnecessary time spent sipping coffee afterward, but it never would have occurred to her to divulge her reasons. With Prue around she felt constrained to behave with the utmost decorum. Fortunately her ankle provided her with a convenient excuse to get back upstairs to her room.

She soon discovered a tiny patio next to the kitchen where heavy vines with sweet-smelling flowers grew up an arbor that had been placed at one side. The air was full of the humming of hundreds of bees that clung heavily to the petals and moved slowly about in the air. After lunch she would pull a deck chair into the arbor's shade and read until the rain began. It was a stifling, airless spot, but the sound of the bees covered that of the waterfall. One afternoon Prue followed her there and stood with her hands in her hip pockets looking at her.

"How can you take this heat?" she asked Aileen.

"Oh, I love it."

"You do?" She paused. "Tell me, do you really like it here, or do you think it's a bloody bore?"

"Why, I think it's absolutely wonderful."

"Mm. It is."

"Don't you like it?"

Prue yawned. "Oh, I'm all for it. But I keep busy. Wherever I can work, I get on, you know."

"Yes, I suppose so," said Aileen. Then she added, "Are you planning on staying long?"

"What the hell do you mean?" said Prue, leaning backward against the house, her hands still behind her. "I live here."

Aileen laughed shortly. To anyone but Prue it would have sounded like a merry, tinkling laugh, but Prue narrowed her eyes and thrust her jaw forward a bit.

"What's so funny?" she demanded.

"I think you're funny. You're so tied up in knots. You get upset so easily. Perhaps you work too hard out there in your little house."

Prue was looking at her with astonishment.

"God Almighty," she said finally, "your I.Q.'s showing, gal."

"Thank you," said Aileen with great seriousness. "Anyway, I think it's fine that you're happy here, and I hope you go on being happy."

"That's what I came to say to you."

"Then everything's fine."

"I can't make you out," said Prue, frowning.

"I don't know what you're talking about," replied Aileen, fingering the pages of her book impatiently. "It's the most pointless conversation I've ever had."

"That I *don't* think," Prue said, going into the kitchen.

The same evening, when her mother came for her usual after-dinner chat, she looked a little unhappy.

"You don't seem to be getting on very well with Prue," she said reproachfully, as she sat down at the foot of the bed.

"Why, we get on perfectly well. Oh. You're talking about this afternoon, probably."

"Yes, I am, probably. Really, Aileen. You simply can't be rude to a woman her age. She's my guest, and you're my guest, and you've got to be civil to each other. But she's always civil and I have a feeling you're not."

Aileen caught her breath and said, "I'm your guest . . ."

"I invited you here for your vacation and I want things pleasant, and I don't see the slightest reason why they shouldn't be."

Suddenly Aileen cried, "She's a maniac!"

Her mother rose and quickly left the room.

In the quiet days that followed, the incident was not mentioned by any of them. Aileen continued to haunt the little patio after lunch.

There came a morning sweeter than the rest, when the untouched early mist hung inside her bedroom, and the confusion of shrill bird cries came down with perfect clarity from the uncut forest. She dressed quickly and went out. There was a white radiance in the air that she had never seen before. She walked along the path that led by the native huts. There was life stirring within; babies were crying and captive parrots and songbirds laughed and sang. The path swung into a stretch of low trees that had been planted to shield the coffee bushes. It was still almost nocturnal in here; the air was streaked with chill, and the vegetable odors were like invisible festoons drooping from the branches as she walked through. A huge bright spider walked slowly across the path at her feet. She stood still and watched it until it had disappeared in the leaves at one side. She put her hand over her heart to feel how insistently it was beating. And she listened to its sound in her head for a moment, not wanting to break into its rhythm by starting to walk again. Then she began to walk ahead fast, following the path upward toward the lightest part of the sky. When it came out suddenly onto an eminence directly above the plantation, she could barely discern the cluster of roofs through the mist. But here the sound of the waterfall was stronger; she supposed she was near the gorge, although there was no sign of it. The path turned here and went along rough open ground upward. She climbed at a steady gait, breathing slowly and deeply, for perhaps half an hour, and was surprised to find that the jungle had been cut away on all sides in this portion of the mountainside. For a time she thought the sky was growing brighter, and that the sun was about to break through, but as the path leveled out and she was able to see for some distance ahead, she saw that the mist was even thicker up here than down below.

At certain points there was a steep declivity on each side of the path. It was impossible to see how deeply the land fell away. There were a few nearby plants and rocks, the highest fronds of a tree fern a little beyond, and white emptiness after that. It was like going along the top of a wall high in the air. Then the path would make a wide turn and go sharply upward and she would see a solitary tree above her at one side.

Suddenly she came up against a row of huts. They were less well made than those down at the plantation, and smaller. The mist was full of woodsmoke; there was the smell of pigs. She stood still. A man was singing. Two small naked children came out of the door of one hut, looked at her a moment in terror, and ran quickly back inside. She walked ahead. The singing came from behind the last hut. When she came opposite the hut, she saw that it was enclosed by a tangled but effective fence of barbed wire which left a runway about six feet wide all the way around. A young man appeared from the farther side of the closed-in space. His shirt and pants were tattered; the brown skin showed in many places. He was singing as he walked toward her, and he continued to sing, looking straight into her face with bright, questioning eyes. She smiled and said, *"Buenos dias."* He made a beckoning gesture, rather too dramatically. She stopped walking and stood still, looking hesitantly back at the other huts. The young man beckoned again and then stepped inside the hut. A moment later he came out, and still staring fascinatedly at her, made more summoning motions. Aileen stood perfectly quiet, not taking her eyes from his face. He walked slowly over to the fence and grasped the wire with both hands, his eyes growing wider as he pressed the barbs into his palms. Then he leaned across, thrusting his head toward her, his eyes fixing hers with incredible intensity. For several seconds they watched each other; then she stepped a little nearer, peering into his face and frowning. At that point with a cry he emptied his mouth of the water he had been holding in it, aiming with force at Aileen's face. Some of it struck her cheek, and the rest the front of her dress. His fingers unclenched themselves from around the wire, and straightening himself, he backed slowly into the hut, watching her face closely all the while.

She stood still an instant, her hand to her cheek. Then she bent down, and picking up a large stone from the path she flung it with all her strength through the door. A terrible cry came from within; it was like nothing she had ever heard. Or yes, she thought as she began to run back past the other huts, it had the indignation and outraged innocence of a small baby, but it was also a grown man's cry. No one appeared as she passed the huts. Soon she was back in the silence of the empty mountainside, but she kept running, and she was astonished to find that she was sobbing as well. She sat down on a rock and calmed herself by watching some ants demolish a bush as they cut away squares of leaf and carried them away in their mouths. The sky was growing brighter now; the sun would soon be through. She went on. By the time she got back to the high spot above the plantation the mist had turned into long clouds that were rolling away down the mountainside into the ravines. She was horrified to see how near she stood to the ugly black edge of the gorge. And the house looked insane down there, leaning out over as if it were trying to see the bottom. Far below the house the vapor rose up from the pool. She followed the sheer sides of the opposite cliff upward with her eye, all the way to the top, a little above the spot where she stood. It made her feel ill, and she stumbled back down to the house with her hand to her forehead, paying no attention to the natives who greeted her from their doorways.

As she ran past the garden a voice called to her. She turned and saw Prue washing her hands in the fountain's basin. She stood still.

"You're up early. You must feel better," said Prue, drying her hands on her hair. "Your mother's been having a fit. Go in and see her."

Aileen stared at Prue a moment before she said, "I was going in. You don't have to tell me."

"Oh, I thought I did."

"You don't have to tell me anything. I think I can manage all right without your help."

"Help isn't exactly what I'd like to give you," said Prue, putting her hands into her pockets. "A swift kick in the teeth would be more like it. How do you think I like to see your mother worrying about you? First you're sick in bed, then you just disappear into the goddamn jungle. D'you think I like to have to keep talking about you, reassuring her every ten minutes? What the hell d'you think life is, one long coming-out party?"

Aileen stared harder, now with unmasked hatred. "I think," she said slowly, "that life is pretty awful. Here especially. And I think you should look once in the mirror and then jump off the terrace. And I think Mother should have her mind examined."

"I see," said Prue, with dire inflection. She lit a cigarette and strode off to her studio. Aileen went into the house and up to her room.

Less than an hour later, her mother knocked at her door. As she came into the room, Aileen could see she had been crying only a moment before.

"Aileen darling, I've got something to say to you," she began apologetically, "and it just breaks my heart to say it. But I've got to."

She stopped, as though waiting for encouragement.

"Mother, what is it?"

"I think you probably know."

"About Prue, I suppose. No?"

23

"It certainly is. I don't know how I can ever make it right with her. She told me what you said to her, and I must say I found it hard to believe. How could you?"

"You mean just now in the garden?"

"I don't know where you said it, but I do know this can't go on. So I'm just forced to say this. . . . You'll have to go. I can't be stirred up this way, and I can tell just how it'll be if you stay on."

"I'm not surprised at all," said Aileen, making a show of calm. "When do you want me to leave?"

"This is terribly painful . . ."

"Oh, stop! It's all right. I've had a vacation and I can get a lot of work done before the term starts. Today? Tomorrow?"

"I think the first of the week. I'll go to Barranquilla with you."

"Would you think I was silly if I had all my meals up here?"

"I think it's a perfect idea, darling, and we can have nice visits together, you and I, between meals."

Now, when the tension should have been over, somehow it was not. During the four nights before she was to leave, Aileen had endless excruciating dreams. She would wake up in the darkness too agonized even to move her hand. It was not fear; she could not recall the dreams. It was rather as if some newly discovered, innermost part of her being were in acute pain. Breathing quickly, she would lie transfixed for long periods listening to the eternal sound of the waterfall, punctuated at great intervals by some slight, nearby nocturnal noise in the trees. Finally, when she had summoned sufficient energy to move, she would change her position in the bed, sigh profoundly, and relax enough to fall back into the ominous world of sleep.

When the final day came, there was a light tapping on her door just after dawn. She got up and unbolted it. Her mother was there, smiling thinly.

"May I come in?"

"Oh. Good morning. Of course. It's early, isn't it?"

Her mother walked across to the window and stood looking down at the misty garden.

"I'm not so well today," she said. "I'm afraid I can't take you to Barranquilla. I'm not up to getting onto a horse today. It's just too much, that three-hour trip to Jamonocal, and then the train and the boat all night. You'll just have to forgive me. I couldn't stand all three. But it won't matter, will it?" she went on, looking up at last. "We'll say good-bye here."

"But, Mother, how can I go alone?"

"Oh, José'll go all the way to Barranquilla with you and be back by Wednesday night. You don't think I'd let you go off by yourself?"

She began to laugh intensely, then stopped suddenly and looked pensive.

"I rather hate to be here two nights without him, but I don't see any other way to get you down there by tomorrow. You can go shipside to Panama. There's usually a seat somewhere. Now, breakfast, breakfast . . ."

Patting Aileen's cheek, she hurried out and downstairs to the kitchen.

The birds' morning song was coming down from the forest; the mist lay ragged in the tops of the great trees up there. Aileen shifted her gaze to the garden at her feet. Suddenly she felt she could not leave; in a sense it was as if she were leaving love behind. She sat down on the bed. "But what is it?" she asked herself desperately. "Not Mother. Not the house. Not the jungle." Automatically she dressed and packed the remaining toilet articles in her overnight case. But the feeling was there, imperious and enveloping in its completeness.

She went downstairs. There was the sound of voices and the clatter of china in the kitchen. Concha and Luz were preparing her breakfast tray. She went out and watched them until everything was ready.

"*Ya se va la señorita?*" said Concha sadly.

She did not answer, but took the tray from her and carried it through the house, out onto the terrace, where she set it on the table. Everything on the terrace was wet with dew and moisture from the gorge. She turned the chair cushion over and sat down to eat. The sound of the waterfall took her appetite away, but she thought, "This is the last time." She felt choked with emotions, but they were too disparate and confused for her to be able to identify any one of them as outstanding. As she sat there eating intently, she was suddenly aware that someone was watching her. She started up and saw Prue standing in the doorway. She was wearing pajamas and a bathrobe, and in her hand she held a glass of water. She looked very sleepy.

"How are you?" she said, sipping her water.

Aileen stood up.

"We're all up bright and early this morning," Prue went on cheerily.

"I'm—leaving. I've got to go. Excuse me, it's late," mumbled Aileen, glancing about furtively.

"Oh, take your time, gal. You haven't said good-bye to your mother yet. And José is still saddling the nags. You've got a lot of grips with you."

"Excuse me," said Aileen, trying to slip past her through the doorway.

"Well, shake," Prue said, reaching for Aileen's hand.

"Get away!" cried Aileen, struggling to keep clear of her. "Don't touch me!" But Prue had succeeded in grasping one frantic arm. She held it fast.

"A dramatic entrance is enough. We don't have to have the same sort of exit. Say good-bye to me like a human being." She twisted the arm a bit, in spite of herself. Aileen leaned against the door and turned very white.

"Feel faint?" said Prue. She let go of her arm, and holding up her glass of water, flicked some of it into Aileen's face with her fingers.

The reaction was instantaneous. Aileen jumped at her with vicious suddenness, kicking, ripping and pounding all at once. The glass fell to the stone floor; Prue was caught off her guard. Mechanically, with rapid, birdlike fury, the girl hammered at the woman's face and head, as she slowly impelled her away from the doorway and across the terrace.

From Prue's lips came several times the word "God." At first she did very little to defend herself; she seemed half asleep as she moved toward the outer edge beneath the onslaught. Then suddenly she threw herself to the floor. Aileen continued to kick her where she lay doubled over, trying to protect her face.

"Nobody! Nobody! Nobody! Nobody can do that to me!" she cried rhythmically as she kicked.

Her voice rose in pitch and volume; she stopped for an instant, and then, raising her head, she uttered the greatest scream of her life. It came back immediately from the black wall of rock across the gorge, straight through the noise of water. The sound of her own voice ended the episode for her, and she began to walk back across the terrace.

Concha and Luz stood frightened in the doorway; it was as if they had come to watch a terrible storm pass over the countryside. They stepped aside as Aileen walked through.

Outside the stable, José was whistling as he finished saddling the horses. The valises were already strapped on the burro.

Still in the midst of her deep dream, Aileen turned her head toward the house as they rode past. For a brief second, between the leaves, she saw the two figures of her mother and Prue standing side by side on the terrace, the wall of the gorge looming behind. Then the horses turned and began to descend the trail.

CALL AT CORAZÓN

"But why would you want a little horror like that to go along with us? It doesn't make sense. You know what they're like."

"I know what they're like," said her husband. "It's comforting to watch them. Whatever happens, if I had that to look at, I'd be reminded of how stupid I was ever to get upset."

He leaned further over the railing and looked intently down at the dock. There were baskets for sale, crude painted toys of hard natural rubber, reptile-hide wallets and belts, and a few whole snakeskins unrolled. And placed apart from these wares, out of the hot sunlight, in the shadow of a crate, sat a tiny, furry monkey. The hands were folded, and the forehead was wrinkled in sad apprehensiveness.

"Isn't he wonderful?"

"I think you're impossible—and a little insulting," she replied.

He turned to look at her. "Are you serious?" He saw that she was.

She went on, studying her sandaled feet and the narrow deck boards beneath them: "You know I don't really mind all this nonsense, or your craziness. Just let me finish." He nodded his head in agreement, looking back at the hot dock and the wretched tin-roofed village beyond. "It goes without saying I don't mind all that, or we wouldn't be here together. You might be here alone . . ."

"You don't take a honeymoon alone," he interrupted.

"*You* might." She laughed shortly.

He reached along the rail for her hand, but she pulled it away, saying, "I'm still talking to you. I expect you to be crazy, and I expect to give in to you all along. I'm crazy too, I know. But I wish there were some

28

way I could just once feel that my giving in meant anything to you. I wish you knew how to be gracious about it."

"You think you humor me so much? I haven't noticed it." His voice was sullen.

"I don't *humor* you at all. I'm just trying to live with you on an extended trip in a lot of cramped little cabins on an endless series of stinking boats."

"What do you mean?" he cried excitedly. "You've always said you loved the boats. Have you changed your mind, or just lost it completely?"

She turned and walked toward the prow. "Don't talk to me," she said. "Go and buy your monkey."

An expression of solicitousness on his face, he was following her. "You know I won't buy it if it's going to make you miserable."

"I'll be more miserable if you don't, so please go and buy it." She stopped and turned. "I'd love to have it. I really would. I think it's sweet."

"I don't get you at all."

She smiled. "I know. Does it bother you very much?"

After he had bought the monkey and tied it to the metal post of the bunk in the cabin, he took a walk to explore the port. It was a town made of corrugated tin and barbed wire. The sun's heat was painful, even with the sky's low-lying cover of fog. It was the middle of the day and few people were in the streets. He came to the edge of the town almost immediately. Here between him and the forest lay a narrow, slow-moving stream, its water the color of black coffee. A few women were washing clothes; small children splashed. Gigantic gray crabs scuttled between the holes they had made in the mud along the bank. He sat down on some elaborately twisted roots at the foot of a tree and took out the notebook he always carried with him. The day before, in a bar at Pedernales, he had written: "Recipe for dissolving the impression of hideousness made by a thing: Fix the attention upon the given object or situation so that the various elements, all familiar, will regroup themselves. Frightfulness is never more than an unfamiliar pattern."

He lit a cigarette and watched the women's hopeless attempts to launder the ragged garments. Then he threw the burning stub at the nearest crab, and carefully wrote: "More than anything else, woman requires strict ritualistic observance of the traditions of sexual behavior. That is her definition of love." He thought of the derision that would be called forth should he make such a statement to the girl back on the ship. After looking at his watch, he wrote hurriedly: "Modern, that is, intellectual education, having been devised by males for males, inhibits and confuses her. She avenges . . ."

Two naked children, coming up from their play in the river, ran screaming past him, scattering drops of water over the paper. He called out to them, but they continued their chase without noticing him. He put his pencil and notebook into his pocket, smiling, and watched them patter after one another through the dust.

When he arrived back at the ship, the thunder was rolling down from the mountains around the harbor. The storm reached the height of its hysteria just as they got under way.

She was sitting on her bunk, looking through the open porthole. The shrill crashes of thunder echoed from one side of the bay to the other as they steamed toward the open sea. He lay doubled up on his bunk opposite, reading.

"Don't lean your head against that metal wall," he advised. "It's a perfect conductor."

She jumped down to the floor and went to the washstand.

"Where are those two quarts of White Horse we got yesterday?"

He gestured. "In the rack on your side. Are you going to drink?"

"I'm going to *have* a drink, yes."

"In this heat? Why don't you wait until it clears, and have it on deck?"

"I want it now. When it clears I won't need it."

She poured the whiskey and added water from the carafe in the wall bracket over the washbowl.

"You realize what you're doing, of course."

She glared at him. "What am I doing?"

He shrugged his shoulders. "Nothing, except just giving in to a passing emotional state. You could read, or lie down and doze."

Holding her glass in one hand, she pulled open the door into the passageway with the other, and went out. The noise of the slamming door startled the monkey, perched on a suitcase. It hesitated a second, and hurried under its master's bunk. He made a few kissing sounds to entice it out, and returned to his book. Soon he began to imagine her alone and unhappy on the deck, and the thought cut into the pleasure of his reading. He forced himself to lie still a few minutes, the open book face down across his chest. The boat was moving at full speed now, and the sound of the motors was louder than the storm in the sky.

Soon he rose and went on deck. The land behind was already hidden by the falling rain, and the air smelled of deep water. She was standing alone by the rail, looking down at the waves, with the empty glass in her hand. Pity seized him as he watched, but he could not walk across to her and put into consoling words the emotion he felt.

Back in the cabin he found the monkey on his bunk, slowly tearing the pages from the book he had been reading.

The next day was spent in leisurely preparation for disembarking and changing of boats: in Villalta they were to take a smaller vessel to the opposite side of the delta.

When she came in to pack after dinner, she stood a moment studying the cabin. "He's messed it up, all right," said her husband, "but I found your necklace behind my big valise, and we'd read all the magazines anyway."

"I suppose this represents Man's innate urge to destroy," she said, kicking a ball of crumpled paper across the floor. "And the next time he tries to bite you, it'll be Man's basic insecurity."

"You don't know what a bore you are when you try to be caustic. If you want me to get rid of him, I will. It's easy enough."

She bent to touch the animal, but it backed uneasily under the bunk. She stood up. "I don't mind him. What I mind is you. *He* can't help being a little horror, but he keeps reminding me that you could if you wanted."

Her husband's face assumed the impassivity that was characteristic of him when he was determined not to lose his temper. She knew he would wait to be angry until she was unprepared for his attack. He said nothing, tapping an insistent rhythm on the lid of a suitcase with his fingernails.

"Naturally I don't really mean you're a horror," she continued.

"Why not mean it?" he said, smiling pleasantly. "What's wrong with criticism? Probably I am, to you. I like monkeys because I see them as little model men. You think men are something else, something spiritual or God knows what. Whatever it is, I notice you're the one who's always being disillusioned and going around wondering how mankind can be so bestial. I think mankind is fine."

31

"Please don't go on," she said. "I know your theories. You'll never convince yourself of them."

When they had finished packing, they went to bed. As he snapped off the light behind his pillow, he said, "Tell me honestly. Do you want me to give him to the steward?"

She kicked off her sheet in the dark. Through the porthole, near the horizon, she could see stars, and the calm sea slipped by just below her. Without thinking she said, "Why don't you drop him overboard?"

In the silence that followed she realized she had spoken carelessly, but the tepid breeze moving with languor over her body was making it increasingly difficult for her to think or speak. As she fell asleep it seemed to her she heard her husband saying slowly, "I believe you would. I believe you would."

The next morning she slept late, and when she went up for breakfast her husband had already finished his and was leaning back, smoking.

"How are you?" he asked brightly. "The cabin steward's delighted with the monkey."

She felt a flush of pleasure. "Oh," she said, sitting down, "did you give it to him? You didn't have to do that." She glanced at the menu; it was the same as every other day. "But I suppose really it's better. A monkey doesn't go with a honeymoon."

"I think you're right," he agreed.

Villalta was stifling and dusty. On the other boat they had grown accustomed to having very few passengers around, and it was an unpleasant surprise to find the new one swarming with people. Their new boat was a two-decked ferry painted white, with an enormous paddle wheel at the stern. On the lower deck, which rested not more than two feet above the surface of the water, passengers and freight stood ready to travel, packed together indiscriminately. The upper deck had a salon and a dozen or so narrow staterooms. In the salon the first-class passengers undid their bundles of pillows and opened their paper bags of food. The orange light of the setting sun flooded the room.

They looked into several of the staterooms.

"They all seem to be empty," she said.

"I can see why. Still, the privacy would be a help."

"This one's double. And it has a screen in the window. This is the best one."

"I'll look for a steward or somebody. Go on in and take over." He pushed the bags out of the passageway where the *cargador* had left them, and went off in search of an employee. In every corner of the boat the people seemed to be multiplying. There were twice as many as there had been a few moments before. The salon was completely full, its floor space occupied by groups of travelers with small children and elderly women, who were already stretched out on blankets and newspapers.

"It looks like Salvation Army headquarters the night after a major disaster," he said as he came back into the stateroom. "I can't find anybody. Anyway, we'd better stay in here. The other cubicles are beginning to fill up."

"I'm not so sure I wouldn't rather be on deck," she announced. "There are hundreds of cockroaches."

"And probably worse," he added, looking at the bunks.

"The thing to do is take those filthy sheets off and just lie on the mattresses." She peered out into the corridor. Sweat was trickling down her neck. "Do you think it's safe?"

"What do you mean?"

"All those people. This old tub."

He shrugged his shoulders.

"It's just one night. Tomorrow we'll be at Ciénaga. And it's almost night now."

She shut the door and leaned against it, smiling faintly.

"I think it's going to be fun," she said.

"The boat's moving!" he cried. "Let's go on deck. If we can get out there."

Slowly the old boat pushed across the bay toward the dark east shore. People were singing and playing guitars. On the bottom deck a cow lowed continuously. And louder than all the sounds was the rush of water made by the huge paddles.

They sat on the deck in the middle of a vociferous crowd, leaning against the bars of the railing, and watched the moon rise above the mangrove swamps ahead. As they approached the opposite side of the bay, it looked as if the boat might plow straight into the shore, but a narrow waterway presently appeared, and the boat slipped cautiously in. The people immediately moved back from the railing, crowding against the opposite wall. Branches from the trees on the bank began to rub against the boat, scraping along the side walls of the cabins, and then whipping violently across the deck.

They pushed their way through the throng and walked across the salon to the deck on the other side of the boat; the same thing was happening there.

"It's crazy," she declared. "It's like a nightmare. Whoever heard of going through a channel no wider than the boat! It makes me nervous. I'm going in and read."

Her husband let go of her arm. "You can never enter into the spirit of a thing, can you?"

"You tell me what the spirit is, and I'll see about entering into it," she said, turning away.

He followed her. "Don't you want to go down onto the lower deck? They seem to be going strong down there. Listen." He held up his hand. Repeated screams of laughter came up from below.

"I certainly don't!" she called, without looking around.

He went below. Groups of men were seated on bulging burlap sacks and wooden crates, matching coins. The women stood behind them, puffing on black cigarettes and shrieking with excitement. He watched them closely, reflecting that with fewer teeth missing they would be a handsome people. "Mineral deficiency in the soil," he commented to himself.

Standing on the other side of a circle of gamblers, facing him, was a muscular young native whose visored cap and faint air of aloofness suggested official position of some sort aboard the boat. With difficulty the traveler made his way over to him, and spoke to him in Spanish.

"Are you an employee here?"

"Yes, sir."

"I am in cabin number eight. Can I pay the supplementary fare to you?"

"Yes, sir."

"Good."

He reached into his pocket for his wallet, at the same time remembering with annoyance that he had left it upstairs locked in a suitcase. The man looked expectant. His hand was out.

"My money is in my stateroom." Then he added, "My wife has it. But if you come up in half an hour I can pay you the fare."

"Yes, sir." The man lowered his hand and merely looked at him. Even though he gave an impression of purely animal force, his broad, somewhat simian face was handsome, the husband reflected. It was surprising when, a moment later, that face betrayed a boyish shyness as the man said, "I am going to spray the cabin for your señora."

"Thank you. Are there many mosquitoes?"

The man grunted and shook the fingers of one hand as if he had just burned them.

"Soon you will see how many." He moved away.

At that moment the boat jolted violently, and there was great merriment among the passengers. He pushed his way to the prow and saw that the pilot had run into the bank. The tangle of branches and roots was a few feet from his face, its complex forms vaguely lighted by the boat's lanterns. The boat backed laboriously and the channel's agitated water rose to deck level and lapped the outer edge. Slowly they nosed along the bank until the prow once more pointed to midstream, and they continued. Then almost immediately the passage curved so sharply that the same thing happened again, throwing him sideways against a sack of something unpleasantly soft and wet. A bell clanged below deck in the interior of the boat; the passengers' laughter was louder.

Eventually they pushed ahead, but now the movement became painfully slow as the sharpness of the curves in the passage increased. Under the water the stumps groaned as the boat forced its sides against them. Branches cracked and broke, falling onto the forward and upper decks. The lantern at the prow was swept into the water.

"This isn't the regular channel," muttered a gambler, glancing up.

Several travelers exclaimed, "What?" almost in unison.

"There's a pile of passages through here. We're picking up cargo at Corazón."

The players retreated to a square inner arena which others were forming by shifting some of the crates. The husband followed them. Here they were comparatively safe from the intruding boughs. The deck was better lighted here, and this gave him the idea of making an entry in his notebook. Bending over a carton marked VERMIFUGO SANTA ROSALIA, he wrote: "November 18. We are moving through the bloodstream of a giant. A very dark night." Here a fresh collision with the land knocked him over, knocked over everyone who was not propped between solid objects.

A few babies were crying, but most of them still slept. He slid down to the deck. Finding his position fairly comfortable, he fell into a dozing state which was broken irregularly by the shouting of the people and the jolting of the boat.

When he awoke later, the boat was quite stationary, the games had ceased, and the people were asleep, a few of the men continuing their conversation in small groups. He lay still, listening. The talk was all about places; they were comparing the unpleasant things to be found in various parts of the republic: insects, weather, reptiles, diseases, lack of food, high prices.

He looked at his watch. It was half past one. With difficulty he got to his feet, and found his way to the stairs. Above, in the salon, the kerosene lamps illumined a vast disorder of prostrate figures. He went into the corridor and knocked on the door marked with an eight. Without waiting for her to answer, he opened the door. It was dark inside. He heard a muffled cough nearby, and decided that she was awake.

"How are the mosquitoes? Did my monkey man come and fix you up?" he asked.

She did not answer, so he lit a match. She was not in the bunk on the left. The match burned his thumb. With the second one, he looked at the right-hand bunk. A tin insecticide sprayer lay there on the mattress; its leak had made a large circle of oil on the bare ticking. The cough was repeated. It was someone in the next cabin.

"Now what?" he said aloud, uncomfortable at finding himself upset to this degree. A suspicion seized him. Without lighting the hanging lamp, he rushed to open her valises, and in the dark felt hurriedly through the flimsy pieces of clothing and the toilet articles. The whiskey bottles were not there.

This was not the first time she had gone on a solitary drinking bout, and it would be easy to find her among the passengers. However, being angry, he decided not to look for her. He took off his shirt and trousers and lay down on the left-hand bunk. His hand touched a bottle standing on the floor by the head of the bunk. He raised himself enough to smell it; it was beer and the bottle was half full. It was hot in the cabin, and he drank the remaining warm, bitter liquid with relish and rolled the bottle across the room.

The boat was not moving, but voices shouted out here and there. An occasional bump could be felt as a sack of something heavy was heaved aboard. He looked through the little square window with the screen in it. In the foreground, dimly illumined by the boat's lanterns, a few dark men, naked save for their ragged underdrawers, stood on a landing made in the mud and stared toward the boat. Through the endless intricacies of roots and trunks behind them he saw a bonfire blazing, but it was far back in the swamp. The air smelled of stagnant water and smoke.

Deciding to take advantage of the relative silence, he lay down and tried to sleep; he was not surprised, however, by the difficulty he found in relaxing. It was always hard to sleep when she was not there in the room. The comfort of her presence was lacking, and there was also the fear of being awakened by her return. When he allowed himself to, he would quickly begin to formulate ideas and translate them into sentences whose recording seemed the more urgent because he was lying comfortably in the dark. Sometimes he thought about her, but only as an unclear figure whose character lent flavor to a succession of backdrops. More often he reviewed the day just completed, seeking to convince himself that it had carried him a bit further away from his childhood. Often for months at a time the strangeness of his dreams persuaded him that at last he had turned the corner, that the dark place had finally been left behind, that he was out of hearing. Then, one evening as he fell asleep, before he had time to refuse, he would be staring closely at a long-forgotten object—a plate, a chair, a pincushion—and the accustomed feeling of infinite futility and sadness would recur.

The motor started up, and the great noise of the water in the paddle wheel recommenced. They pushed off from Corazón. He was pleased. "Now I shan't hear her when she comes in and bangs around," he thought, and fell into a light sleep.

He was scratching his arms and legs. The long-continued, vague malaise eventually became full consciousness, and he sat up angrily. Above the sounds made by the boat he could hear another sound, one which came through the window: an incredibly high and tiny tone, tiny but constant in pitch and intensity. He jumped down from the berth and went to the window. The channel was wider here, and the overhanging vegetation no longer touched the sides of the boat. In the air, nearby, far away, everywhere, was the thin wail of mosquito wings. He was aghast, and completely delighted by the novelty of the phenomenon. For a moment he watched the tangled black wilderness slip past. Then with the itching he remembered the mosquitoes inside the cabin. The screen did not reach quite to the top of the window; there was ample space for them to crawl in. Even there in the dark as he moved his fingers along the frame to find the handle he could feel them; there were that many.

Now that he was fully awake, he lighted a match and went to her bunk. Of course she was not there. He lifted the Flit gun and shook it. It was empty, and as the match went out, he saw that the spot on the mattress had spread even further.

"Son of a bitch!" he whispered, and going back to the window he tugged the screen vigorously upward to close the crack. As he let go of it, it fell out into the water, and almost immediately he was conscious of the soft caress of tiny wings all about his head. In his undershirt and trousers he rushed out into the corridor. Nothing had changed in the salon. Almost everyone was asleep. There were screen doors giving onto the deck. He inspected them: they appeared to be more firmly installed. A few mosquitoes brushed against his face, but it was not the horde. He edged in between two women who were sleeping sitting with their backs against the wall, and stayed there in acute discomfort until again he dozed. It was not long before he opened his eyes to find the dim light of dawn in the air. His neck ached. He arose and went out onto the deck, to which most of the people from the salon had already crowded.

The boat was moving through a wide estuary dotted with clumps of plants and trees that rose out of the shallow water. Along the edges of the small islands stood herons, so white in the early gray light that their brightness seemed to come from inside them.

It was half past five. At this moment the boat was due in Ciénaga, where it was met on its weekly trip by the train that went into the interior. Already a thin spit of land ahead was being identified by eager watchers. Day was coming up swiftly; sky and water were the same color. The deck reeked of the greasy smell of mangoes as people began to breakfast.

And now at last he began to feel pangs of anxiety as to where she might be. He determined to make an immediate and thorough search of the boat. She would be instantly recognizable in any group. First, he looked methodically through the salon, then he exhausted the possibilities on the upper decks. Then he went downstairs, where the gambling had already begun again. Toward the stern, roped to two flimsy iron posts, stood the cow, no longer bellowing. Nearby was an improvised lean-to, probably the crew's quarters. As he passed the small door, he peered through the low transom above it, and saw her lying beside a man on the floor. Automatically he walked on; then he turned and went back. The two were asleep, and half-clothed. In the warm air that came through the screened transom there was the smell of whiskey that had been drunk and whiskey that had been spilled.

He went upstairs, his heart beating violently. In the cabin, he closed her two valises, packed his own, set them all together by the door and laid the raincoats on top of them. He put on his shirt, combed his hair carefully, and went on deck. Ciénaga was there ahead, in the mountains' morning shadow: the dock, a line of huts against the jungle behind, and the railway station to the right beyond the village.

As they docked, he signaled the two urchins who were waving for his attention, screaming, *"Equipajes!"* They fought a bit with one another until he made them see his two fingers held aloft. Then to make them certain, he pointed at each of them in turn, and they grinned. Still grinning, they stood beside him with the bags and coats, and he was among the first of the upper-deck passengers to get on land. They went down the street to the station with the parrots screaming at them from each thatched gable along the way.

On the crowded, waiting train, with the luggage finally in the rack, his heart beat harder than ever, and he kept his eyes painfully on the long dusty street that led back to the dock. At the far end, as the whistle blew, he thought he saw a figure in white running among the dogs and children toward the station, but the train started up as he watched, and the street was lost to view. He took out his notebook, and sat with it on his lap, smiling at the shining green landscape that moved with increasing speed past the window.

PAGES FROM COLD POINT

Our civilization is doomed to a short life: its component parts are too heterogeneous. I personally am content to see everything in the process of decay. The bigger the bombs, the quicker it will be done. Life is visually too hideous for one to make the attempt to preserve it. Let it go. Perhaps some day another form of life will come along. Either way, it is of no consequence. At the same time, I am still a part of life, and I am bound by this to protect myself to whatever extent I am able. And so I am here. Here in the Islands vegetation still has the upper hand, and man has to fight even to make his presence seen at all. It is beautiful here, the trade winds blow all year, and I suspect that bombs are extremely unlikely to be wasted on this unfrequented side of the island, if indeed on any part of it.

I was loath to give up the house after Hope's death. But it was the obvious move to make. My university career always having been an utter farce (since I believe no reason inducing a man to "teach" can possibly be a valid one), I was elated by the idea of resigning, and as soon as her affairs had been settled and the money properly invested, I lost no time in doing so.

I think that week was the first time since childhood that I had managed to recapture the feeling of there being a content in existence. I went from one pleasant house to the next, making my adieux to the English quacks, the Philosophy fakirs and so on—even to those colleagues with whom I was merely on speaking terms. I watched the envy in their faces when I announced my departure by Pan American on Saturday morning; and the greatest pleasure I felt in all this was in being able to answer, "Nothing," when I was asked, as invariably I was, what I intended to do.

When I was a boy people used to refer to Charles as "Big Brother C.," although he is only a scant year older than I. To me now he is merely "Fat Brother C.," a successful lawyer. His thick, red face and hands, his back-slapping joviality and his fathomless hypocritical prudery—these are the qualities which make him truly repulsive to me. There is also the fact that he once looked not unlike the way Racky does now. And after all, he still is my big brother, and disapproves openly of everything I do. The loathing I feel for him is so strong that for years I have not been able to swallow a morsel of food or a drop of liquid in his presence without making a prodigious effort. No one knows this but me— certainly not Charles, who would be the last one I should tell about it. He came up on the late train two nights before I left. He got quickly to the point—as soon as he was settled with a highball.

"So you're off for the wilds," he said, sitting forward in his chair like a salesman.

"If you can call it the wilds," I replied. "Certainly it's not wild like Mitichi." (He has a lodge in northern Quebec.) "I consider it really civilized."

He drank and smacked his lips together stiffly, bringing the glass down hard on his knee.

"And Racky. You're taking him along?"

"Of course."

"Out of school. Away. So he'll see nobody but you. You think that's good."

I looked at him. "I do," I said.

"By God, if I could stop you legally, I would!" he cried, jumping up and putting his glass on the mantel. I was trembling inwardly with excitement, but I merely sat and watched him. He went on. "You're not fit to have custody of the kid!" he shouted. He shot a stern glance at me over his spectacles.

"You think not?" I said gently.

Again he looked at me sharply. "D'ye think I've forgotten?"

I was understandably eager to get him out of the house as soon as I could. As I piled and sorted letters and magazines on the desk, I said: "Is that all you came to tell me? I have a good deal to do tomorrow and I must get some sleep. I probably shan't see you at breakfast. Agnes'll see that you eat in time to make the early train."

41

All he said was: "God! Wake up! Get wise to yourself! You're not fooling anybody, you know."

That kind of talk is typical of Charles. His mind is slow and obtuse; he constantly imagines that everyone he meets is playing some private game of deception with him. He is so utterly incapable of following the functioning of even a moderately evolved intellect that he finds the will to secretiveness and duplicity everywhere.

"I haven't time to listen to that sort of nonsense," I said, preparing to leave the room.

But he shouted, "You don't want to listen! No! Of course not! You just want to do what you want to do. You just want to go on off down there and live as you've a mind to, and to hell with the consequences!" At this point I heard Racky coming downstairs. C. obviously heard nothing, and he raved on. "But just remember, I've got your number all right, and if there's any trouble with the boy I'll know who's to blame."

I hurried across the room and opened the door so he could see that Racky was there in the hallway. That stopped his tirade. It was hard to know whether Racky had heard any of it or not. Although he is not a quiet young person, he is the soul of discretion, and it is almost never possible to know any more about what goes on inside his head than he intends one to know.

I was annoyed that C. should have been bellowing at me in my own house. To be sure, he is the only one from whom I would accept such behavior, but then, no father likes to have his son see him take criticism meekly. Racky simply stood there in his bathrobe, his angelic face quite devoid of expression, saying: "Tell Uncle Charley good night for me, will you? I forgot."

I said I would, and quickly shut the door. When I thought Racky was back upstairs in his room, I bade Charles good night. I have never been able to get out of his presence fast enough. The effect he has on me dates from an early period of our lives, from days I dislike to recall.

Racky is a wonderful boy. After we arrived, when we found it impossible to secure a proper house near any town where he might have the company of English boys and girls his own age, he showed no sign of chagrin, although he must have been disappointed. Instead, as we went out of the renting office into the glare of the street, he grinned and said: "Well, I guess we'll have to get bikes, that's all."

The few available houses near what Charles would have called "civilization" turned out to be so ugly and so impossibly confining in atmosphere that we decided immediately on Cold Point, even though it was across the island and quite isolated on its seaside cliff. It was beyond a doubt one of the most desirable properties on the island, and Racky was as enthusiastic about its splendors as I.

"You'll get tired of being alone out there, just with me," I said to him as we walked back to the hotel.

"Aw, I'll get along all right. When do we look for the bikes?"

At his insistence we bought two the next morning. I was sure I should not make much use of mine, but I reflected that an extra bicycle might be convenient to have around the house. It turned out that the servants all had their own bicycles, without which they would not have been able to get to and from the village of Orange Walk, eight miles down the shore. So for a while I was forced to get astride mine each morning before breakfast and pedal madly along beside Racky for a half hour. We would ride through the cool early air, under the towering silk-cotton trees near the house, and out to the great curve in the shoreline where the waving palms bend landward in the stiff breeze that always blows there. Then we would make a wide turn and race back to the house, loudly discussing the degrees of our desires for the various items of breakfast we knew were awaiting us there on the terrace. Back home we would eat in the wind, looking out over the Caribbean, and talk about the news in yesterday's local paper, brought to us by Isiah each morning from Orange Walk. Then Racky would disappear for the whole morning on his bicycle, riding furiously along the road in one direction or the other until he had discovered an unfamiliar strip of sand along the shore that he could consider a new beach. At lunch he would describe it in detail to me, along with a recounting of all the physical hazards involved in hiding the bicycle in among the trees, so that natives passing along the road on foot would not spot it, or in climbing down unscalable cliffs that turned out to be much higher than they had appeared at first sight, or in measuring the depth of the water preparatory to diving from the rocks, or in judging the efficacy of the reef in barring sharks and barracuda. There is never any element of bragadoccio in Racky's relating of his exploits—only the joyous excitement he derives from telling how he satisfies his inexhaustible curiosity. And his mind shows its alertness in all directions at once. I do not mean to say that I expect him to be an "intellectual." That is no affair of mine, nor do I have any particular interest in whether he turns out to be a thinking man or not. I know he will always have a certain boldness of manner and a great purity of spirit in judging values. The former will prevent his becoming what I call a "victim": he never will be brutalized by realities. And his unerring sense of balance in ethical considerations will shield him from the paralyzing effects of present-day materialism.

For a boy of sixteen Racky has an extraordinary innocence of vision. I do not say this as a doting father, although God knows I can never even think of the boy without that familiar overwhelming sensation of delight and gratitude for being vouchsafed the privilege of sharing my life with him. What he takes so completely as a matter of course, our daily life here together, is a source of never-ending wonder to me; and I reflect upon it a good part of each day, just sitting here being conscious of my great good fortune in having him all to myself, beyond the reach of prying eyes and malicious tongues. (I suppose I am really thinking of C. when I write that.) And I believe that a part of the charm of sharing Racky's life with him consists precisely in his taking it all so utterly for granted. I have never asked him whether he likes being here—it is so patent that he does, very much. I think if he were to turn to me one day and tell me how happy he is here, that somehow, perhaps, the spell might be broken. Yet if he were to be thoughtless and inconsiderate, or even unkind to me, I feel that I should be able only to love him the more for it.

I have reread that last sentence. What does it mean? And why should I even imagine it could mean anything more than it says?

Still, much as I may try, I can never believe in the gratuitous, isolated fact. What I must mean is that I feel that Racky already has been in some way inconsiderate. But in what way? Surely I cannot resent his bicycle treks; I cannot expect him to want to stay and sit talking with me all day. And I never worry about his being in danger; I know he is more capable than most adults of taking care of himself, and that he is no more likely than any native to come to harm crawling over the cliffs or swimming in the bays. At the same time there is no doubt in my mind that something about our existence annoys me. I must resent some detail in the pattern, whatever that pattern may be. Perhaps it is just his youth, and I am envious of the lithe body, the smooth skin, the animal energy and grace.

For a long time this morning I sat looking out to sea, trying to solve that small puzzle. Two white herons came and perched on a dead stump east of the garden. They stayed a long time there without stirring. I would turn my head away and accustom my eyes to the bright sea horizon, then I would look suddenly at them to see if they had shifted position, but they would always be in the same attitude. I tried to imagine the black stump without them—a purely vegetable landscape—but it was impossible. All the while I was slowly forcing myself to accept a ridiculous explanation of my annoyance with Racky. It had made itself manifest to me only yesterday, when instead of appearing for lunch, he sent a young colored boy from Orange Walk to say that he would be lunching in the village. I could not help noticing that the boy was riding Racky's bicycle. I had been waiting lunch a good half hour for him, and I had Gloria serve immediately as the boy rode off, back to the village. I was curious to know in what sort of place and with whom Racky could be eating, since Orange Walk, as far as I know, is inhabited exclusively by Negroes, and I was sure Gloria would be able to shed some light on the matter, but I could scarcely ask her. However, as she brought on the dessert, I said: "Who was that boy that brought the message from Mister Racky?"

She shrugged her shoulders. "A young lad of Orange Walk. He's named Wilmot."

When Racky returned at dusk, flushed from his exertion (for he never rides casually), I watched him closely. His behavior struck my already suspicious eye as being one of false heartiness and a rather forced good humor. He went to his room early and read for quite a while before turning off his light. I took a long walk in the almost day-bright moonlight, listening to the songs of the night insects in the trees. And I sat for a while in the dark on the stone railing of the bridge across Black River. (It is really only a brook that rushes down over the rocks from the mountain a few miles inland, to the beach near the house.) In the night it always sounds louder and more important than it does in the daytime. The music of the water over the stones relaxed my nerves, although why

I had need of such a thing I find it difficult to understand, unless I was really upset by Racky's not having come home for lunch. But if that were true it would be absurd, and moreover, dangerous—just the sort of thing the parent of an adolescent has to beware of and fight against, unless he is indifferent to the prospect of losing the trust and affection of his offspring permanently. Racky must stay out whenever he likes, with whom he likes, and for as long as he likes, and I must not think twice about it, much less mention it to him, or in any way give the impression of prying. Lack of confidence on the part of a parent is the one unforgivable sin.

Although we still take our morning dip together on arising, it is three weeks since we have been for the early spin. One morning I found that Racky had jumped onto his bicycle in his wet trunks while I was still swimming, and gone by himself, and since then there has been an unspoken agreement between us that such is to be the procedure; he will go alone. Perhaps I held him back; he likes to ride so fast.

Young Peter, the smiling gardener from Saint Ives Cove, is Racky's special friend. It is amusing to see them together among the bushes, crouched over an anthill or rushing about trying to catch a lizard, almost of an age the two, yet so disparate—Racky with his tan skin looking almost white in contrast to the glistening black of the other. Today I know I shall be alone for lunch, since it is Peter's day off. On such days they usually go together on their bicycles into Saint Ives Cove, where Peter keeps a small rowboat. They fish along the coast there, but they have never returned with anything so far.

Meanwhile I am here alone, sitting on the rocks in the sun, from time to time climbing down to cool myself in the water, always conscious of the house behind me under the high palms, like a large glass boat filled with orchids and lilies. The servants are clean and quiet, and the work seems to be accomplished almost automatically. The good, black servants are another blessing of the islands; the British, born here in this paradise, have no conception of how fortunate they are. In fact, they do nothing but complain. One must have lived in the United States to appreciate the wonder of this place. Still, even here ideas are changing each day. Soon the people will decide that they want their land to be a part of today's monstrous world, and once that happens, it will be all over. As soon as you have that desire, you are infected with the deadly virus, and you begin to show the symptoms of the disease. You live in terms of time and money, and you think in terms of society and progress. Then all that is left for you is to kill the other people who think the same way, along with a good many of those who do not, since that is the final manifestation of the malady. Here for the moment at any rate, one has a feeling of staticity—existence ceases to be like those last few seconds in the hourglass when what is left of the sand suddenly begins to rush through to the bottom all at once. For the moment, it seems suspended. And if it seems, it is. Each wave at my feet, each birdcall in the forest at my back, does *not* carry me one step nearer the final disaster. The disaster is certain, but it will suddenly have happened, that is all. Until then, time stays still.

I am upset by a letter in this morning's mail: the Royal Bank of Canada requests that I call in person at its central office to sign the deposit slips and other papers for a sum that was cabled from the bank in Boston. Since the central office is on the other side of the island, fifty miles away, I shall have to spend the night over there and return the following day. There is no point in taking Racky along. The sight of "civilization" might awaken a longing for it in him; one never knows. I am sure it would have in me when I was his age. And if that should once start, he would merely be unhappy, since there is nothing for him but to stay here with me, at least for the next two years, when I hope to renew the lease, or, if things in New York pick up, buy the place. I am sending word by Isiah when he goes home into Orange Walk this evening, to have the McCoigh car call for me at seven-thirty tomorrow morning. It is an enormous old open Packard, and Isiah can save the ride out to work here by piling his bicycle into the back and riding with McCoigh.

The trip across the island was beautiful, and would have been highly enjoyable if my imagination had not played me a strange trick at the very outset. We stopped in Orange Walk for gasoline, and while that was being seen to, I got out and went to the corner store for some cigarettes. Since it was not yet eight o'clock, the store was still closed, and I hurried up the side street to the other little shop which I thought might be open. It was, and I bought my cigarettes. On the way back to the corner I noticed a large black woman leaning with her arms on the gate in front of her tiny house, staring into the street. As I passed by her, she looked straight into my face and said something with the strange accent of the island. It was said in what seemed an unfriendly tone, and ostensibly was directed at me, but I had no notion what it was. I got back into the car and the driver started it. The sound of the words had stayed in my head, however, as a bright shape outlined by darkness is likely to stay in the mind's eye, in such a way that when one shuts one's eyes one can see the exact contour of the shape. The car was already roaring up the hill toward the overland road when I suddenly reheard the very words. And they were: "Keep your boy at home, mahn." I sat perfectly rigid for a moment as the open countryside rushed past. Why should I think she had said that? Immediately I decided that I was giving an arbitrary sense to a phrase I could not have understood even if I had been paying strict attention. And then I wondered why my subconscious should have chosen that sense, since now that I whispered the words over to myself they failed to connect with any anxiety to which my mind might have been disposed. Actually I have never given a thought to Racky's wanderings about Orange Walk. I can find no such preoccupation no matter how I put the question to myself. Then, could she really have said those words? All the way through the mountains I pondered the question, even though it was obviously a waste of energy. And soon I could no longer hear the sound of her voice in my memory: I had played the record over too many times, and worn it out.

Here in the hotel a gala dance is in progress. The abominable orchestra, comprising two saxophones and one sour violin, is playing directly under my window in the garden, and the serious-looking couples slide about on the waxed concrete floor of the terrace, in the light of strings of paper lanterns. I suppose it is meant to look Japanese.

At this moment I wonder what Racky is doing there in the house with only Peter and Ernest the watchman to keep him company. I wonder if he is asleep. The house, which I am accustomed to think of as smiling and benevolent in its airiness, could just as well be in the most sinister and remote regions of the globe, now that I am here. Sitting here with the absurd orchestra bleating downstairs, I picture it to myself, and it strikes me as terribly vulnerable in its isolation. In my mind's eye I see the moonlit point with its tall palms waving restlessly in the wind, its dark cliffs licked by the waves below. Suddenly, although I struggle against the sensation, I am inexpressibly glad to be away from the house, helpless there, far on its point of land, in the silence of the night. Then I remember that the night is seldom silent. There is the loud sea at the base of the rocks, the droning of the thousands of insects, the occasional cries of the night birds—all the familiar noises that make sleep so sound. And Racky is there surrounded by them as usual, not even hearing them. But I feel profoundly guilty for having left him, unutterably tender and sad at the thought of him, lying there alone in the house with the two Negroes the only human beings within miles. If I keep thinking of Cold Point I shall be more and more nervous.

I am not going to bed yet. They are all screaming with laughter down there, the idiots; I could never sleep anyway. The bar is still open. Fortunately it is on the street side of the hotel. For once I need a few drinks.

Much later, but I feel no better; I may be a little drunk. The dance is over and it is quiet in the garden, but the room is too hot.

As I was falling asleep last night, all dressed, and with the overhead light shining sordidly in my face, I heard the black woman's voice again, more clearly even than I did in the car yesterday. For some reason this morning there is no doubt in my mind that the words I heard are the words she said. I accept that and go on from there. Suppose she did tell me to keep Racky home. It could only mean that she, or someone else in Orange Walk, has had a childish altercation with him; although I must say it is hard to conceive of Racky's entering into any sort of argument or feud with those people. To set my mind at rest (for I do seem to be taking the whole thing with great seriousness), I am going to stop in the village this afternoon before going home, and try to see the woman. I am extremely curious to know what she could have meant.

I had not been conscious until this evening when I came back to Cold Point how powerful they are, all those physical elements that go to make up its atmosphere: the sea and wind sounds that isolate the house from the road, the brilliancy of the water, sky and sun, the bright colors and strong odors of the flowers, the feeling of space both outside and within the house. One naturally accepts these things when one is living here. This afternoon when I returned I was conscious of them all over again, of their existence and their strength. All of them together are like a powerful drug; coming back made me feel as though I had been disintoxicated and were returning to the scene of my former indulgences. Now at eleven it is as if I had never been absent an hour. Everything is the same as always, even to the dry palm branch that scrapes against the window screen by my night table. And indeed, it is only thirty-six hours since I was here; but I always expect my absence from a place to bring about irremediable changes.

Strangely enough, now that I think of it, I feel that something *has* changed since I left yesterday morning, and that is the general attitude of the servants—their collective aura, so to speak. I noticed that difference immediately upon arriving back, but was unable to define it. Now I see it clearly. The network of common understanding which slowly spreads itself through a well-run household has been destroyed. Each person is by himself now. No unfriendliness, however, that I can see. They all behave with the utmost courtesy, excepting possibly Peter, who struck me as looking unaccustomedly glum when I encountered him in the kitchen after dinner. I meant to ask Racky if he had noticed it, but I forgot and he went to bed early.

In Orange Walk I made a brief stop on the pretext to McCoigh that I wanted to see the seamstress in the side street. I walked up and back in front of the house where I had seen the woman, but there was no sign of anyone.

As for my absence, Racky seems to have been perfectly content, having spent most of the day swimming off the rocks below the terrace. The insect sounds are at their height now, the breeze is cooler than usual, and I shall take advantage of these favorable conditions to get a good long night's rest.

Today has been one of the most difficult days of my life. I arose early, we had breakfast at the regular time, and Racky went off in the direction of Saint Ives Cove. I lay in the sun on the terrace for a while, listening to the noises of the household's regime. Peter was all over the property, collecting dead leaves and fallen blossoms in a huge basket and carrying them off to the compost heap. He appeared to be in an even fouler humor than last night. When he came near to me at one point on his way to another part of the garden I called to him. He set the basket down and stood looking at me; then he walked across the grass toward me slowly—reluctantly, it seemed to me.

"Peter, is everything all right with you?"

"Yes, sir."

"No trouble at home?"

"Oh, no, sir."

"Good."

"Yes, sir."

He went back to his work. But his face belied his words. Not only did he seem to be in a decidedly unpleasant temper; out here in the sunlight he looked positively ill. However, it was not my concern, if he refused to admit it.

When the heavy heat of the sun reached the unbearable point for me, I got out of my chair and went down the side of the cliff along the series of steps cut there into the rock. A level platform is below, and a diving board, for the water is deep. At each side, the rocks spread out and the waves break over them, but by the platform the wall of rock is vertical and the water merely hits against it below the springboard. The place is a tiny amphitheatre, quite cut off in sound and sight from the house. There too I like to lie in the sun; when I climb out of the water I often remove my trunks and lie stark naked on the springboard. I regularly make fun of Racky because he is embarrassed to do the same. Occasionally he will do it, but never without being coaxed. I was spread out there without a stitch on, being lulled by the slapping of the water, when an unfamiliar voice very close to me said: "Mister Norton?"

I jumped with nervousness, nearly fell off the springboard, and sat up, reaching at the same time, but in vain, for my trunks, which were lying on the rock practically at the feet of a middle-aged mulatto gentleman. He was in a white duck suit, and wore a high collar with a black tie, and it seemed to me that he was eyeing me with a certain degree of horror.

My next reaction was one of anger at being trespassed upon in this way. I rose and got the trunks, however, donning them calmly and saying nothing more meaningful than: "I didn't hear you come down the steps."

"Shall we go up?" said my caller. As he led the way, I had a definite premonition that he was here on an unpleasant errand. On the terrace we sat down, and he offered me an American cigarette which I did not accept.

"This is a delightful spot," he said, glancing out to sea and then at the end of his cigarette, which was only partially aglow. He puffed at it.

I said, "Yes," waiting for him to go on; presently he did.

"I am from the constabulary of this parish. The police, you see." And seeing my face, "This is a friendly call. But still it must be taken as a warning, Mister Norton. It is very serious. If anyone else comes to you about this it will mean trouble for you, heavy trouble. That's why I want to see you privately this way and warn you personally. You see."

I could not believe I was hearing his words. At length I said faintly: "But what about?"

"This is not an official call. You must not be upset. I have taken it upon myself to speak to you because I want to save you deep trouble."

"But I *am* upset!" I cried, finding my voice at last. "How can I help being upset, when I don't know what you're talking about?"

He moved his chair close to mine, and spoke in a very low voice.

"I have waited until the young man was away from the house so we could talk in private. You see, it is about him."

Somehow that did not surprise me. I nodded.

"I will tell you very briefly. The people here are simple country folk. They make trouble easily. Right now they are all talking about the young man you have living here with you. He is your son, I hear." His inflection here was skeptical.

"Certainly he's my son."

His expression did not change, but his voice grew indignant. "Whoever he is, that is a bad young man."

"What do you mean?" I cried, but he cut in hotly: "He may be your son; he may not be. I don't care who he is. That is not my affair. But he is bad through and through. We don't have such things going on here, sir. The people in Orange Walk and Saint Ives Cove are very cross now. You don't know what these folk do when they are aroused."

I thought it my turn to interrupt. "Please tell me why you say my son is bad. What has he done?" Perhaps the earnestness in my voice reached him, for his face assumed a gentler aspect. He leaned still closer to me and almost whispered.

"He has no shame. He does what he pleases with all the young boys, and the men too, and gives them a shilling so they won't tell about it.

But they talk. Of course they talk. Every man for twenty miles up and down the coast knows about it. And the women too, they know about it." There was a silence.

I had felt myself preparing to get to my feet for the last few seconds because I wanted to go into my room and be alone, to get away from that scandalized stage whisper. I think I mumbled "Good morning" or "Thank you," as I turned away and began walking toward the house. But he was still beside me, still whispering like an eager conspirator into my ear: "Keep him home, Mister Norton. Or send him away to school, if he is your son. But make him stay out of these towns. For his own sake."

I shook hands with him and went to lie on my bed. From there I heard his car door slam, heard him drive off. I was painfully trying to formulate an opening sentence to use in speaking to Racky about this, feeling that the opening sentence would define my stand. The attempt was merely a sort of therapeutic action, to avoid thinking about the thing itself. Every attitude seemed impossible. There was no way to broach the subject. I suddenly realized that I should never be able to speak to him directly about it. With the advent of this news he had become another person—an adult, mysterious and formidable. To be sure, it did occur to me that the mulatto's story might not be true, but automatically I rejected the doubt. It was as if I wanted to believe it, almost as if I had already known it, and he had merely confirmed it.

Racky returned at midday, panting and grinning. The inevitable comb appeared and was used on the sweaty, unruly locks. Sitting down to lunch, he exclaimed: "Gosh! Did I find a swell beach this morning! But what a job to get to it!" I tried to look unconcerned as I met his gaze; it was as if our positions had been reversed, and I were hoping to stem his rebuke. He prattled on about thorns and vines and his machete. Throughout the meal I kept telling myself: "Now is the moment. You must say something." But all I said was: "More salad? Or do you want dessert now?" So the lunch passed and nothing happened. After I had finished my coffee I went into my bedroom and looked at myself in the large mirror. I saw my eyes trying to give their reflected brothers a little courage. As I stood there I heard a commotion in the other wing of the house: voices, bumpings, the sound of a scuffle. Above the noise came Gloria's sharp voice, imperious and excited: "No, mahn! Don't strike him!" And louder: "Peter, mahn, no!"

I went quickly toward the kitchen, where the trouble seemed to be, but on the way I was run into by Racky, who staggered into the hallway with his hands in front of his face.

"What is it, Racky?" I cried.

He pushed past me into the living room without moving his hands away from his face; I turned and followed him. From there he went into his own room, leaving the door open behind him. I heard him in his bathroom running the water. I was undecided what to do. Suddenly Peter appeared in the hall doorway, his hat in his hand. When he raised his head, I was surprised to see that his cheek was bleeding. In his eyes was a strange, confused expression of transient fear and deep hostility. He looked down again.

"May I please talk with you, sir?"

"What was all the racket? What's been happening?"

"May I talk with you outside, sir?" He said it doggedly, still not looking up.

In view of the circumstances, I humored him. We walked slowly up the cinder road to the main highway, across the bridge, and through the forest while he told me his story. I said nothing.

At the end he said: "I never wanted to, sir, even the first time, but after the first time I was afraid, and Mister Racky was after me every day."

I stood still, and finally said: "If you had only told me this the first time it happened, it would have been much better for everyone."

He turned his hat in his hands, studying it intently. "Yes, sir. But I didn't know what everyone was saying about him in Orange Walk until today. You know I always go to the beach at Saint Ives Cove with Mister Racky on my free days. If I had known what they were all saying I wouldn't have been afraid, sir. And I wanted to keep on working here. I needed the money." Then he repeated what he had already said three times. "Mister Racky said you'd see about it that I was put in the jail. I'm a year older than Mister Racky, sir."

"I know, I know," I said impatiently; and deciding that severity was what Peter expected of me at this point I added: "You had better get your things together and go home. You can't work here any longer, you know."

The hostility in his face assumed terrifying proportions as he said: "If you killed me I would not work anymore at Cold Point, sir."

I turned and walked briskly back to the house, leaving him standing there in the road. It seems he returned at dusk, a little while ago, and got his belongings.

In his room Racky was reading. He had stuck some adhesive tape on his chin and over his cheekbone.

"I've dismissed Peter," I announced. "He hit you, didn't he?"

He glanced up. His left eye was swollen, but not yet black.

"He sure did. But I landed him one, too. And I guess I deserved it anyway."

I rested against the table. "Why?" I asked nonchalantly.

"Oh, I had something on him from a long time back that he was afraid I'd tell you."

"And just now you threatened to tell me?"

"Oh, no! He said he was going to quit the job here, and I kidded him about being yellow."

"Why did he want to quit? I thought he liked the job."

"Well, he did, I guess, but he didn't like me." Racky's candid gaze betrayed a shade of pique. I still leaned against the table.

I persisted. "But I thought you two got on fine together. You seemed to."

"Nah. He was just scared of losing his job. I had something on him. He was a good guy, though; I liked him all right." He paused. "Has he gone yet?" A strange quaver crept into his voice as he said the last words, and I understood that for the first time Racky's heretofore impeccable histrionics were not quite equal to the occasion. He was very much upset at losing Peter.

"Yes, he's gone," I said shortly. "He's not coming back, either." And as Racky, hearing the unaccustomed inflection in my voice, looked up at me suddenly with faint astonishment in his young eyes, I realized that this was the moment to press on, to say: "What did you have on him?" But as if he had arrived at the same spot in my mind a fraction of a second earlier, he proceeded to snatch away my advantage by jumping up, bursting into loud song, and pulling off all his clothes simultaneously. As he stood before me naked, singing at the top of his lungs, and stepped into his swimming trunks, I was conscious that again I should be incapable of saying to him what I must say.

He was in and out of the house all afternoon: some of the time he read in his room, and most of the time he was down on the diving board. It is strange behavior for him; if I could only know what is in his mind. As evening approached, my problem took on a purely obsessive character. I walked to and fro in my room, always pausing at one end to look out the window over the sea, and at the other end to glance at my face in the mirror. As if that could help me! Then I took a drink. And another. I thought I might be able to do it at dinner, when I felt fortified by the whiskey. But no. Soon he will have gone to bed. It is not that I expect to confront him with any accusations. That I know I never can do. But I must find a way to keep him from his wanderings, and I must offer a reason to give him, so that he will never suspect that I know.

We fear for the future of our offspring. It is ludicrous, but only a little more palpably so than anything else in life. A length of time has passed; days which I am content to have known, even if now they are over. I think that this period was what I had always been waiting for life to offer, the recompense I had unconsciously but firmly expected, in return for having been held so closely in the grip of existence all these years.

That evening seems long ago only because I have recalled its details so many times that they have taken on the color of legend. Actually my problem already had been solved for me then, but I did not know it. Because I could not perceive the pattern, I foolishly imagined that I must cudgel my brains to find the right words with which to approach Racky. But it was he who came to me. That same evening, as I was about to go out for a solitary stroll which I thought might help me hit upon a formula, he appeared at my door.

"Going for a walk?" he asked, seeing the stick in my hand.

The prospect of making an exit immediately after speaking with him made things seem simpler. "Yes," I said, "but I'd like to have a word with you first."

"Sure. What?" I did not look at him because I did not want to see the watchful light I was sure was playing in his eyes at this moment. As I spoke I tapped with my stick along the designs made by the tiles in the floor. "Racky, would you like to go back to school?"

"Are you kidding? You know I hate school."

I glanced up at him. "No, I'm not kidding. Don't look so horrified.

You'd probably enjoy being with a bunch of fellows your own age."
(That was not one of the arguments I had meant to use.)

"I might like to be with guys my own age, but I don't want to have
to be in school to do it. I've had school enough."

I went to the door and said lamely: "I thought I'd get your reactions."
He laughed. "No, thanks."

"That doesn't mean you're not going," I said over my shoulder as I
went out.

On my walk I pounded the highway's asphalt with my stick, stood
on the bridge having dramatic visions which involved such eventualities
as our moving back to the States, Racky's having a bad spill on his bicycle
and being paralyzed for some months, and even the possibility of my
letting events take their course, which would doubtless mean my having
to visit him now and then in the governmental prison with gifts of food,
if it meant nothing more tragic and violent. "But none of these things
will happen," I said to myself, and I knew I was wasting precious time;
he must not return to Orange Walk tomorrow.

I went back toward the point at a snail's pace. There was no moon and
very little breeze. As I approached the house, trying to tread lightly on
the cinders so as not to awaken the watchful Ernest and have to explain
to him that it was only I, I saw that there were no lights in Racky's room.
The house was dark save for the dim lamp on my night table. Instead
of going in, I skirted the entire building, colliding with bushes and
getting my face sticky with spiderwebs, and went to sit awhile on the
terrace where there seemed to be a breath of air. The sound of the sea
was far out on the reef, where the breakers sighed. Here below, there were
only slight watery chugs and gurgles now and then. It was unusually low
tide. I smoked three cigarettes mechanically, having ceased even to think,
and then, my mouth tasting bitter from the smoke, I went inside.

My room was airless. I flung my clothes onto a chair and looked at
the night table to see if the carafe of water was there. Then my mouth
opened. The top sheet of my bed had been stripped back to the foot. There
on the far side of the bed, dark against the whiteness of the lower sheet,
lay Racky asleep on his side, and naked.

I stood looking at him for a long time, probably holding my breath,
for I remember feeling a little dizzy at one point. I was whispering to

myself, as my eyes followed the curve of his arm, shoulder, back, thigh, leg: "A child. A child." Destiny, when one perceives it clearly from very near, has no qualities at all. The recognition of it and the consciousness of the vision's clarity leave no room on the mind's horizon. Finally I turned off the light and softly lay down. The night was absolutely black.

He lay perfectly quiet until dawn. I shall never know whether or not he was really asleep all that time. Of course he couldn't have been, and yet he lay so still. Warm and firm, but still as death. The darkness and silence were heavy around us. As the birds began to sing, I sank into a soft, enveloping slumber; when I awoke in the sunlight later, he was gone.

I found him down by the water, cavorting alone on the springboard; for the first time he had discarded his trunks without my suggesting it. All day we stayed together around the terrace and on the rocks, talking, swimming, reading, and just lying flat in the hot sun. Nor did he return to his room when night came. Instead, after the servants were asleep, we brought three bottles of champagne in and set the pail on the night table.

Thus it came about that I was able to touch on the delicate subject that still preoccupied me, and profiting by the new understanding between us, I made my request in the easiest, most natural fashion.

"Racky, would you do me a tremendous favor if I asked you?"

He lay on his back, his hands beneath his head. It seemed to me his regard was circumspect, wanting in candor.

"I guess so," he said. "What is it?"

"Will you stay around the house for a few days—a week, say? Just to please me? We can take some rides together, as far as you like. Would you do that for me?"

"Sure thing," he said, smiling.

I was temporizing, but I was desperate.

Perhaps a week later—(it is only when one is not fully happy that one is meticulous about time, so that it may have been more or less)—we were having breakfast. Isiah stood by, in the shade, waiting to pour us more coffee.

"I noticed you had a letter from Uncle Charley the other day," said Racky. "Don't you think we ought to invite him down?"

My heart began to beat with great force.

"Here? He'd hate it here," I said casually. "Besides, there's no room. Where would he sleep?" Even as I heard myself saying the words, I knew that they were the wrong ones, that I was not really participating in the conversation. Again I felt the fascination of complete helplessness that comes when one is suddenly a conscious onlooker at the shaping of one's fate.

"In my room," said Racky. "It's empty."

I could see more of the pattern at that moment than I had ever suspected existed. "Nonsense," I said. "This is not the sort of place for Uncle Charley."

Racky appeared to be hitting on an excellent idea. "Maybe if I wrote and invited him," he suggested, motioning to Isiah for more coffee.

"Nonsense," I said again, watching still more of the pattern reveal itself, like a photographic print becoming constantly clearer in a tray of developing solution.

Isiah filled Racky's cup and returned to the shade. Racky drank slowly, pretending to be savoring the coffee.

"Well, it won't do any harm to try. He'd appreciate the invitation," he said speculatively.

For some reason, at this juncture I knew what to say, and as I said it, I knew what I was going to do.

"I thought we might fly over to Havana for a few days next week."

He looked guardedly interested, and then he broke into a wide grin. "Swell!" he cried. "Why wait till next week?"

The next morning the servants called "Good-bye" to us as we drove up the cinder road in the McCoigh car. We took off from the airport at six that evening. Racky was in high spirits; he kept the stewardess engaged in conversation all the way to Camagüey.

He was delighted also with Havana. Sitting in the bar at the Nacional, we continued to discuss the possibility of having C. pay us a visit at the island. It was not without difficulty that I eventually managed to persuade Racky that writing him would be inadvisable.

We decided to look for an apartment right there in Vedado for Racky. He did not seem to want to come back here to Cold Point. We also decided that living in Havana he would need a larger income than I. I am already having the greater part of Hope's estate transferred to his name in the form of a trust fund which I shall administer until he is of age. It was his mother's money, after all.

We bought a new convertible, and he drove me out to Rancho Boyeros in it when I took my plane. A Cuban named Claudio with very white teeth, whom Racky had met in the pool that morning, sat between us.

We were waiting in front of the landing field. An official finally unhooked the chain to let the passengers through. "If you get fed up, come to Havana," said Racky, pinching my arm.

The two of them stood together behind the rope, waving to me, their shirts flapping in the wind as the plane started to move.

The wind blows by my head; between each wave there are thousands of tiny licking and chopping sounds as the water hurries out of the crevices and holes; and a part-floating, part-submerged feeling of being in the water haunts my mind even as the hot sun burns my face. I sit here and I read, and I wait for the pleasant feeling of repletion that follows a good meal, to turn slowly, as the hours pass along, into the even more delightful, slightly stirring sensation deep within, which accompanies the awakening of the appetite.

I am perfectly happy here in reality, because I still believe that nothing very drastic is likely to befall this part of the island in the near future.

THE CIRCULAR VALLEY

The abandoned monastery stood on a slight eminence of land in the middle of a vast clearing. On all sides the ground sloped gently downward toward the tangled, hairy jungle that filled the circular valley, ringed about by sheer, black cliffs. There were a few trees in some of the courtyards, and the birds used them as meeting places when they flew out of the rooms and corridors where they had their nests. Long ago bandits had taken whatever was removable out of the building. Soldiers had used it once as headquarters, had, like the bandits, built fires in the great windy rooms so that afterward they looked like ancient kitchens. And now that everything was gone from within, it seemed that never again would anyone come near the monastery. The vegetation had thrown up a protecting wall; the first story was soon quite hidden from view by small trees which dripped vines to lasso the cornices of the windows. The meadows roundabout grew dank and lush; there was no path through them.

At the higher end of the circular valley a river fell off the cliffs into a great cauldron of vapor and thunder below; after this it slid along the base of the cliffs until it found a gap at the other end of the valley, where it hurried discreetly through with no rapids, no cascades—a great thick black rope of water moving swiftly downhill between the polished flanks of the canyon. Beyond the gap the land opened out and became smiling; a village nestled on the side hill just outside. In the days of the monastery it was there that the friars had got their provisions, since the Indians would not enter the circular valley. Centuries ago when the building had been constructed the Church had imported the workmen from another part of the country. These were traditional enemies of the tribes there-

61

abouts, and had another language; there was no danger that the inhabitants would communicate with them as they worked at setting up the mighty walls. Indeed, the construction had taken so long that before the east wing was completed the workmen had all died, one by one. Thus it was the friars themselves who had closed off the end of the wing with blank walls, leaving it that way, unfinished and blind-looking, facing the black cliffs.

Generation after generation, the friars came, fresh-cheeked boys who grew thin and gray, and finally died, to be buried in the garden beyond the courtyard with the fountain. One day not long ago they had all left the monastery; no one knew where they had gone, and no one thought to ask. It was shortly after this that the bandits, and then the soldiers had come. And now, since the Indians do not change, still no one from the village went up through the gap to visit the monastery. The Atlájala lived there; the friars had not been able to kill it, had given up at last and gone away. No one was surprised, but the Atlájala gained in prestige by their departure. During the centuries the friars had been there in the monastery, the Indians had wondered why it allowed them to stay. Now, at last, it had driven them out. It always had lived there, they said, and would go on living there because the valley was its home, and it could never leave.

In the early morning the restless Atlájala would move through the halls of the monastery. The dark rooms sped past, one after the other. In a small patio, where eager young trees had pushed up the paving stones to reach the sun, it paused. The air was full of small sounds: the movements of butterflies, the falling to the ground of bits of leaves and flowers, the air following its myriad courses around the edges of things, the ants pursuing their endless labors in the hot dust. In the sun it waited, conscious of each gradation in sound and light and smell, living in the awareness of the slow, constant disintegration that attacked the morning and transformed it into afternoon. When evening came, it often slipped above the monastery roof and surveyed the darkening sky: the waterfall would roar distantly. Night after night, along the procession of years, it had hovered here above the valley, darting down to become a bat, a leopard, a moth for a few minutes or hours, returning to rest immobile in the center of the space enclosed by the cliffs. When the monastery had been built, it had taken to frequenting the rooms, where it had observed for the first time the meaningless gestures of human life.

And then one evening it had aimlessly become one of the young friars. This was a new sensation, strangely rich and complex, and at the same time unbearably stifling, as though every other possibility besides that of being enclosed in a tiny, isolated world of cause and effect had been removed forever. As the friar, it had gone and stood in the window, looking out at the sky, seeing for the first time, not the stars, but the space between and beyond them. Even at that moment it had felt the urge to leave, to step outside the little shell of anguish where it lodged for the moment, but a faint curiosity had impelled it to remain a little longer and partake a little further of the unaccustomed sensation. It held on; the friar raised his arms to the sky in an imploring gesture. For the first time the Atlájala sensed opposition, the thrill of a struggle. It was delicious to feel the young man striving to free himself of its presence, and it was immeasurably sweet to remain there. Then with a cry the friar had rushed to the other side of the room and seized a heavy leather whip hanging on the wall. Tearing off his clothing he had begun to carry out a ferocious self-beating. At the first blow of the lash the Atlájala had been on the point of letting go, but then it realized that the immediacy of that intriguing inner pain was only made more manifest by the impact of the blows from without, and so it stayed and felt the young man grow weak under his own lashing. When he had finished and said a prayer, he crawled to his pallet and fell asleep weeping, while the Atlájala slipped out obliquely and entered into a bird which passed the night sitting in a great tree on the edge of the jungle, listening intently to the night sounds, and uttering a scream from time to time.

Thereafter the Atlájala found it impossible to resist sliding inside the bodies of the friars; it visited one after the other, finding an astonishing variety of sensation in the process. Each was a separate world, a separate experience, because each had different reactions when he became conscious of the other being within him. One would sit and read or pray, one would go for a long troubled walk in the meadows, around and around the building, one would find a comrade and engage in an absurd but bitter quarrel, a few wept, some flagellated themselves or sought a friend to wield the lash for them. Always there was a rich profusion of perceptions for the Atlájala to enjoy, so that it no longer occurred to it to frequent the bodies of insects, birds and furred animals, nor even to leave the monastery and move in the air above. Once it almost got into difficulties when an old friar it was occupying suddenly fell back dead. That was a hazard it ran in the frequenting of men: they seemed not to know when they were doomed, or if they did know, they pretended with such strength not to know, that it amounted to the same thing. The other beings knew beforehand, save when it was a question of being seized unawares and devoured. And that the Atlájala was able to prevent: a bird in which it was staying was always avoided by the hawks and eagles.

When the friars left the monastery, and, following the government's orders, doffed their robes, dispersed and became workmen, the Atlájala was at a loss to know how to pass its days and nights. Now everything was as it had been before their arrival: there was no one but the creatures that always had lived in the circular valley. It tried a giant serpent, a deer, a bee: nothing had the savor it had grown to love. Everything was the same as before, but not for the Atlájala; it had known the existence of man, and now there were no men in the valley—only the abandoned building with its empty rooms to make man's absence more poignant.

Then one year bandits came, several hundred of them in one stormy afternoon. In delight it tried many of them as they sprawled about cleaning their guns and cursing, and it discovered still other facets of sensation: the hatred they felt for the world, the fear they had of the soldiers who were pursuing them, the strange gusts of desire that swept through them as they sprawled together drunk by the fire that smoldered in the center of the floor and the insufferable pain of jealousy which the nightly orgies seem to awaken in some of them. But the bandits did not stay long. When they had left, the soldiers came in their wake. It felt very much the same way to be a soldier as to be a bandit. Missing were the strong fear and the hatred, but the rest was almost identical. Neither the bandits nor the soldiers appeared to be at all conscious of its presence in them; it could slip from one man to another without causing any change in their behavior. This surprised it, since its effect on the friars had been so definite, and it felt a certain disappointment at the impossibility of making its existence known to them.

Nevertheless, the Atlájala enjoyed both bandits and soldiers immensely, and was even more desolate when it was left alone once again. It would become one of the swallows that made their nests in the rocks beside the top of the waterfall. In the burning sunlight it would plunge again and again into the curtain of mist that rose from far below, sometimes uttering exultant cries. It would spend a day as a plant louse, crawling slowly along the underside of the leaves, living quietly in the huge green world down there which is forever hidden from the sky. Or at night, in the velvet body of a panther, it would know the pleasure of the kill. Once for a year it lived in an eel at the bottom of the pool below the waterfall, feeling the mud give slowly before it as it pushed ahead with its flat nose; that was a restful period, but afterward the desire to know again the mysterious life of man had returned—an obsession of which it was useless to try to rid itself. And now it moved restlessly through the ruined rooms, a mute presence, alone, and thirsting to be incarnate once again, but in man's flesh only. And with the building of highways through the country it was inevitable that people should come once again to the circular valley.

A man and a woman drove their automobile as far as a village down in a lower valley; hearing about the ruined monastery and the waterfall that dropped over the cliffs into the great amphitheatre, they determined to see these things. They came on burros as far as the village outside the gap, but there the Indians they had hired to accompany them refused to go any farther, and so they continued alone, upward through the canyon and into the precinct of the Atlájala.

It was noon when they rode into the valley; the black ribs of the cliffs glistened like glass in the sun's blistering downward rays. They stopped the burros by a cluster of boulders at the edge of the sloping meadows. The man got down first, and reached up to help the woman off. She leaned forward, putting her hands on his face, and for a long moment they kissed. Then he lifted her to the ground and they climbed hand in hand up over the rocks. The Atlájala hovered near them, watching the woman closely: she was the first ever to have come into the valley. The two sat beneath a small tree on the grass, looking at one another, smiling. Out of habit, the Atlájala entered into the man. Immediately, instead of existing in the midst of the sunlit air, the bird calls and the plant odors, it was conscious only of the woman's beauty and her terrible imminence. The waterfall, the earth, and the sky itself receded, rushed into nothingness, and there were only the woman's smile and her arms and her odor. It was a world more suffocating and painful than the Atlájala had thought possible. Still, while the man spoke and the woman answered, it remained within.

"Leave him. He doesn't love you."

"He would kill me."

"But I love you. I need you with me."

"I can't. I'm afraid of him."

The man reached out to pull her to him; she drew back slightly, but her eyes grew large.

"We have today," she murmured, turning her face toward the yellow walls of the monastery.

The man embraced her fiercely, crushing her against him as though the act would save his life. "No, no, no. It can't go on like this," he said. "No."

The pain of his suffering was too intense; gently the Atlájala left the man and slipped into the woman. And now it would have believed itself to be housed in nothing, to be in its own spaceless self, so completely was it aware of the wandering wind, the small flutterings of the leaves, and the bright air that surrounded it. Yet there was a difference: each element was magnified in intensity, the whole sphere of being was immense, limitless. Now it understood what the man sought in the woman, and it knew that he suffered because he never would attain that sense of completion he sought. But the Atlájala, being one with the woman, had attained it, and being aware of possessing it, trembled with delight. The woman shuddered as her lips met those of the man. There on the grass in the shade of the tree their joy reached new heights; the Atlájala, knowing them both, formed a single channel between the secret springs of their desires. Throughout, it remained within the woman, and began vaguely to devise ways of keeping her, if not inside the valley, at least nearby, so that she might return.

In the afternoon, with dreamlike motions, they walked to the burros and mounted them, driving them through the deep meadow grass to the monastery. Inside the great courtyard they halted, looking hesitantly at the ancient arches in the sunlight, and at the darkness inside the doorways.

"Shall we go in?" said the woman.

"We must get back."

"I want to go in," she said. (The Atlájala exulted.) A thin gray snake slid along the ground into the bushes. They did not see it.

The man looked at her perplexedly. "It's late," he said.

But she jumped down from her burro by herself and walked beneath the arches into the long corridor within. (Never had the rooms seemed so real as now when the Atlájala was seeing them through her eyes.)

They explored all the rooms. Then the woman wanted to climb up into the tower, but the man took a determined stand.

"We must go back now," he said firmly, putting his hand on her shoulder.

"This is our only day together, and you think of nothing but getting back."

"But the time . . ."

"There is a moon. We won't lose the way."

He would not change his mind. "No."

"As you like," she said. "I'm going up. You can go back alone if you like."

The man laughed uneasily. "You're mad." He tried to kiss her.

She turned away and did not answer for a moment. Then she said: "You want me to leave my husband for you. You ask everything from me, but what do you do for me in return? You refuse even to climb up into a little tower with me to see the view. Go back alone. Go!"

She sobbed and rushed toward the dark stairwell. Calling after her, he followed, but stumbled somewhere behind her. She was as sure of foot as if she had climbed the many stone steps a thousand times before, hurrying up through the darkness, around and around.

In the end she came out at the top and peered through the small apertures in the cracking walls. The beams which had supported the bell had rotted and fallen; the heavy bell lay on its side in the rubble, like a dead animal. The waterfall's sound was louder up here; the valley was nearly full of shadow. Below, the man called her name repeatedly. She did not answer. As she stood watching the shadow of the cliffs slowly overtake the farthest recesses of the valley and begin to climb the naked rocks to the east, an idea formed in her mind. It was not the kind of idea which she would have expected of herself, but it was there, growing and inescapable. When she felt it complete there inside her, she turned and went lightly back down. The man was sitting in the dark near the bottom of the stairs, groaning a little.

"What is it?" she said.

"I hurt my leg. Now are you ready to go or not?"

"Yes," she said simply. "I'm sorry you fell."

Without saying anything he rose and limped after her out into the courtyard where the burros stood. The cold mountain air was beginning to flow down from the tops of the cliffs. As they rode through the meadow she began to think of how she would broach the subject to him. (It must be done before they reached the gap. The Atlájala trembled.)

"Do you forgive me?" she asked him.

"Of course," he laughed.

"Do you love me?"

"More than anything in the world."

"Is that true?"

He glanced at her in the failing light, sitting erect on the jogging animal.

"You know it is," he said softly.

She hesitated.

"There is only one way, then," she said finally.

"But what?"

"I'm afraid of him. I won't go back to him. You go back. I'll stay in the village here." (Being that near, she would come each day to the monastery.) "When it is done, you will come and get me. Then we can go somewhere else. No one will find us."

The man's voice sounded strange. "I don't understand."

"You do understand. And that is the only way. Do it or not, as you like. It is the only way."

They trotted along for a while in silence. The canyon loomed ahead, black against the evening sky.

Then the man said, very clearly: "Never."

A moment later the trail led out into an open space high above the swift water below. The hollow sound of the river reached them faintly. The light in the sky was almost gone; in the dusk the landscape had taken on false contours. Everything was gray—the rocks, the bushes, the trail— and nothing had distance or scale. They slowed their pace.

His word still echoed in her ears.

"I won't go back to him!" she cried with sudden vehemence. "You can go back and play cards with him as usual. Be his good friend the same as always. I won't go. I can't go on with both of you in the town." (The plan was not working; the Atlájala saw it had lost her, yet it still could help her.)

"You're very tired," he said softly.

He was right. Almost as he said the words, that unaccustomed exhilaration and lightness she had felt ever since noon seemed to leave her; she hung her head wearily, and said: "Yes, I am."

At the same moment the man uttered a sharp, terrible cry; she looked up in time to see his burro plunge from the edge of the trail into the grayness below. There was a silence, and then the faraway sound of many stones sliding downward. She could not move or stop the burro; she sat dumbly, letting it carry her along, an inert weight on its back.

For one final instant, as she reached the pass which was the edge of its realm, the Atlájala alighted tremulously within her. She raised her head and a tiny exultant shiver passed through her; then she let it fall forward once again.

Hanging in the dim air above the trail, the Atlájala watched her indistinct figure grow invisible in the gathering night. (If it had not been able to hold her there, still it had been able to help her.)

A moment later it was in the tower, listening to the spiders mend the webs that she had damaged. It would be a long, long time before it would bestir itself to enter into another being's awareness. A long, long time—perhaps forever.

THE DELICATE PREY

There were three Filala who sold leather in Tabelbala—two brothers and the young son of their sister. The two older merchants were serious, bearded men who liked to engage in complicated theological discussions during the slow passage of the hot hours in their *hanoute* near the marketplace; the youth naturally occupied himself almost exclusively with the black-skinned girls in the small *quartier réservé*. There was one who seemed more desirable than the others, so that he was a little sorry when the older men announced that soon they would all leave for Tessalit. But nearly every town has its *quartier*, and Driss was reasonably certain of being able to have any lovely resident of any *quartier*, whatever her present emotional entanglements; thus his chagrin at hearing of the projected departure was short-lived.

The three Filala waited for the cold weather before starting out for Tessalit. Because they wanted to get there quickly they chose the western-most trail, which is also the one leading through the most remote regions, contiguous to the lands of the plundering Reguibat tribes. It was a long time since the uncouth mountain men had swept down from the *hammada* upon a caravan; most people were of the opinion that since the war of the Sarrho they had lost the greater part of their arms and ammunition, and, more important still, their spirit. And a tiny group of three men and their camels could scarcely awaken the envy of the Reguibat, tradition-ally rich with loot from all Río de Oro and Mauretania.

Their friends in Tabelbala, most of them other Filali leather merchants, walked beside them sadly as far as the edge of the town; then they bade them farewell, and watched them mount their camels to ride off slowly toward the bright horizon.

"If you meet any Reguibat, keep them ahead of you!" they called.

The danger lay principally in the territory they would reach only three or four days' journey from Tabelbala; after a week the edge of the land haunted by the Reguibat would be left entirely behind. The weather was cool save at midday. They took turns sitting guard at night; when Driss stayed awake he brought out a small flute whose piercing notes made the older uncle frown with annoyance, so that he asked him to go and sit at some distance from the sleeping-blankets. All night he sat playing whatever sad songs he could call to mind; the bright ones in his opinion belonged to the *quartier,* where one was never alone.

When the uncles kept watch, they sat quietly, staring ahead of them into the night. There were just the three of them.

And then one day a solitary figure appeared, moving toward them across the lifeless plain from the west. One man on a camel; there was no sign of any others, although they scanned the wasteland in every direction. They stopped for a while; he altered his course slightly. They went ahead; he changed it again. There was no doubt that he wanted to speak with them.

"Let him come," grumbled the older uncle, glaring about the empty horizon once more. "We each have a gun."

Driss laughed. To him it seemed absurd even to admit the possibility of trouble from one lone man.

When finally the figure arrived within calling distance, it hailed them in a voice like a muezzin's: *"S'l'm aleikoum!"* They halted, but did not dismount, and waited for the man to draw nearer. Soon he called again; this time the older uncle replied, but the distance was still too great for his voice to carry, and the man did not hear his greeting. Presently he was close enough for them to see that he did not wear Reguiba attire. They muttered to one another: "He comes from the north, not the west." And they all felt glad. However, even when he came up beside them they remained on the camels, bowing solemnly from where they sat, and always searching in the new face and in the garments below it for some false note which might reveal the possible truth—that the man was a scout for the Reguibat, who would be waiting up on the *hammada* only a few hours distant, or even now moving parallel to the trail, closing in upon them in such a manner that they would not arrive at a point within visibility until after dusk.

Certainly the stranger himself was no Reguiba; he was quick and jolly, with light skin and very little beard. It occurred to Driss that he did not like his small, active eyes which seemed to take in everything and give out nothing, but this passing reaction became only a part of the general initial distrust, all of which was dissipated when they learned that the man was a Moungari. Moungar is a holy place in that part of the world, and its few residents are treated with respect by the pilgrims who go to visit the ruined shrine nearby.

The newcomer took no pains to hide the fear he had felt at being alone in the region, or the pleasure it gave him to be now with three other men. They all dismounted and made tea to seal their friendship, the Moungari furnishing the charcoal.

During the third round of glasses he made the suggestion that since he was going more or less in their direction he accompany them as far as Taoudeni. His bright black eyes darting from one Filali to the other, he explained that he was an excellent shot, that he was certain he could supply them all with some good gazelle meat en route, or at least an *aoudad.* The Filala considered; the oldest finally said: "Agreed." Even if the Moungari turned out to have not quite the hunting prowess he claimed for himself, there would be four of them on the voyage instead of three.

Two mornings later, in the mighty silence of the rising sun, the Moungari pointed at the low hills that lay beside them to the east: "*Timma.* I know this land. Wait here. If you hear me shoot, then come, because that will mean there are gazelles."

The Moungari went off on foot, climbing up between the boulders and disappearing behind the nearest crest. "He trusts us," thought the Filala. "He has left his *mehari,* his blankets, his packs." They said nothing, but each knew that the others were thinking the same as he, and they all felt warmly toward the stranger. They sat waiting in the early-morning chill while the camels grumbled.

It seemed unlikely that there would prove to be any gazelles in the region, but if there should be any, and the Moungari were as good a hunter as he claimed to be, then there was a chance they would have a *mechoui* of gazelle that evening, and that would be very fine.

Slowly the sun mounted in the hard blue sky. One camel lumbered up and went off, hoping to find a dead thistle or a bush between the rocks, something left over from a year when rain might have fallen. When it had disappeared, Driss went in search of it and drove it back to the others, shouting: *"Hut!"*

He sat down. Suddenly there came a shot, a long empty interval, and then another shot. The sounds were fairly distant, but perfectly clear in the absolute silence. The older brother said: "I shall go. Who knows? There may be many gazelles."

He clambered up the rocks, his gun in his hand, and was gone.

Again they waited. When the shots sounded this time, they came from two guns.

"Perhaps they have killed one!" Driss cried.

"Yemkin. With Allah's aid," replied his uncle, rising and taking up his gun. "I want to try my hand at this."

Driss was disappointed: he had hoped to go himself. If only he had got up a moment ago, it might have been possible, but even so it was likely that he would have been left behind to watch the *mehara.* In any case, now it was too late; his uncle had spoken.

"Good."

His uncle went off singing a song from Tafilalet: it was about date palms and hidden smiles. For several minutes Driss heard snatches of the song, as the melody reached the high notes. Then the sound was lost in the enveloping silence.

He waited. The sun began to be very hot. He covered his head with his burnoose. The camels looked at each other stupidly, craning their necks, baring their brown and yellow teeth. He thought of playing his flute, but it did not seem the right moment: he was too restless, too eager to be up there with his gun, crouching behind the rocks, stalking the delicate prey. He thought of Tessalit and wondered what it would be like. Full of blacks and Touareg, certainly more lively than Tabelbala, because of the road that passed through it. There was a shot. He waited for others, but no more came this time. Again he imagined himself there among the boulders, taking aim at a fleeing beast. He pulled the trigger, the animal fell. Others appeared, and he got them all. In the dark the travelers sat around the fire gorging themselves with the rich roasted flesh, their faces gleaming with grease. Everyone was happy, and even the Moungari admitted that the young Filali was the best hunter of them all.

In the advancing heat he dozed, his mind playing over a landscape made of soft thighs and small hard breasts rising like sand dunes; wisps of song floated like clouds in the sky, and the air was thick with the taste of fat gazelle meat.

He sat up and looked around quickly. The camels lay with their necks stretched along the ground in front of them. Nothing had changed. He stood up, uneasily scanned the stony landscape. While he had slept, a hostile presence had entered into his consciousness. Translating into thought what he already sensed, he cried out. Since first he had seen those small, active eyes he had felt mistrust of their owner, but the fact that his uncles had accepted him had pushed suspicion away into the dark of his mind. Now, unleashed in his slumber, it had bounded back. He turned toward the hot hillside and looked intently between the boulders, into the black shadows. In memory he heard again the shots up among the rocks, and he knew what they had meant. Catching his breath in a sob, he ran to mount his *mehari,* forced it up, and already had gone several hundred paces before he was aware of what he was doing. He stopped the animal to sit quietly a moment, glancing back at the campsite with fear and indecision. If his uncles were dead, then there was nothing to do but get out into the open desert as quickly as possible, away from the rocks that could hide the Moungari while he took aim.

And so, not knowing the way to Tessalit, and without sufficient food or water, he started ahead, lifting one hand from time to time to wipe away the tears.

For two or three hours he continued that way, scarcely noticing where the *mehari* walked. All at once he sat erect, uttered an oath against himself, and in a fury turned the beast around. At that very moment his uncles might be seated in the camp with the Moungari, preparing a *mechoui* and a fire, sadly asking themselves why their nephew had deserted them. Or perhaps one would already have set out in search of him. There would be no possible excuse for his conduct, which had been the result of an absurd terror. As he thought about it, his anger against himself mounted: he had behaved in an unforgivable manner. Noon had passed; the sun was in the west. It would be late when he got back. At the prospect of the inevitable reproaches and the mocking laughter that would greet him, he felt his face grow hot with shame, and he kicked the *mehari*'s flanks viciously.

A good while before he arrived at the camp he heard singing. This surprised him. He halted and listened: the voice was too far away to be identified, but Driss felt certain it was the Moungari's. He continued around the side of the hill to a spot in full view of the camels. The singing stopped, leaving silence. Some of the packs had been loaded back on to the beasts, preparatory to setting out. The sun had sunk low, and the shadows of the rocks were stretched out along the earth. There was no sign that they had caught any game. He called out, ready to dismount. Almost at the same instant there was a shot from very nearby, and he heard the small rushing sound of a bullet go past his head. He seized his gun. There was another shot, a sharp pain in his arm, and his gun slipped to the ground.

For a moment he sat there holding his arm, dazed. Then swiftly he leapt down and remained crouching among the stones, reaching out with his good arm for the gun. As he touched it, there was a third shot, and the rifle moved along the ground a few inches toward him in a small cloud of dust. He drew back his hand and looked at it: it was dark and blood dripped from it. At that moment the Moungari bounded across the open space between them. Before Driss could rise the man was upon him, had pushed him back down to the ground with the barrel of his rifle. The untroubled sky lay above; the Moungari glanced up at it defiantly. He straddled the supine youth, thrusting the gun into his neck just below the chin, and under his breath he said: "Filali dog!"

Driss stared up at him with a certain curiosity. The Moungari had the upper hand; Driss could only wait. He looked at the face in the sun's light, and discovered a peculiar intensity there. He knew the expression: it comes from hashish. Carried along on its hot fumes, a man can escape very far from the world of meaning. To avoid the malevolent face he rolled his eyes from side to side. There was only the fading sky. The gun was choking him a little. He whispered: "Where are my uncles?"

The Moungari pushed harder against his throat with the gun, leaned partially over and with one hand ripped away his *serouelles*, so that he lay naked from the waist down, squirming a little as he felt the cold stones beneath him.

Then the Moungari drew forth rope and bound his feet. Taking two steps to his head, he abruptly faced in the other direction, and thrust the gun into his navel. Still with one hand he slipped the remaining garments off over the youth's head and lashed his wrists together. With an old barber's razor he cut off the superfluous rope. During this time Driss called his uncles by name, loudly, first one and then the other.

The man moved and surveyed the young body lying on the stones. He ran his finger along the razor's blade; a pleasant excitement took possession of him. He stepped over, looked down, and saw the sex that sprouted from the base of the belly. Not entirely conscious of what he was doing, he took it in one hand and brought his other arm down with the motion of a reaper wielding a sickle. It was swiftly severed. A round, dark hole was left, flush with the skin; he stared a moment, blankly. Driss was screaming. The muscles all over his body stood out, moved.

Slowly the Moungari smiled, showing his teeth. He put his hand on the hard belly and smoothed the skin. Then he made a small vertical incision there, and using both hands, studiously stuffed the loose organ in until it disappeared.

As he was cleaning his hands in the sand, one of the camels uttered a sudden growling gurgle. The Moungari leapt up and wheeled about savagely, holding his razor high in the air. Then, ashamed of his nervousness, feeling that Driss was watching and mocking him (although the youth's eyes were unseeing with pain), he kicked him over on to his stomach where he lay making small spasmodic movements. And as the Moungari followed these with his eyes, a new idea came to him. It would be pleasant to inflict an ultimate indignity upon the young Filali. He threw himself down; this time he was vociferous and leisurely in his enjoyment. Eventually he slept.

At dawn he awoke and reached for his razor, lying on the ground nearby. Driss moaned faintly. The Moungari turned him over and pushed the blade back and forth with a sawing motion into his neck until he was certain he had severed the windpipe. Then he rose, walked away, and finished the loading of the camels he had started the day before. When this was done he spent a good while dragging the body over to the base of the hill and concealing it there among the rocks.

In order to transport the Filala's merchandise to Tessalit (for in Taoudeni there would be no buyers) it was necessary to take their *mehara* with him. It was nearly fifty days later when he arrived. Tessalit is a small town. When the Moungari began to show the leather around, an old Filali living there, whom the people called Ech Chibani, got wind of his presence. As a prospective buyer he came to examine the hides, and the

Moungari was unwise enough to let him see them. Filali leather is unmistakable, and only the Filala buy and sell it in quantity. Ech Chibani knew the Moungari had come by it illicitly, but he said nothing. When a few days later another caravan arrived from Tabelbala with friends of the three Filala who asked after them and showed great distress on hearing that they never had arrived, the old man went to the Tribunal. After some difficulty he found a Frenchman who was willing to listen to him. The next day the commandant and two subordinates paid the Moungari a visit. They asked him how he happened to have the three extra *mehara,* which still carried some of their Filali trappings; his replies took a devious turn. The Frenchmen listened seriously, thanked him, and left. He did not see the commandant wink at the others as they went out into the street. And so he remained sitting in his courtyard, not knowing that he had been judged and found guilty.

The three Frenchmen went back to the Tribunal, where the newly arrived Filali merchants were sitting with Ech Chibani. The story had an old pattern; there was no doubt at all about the Moungari's guilt. "He is yours," said the commandant. "Do what you like with him."

The Filala thanked him profusely, held a short conference with the aged Chibani, and strode out in a group. When they arrived at the Moungari's dwelling he was making tea. He looked up, and a chill moved along his spine. He began to scream his innocence at them; they said nothing, but at the point of a rifle bound him and tossed him into a corner, where he continued to babble and sob. Quietly they drank the tea he had been brewing, made some more, and went out at twilight. They tied him to one of the *mehara,* and mounting their own, moved in a silent procession (silent save for the Moungari) out through the town gate into the infinite wasteland beyond.

Half the night they continued, until they were in a completely unfrequented region of the desert. While he lay raving, bound to the camel, they dug a well-like pit, and when they had finished they lifted him off, still trussed tightly, and stood him in it. Then they filled all the space around his body with sand and stones, until only his head remained above the earth's surface. In the faint light of the new moon his shaved pate without its turban looked rather like a rock. And still he pleaded with them, calling upon Allah and Sidi Ahmed Ben Moussa to witness his innocence. But he might have been singing a song for all the attention they paid to his words. Presently they set off for Tessalit; in no time they were out of hearing.

When they had gone the Moungari fell silent, to wait through the cold hours for the sun that would bring first warmth, then heat, thirst, fire, visions. The next night he did not know where he was, did not feel the cold. The wind blew dust along the ground into his mouth as he sang.

AT PASO ROJO

When old Señora Sanchez died, her two daughters Lucha and Chalía decided to visit their brother at his ranch. Out of devotion they had agreed never to marry while their mother lived, and now that she was gone and they were both slightly over forty there seemed just as little likelihood of a wedding in the family as there ever had. They would probably not admit this even to themselves, however. It was with complete understanding of his two sisters that Don Federico suggested they leave the city and go down to Paso Rojo for a few weeks.

Lucha arrived in black crêpe. To her, death was one of the things that happen in life with a certain regularity, and it therefore demanded outward observance. Otherwise her life was in no way changed, save that at the ranch she would have to get used to a whole new staff of servants.

"Indians, poor things, animals with speech," she said to Don Federico the first night as they sat having coffee. A barefooted girl had just carried the dessert dishes out.

Don Federico smiled. "They are good people," he said deliberately. Living at the ranch so long had lowered his standards, it was said, for even though he had always spent a month or so of each year in the capital, he had grown increasingly indifferent to the social life there.

"The ranch is eating his soul little by little," Lucha used to say to Señora Sanchez.

Only once the old lady had replied. "If his soul is to be eaten, then let the ranch do it."

She looked around the primitive dining room with its dry decorations of palm leaves and branches. "He loves it here because everything is his,"

79

she thought, "and some of the things could never have been his if he had not purposely changed to fit them." That was not a completely acceptable thought. She knew the ranch had made him happy and tolerant and wise; to her it seemed sad that he could not have been those things without losing his civilized luster. And that he certainly had lost. He had the skin of a peasant—brown and lined everywhere. He had the slowness of speech of men who have lived for long periods of time in the open. And the inflections of his voice suggested the patience that can come from talking to animals rather than to human beings. Lucha was a sensible woman; still, she could not help feeling a certain amount of regret that her little brother, who at an earlier point in his life had been the best dancer among the members of the country club, should have become the thin, sad-faced, quiet man who sat opposite her.

"You've changed a great deal," she suddenly said, shaking her head from side to side slowly.

"Yes. You change here. But it's a good place."

"Good, yes. But so sad," she said.

He laughed. "Not sad at all. You get used to the quiet. And then you find it's not quiet at all. But you never change much, do you? Chalía's the one who's different. Have you noticed?"

"Oh, Chalía's always been crazy. She doesn't change either."

"Yes. She is very much changed." He looked past the smoking oil lamp, out into the dark. "Where is she? Why doesn't she take coffee?"

"She has insomnia. She never takes it."

"Maybe our nights will put her to sleep," said Don Federico.

Chalía sat on the upper veranda in the soft night breeze. The ranch stood in a great clearing that held the jungle at bay all about, but the monkeys were calling from one side to the other, as if neither clearing nor ranch house existed. She had decided to put off going to bed—that way there was less darkness to be borne in case she stayed awake. The lines of a poem she had read on the train two days before were still in her mind: "Aveces la noche. . . . Sometimes the night takes you with it, wraps you up and rolls you along, leaving you washed in sleep at the morning's edge." Those lines were comforting. But there was the terrible line yet to come: "And sometimes the night goes on without you." She tried to jump from the image of the fresh sunlit morning to a completely

80

alien idea: the waiter at the beach club in Puntarenas, but she knew the other thought was waiting there for her in the dark.

She had worn riding breeches and a khaki shirt open at the neck, on the trip from the capital, and she had announced to Lucha her intention of going about in those clothes the whole time she was at Paso Rojo. She and Lucha had quarreled at the station.

"Everyone knows Mamá has died," said Lucha, "and the ones who aren't scandalized are making fun of you."

With intense scorn in her voice Chalía had replied, "You have asked them, I suppose."

On the train as it wound through the mountains toward *tierra caliente* she had suddenly said, apropos of nothing: "Black doesn't become me." Really upsetting to Lucha was the fact that in Puntarenas she had gone off and bought some crimson nail polish which she had painstakingly applied herself in the hotel room.

"You can't, Chalía!" cried her sister, wide-eyed. "You've never done it before. Why do you do it now?"

Chalía had laughed immoderately. "Just a whim!" she had said, spreading her decorated hands in front of her.

Loud footsteps came up the stairs and along the veranda, shaking it slightly. Her sister called: "Chalía!"

She hesitated an instant, then said, "Yes."

"You're sitting in the dark! Wait. I'll bring out a lamp from your room. What an idea!"

"We'll be covered with insects," objected Chalía, who, although her mood was not a pleasant one, did not want it disturbed.

"Federico says no!" shouted Lucha from inside. "He says there are no insects! None that bite, anyway!"

Presently she appeared with a small lamp which she set on a table against the wall. She sat down in a nearby hammock and swung herself softly back and forth, humming. Chalía frowned at her, but she seemed not to notice.

"What heat!" exclaimed Lucha finally.

"Don't exert yourself so much," suggested Chalía.

They were quiet. Soon the breeze became a strong wind, coming from the direction of the distant mountains; but it too was hot, like the breath of a great animal. The lamp flickered, threatened to go out. Lucha got up and turned it down. As Chalía moved her head to watch her, her attention was caught by something else, and she quickly shifted her gaze to the wall. Something enormous, black and swift had been there an instant ago; now there was nothing. She watched the spot intently. The wall was faced with small stones which had been plastered over and whitewashed indifferently, so that the surface was very rough and full of large holes. She rose suddenly and approaching the wall, peered at it closely. All the holes, large and small, were lined with whitish funnels. She could see the long, agile legs of the spiders that lived inside, sticking out beyond some of the funnels.

"Lucha, this wall is full of monsters!" she cried. A beetle flew near to the lamp, changed its mind and lighted on the wall. The nearest spider darted forth, seized it and disappeared into the wall with it.

"Don't look at them," advised Lucha, but she glanced about the floor near her feet apprehensively.

Chalía pulled her bed into the middle of the room and moved a small table over to it. She blew out the lamp and lay back on the hard mattress. The sound of the nocturnal insects was unbearably loud—an endless, savage scream above the noise of the wind. All the vegetation out there was dry. It made a million scraping sounds in the air as the wind swept through it. From time to time the monkeys called to each other from different sides. A night bird scolded occasionally, but its voice was swallowed up in the insistent insect song and the rush of wind across the hot countryside. And it was absolutely dark.

Perhaps an hour later she lit the lamp by her bed, rose, and in her nightgown went to sit on the veranda. She put the lamp where it had been before, by the wall, and turned her chair to face it. She sat watching the wall until very late.

At dawn the air was cool, full of the sound of continuous lowing of cattle, nearby and far. Breakfast was served as soon as the sky was completely light. In the kitchen there was a hubbub of women's voices. The dining room smelled of kerosene and oranges. A great platter heaped with thick slices of pale pineapple was in the center of the table. Don Federico sat at the end, his back to the wall. Behind him was a small niche, bright with candles, and the Virgin stood there in a blue and silver gown.

"Did you sleep well?" said Don Federico to Lucha.

"Ah, wonderfully well!"

"And you?" to Chalía.

"I never sleep well," she said.

A hen ran distractedly into the room from the veranda and was chased out by the serving girl. Outside the door a group of Indian children stood guard around a square of clothesline along which was draped a red assortment of meat: strips of flesh and loops of internal organs. When a vulture swooped low, the children jumped up and down, screaming in chorus, and drove it into the air again. Chalía frowned at their noise. Don Federico smiled.

"This is all in your honor," he said. "We killed a cow yesterday. Tomorrow all that will be gone."

"Not the vultures!" exclaimed Lucha.

"Certainly not. All the cowboys and servants take some home to their families. And they manage to get rid of quite a bit of it themselves."

"You're too generous," said Chalía. "It's bad for them. It makes them dissatisfied and unhappy. But I suppose if you didn't give it to them, they'd steal it anyway."

Don Federico pushed back his chair.

"No one here has ever stolen anything from me." He rose and went out.

After breakfast while it was still early, before the sun got too high in the sky, he regularly made a two-hour tour of the ranch. Since he preferred to pay unexpected visits to the vaqueros in charge of the various districts, he did not always cover the same regions. He was explaining this to Lucha as he untethered his horse outside the high barbed-wire fence that enclosed the house. "Not because I hope to find something wrong. But this is the best way always to find everything right."

Like Chalía, Lucha was skeptical of the Indians' ability to do anything properly. "A very good idea," she said. "I'm sure you are much too lenient with those boys. They need a strong hand and no pity."

Above the high trees that grew behind the house the red and blue macaws screamed, endlessly repeating their elliptical path in the sky. Lucha looked up in their direction and saw Chalía on the upper porch, tucking a khaki shirt into her breeches.

"Rico, wait! I want to go with you," she called, and rushed into her room.

Lucha turned back to her brother. "You won't take her? She couldn't! With Mamá . . ."

Don Federico cut her short, so as not to hear what would have been painful to him. "You both need fresh air and exercise. Come, both of you."

Lucha was silent a moment, looking aghast into his face. Finally she said, "I couldn't," and moved away to open the gate. Several cowboys were riding their horses slowly up from the paddock toward the front of the house. Chalía appeared on the lower porch and hurried to the gate, where Lucha stood looking at her.

"So you're going horseback riding," said Lucha. Her voice had no expression.

"Yes. Are you coming? I suppose not. We should be back soon; no, Rico?"

Don Federico disregarded her, saying to Lucha: "It would be good if you came."

When she did not reply, but went through the gate and shut it, he had one of the cowboys dismount and help Chalía onto his horse. She sat astride the animal beaming down at the youth.

"Now, you can't come. You have no horse!" she cried, pulling the reins taut violently so that the horse stood absolutely still.

"Yes, señora. I shall go with the señores." His speech was archaic and respectful, the speech of the rustic Indian. Their soft, polite words always annoyed her, because she believed, quite erroneously, that she could detect mockery underneath. "Like parrots who've been taught two lines of Góngora!" she would laugh, when the subject was being discussed. Now she was further nettled by hearing herself addressed as señora. "The idiot!" she thought. "He should know that I'm not married." But when she looked down at the cowboy again she noticed his white teeth and his very young face. She smiled, saying, "How hot it is already," and undid the top button of her shirt.

The boy ran to the paddock and returned immediately, riding a larger and more nervous horse. This was a joke to the other cowboys, who started ahead, laughing. Don Federico and Chalía rode side by side, and the boy went along behind them, by turns whistling a tune and uttering soothing words to his skittish horse.

The party went across the mile or so of open space that lay between the house and the jungle. Then the high grass swept the riders' legs as the horses went downward to the river, which was dry save for a narrow stream of water in the middle. They followed the bed downstream, the vegetation increasing the height along the banks as they progressed. Chalía had enameled her fingernails afresh before starting out and was in a good humor. She was discussing the administration of the ranch with Don Federico. The expenses and earning capacity interested her particularly, although she had no clear idea of the price of anything. She had worn an enormous soft straw sombrero whose brim dropped to her shoulders as she rode. Every few minutes she turned around and waved to the cowboy who still remained behind, shouting to him: "Muchacho! You're not lost yet?"

Presently the river was divided into two separate beds by a large island which loomed ahead of them, its upper reaches a solid wall of branches and vines. At the foot of the giant trees among some gray boulders was a score or so of cows, looking very small indeed as they lay hunched up in the mud or ambled about seeking the thickest shade. Don Federico galloped ahead suddenly and conferred loudly with the other vaqueros. Almost simultaneously Chalía drew in her reins and brought her horse to a halt. The boy was quickly abreast of her. As he came up she called to him: "It's hot, isn't it?"

The men rode on ahead. He circled around her. "Yes, señora. But that is because we are in the sun. There"—he indicated the island—"it is shady. Now they are almost there."

She said nothing, but took off her hat and fanned herself with the brim. As she moved her hand back and forth she watched her red nails. "What an ugly color," she murmured.

"What, señora?"

"Nothing." She paused. "Ah, what heat!"

"Come, señora. Shall we go on?"

Angrily she crumpled the crown of the sombrero in her fist. "I am not señora," she said distinctly, looking at the men ahead as they rode up to the cows and roused them from their lethargy. The boy smiled. She went on. "I am señorita. That is not the same thing. Or perhaps you think it is?"

The boy was puzzled; he was conscious of her sudden emotion, but he had no idea of its cause. "Yes, señorita," he said politely, without conviction. And he added, with more assurance, "I am Roberto Paz, at your orders."

The sun shone down upon them from above and was reflected by the mica in the stones at their feet. Chalía undid another button of her shirt. "It's hot. Will they come back soon?"

"No, señorita. They return by the road. Shall we go?" He turned his horse toward the island ahead.

"I don't want to be where the cows are," said Chalía with petulance. "They have *garrapatas*. The *garrapatas* get under your skin."

Roberto laughed indulgently. "The *garrapatas* will not molest you if you stay on your horse, señorita."

"But I want to get down and rest. I'm so tired!" The discomfort of the heat became pure fatigue as she said the words; this made it possible for the annoyance she felt with him to transform itself into a general state of self-pity and depression that came upon her like a sudden pain. Hanging her head she sobbed: *"Ay, madre mía!* My poor mamá!" She stayed that way a moment, and her horse began to walk slowly toward the trees at the side of the riverbed.

Roberto glanced perplexedly in the direction the others had taken. They had all passed out of sight beyond the head of the island; the cows were lying down again. "The señorita should not cry."

She did not reply. Since the reins continued slack, her horse proceeded at a faster pace toward the forest. When it had reached the shade at the edge of the stream, the boy rode quickly to her side. "Señorita!" he cried.

She sighed and looked up at him, her hat still in her hand. "I'm very tired," she repeated. "I want to get down and rest."

There was a path leading into the forest. Roberto went ahead to lead the way, hacking at stray vines and bushes with his machete. Chalía followed, sitting listlessly in the saddle, calmed by the sudden entrance into the green world of silence and comparative coolness.

They rode slowly upward through the forest for a quarter of an hour or so without saying anything to each other. When they came to a gate

Roberto opened it without dismounting and waited for Chalía to pass through. As she went by him she smiled and said: "How nice it is here."

He replied, rather curtly, she thought: "Yes, señorita."

Ahead, the vegetation thinned, and beyond lay a vast, open, slightly undulating expanse of land, decorated here and there, as if by intent, with giant white-trunked ceiba trees. The hot wind blew across this upland terrain, and the cry of cicadas was in the air. Chalía halted her horse and jumped down. The tiny thistlelike plants that covered the ground crackled under her boots. She seated herself carefully in the shade at the very edge of the open land.

Roberto tied the two horses to a tree and stood looking at her with the alert, hostile eyes of the Indian who faces what he does not understand.

"Sit down. Here," she said.

Stonily he obeyed, sitting with his legs straight on the earth in front of him, his back very erect. She rested her hand on his shoulder. *"Qué calor,"* she murmured.

She did not expect him to answer, but he did, and his voice sounded remote. "It is not my fault, señorita."

She slipped her arm around his neck and felt the muscles grow tense. She rubbed her face over his chest; he did not move or say anything. With her eyes shut and her head pressing hard against him, she felt as if she were hanging to consciousness only by the ceaseless shrill scream of the cicadas. She remained thus, leaning over more heavily upon him as he braced himself with his hands against the earth behind him. His face had become an impenetrable mask; he seemed not to be thinking of anything, not even to be present.

Breathing heavily, she raised her head to look at him, but found she did not have the courage to reach his eyes with her gaze. Instead she watched his throat and finally whispered, "It doesn't matter what you think of me. It's enough for me to hold you like this."

He turned his head stiffly away from her face, looking across the landscape to the mountains. Gruffly he said, "My brother could come by this place. We must go back to the river."

She tried to bury her face in his chest, to lose herself once more in the delicious sensation. Without warning, he moved quickly and stood up, so that she tumbled forward with her face against the ground.

The surprise of her little fall changed her mood instantly. She sprang up, dashed blindly for the nearer of the two horses, was astride it in an instant, and before he could cry, "It's the bad horse!" had pounded the animal's flanks with her heels. It raised its head wildly; with a violent bound it began to gallop over the countryside. At the first movement she realized dimly that there had been a change, that it was not the same horse, but in her excitement she let her observation stop there. She was delighted to be moving swiftly across the plain against the hot wind. Roberto was left behind.

"*Idiota!*" she screamed into the air. "*Idiota! Idiota!*" with all her might. Ahead of her a tremendous vulture, panic-stricken at the approaching hoof sounds, flapped clumsily away into the sky.

The saddle, having been strapped on for less vigorous action, began to slip. She gripped the pommel with one hand, and seizing her shirt with the other gave it a convulsive tug that ripped it completely open. A powerful feeling of exultation came to her as she glanced down and saw her own skin white in the sunlight.

In the distance to one side, she dimly saw some palm trees reaching above a small patch of lower vegetation. She shut her eyes: the palms looked like shiny green spiders. She was out of breath from the jolting. The sun was too hot. The saddle kept slipping further; she could not right it. The horse showed no sign of being aware of her existence. She pulled on the reins as hard as she could without falling over backward, but it had no effect on the horse, which continued to run at top speed, following no path and missing some of the trees by what seemed no more than inches.

"Where shall I be in an hour?" she asked herself. "Dead, perhaps?" The idea of death did not frighten her the way it did some people. She was afraid of the night because she could not sleep; she was not afraid of life and death because she did not feel implicated to any extent in either one. Only other people lived and died, had their lives and deaths. She, being inside herself, existed merely as herself and not as a part of anything else. People, animals, flowers and stones were objects, and they all belonged to the world outside. It was their juxtapositions that made hostile or friendly patterns. Sometimes she looked at her own hands and feet for several minutes, trying to fight off an indefinite sensation they gave her of belonging also to the world outside. But this never troubled her deeply. The impressions were received and accepted without question; at most she could combat them when they were too strong for her comfort.

Here in the hot morning sun, being pulled forward through the air, she began to feel that almost all of her had slipped out of the inside world, that only a tiny part of her was still she. The part that was left was full of astonishment and disbelief; the only discomfort now lay in having to accept the fact of the great white tree trunks that continued to rush by her.

She tried several times to make herself be elsewhere: in her rose garden at home, in the hotel dining room at Puntarenas, even as a last resort which might prove feasible since it too had been unpleasant, in her bed back at the ranch, with the dark around her.

With a great bound, the horse cleared a ditch. The saddle slipped completely around and hung underneath. Having no pommel to cling to, she kept on as best she could, clutching the horse's flanks with her legs and always pulling on the reins. Suddenly the animal slowed down and stepped briskly into a thicket. There was a path of sorts; she suspected it was the same one they had used coming from the river. She sat listlessly, waiting to see where the horse would go.

Finally it came out into the riverbed as she had expected, and trotted back to the ranch. The sun was directly overhead when they reached the paddock. The horse stood outside, waiting to be let in, but it seemed that no one was around. Making a great effort, she slid down to the ground and found she had difficulty in standing because her legs were trembling so. She was furious and ashamed. As she hobbled toward the house she was strongly hoping Lucha would not see her. A few Indian girls appeared to be the only people about. She dragged herself upstairs and shut herself in her room. The bed had been pushed back against the wall, but she did not have the force to pull it out into the center where she wanted it.

When Don Federico and the others returned, Lucha, who had been reading downstairs, went to the gate. "Where's Chalía?" she cried.

"She was tired. One of the boys brought her back a while ago," he said. "It's just as well. We went halfway to Las Cañas."

Chalía had her lunch in bed and slept soundly until late in the afternoon. When she emerged from her room onto the veranda, a woman was dusting the rocking chairs and arranging them in a row against the wall.

"Where's my sister?" demanded Chalía.

"Gone to the village in the truck with the señor," the woman replied, going to the head of the stairs and beginning to dust them one by one, as she went down backward.

Chalía seated herself in a chair and put her feet up on the porch railing, reflecting as she did so that if Lucha had been there she would have disapproved of the posture. There was a bend in the river—the only part of it that came within sight of the house—just below her, and a portion of the bank was visible to her through the foliage from where she sat. A large breadfruit tree spread its branches out almost to the opposite side of the stream. There was a pool at the turn, just where the tree's trunk grew out of the muddy bank. An Indian sauntered out of the undergrowth and calmly removed his trousers, then his shirt. He stood there a moment, stark naked, looking at the water, before he walked into it and began to splash and swim. When he had finished bathing he stood again on the bank, smoothing his blue-black hair. Chalía was puzzled, knowing that few Indians would be so immodest as to bathe naked in full view of the upstairs veranda. With a sudden strange sensation as she watched him, she realized it was Roberto and that he was wholly conscious of her presence at that moment.

"He knows Rico is gone and that no one can see him from downstairs," she thought, resolving to tell her brother when he came home. The idea of vengeance upon the boy filled her with a delicious excitement. She watched his deliberate movements as he dressed. He sat down on a rock with only his shirt on and combed his hair. The late-afternoon sun shone through the leaves and gave his brown skin an orange cast. When finally he had gone away without once glancing up at the house, she rose and went into her room. Maneuvering the bed into the middle of the floor once more, she began to walk around it; her mood was growing more and more turbulent as she circled about the room.

She heard the truck door slam, and a moment later, voices downstairs. With her finger to her temple, where she always put it when her heart was beating very fast, she slipped out onto the veranda and downstairs. Don Federico was in the commissary, which he opened for a half hour each morning and evening. Chalía stepped inside the door, her mouth already open, feeling the words about to burst from her lungs. Two children were pushing their copper coins along the counter, pointing at the candy they wanted. By the lamp a woman was looking at a bolt of goods. Don Federico was on a ladder, getting down another bolt. Chalía's mouth closed slowly. She looked down at her brother's desk by the door beside her, where he kept his ledgers and bills. In an open cigar box almost touching her hand was a pile of dirty bank notes. She was back in the room before she knew it. She shut the door and saw that she had four ten-colón notes in her hand. She stuffed them into her breeches pocket.

At dinner they made fun of her for having slept all the afternoon, telling her that now she would lie awake again all night.

She was busy eating. "If I do, so much the worse," she said, without looking up.

"I've arranged a little concert after dinner," said Don Federico. Lucha was ecstatic. He went on: "The cowboys have some friends here, over from Bagaces, and Raul has finished building his marimba."

The men and boys began to assemble soon after dinner. There was laughter, and guitars were strummed in the dark on the terrace. The two sisters went to sit at the end near the dining room, Don Federico was in the middle with the vaqueros, and the servants were ranged at the kitchen end. After several solo songs by various men with guitars, Raul and a friend began to play the marimba. Roberto was seated on the floor among the cowboys who were not performing.

"Suppose we all dance," said Don Federico, jumping up and seizing Lucha. They moved about together at one end of the terrace for a moment, but no one else stirred.

"*A bailar!*" Don Federico shouted, laughing.

Several of the girls started to dance timidly in couples, with loud giggling. None of the men would budge. The marimba players went on pounding out the same piece over and over again. Don Federico danced with Chalía, who was stiff from her morning ride; soon she excused herself and left. Instead of going upstairs to bed she crossed onto the front veranda and sat looking across the vast moonlit clearing. The night was thick with eternity. She could feel it there, just beyond the gate. Only the monotonous, tinkling music kept the house within the confines of time, saved it from being engulfed. As she listened to the merrymaking progress, she had the impression that the men were taking more part in it. "Rico has probably opened them a bottle of rum," she thought with fury.

At last it sounded as though everyone were dancing. Her curiosity having risen to a high pitch, she was about to rise and return to the terrace, when a figure appeared at the other end of the veranda. She needed no one to tell her it was Roberto. He was walking soundlessly toward her; he seemed to hesitate as he came up to her, then he squatted down by her chair and looked up at her. She had been right: he smelled of rum.

"Good evening, señorita."

She felt impelled to remain silent. Nevertheless, she said, "Good evening." She put her hand into her pocket, saying to herself that she must do this correctly and quickly.

As he crouched there with his face shining in the moonlight, she bent forward and passed her hand over his smooth hair. Keeping her fingers on the back of his neck, she leaned still further forward and kissed his lips. The rum was very strong. He did not move. She began to whisper in his ear, very low: "Roberto, I love you. I have a present for you. Forty *colones*. Here."

He turned his head swiftly and said out loud, "Where?"

She put the bills into his hand, still holding his head, and whispered again: "Sh! Not a word to anyone. I must go now. I'll give you more tomorrow night." She let go of him.

He rose and went out the gate. She went straight upstairs to bed, and as she went to sleep the music was still going on.

Much later she awoke and lit her lamp. It was half past four. Day would soon break. Feeling full of an unaccustomed energy, Chalía dressed, extinguished the lamp and went outdoors, shutting the gate quietly behind her. In the paddock the horses stirred. She walked by it and started along the road to the village. It was a very silent hour: the night insects had ceased their noises and the birds had not yet begun their early-morning twitter. The moon was low in the sky, so that it remained behind the trees most of the time. Ahead of her Venus flared like a minor moon. She walked quickly, with only a twinge of pain now and then in her hip.

Something dark lying in the road ahead of her made her stop walking. It did not move. She watched it closely, stepping cautiously toward it, ready to run the other way. As her eyes grew accustomed to its form, she saw that it was a man lying absolutely still. And as she drew near, she knew it was Roberto. She touched his arm with her foot. He did not respond. She leaned over and put her hand on his chest. He was breathing deeply, and the smell of liquor was almost overpowering. She straightened and kicked him lightly in the head. There was a tiny groan from far within. This also, she said to herself, would have to be done quickly. She felt wonderfully light and powerful as she slowly maneuvered his body with her feet to the right-hand side of the road. There was a small cliff there, about twenty feet high. When she got him to the edge, she waited a while, looking at his features in the moonlight. His mouth was open a little, and the white teeth peeked out from behind the lips. She smoothed his forehead a few times and with a gentle push rolled him over the edge. He fell very heavily, making a strange animal sound as he hit.

She walked back to the ranch at top speed. It was getting light when she arrived. She went into the kitchen and ordered her breakfast, saying: "I'm up early." The entire day she spent around the house, reading and talking to Lucha. She thought Don Federico looked preoccupied when he set out on his morning tour of inspection, after closing the commissary. She thought he still did when he returned; she told him so at lunch.

"It's nothing," he said. "I can't seem to balance my books."

"And you've always been such a good mathematician," said Chalía.

During the afternoon some cowboys brought Roberto in. She heard the commotion in the kitchen and the servants' cries of *"Ay, Dios!"* She went out to watch. He was conscious, lying on the floor with all the other Indians staring at him.

"What's the matter?" she said.

One of the cowboys laughed. "Nothing of importance. He had too much—" the cowboy made a gesture of drinking from a bottle, "and fell off the road. Nothing but bruises, I think."

After dinner Don Federico asked Chalía and Lucha into his little private office. He looked drawn, and he spoke more slowly than usual.

93

As Chalía entered she saw that Roberto was standing inside the door. He did not look at her. Lucha and Chalía sat down; Don Federico and Roberto remained standing.

"This is the first time anyone has done this to me," said Don Federico, looking down at the rug, his hands locked behind him. "Roberto has stolen from me. The money is missing. Some of it is in his pocket still, more than his monthly wages. I know he has stolen it because he had no money yesterday and because"—he turned to Chalía—"because he can account for having it only by lying. He says you gave it to him. Did you give Roberto any money yesterday?"

Chalía looked puzzled. "No," she said. "I thought of giving him a *colón* when he brought me back from the ride yesterday morning. But then I thought it would be better to wait until we were leaving to go back to the city. Was it much? He's just a boy."

Don Federico said: "It was forty *colones*. But that's the same as forty *centavos*. Stealing . . ."

Chalía interrupted him. "Rico!" she exclaimed. "Forty *colones!* That's a great deal! Has he spent much of it? You could take it out of his wages little by little." She knew her brother would say what he did say, a moment later.

"Never! He'll leave tonight. And his brother with him."

In the dim light Chalía could see the large purple bruise on Roberto's forehead. He kept his head lowered and did not look up, even when she and Lucha rose and left the room at a sign from their brother. They went upstairs together and sat down on the veranda.

"What barbarous people they are!" said Lucha indignantly. "Poor Rico may learn someday how to treat them. But I'm afraid one of them will kill him first."

Chalía rocked back and forth, fanning herself lazily. "With a few more lessons like this he may change," she said. "What heat!"

They heard Don Federico's voice below by the gate. Firmly it said, *"Adiós."* There were muffled replies and the gate was closed. Don Federico joined his sisters on the veranda. He sat down sadly.

"I didn't like to send them away on foot at night," he said, shaking his head. "But that Roberto is a bad one. It was better to have him go once and for all, quickly. Juan is good, but I had to get rid of him too, of course."

"*Claro, claro,*" said Lucha absently. Suddenly she turned to her brother full of concern. "I hope you remembered to take away the money you said he still had in his pocket."

"Yes, yes," he assured her, but from the tone of his voice she knew he had let the boy keep it.

Don Federico and Lucha said good night and went to bed. Chalía sat up a while, looking vaguely at the wall with the spiders in it. Then she yawned and took the lamp into her room. Again the bed had been pushed back against the wall by the maid. Chalía shrugged her shoulders, got into the bed where it was, blew out the lamp, listened for a few minutes to the night sounds, and went peacefully to sleep, thinking of how surprisingly little time it had taken her to get used to life at Paso Rojo, and even, she had to admit now, to begin to enjoy it.

PASTOR DOWE AT TACATÉ

Pastor Dowe delivered his first sermon in Tacaté on a bright Sunday morning shortly after the beginning of the rainy season. Almost a hundred Indians attended, and some of them had come all the way from Balaché in the valley. They sat quietly on the ground while he spoke to them for an hour or so in their own tongue. Not even the children became restive; there was the most complete silence as long as he kept speaking. But he could see that their attention was born of respect rather than of interest. Being a conscientious man he was troubled to discover this.

When he had finished the sermon, the notes for which were headed "Meaning of Jesus," they slowly got to their feet and began wandering away, quite obviously thinking of other things. Pastor Dowe was puzzled. He had been assured by Dr. Ramos of the University that his mastery of the dialect was sufficient to enable his prospective parishioners to follow his sermons, and he had had no difficulty conversing with the Indians who had accompanied him up from San Gerónimo. He stood sadly on the small thatch-covered platform in the clearing before his house and watched the men and women walking slowly away in different directions. He had the sensation of having communicated absolutely nothing to them.

All at once he felt he must keep the people here a little longer, and he called out to them to stop. Politely they turned their faces toward the pavilion where he stood, and remained looking at him, without moving. Several of the smaller children were already playing a game, and were darting about silently in the background. The pastor glanced at his wrist watch and spoke to Nicolás, who had been pointed out to him as one

96

of the most intelligent and influential men in the village, asking him to come up and stand beside him.

Once Nicolás was next to him, he decided to test him with a few questions. "Nicolás," he said in his dry, small voice, "what did I tell you today?"

Nicolás coughed and looked over the heads of the assembly to where an enormous sow was rooting in the mud under a mango tree. Then he said: "Don Jesucristo."

"Yes," agreed Pastor Dowe encouragingly. *"Bai,* and Don Jesucristo what?"

"A good man," answered Nicolás with indifference.

"Yes, yes, but what more?" Pastor Dowe was impatient; his voice rose in pitch.

Nicolás was silent. Finally he said, "Now I go," and stepped carefully down from the platform. The others again began to gather up their belongings and move off. For a moment Pastor Dowe was furious. Then he took his notebook and his Bible and went into the house.

At lunch Mateo, who waited on table, and whom he had brought with him from Ocosingo, stood leaning against the wall smiling.

"Señor," he said, "Nicolás says they will not come again to hear you without music."

"Music!" cried Pastor Dowe, setting his fork on the table. "Ridiculous! What music? We have no music."

"He says the father at Yalactín used to sing."

"Ridiculous!" said the pastor again. "In the first place I can't sing, and in any case it's unheard of! *Inaudito!"*

"Sí, verdad?" agreed Mateo.

The pastor's tiny bedroom was breathlessly hot, even at night. However, it was the only room in the little house with a window on the outside; he could shut the door onto the noisy patio where by day the servants invariably gathered for their work and their conversations. He lay under the closed canopy of his mosquito net, listening to the barking of the dogs in the village below. He was thinking about Nicolás. Apparently Nicolás had chosen for himself the role of envoy from the village to the mission. The pastor's thin lips moved. "A troublemaker," he whispered to himself. "I'll speak with him tomorrow."

Early the next morning he stood outside Nicolás's hut. Each house in Tacaté had its own small temple: a few tree trunks holding up some thatch to shelter the offerings of fruit and cooked food. The pastor took care not to go near the one that stood nearby; he already felt enough like a pariah, and Dr. Ramos had warned him against meddling of that sort. He called out.

A little girl about seven years old appeared in the doorway of the house. She looked at him wildly a moment with huge round eyes before she squealed and disappeared back into the darkness. The pastor waited and called again. Presently a man came around the hut from the back and told him that Nicolás would return. The pastor sat down on a stump. Soon the little girl stood again in the doorway; this time she smiled coyly. The pastor looked at her severely. It seemed to him she was too old to run about naked. He turned his head away and examined the thick red petals of a banana blossom hanging nearby. When he looked back she had come out and was standing near him, still smiling. He got up and walked toward the road, his head down, as if deep in thought. Nicolás entered through the gate at that moment, and the pastor, colliding with him, apologized.

"Good," grunted Nicolás. "What?"

His visitor was not sure how he ought to begin. He decided to be pleasant.

"I am a good man," he smiled.

"Yes," said Nicolás. "Don Jesucristo is a good man."

"No, no, no!" cried Pastor Dowe.

Nicolás looked politely confused, but said nothing.

Feeling that his command of the dialect was not equal to this sort of situation, the pastor wisely decided to begin again. "Hachakyum made the world. Is that true?"

Nicolás nodded in agreement, and squatted down at the pastor's feet, looking up at him, his eyes narrowed against the sun.

"Hachakyum made the sky," the pastor began to point, "the mountains, the trees, those people there. Is that true?"

Again Nicolás assented.

"Hachakyum is good. Hachakyum made you. True?" Pastor Dowe sat down again on the stump.

Nicolás spoke finally, "All that you say is true."

The pastor permitted himself a pleased smile and went on. "Ha-chakyum made everything and everyone because He is mighty and good."

Nicolás frowned. "No!" he cried. "That is not true! Hachakyum did not make everyone. He did not make you. He did not make guns or Don Jesucristo. Many things He did not make!"

The pastor shut his eyes a moment, seeking strength. "Good," he said at last in a patient voice. "Who made the other things? Who made me? Please tell me."

Nicolás did not hesitate. "Metzabok."

"But who is Metzabok?" cried the pastor, letting an outraged note show in his voice. The word for God he had always known only as Hachakyum.

"Metzabok makes all the things that do not belong here," said Nicolás.

The pastor rose, took out his handkerchief and wiped his forehead. "You hate me," he said, looking down at the Indian. The word was too strong, but he did not know how to say it any other way.

Nicolás stood up quickly and touched the pastor's arm with his hand. "No. That is not true. You are a good man. Everyone likes you."

Pastor Dowe backed away in spite of himself. The touch of the brown hand was vaguely distasteful to him. He looked beseechingly into the Indian's face and said, "But Hachakyum did not make me?"

"No."

There was a long pause.

"Will you come next time to my house and hear me speak?"

Nicolás looked uncomfortable.

"Everyone has work to do," he said.

"Mateo says you want music," began the pastor.

Nicolás shrugged. "To me it is not important. But the others will come if you have music. Yes, that is true. They like music."

"But *what* music?" cried the pastor in desperation.

"They say you have a *bitrola*."

The pastor looked away, thinking: "There is no way to keep anything from these people." Along with all his other household goods and the things left behind by his wife when she died, he had brought a little portable phonograph. It was somewhere in the storeroom piled with the empty valises and cold-weather garments.

"Tell them I will play the *bitrola*," he said, going out the gate.

The little girl ran after him and stood watching him as he walked up the road.

On his way through the village the pastor was troubled by the reflection that he was wholly alone in this distant place, alone in his struggle to bring the truth to its people. He consoled himself by recalling that it is only in each man's own consciousness that the isolation exists; objectively man is always a part of something.

When he arrived home he sent Mateo to the storeroom to look for the portable phonograph. After a time the boy brought it out, dusted it and stood by while the pastor opened the case. The crank was inside. He took it out and wound the spring. There were a few records in the compartment at the top. The first he examined were "Let's Do It," "Crazy Rhythm," and "Strike Up the Band," none of which Pastor Dowe considered proper accompaniments to his sermons. He looked further. There was a recording of Al Jolson singing "Sonny Boy" and a cracked copy of "She's Funny That Way." As he looked at the labels he remembered how the music on each disk had sounded. Unfortunately Mrs. Dowe had disliked hymn music; she had called it "mournful."

"So here we are," he sighed, "without music."

Mateo was astonished. "It does not play?"

"I can't play them this music for dancing, Mateo."

"*Cómo nó, señor!* They will like it very much!"

"No, Mateo!" said the pastor forcefully, and he put on "Crazy Rhythm" to illustrate his point. As the thin metallic tones issued from the instrument, Mateo's expression changed to one of admiration bordering on beatitude. "*Qué bonito!*" he said reverently. Pastor Dowe lifted the tone arm and the hopping rhythmical pattern ceased.

"It cannot be done," he said with finality, closing the lid.

Nevertheless on Saturday he remembered that he had promised Nicolás there would be music at the service, and he decided to tell Mateo to carry the phonograph out to the pavilion in order to have it there in case the demand for it should prove to be pressing. This was a wise precaution, because the next morning when the villagers arrived they were talking of nothing but the music they were to hear.

His topic was "The Strength of Faith," and he had got about ten minutes into the sermon when Nicolás, who was squatting directly in front of him, quietly stood up and raised his hand. Pastor Dowe frowned and stopped talking.

Nicolás spoke: "Now music, then talk. Then music, then talk. Then music." He turned around and faced the others. "That is a good way." There were murmurs of assent, and everyone leaned a bit farther forward on his haunches to catch whatever musical sounds might issue from the pavilion.

The pastor sighed and lifted the machine onto the table, knocking off the Bible that lay at the edge. "Of course," he said to himself with a faint bitterness. The first record he came to was "Crazy Rhythm." As it started to play, an infant nearby, who had been singsonging a series of meaningless sounds, ceased making its parrotlike noises, remaining silent and transfixed as it stared at the platform. Everyone sat absolutely quiet until the piece was over. Then there was a hubbub of approbation. "Now more talk," said Nicolás, looking very pleased.

The pastor continued. He spoke a little haltingly now, because the music had broken his train of thought, and even by looking at his notes he could not be sure just how far he had got before the interruption. As he continued, he looked down at the people sitting nearest him. Beside Nicolás he noticed the little girl who had watched him from the doorway, and he was gratified to see that she was wearing a small garment which managed to cover her. She was staring at him with an expression he interpreted as one of fascinated admiration.

Presently, when he felt that his audience was about to grow restive (even though he had to admit that they never would have shown it outwardly) he put on "Sonny Boy." From the reaction it was not difficult to guess that this selection was finding less favor with its listeners. The general expression of tense anticipation at the beginning of the record soon relaxed into one of routine enjoyment of a less intense degree. When the piece was finished, Nicolás got to his feet again and raised his hand solemnly, saying: "Good. But the other music is more beautiful."

The pastor made a short summation, and, after playing "Crazy Rhythm" again, he announced that the service was over.

In this way "Crazy Rhythm" became an integral part of Pastor Dowe's weekly service. After a few months the old record was so badly worn that he determined to play it only once at each gathering. His flock submitted to this show of economy with bad grace. They complained, using Nicolás as emissary.

"But the music is old. There will be no more if I use it all," the pastor explained.

Nicolás smiled unbelievingly. "You say that. But you do not want us to have it."

The following day, as the pastor sat reading in the patio's shade, Mateo again announced Nicolás, who had entered through the kitchen and, it appeared, had been conversing with the servants there. By now the pastor had learned fairly well how to read the expressions on Nicolás's face; the one he saw there now told him that new exactions were at hand.

Nicolás looked respectful. "Señor," he said, "we like you because you have given us music when we asked you for it. Now we are all good friends. We want you to give us salt."

"Salt?" exclaimed Pastor Dowe, incredulous. "What for?"

Nicolás laughed good-naturedly, making it clear that he thought the pastor was joking with him. Then he made a gesture of licking. "To eat," he said.

"Ah, yes," murmured the pastor, recalling that among the Indians rock salt is a scarce luxury.

"But we have no salt," he said quickly.

"Oh, yes, señor. There." Nicolás indicated the kitchen.

The pastor stood up. He was determined to put an end to this haggling, which he considered a demoralizing element in his official relationship with the village. Signaling for Nicolás to follow, he walked into the kitchen, calling as he entered, "Quintina, show me our salt."

Several of the servants, including Mateo, were standing in the room. It was Mateo who opened a low cupboard and disclosed a great stack of grayish cakes piled on the floor. The pastor was astonished. "So many kilos of salt!" he exclaimed. *Cómo se hace?*

Mateo calmly told him it had been brought with them all the way from Ocosingo. "For us," he added, looking about at the others.

Pastor Dowe seized upon this, hoping it was meant as a hint and could be recognized as one. "Of course," he said to Nicolás. "This is for my house."

Nicolás looked unimpressed. "You have enough for everyone in the

village," he remarked. "In two Sundays you can get more from Ocosingo. Everyone will be very happy all the time that way. Everyone will
come each time you speak. You give them salt and make music."

Pastor Dowe felt himself beginning to tremble a little. He knew he
was excited and so he was careful to make his voice sound natural.

"I will decide, Nicolás," he said. "Good-bye."

It was clear that Nicolás in no way regarded these words as a dismissal.
He answered, "Good-bye," and leaned back against the wall calling,
"Marta!" The little girl, of whose presence in the room the pastor now
became conscious, moved out from the shadows of a corner. She held
what appeared to him to be a large doll, and was being very solicitous
of it. As the pastor stepped out into the bright patio, the picture struck
him as false, and he turned around and looked back into the kitchen,
frowning. He remained in the doorway in an attitude of suspended action
for a moment, staring at little Marta. The doll, held lovingly in the child's
arms, and swaddled in a much-used rag, was making spasmodic movements.

The pastor's ill humor was with him; probably he would have shown
it no matter what the circumstances. "What is it?" he demanded indignantly. As if in answer the bundle squirmed again, throwing off part of
the rag that covered it, and the pastor saw what looked to him like a
comic-strip caricature of Red Riding Hood's wolf peering out from
under the grandmother's nightcap. Again Pastor Dowe cried, "What is
it?"

Nicolás turned from his conversation, amused, and told Marta to hold
it up and uncover it so the señor could see it. This she did, pulling away
the wrapping and exposing to view a lively young alligator which, since
it was being held more or less on its back, was objecting in a routine
fashion to the treatment by rhythmically paddling the air with its little
black feet. Its rather long face seemed, however, to be smiling.

"Good heavens!" cried the pastor in English. The spectacle struck him
as strangely scandalous. There was a hidden obscenity in the sight of the
mildly agitated little reptile with its head wrapped in a rag, but Marta
was still holding it out toward him for his inspection. He touched the
smooth scales of its belly with his fingers, and withdrew his hand, saying,
"Its jaws should be bound. It will bite her."

Mateo laughed. "She is too quick," and then said it in dialect to

103

Nicolás, who agreed, and also laughed. The pastor patted Marta on the head as she returned the animal to her bosom and resumed cradling it tenderly.

Nicolás's eyes were on him. "You like Marta?" he asked seriously.

The pastor was thinking about the salt. "Yes, yes," he said with the false enthusiasm of the preoccupied man. He went to his bedroom and shut the door. Lying on the narrow bed in the afternoon was the same as lying on it at night: there was the same sound of dogs barking in the village. Today there was also the sound of wind going past the window. Even the canopy of mosquito netting swayed a little from time to time as the air came into the room. The pastor was trying to decide whether or not to give in to Nicolás. When he got very sleepy, he thought: "After all, what principle am I upholding in keeping it from them? They want music. They want salt. They will learn to want God." This thought proved relaxing to him, and he fell asleep to the sound of the dogs barking and the wind shrilling past the window.

During the night the clouds rolled down off the mountains into the valley, and when dawn came they remained there, impaled on the high trees. The few birds that made themselves heard sounded as though they were singing beneath the ceiling of a great room. The wet air was thick with woodsmoke, but there was no noise from the village; a wall of cloud lay between it and the mission house.

From his bed, instead of the wind passing the window, the pastor heard the slow drops of water falling upon the bushes from the eaves. He lay still awhile, lulled by the subdued chatter of the servants' voices in the kitchen. Then he went to the window and looked out into the grayness. Even the nearest trees were invisible; there was a heavy odor of earth. He dressed, shivering as the damp garments touched his skin. On the table lay a newspaper:

BARCELONA BOMBARDEADO POR
DOSCIENTOS AVIONES

As he shaved, trying to work up a lather with the tepid water Quintina had brought him, full of charcoal ashes, it occurred to him that he would like to escape from the people of Tacaté and the smothering feeling they gave him of being lost in antiquity. It would be good to be free from that infinite sadness even for a few hours.

He ate a larger breakfast than usual and went outside to the sheltered platform, where he sat down in the dampness and began to read the Seventy-eighth Psalm, which he had thought of using as the basis of a sermon. As he read he looked out at the emptiness in front of him. Where he knew the mango tree stood he could see only the white void, as if the land dropped away at the platform's edge for a thousand feet or more.

"He clave the rocks in the wilderness, and gave them drink as out of the great depths." From the house came the sound of Quintina's giggling. "Mateo is probably chasing her around the patio," thought the pastor; wisely he had long since given up expecting any Indian to behave as he considered an adult should. Every few seconds on the other side of the pavilion a turkey made its hysterical gobbling sound. The pastor spread his Bible out on the table, put his hands to his ears, and continued to read: "He caused an east wind to blow in the heaven: and by His power He brought in the south wind."

"Passages like that would sound utterly pagan in the dialect," he caught himself thinking. He unstopped his ears and reflected: "But to their ears *everything* must have a pagan sound. Everything I say is transformed on the way to them into something else." This was a manner of thinking that Pastor Dowe had always taken pains to avoid. He fixed his eyes on the text with determination, and read on. The giggling in the house was louder; he could hear Mateo too now. "He sent divers sorts of flies among them; . . . and frogs, which destroyed them." The door into the patio was opened and the pastor heard Mateo coughing as he stood looking out. "He certainly has tuberculosis," said the pastor to himself, as the Indian spat repeatedly. He shut his Bible and took off his glasses, feeling about on the table for their case. Not encountering it, he rose, and taking a step forward, crushed it under his heel. Compassionately, he stooped down and picked it up. The hinges were snapped and the metal sides under their artificial leather covering were bent out of shape. Mateo could have hammered it back into a semblance of its form, but Pastor Dowe preferred to think: "All things have their death." He had had the case eleven years. Briefly he summed up its life: the sunny afternoon when he had bought it on the little side street in downtown Havana; the busy years in the hills of southern Brazil; the time in Chile when he had dropped the case, with a pair of dark glasses in it, out the bus window, and everyone in the bus had got out and helped him look for it; the depressing year in Chicago when for some reason he had left it in a bureau drawer most of the time and had carried his glasses loose in his coat pocket. He remembered some of the newspaper clippings he had kept in the case, and many of the little slips of paper with ideas jotted down on them. He looked tenderly down at it, thinking: "And so this is the place and time, and these are the circumstances of its death." For some reason he was happy to have witnessed this death; it was comforting to know exactly how the case had finished its existence. He still looked at it with sadness for a moment. Then he flung it out into the white air as if the precipice were really there. With his Bible under his arm he strode to the door and brushed past Mateo without saying a word. But as he walked into his room it seemed to him that Mateo had looked at him in a strange fashion, as if he knew something and were waiting to see when the pastor would find out, too.

Back in his suffocating little room the pastor felt an even more imperious need to be alone for a time. He changed his shoes, took his cane and went out into the fog. In this weather there was only one path practicable, and that led downward through the village. He stepped ahead over the stones with great caution, for although he could discern the ground at his feet and the spot where he put the tip of his cane each time, beyond that on all sides was mere whiteness. Walking along thus, he reflected, was like trying to read a text with only one letter visible at a time. The wood smoke was sharp in the still air.

For perhaps half an hour Pastor Dowe continued this way, carefully putting one foot before the other. The emptiness around him, the lack of all visual detail, rather than activating his thought, served to dull his perceptions. His progress over the stones was laborious but strangely relaxing. One of the few ideas that came into his head as he moved along was that it would be pleasant to pass through the village without anyone's noticing him, and it seemed to him that it might be managed; even at ten feet he would be invisible. He could walk between the huts and hear the babies crying, and when he came out at the other end no one would know he had been there. He was not sure where he would go then.

The way became suddenly rougher as the path went into a zigzagging descent along the steep side of a ravine. He had reached the bottom before he raised his head once. "Ah," he said, standing still. The fog was now above him, a great gray quilt of cloud. He saw the giant trees that stood around him and heard them dripping slowly in a solemn, uneven chorus onto the wild coca leaves beneath.

"There is no such place as this on the way to the village," thought the pastor. He was mildly annoyed, but more astonished, to find himself standing by these trees that looked like elephants and were larger than any other trees he had seen in the region. Automatically he turned around in the path and started back up the slope. Beside the overpowering sadness of the landscape, now that it was visible to him, the fog up there was a comfort and a protection. He paused for a moment to stare back at the fat, spiny tree trunks and the welter of vegetation beyond. A small sound behind him made him turn his head.

Two Indians were trotting down the path toward him. As they came up they stopped and looked at him with such expectancy on their dark little faces that Pastor Dowe thought they were going to speak. Instead the one ahead made a grunting sound and motioned to the other to follow. There was no way of effecting a detour around the pastor, so they brushed violently against him as they went by. Without once looking back they hurried on downward and disappeared among the green coca leaves.

This unlikely behavior on the part of the two natives vaguely intrigued him; on an impulse he determined to find an explanation for it. He started after them.

Soon he had gone beyond the spot where he had turned back a moment ago. He was in the forest; the plant odor was almost unbearable—a smell of living and dead vegetation in a world where slow growth and slow death are simultaneous and inseparable. He stopped once and listened for footsteps. Apparently the Indians had run on ahead of him; nevertheless he continued on his way. Since the path was fairly wide and well broken in, it was only now and then that he came into contact with a hanging tendril or a projecting branch.

The posturing trees and vines gave the impression of having been arrested in furious motion, and presented a monotonous succession of tortured tableaux vivants. It was as if, for the moment while he watched, the desperate battle for air had been suspended and would be resumed only when he turned away his head. As he looked, he decided that it was precisely this unconfirmable quality of surreptitiousness which made the place so disquieting. Now and then, high above his head, a blood-colored butterfly would float silently through the gloom from one tree trunk to another. They were all alike; it seemed to him that it must be always the same insect. Several times he passed the white grillwork of great spiderwebs flung across between the plants like gates painted on the dark wall behind. But all the webs looked uninhabited. The large, leisurely drops of water still continued to fall from above; even if it had been raining hard, the earth could not have been wetter.

The pastor was astigmatic, and since he was beginning to be dizzy from watching so many details, he kept his eyes looking straight ahead as he walked, deviating his gaze only when he had to avoid the plant life that had grown across the path. The floor of the forest continued flat. Suddenly he became aware that the air around him was reverberating with faint sounds. He stood still, and recognized the casual gurgle a deep stream makes from time to time as it moves past its banks. Almost immediately ahead of him was the water, black and wide, and considering its proximity, incredibly quiet in its swift flowing. A few paces before him a great dead tree, covered with orange fungus, lay across the path. The pastor's glance followed the trunk to the left; at the small end, facing him, sat the two Indians. They were looking at him with interest, and he knew they had been waiting for him. He walked over to them, greeted them. They replied solemnly, never taking their shining eyes from his face.

As if they had rehearsed it, they both rose at the same instant and walked to the water's edge, where they stood looking down. Then one of them glanced back at the pastor and said simply, "Come." As he made his way around the log he saw that they were standing by a long bamboo raft which was beached on the muddy bank. They lifted it and dropped one end into the stream.

"Where are you going?" asked the pastor. For reply they lifted their short brown arms in unison and waved them slowly in the direction of downstream. Again the one who had spoken before said, "Come." The pastor, his curiosity aroused, looked suspiciously at the delicate raft, and back at the two men. At the same time he felt that it would be pleasanter to be riding with them than to go back through the forest. Impatiently he again demanded, "Where are you going? Tacaté?"

"Tacaté," echoed the one who up to this point had not spoken.

"Is it strong?" queried the pastor, stooping to push lightly on a piece of bamboo. This was merely a formality; he had perfect faith in the Indians' ability to master the materials of the jungle.

"Strong," said the first. "Come."

The pastor glanced back into the wet forest, climbed onto the raft, and sat doubled up on its bottom in the stern. The two quickly jumped aboard and pushed the frail craft from the bank with a pole.

Then began a journey which almost at once Pastor Dowe regretted having undertaken. Even as the three of them shot swiftly ahead, around the first bend in the stream, he wished he had stayed behind and could be at this moment on his way up the side of the ravine. And as they sped on down the silent waterway he continued to reproach himself for having come along without knowing why. At each successive bend in the tunnellike course, he felt farther from the world. He found himself straining in a ridiculous effort to hold the raft back: it glided far too easily along the top of the black water. Farther from the world, or did he mean farther from God? A region like this seemed outside God's jurisdiction. When he had reached that idea he shut his eyes. It was an absurdity, manifestly impossible—in any case, inadmissible—yet it had occurred to him and was remaining with him in his mind. "God is always with me," he said to himself silently, but the formula had no effect. He opened his eyes quickly and looked at the two men. They were facing him, but he had the impression of being invisible to them; they could see only the quickly dissipated ripples left behind on the surface of the water, and the irregular arched ceiling of vegetation under which they had passed.

The pastor took his cane from where it was lying hidden, and gesticulated with it as he asked, "Where are we going?" Once again they both pointed vaguely into the air, over their shoulders, as if the question were of no interest, and the expression on their faces never changed. Loath to let even another tree go past, the pastor mechanically immersed his cane in the water as though he would stop the constant forward thrusting of the raft; he withdrew it immediately and laid it dripping across the bottom. Even that much contact with the dark stream was unpleasant to him. He tried to tell himself that there was no reason for his sudden spiritual collapse, but at the same time it seemed to him that he could feel the innermost fibers of his consciousness in the process of relaxing. The journey downstream was a monstrous letting go, and he fought against it with all his power. "Forgive me, O God, I am leaving You behind. Forgive me for leaving You behind." His nails pressed into his palms as he prayed.

And so he sat in agonized silence while they slid ahead through the forest and out into a wide lagoon where the gray sky was once more visible. Here the raft went much more slowly, and the Indians propelled it gently with their hands toward the shore where the water was shallow. Then one of them poled it along with the bamboo stick. The pastor did not notice the great beds of water hyacinths they passed through, nor the silken sound made as they rubbed against the raft. Out here under the low-hanging clouds there was occasionally a bird cry or a sudden rustle in the high grass by the water's edge. Still the pastor remained sunk within himself, feeling, rather than thinking: "Now it is done. I have passed over into the other land." And he remained so deeply preoccupied with this emotional certainty that he was not aware of it when they approached a high escarpment rising sheer from the lagoon, nor when they drew up onto the sand of a small cove at one side of the cliff. When he looked up the two Indians were standing on the sand, and one of them was saying, "Come." They did not help him get ashore; he did this with some difficulty, although he was conscious of none.

As soon as he was on land they led him along the foot of the cliff that curved away from the water. Following a tortuous track beaten through the undergrowth they came out all at once at the very foot of the wall of rock.

There were two caves—a small one opening to the left, and a wider, higher one to the right. They halted outside the smaller. "Go in," they said to the pastor. It was not very light inside, and he could see very little. The two remained at the entrance. "Your god lives here," said one. "Speak with him."

The pastor was on his knees. "O Father, hear my voice. Let my voice come through to you. I ask it in Jesus' name. . . ." The Indian was calling to him, "Speak in our tongue." The pastor made an effort, and began a halting supplication in the dialect. There were grunts of satisfaction outside. The concentration demanded in order to translate his thoughts into the still unfamiliar language served to clear his mind somewhat. And the comforting parallel between this prayer and those he offered for his congregation helped to restore his calm. As he continued to speak, always with fewer hesitations, he felt a great rush of strength going through him. Confidently he raised his head and went on praying, his eyes on the wall in front of him. At the same moment he heard the cry: "Metzabok hears you now. Say more to him."

The pastor's lips stopped moving, and his eyes saw for the first time the red hand painted on the rock before him, and the charcoal, the ashes, the flower petals and the wooden spoons strewn about. But he had no sensation of horror; that was over. The important thing now was that he felt strong and happy. His spiritual condition was a physical fact. Having prayed to Metzabok was also a fact, of course, but his deploring of it was in purely mental terms. Without formulating the thought, he decided that forgiveness would be forthcoming when he asked God for it.

To satisfy the watchers outside the cave he added a few formal phrases to his prayer, rose, and stepped out into the daylight. For the first time he noticed a certain animation in the features of the two little men. One said, "Metzabok is very happy." The other said, "Wait." Whereupon they both hurried over to the larger of the two apertures and disappeared inside. The pastor sat on a rock, resting his chin on the hand that held the head of his cane. He was still suffused with the strange triumphant sensation of having returned to himself.

He heard them muttering for a quarter of an hour or so inside the cave. Presently they came out, still looking very serious. Moved by curiosity, the pastor risked a question. He indicated the larger cave with a finger and said, "Hachakyum lives there?" Together they assented. He wanted to go further and ask if Hachakyum approved of his having spoken with Metzabok, but he felt the question would be imprudent; besides, he was certain the answer would be in the affirmative.

They arrived back in the village at nightfall, after having walked all the way. The Indians' gait had been far too swift for Pastor Dowe, and they had stopped only once to eat some sapotes they had found under the trees. He asked to be taken to the house of Nicolás. It was raining lightly when they reached the hut. The pastor sat down in the doorway beneath the overhanging eaves of cane. He felt utterly exhausted; it had been one of the most tiring days of his life, and he was not home yet.

His two companions ran off when Nicolás appeared. Evidently he already knew of the visit to the cave. It seemed to the pastor that he had never seen his face so full of expression or so pleasant. *"Utz, utz,"* said Nicolás. "Good, good. You must eat and sleep."

After a meal of fruit and maize cakes, the pastor felt better. The hut was filled with wood smoke from the fire in the corner. He lay back in a low hammock which little Marta, casually pulling on a string from time to time, kept in gentle motion. He was overcome with a desire to sleep, but his host seemed to be in a communicative mood, and he wanted to profit by it. As he was about to speak, Nicolás approached, carrying a rusty tin biscuit box. Squatting beside the hammock he said in a low voice: "I will show you my things." The pastor was delighted; this bespoke a high degree of friendliness. Nicolás opened the box and took out some sample-size squares of printed cloth, an old vial of quinine tablets, a torn strip of newspaper, and four copper coins. He gave the pastor time to examine each carefully. At the bottom of the box were a good many orange and blue feathers which Nicolás did not bother to take out. The pastor realized that he was seeing the treasures of the household, that these items were rare objects of art. He looked at each thing with great seriousness, handing it back with a verbal expression of admiration. Finally he said: "Thank you," and fell back into the hammock. Nicolás returned the box to the women sitting in the corner. When he came back over to the pastor he said: "Now we sleep."

"Nicolás," asked the pastor, "is Metzabok bad?"

"Bai, señor. Sometimes very bad. Like a small child. When he does not get what he wants right away, he makes fires, fever, wars. He can be very good, too, when he is happy. You should speak with him every day. Then you will know him."

"But you never speak with him."

"Bai, we do. Many do, when they are sick or unhappy. They ask him to take away the trouble. I never speak with him"——Nicolás looked pleased——"because Hachakyum is my good friend and I do not need Metzabok. Besides, Metzabok's home is far——three hours' walk. I can speak with Hachakyum here." The pastor knew he meant the little altar outside. He nodded and fell asleep.

The village in the early morning was a chaos of shrill sounds: dogs, parrots and cockatoos, babies, turkeys. The pastor lay still in his hammock awhile listening, before he was officially wakened by Nicolás. "We must go now, señor," he said. "Everyone is waiting for you."

The pastor sat up, a little bit alarmed. "Where?" he cried.

"You speak and make music today."

"Yes, yes." He had quite forgotten it was Sunday.

The pastor was silent, walking beside Nicolás up the road to the mission. The weather had changed, and the early sun was very bright. "I have been fortified by my experience," he was thinking. His head was clear; he felt amazingly healthy. The unaccustomed sensation of vigor gave him a strange nostalgia for the days of his youth. "I must always have felt like this then. I remember it," he thought.

At the mission there was a great crowd—many more people than he had ever seen attend a sermon at Tacaté. They were chatting quietly, but when he and Nicolás appeared there was an immediate hush. Mateo was standing in the pavilion waiting for him, with the phonograph open. With a pang the pastor realized he had not prepared a sermon for his flock. He went into the house for a moment, and returned to seat himself at the table in the pavilion, where he picked up his Bible. He had left his few notes in the book, so that it opened to the Seventy-eighth Psalm. "I shall read them that," he decided. He turned to Mateo. "Play the *disco*," he said. Mateo put on "Crazy Rhythm." The pastor quickly made a few pencil alterations in the text of the psalm, substituting the names of minor local deities, like Usukun and Sibanaa for such names as Jacob and Ephraim, and local place names for Israel and Egypt. And he wrote the word Hachakyum each time the word God or the Lord appeared. He had not finished when the record stopped. "Play it again," he commanded. The audience was delighted, even though the sound was abominably scratchy. When the music was over for the second time, he stood and began to paraphrase the psalm in a clear voice. "The children of Sibanaa, carrying bows to shoot, ran into the forest to hide when the enemy came. They did not keep their promises to Hachakyum, and they would not live as He told them to live." The audience was electrified. As he spoke, he looked down and saw the child Marta staring up at him. She had let go of her baby alligator, and it was crawling with a surprising speed toward the table where he sat. Quintina, Mateo and the two maids were piling up the bars of salt on the ground to one side. They kept returning to the kitchen for more. He realized that what he was saying doubtless made no sense in terms of his listeners' religion, but it was a story of the unleashing of divine displeasure upon an unholy people, and they were enjoying it vastly. The alligator, trailing its rags, had crawled to within a few inches of the pastor's feet, where it remained quiet, content to be out of Marta's arms.

Presently, while he was still speaking, Mateo began to hand out the salt, and soon they all were running their tongues rhythmically over the large rough cakes, but continuing to pay strict attention to his words. When he was about to finish, he motioned to Mateo to be ready to start the record again the minute he finished; on the last word he lowered his arm as a signal, and "Crazy Rhythm" sounded once more. The alligator began to crawl hastily toward the far end of the pavilion. Pastor Dowe bent down and picked it up. As he stepped forward to hand it to Mateo, Nicolás rose from the ground, and taking Marta by the hand, walked over into the pavilion with her.

"Señor," he said, "Marta will live with you. I give her to you."

"What do you mean?" cried the pastor in a voice which cracked a little. The alligator squirmed in his hand.

"She is your wife. She will live here."

Pastor Dowe's eyes grew very wide. He was unable to say anything for a moment. He shook his hands in the air and finally he said "No" several times.

Nicolás's face grew unpleasant. "You do not like Marta?"

"Very much. She is beautiful." The pastor sat down slowly on his chair. "But she is a little child."

Nicolás frowned with impatience. "She is already large."

"No, Nicolás. No. No."

Nicolás pushed his daughter forward and stepped back several paces, leaving her there by the table. "It is done," he said sternly. "She is your wife. I have given her to you."

Pastor Dowe looked out over the assembly and saw the unspoken approval in all the faces. "Crazy Rhythm" ceased to play. There was silence. Under the mango tree he saw a woman toying with a small, shiny object. Suddenly he recognized his glasses case; the woman was stripping the Leatheroid fabric from it. The bare aluminum with its dents flashed in the sun. For some reason even in the middle of this situation he found himself thinking: "So I was wrong. It is not dead. She will keep it, the way Nicolás has kept the quinine tablets."

He looked down at Marta. The child was staring at him quite without expression. Like a cat, he reflected.

Again he began to protest. "Nicolás," he cried, his voice very high, "this is impossible!" He felt a hand grip his arm, and turned to receive a warning glance from Mateo.

Nicolás had already advanced toward the pavilion, his face like a thundercloud. As he seemed about to speak, the pastor interrupted him quickly. He had decided to temporize. "She may stay at the mission today," he said weakly.

"She is your wife," said Nicolás with great feeling. "You cannot send her away. You must keep her."

"Diga que sí," Mateo was whispering. "Say yes, señor."

"Yes," the pastor heard himself saying. "Yes. Good." He got up and walked slowly into the house, holding the alligator with one hand and pushing Marta in front of him with the other. Mateo followed and closed the door after them.

"Take her into the kitchen, Mateo," said the pastor dully, handing the little reptile to Marta. As Mateo went across the patio leading the child by the hand, he called after him. "Leave her with Quintina and come to my room."

He sat down on the edge of his bed, staring ahead of him with unseeing eyes. At each moment his predicament seemed to him more terrible. With relief he heard Mateo knock. The people outdoors were slowly leaving. It cost him an effort to call out, *"Adelante."* When Mateo had come in, the pastor said, "Close the door."

"Mateo, did you know they were going to do this? That they were going to bring that child here?"

"Sí, señor."

"You knew it! But why didn't you say anything? Why didn't you tell me?"

Mateo shrugged his shoulders, looking at the floor. "I didn't know it would matter to you," he said. "Anyway, it would have been useless."

"Useless? Why? You could have stopped Nicolás," said the pastor, although he did not believe it himself.

Mateo laughed shortly. "You think so?"

"Mateo, you must help me. We must oblige Nicolás to take her back."

Mateo shook his head. "It can't be done. These people are very severe. They never change their laws."

"Perhaps a letter to the administrator at Ocosingo . . ."

"No, señor. That would make still more trouble. You are not a Catholic." Mateo shifted on his feet and suddenly smiled thinly. "Why not let her stay? She doesn't eat much. She can work in the kitchen. In two years she will be very pretty."

The pastor jumped, and made such a wide and vehement gesture with his hands that the mosquito netting, looped above his head, fell down about his face. Mateo helped him disentangle himself. The air smelled of dust from the netting.

"You don't understand anything!" shouted Pastor Dowe, beside himself. "I can't talk to you! I don't want to talk to you! Go out and leave me alone." Mateo obediently left the room.

Pounding his left palm with his right fist, over and over again, the pastor stood in his window before the landscape that shone in the strong sun. A few women were still eating under the mango tree; the rest had gone back down the hill.

He lay on his bed throughout the long afternoon. When twilight came he had made his decision. Locking his door, he proceeded to pack what personal effects he could into his smallest suitcase. His Bible and notebooks went on top with his toothbrush and Atabrine tablets. When Quintina came to announce supper he asked to have it brought to his bed, taking care to slip the packed valise into the closet before he unlocked the door for her to enter. He waited until the talking had ceased all over the house, until he knew everyone was asleep. With the small bag not too heavy in one hand he tiptoed into the patio, out through the door into the fragrant night, across the open space in front of the pavilion, under the mango tree and down the path leading to Tacaté. Then he began to walk fast, because he wanted to get through the village before the moon rose.

There was a chorus of dogs barking as he entered the village street. He began to run, straight through to the other end. And he kept running even then, until he had reached the point where the path, wider here, dipped beneath the hill and curved into the forest. His heart was beating rapidly from the exertion. To rest, and to try to be fairly certain he was not being followed, he sat down on his little valise in the center of the path. There he remained a long time, thinking of nothing, while the night went on and the moon came up. He heard only the light wind among the leaves and vines. Overhead a few bats reeled soundlessly back and forth. At last he took a deep breath, got up, and went on.

SEÑOR ONG AND SEÑOR HA

At the end of the town's long street a raw green mountain cut across the sky at a forty-five-degree angle, its straight slope moving violently from the cloudy heights down into the valley where the river ran. In the valley, although the land was fertile, there were no farms or orchards because the people of the town were lazy and did not want to bother clearing away the rocks that strewed the ground. And then, it was always too hot for that sort of work, and everybody had malaria there, so that long ago the town had fallen into its little pattern of living off the Indians who came down from the mountains with food and went back with cheap cloth, machetes and things like mirrors or empty bottles. Life always had been easy; although no one in the town was rich, still, no one ever went hungry. Almost every house had some papayas and a mango tree beside it, and there were plenty of avocados and pineapples to be had in the market for next to nothing.

Some of this had changed when the government had begun the building of the great dam up above. No one seemed to know exactly where the dam was; they were building it somewhere up in the mountains; already the water had covered several villages, and now after six years the construction was still going on. This last was the important part because it meant that when the Indians came down from above they now brought with them not only food but money. Thus it had come about that certain people in the town had suddenly found themselves rich. They could scarcely believe it themselves, but there was the money, and still the Indians went on coming down and leaving more and more of it on the counters of their shops. They did not know what to do with all these unexpected pesos. Most of them bought huge radios which they kept

117

going from early morning until night, all tuned in full strength to Tapachula, so that when they walked the length of the main street they were never out of earshot of the program and could follow it without a break. But still they had money. Pepe Jimenez had bought a bright new automobile in the capital, but by the time he had arrived back in town with it, after driving it over the sixty miles of trail from Mapastenango, it was no longer an object to excite admiration, and he felt that he had made an unwise purchase. Even the main street was too bumpy and muddy for him to drive it up and down, and so it stood rusting in front of Mi Esperanza, the bar by the bridge. When they came out of school Nicho and his companions would play in it, pretending it was a fort. But then a group of larger boys from the upper end of the town had come one day and appropriated the car for their own games, so that the boys who lived by the river no longer dared to approach it.

Nicho lived with his aunt in a small house whose garden ended in a wilderness of plants and vines; just below them rushed the river, dashing sideways from boulder to boulder in its shallow mist-filled canyon. The house was clean and simple, and they lived quietly. Nicho's aunt was a woman of too easygoing a nature. Being conscious of this, she felt that one way of giving her dead sister's child the proper care was to attempt to instill discipline in him; the discipline consisted in calling him by his true name, which was Dionisio.

Nor did she have any conception of discipline as far as her own living was concerned, so that the boy was not astonished when the day came that she said to him: "Dionisio, you will have to stop going to school. We have no more money. Don Anastasio will hire you at ten pesos a month to work in his store, and you can get the noonday meal there too. *Lástima,* but there is no money!"

For a week Nicho sat in the shop learning the prices of the articles that Don Anastasio sold, and then one evening when he went home he found a strange-looking man in the house, sitting in the other rocking chair opposite his aunt. The man looked a little like some of the Indians that came down from the furthest and highest mountains, but his skin was lighter, he was plumper and softer-seeming, and his eyes were almost shut. He smiled at the boy, but not in a way that Nicho thought very friendly, and shook hands without getting up from his chair. That night his aunt looked really quite happy, and as they were getting ready for bed she said to him: "Señor Ong is coming to live with us. You will not have to work anymore. God has been good to us."

But it occurred to Nicho that if Señor Ong was to live with them, he would prefer to go on working at Don Anastasio's, in order not to be around the house and so have to see Señor Ong so much. Tactfully he said: "I like Don Anastasio." His aunt looked at him sharply. "Señor Ong does not want you to work. He is a proud man, and rich enough to feed us both. It is nothing for him. He showed me his money."

Nicho was not at all pleased, and he went to sleep slowly, his mind full of misgivings. He was afraid that one day he would fight with Señor Ong. And besides, what would his friends say? Señor Ong was such a strange-looking man. But the very next morning he arrived from the Hotel Paraiso with three boys whom Nicho knew, and each boy carried a large bag on his head. From the garden he watched them accept the generous tips Señor Ong gave them and then run off to school without waiting to see whether Nicho wanted to speak to them or not. "Very bad," he said to himself as he kicked a stone around and around the bare earth floor of the garden. A little while later he went down to the river and sat on top of the highest boulder watching the milky water that churned beneath him. One of his five cockatoos was screaming from the tangle of leaves on the banks. *"Callate!"* he yelled at it; his own ill humor annoyed him as much as Señor Ong's arrival.

And everything turned out much as he had feared—only worse. Two days later, one of the boys from the upper end of the street said to him in passing: *"Hola, Chale!"* He replied to the greeting automatically and walked on, but a second later he said to himself: *"Chale?* But that means Chinaman! Chink!" Of course. Señor Ong must be a Chinaman. He turned to look at the boy and thought of hitting him in the back with a stone. Then he hung his head and walked on slowly. Nothing would do any good.

Little by little the joke spread, and soon even his own friends called him *Chale* when they met him, and although it was really he who had become less friendly, he imagined that they all were avoiding him, that no one wanted to see him anymore, and he spent most of his time playing by the river. The water's sound was deafening, but at the same time it made him feel a little bit better.

Neither Señor Ong nor his aunt paid much attention to him, save for their constant mealtime demands that he eat. "Now that we have more food than we need, you don't want to eat it," said his aunt angrily. "Eat, Dionisio," smiled Señor Ong. *"Bien,"* said Nicho, full of resentment, but in a tone of mock resignation, and pulled off a small piece of tortilla which he chewed very slowly.

There seemed to be no question of his returning to school; at least, the subject was never mentioned, for which he was most grateful, since he had no desire to be back in the midst of his friends just to hear them call him *Chale.* The name by itself would have been bearable if only it had not implied the ridicule of his home life; his powerlessness to change that condition seemed much more shameful than any state of affairs for which he himself might have been at fault. And so he spent his days down by the river, jumping like a goat across the rocks, throwing stones to frighten the vultures away from the carcasses the water left for them, finding deep pools to swim in, and following the river downstream to lie idly naked on the rocks in the hot sun. No matter how pleasant to him Señor Ong might be—and already he had given him candy on several occasions, as well as a metal pencil with red lead in it—he could not bring himself to accept his being a part of the household. And then there were the singular visits of strange, rich townspeople, persons whom his aunt never had known, but who now appeared to find it quite natural to come to the house, stay for five or ten minutes talking to Señor Ong, and then go away again without so much as asking after his aunt, who always made a point of being in the back of the house or in the garden when they came. He could not understand that at all. It was still her house. Or perhaps not! Maybe she had given it to Señor Ong. Women often were crazy. He did not dare ask her. Once he was able to bring himself to inquire about the people, who kept coming in increasing numbers. She had answered: "They are friends of Señor Ong," and had looked at him with an expression which seemed to say: "Is that enough for you, busybody?" He was more than ever convinced that there was something more to know about the visitors. Then he met Luz, and being no longer alone, he ceased for a time to think about them.

When, one windy day, he had first seen her standing on the bridge, her bright head shining against the black mountains behind, he had stopped walking and stood perfectly still in order to look more carefully: he thought there was a mistake in his seeing. Never would he have

120

believed it possible for anyone to look that way. Her hair was a silky white helmet on the top of her head, her whole face was white, almost as if she had covered it with paint, her brows and lashes, and even her eyes, were light to the point of not existing. Only her pale pink lips seemed real. She clutched the railing of the bridge tightly, an expression of intense preoccupation—or perhaps faint pain—on her face as she peered out from beneath her inadequate white brows. And her head moved slowly up and down as if it were trying to find an angle of vision which would be bearable for those feeble eyes that suffered behind their white lashes.

A few weeks back he merely would have stood looking at this apparition; now he watched intently until the girl, who was about his own age, seemed on the point of pitching forward into the road, and then he hurried toward her and firmly took her arm. In an instant she drew back, squinting into his face.

"Who?" she said, confused.

"Me. What's the matter?"

She relaxed, let herself be led along. "Nothing," she answered after a moment. Nicho walked with her down the path to the river. When they got to the shade, the heavy lines in her forehead disappeared. "The sun hurts your eyes?" he asked her, and she said that it did. Under a giant breadfruit tree there were clean gray rocks; they sat down and he began a series of questions. She answered placidly; her name was Luz; she had come with her sister only two days ago from San Lucas; she would stay on with her grandfather here because her parents were having quarrels at home. All her replies were given while she gazed out across the landscape, yet Nicho was sure she could not see the feathery trees across the river or the mountains beyond. He asked her: "Why don't you look at me when you talk to me?"

She put her hand in front of her face. "My eyes are ugly."

"It's not true!" he declared with indignation. Then, "They're beautiful," he added, after looking at them carefully for a moment.

She saw that he was not making fun of her, and straightway decided that she liked him more than any boy she had ever known.

That night he told his aunt about Luz, and as he described the colors in her face and hair he saw her look pleased. *"Una hija del sol!"* she exclaimed. "They bring good luck. You must invite her here tomorrow.

I shall prepare her a good *refresco de tamarindo.*" Nicho said he would, but he had no intention of subjecting his friend to his aunt's interested scrutiny. And while he was not at all astonished to hear that albinos had special powers, he thought it selfish of his aunt to want to profit immediately by those which Luz might possess.

The next day when he went to the bridge and found Luz standing there, he was careful to lead her through a hidden lane down to the water, so that she might remain unseen as they passed near the house. The bed of the river lay largely in the shadows cast by the great trees that grew along its sides. Slowly the two children wandered downstream, jumping from rock to rock. Now and then they startled a vulture, which rose at their approach like a huge cinder, swaying clumsily in the air while they walked by, to realight in the same spot a moment later. There was a particular place that he wanted to show her, where the river widened and had sandy shores, but it lay a good way downstream, so that it took them a long time to get there. When they arrived, the sun's light was golden and the insects had begun to call. On the hill, invisible behind the thick wall of trees, the soldiers were having machine-gun practice: the blunt little berries of sound came in clusters at irregular intervals. Nicho rolled his trouser legs up high above his knees and waded well out into the shallow stream. "Wait!" he called to her. Bending, he scooped up a handful of sand from the riverbed. His attitude as he brought it back for her to see was so triumphant that she caught her breath, craned her neck to see it before he had arrived. "What is it?" she asked.

"Look! Silver!" he said, dropping the wet sand reverently into her outstretched palm. The tiny grains of mica glistened in the late sunlight.

"*Qué precioso!*" she cried in delight. They sat on some roots by the water. When the sand was drier, she poured it carefully into the pocket of her dress.

"What are you going to do with it?" he asked her.

"Give it to my grandfather."

"No, no!" he exclaimed. "You don't give away silver. You hide it. Don't you have a place where you hide things?"

Luz was silent; she never had thought of hiding anything. "No," she said presently, and she looked at him with admiration.

He took her hand. "I'll give you a special place in my garden where you can hide everything you want. But you must never tell anyone."

"Of course not." She was annoyed that he should think her so stupid. For a while she had been content just to sit there with Nicho beside her; now she was impatient to get back and deposit the treasure. He tried to persuade her to stay a little longer, saying that there would be time enough if they returned later, but she had stood up and would not sit down again. They climbed upstream across the boulders, coming suddenly upon a pool where two young women stood thigh-deep washing clothes, naked save for the skirts wrapped round their waists, long full skirts that floated gently in the current. The women laughed and called out a greeting. Luz was scandalized.

"They should be ashamed!" she cried. "In San Lucas if a woman did that, everyone would throw stones at her until she was buried under them!"

"Why?" said Nicho, thinking that San Lucas must be a very wicked town.

"Because they would," she answered, still savoring the shock and shame she had felt at the sight of the golden breasts in the sunlight.

When they got back to town they turned into the path that led to Nicho's house, and while they were still in the jungle end of the garden, Nicho stopped and indicated a dead tree whose trunk had partially decayed. With the gesture of a conspirator he pulled aside the fringed curtain of vines that hung down across most of it, revealing several dark holes. Reaching into one of them, he pulled out a bright tin can, flicked off the belligerent ants that raced wildly around it, and held it forth to her.

"Put it in here," he whispered.

It took a while to transfer all the sand from her pocket to the can; when it was done he replaced it inside the dark trunk and let the vines fall straight again to cover the place. Then he conducted Luz quickly up through the garden, around the house, into the street. His aunt, having caught sight of them, called: "Dionisio!" But he pretended not to have heard her and pushed Luz ahead of him nervously. He was suddenly in terror lest Luz see Señor Ong; that was something which must be avoided at any cost.

"Dionisio!" She was still calling; she had come out and was standing in front of the door, looking down the street after them, but he did not turn around. They reached the bridge. It was out of sight of the house.

"*Adiós*," he said.

"*Hasta mañana*," she answered, peering up at him with her strange air of making a great effort. He watched her walk up the street, moving her head from side to side as if there were a thousand things to see, when in reality there were only a few pigs and some chickens roaming about.

At the evening meal his aunt eyed him reproachfully. He averted her gaze; she did not mention his promise to bring Luz to the house for *refrescos*. That night he lay on his mat watching the phosphorescent beetles. His room gave on the patio; it had only three walls. The fourth side was wide open. Branches of the lemon tree reached in and rubbed against the wall above his head; up there, too, was a huge unfolding banana leaf which was pushing its way further into the room each day. Now the patio was dizzy with the beetles' sharp lights. Crawling on the plants or flying frantically between them, they flashed their signals on and off with maddening insistence. In the neighboring room his aunt and Señor Ong occupied the bed of the house, enjoying the privacy of quarters that were closed in on all four sides. He listened: the wind was rising. Nightly it appeared and played on the leaves of the trees, dying away again before dawn. Tomorrow he would take Luz down to the river to get more silver. He hoped Señor Ong had not been spying when he had uncovered the holes in the tree trunk. The mere thought of such a possibility set him to worrying, and he twisted on his mat from one side to the other.

Presently he decided to go and see if the silver was still there. Once he had assured himself either that it was safe or that it had been stolen, he would feel better about it. He sat up, slipped into his trousers, and stepped out into the patio. The night was full of life and motion; leaves and branches touched, making tiny sighs. Singing insects droned in the trees overhead; everywhere the bright beetles flashed. As he stood there feeling the small wind wander over him he became aware of other sounds in the direction of the *sala*. The light was on there, and for a moment he thought that perhaps Señor Ong had a late visitor, since that was the room where he received his callers. But he heard no voices. Avoiding the lemon tree's sharp twigs, he made his way soundlessly to the closed doors and peered between them.

There was a square niche in the *sala* wall across which, when he had first arrived, Señor Ong had tacked a large calendar. This bore a colored picture of a smiling Chinese girl. She wore a blue bathing suit and white fur-topped boots, and she sat by a pool of shiny pink tiles. Over her head in a luminous sky a gigantic four-motored plane bore down upon her, and further above, in a still brighter area of the heavens, was the benevolent face of Generalissimo Chiang. Beneath the picture were the words: ABARROTES FINOS. *Sun Man Ngai, Huixtla, Chis.* The calendar was the one object Señor Ong had brought with him that Nicho could wholeheartedly admire; he knew every detail of the picture by heart. Its presence had transformed the *sala* from a dull room with two old rocking chairs and a table to a place where anything might happen if one waited long enough. And now as he peeked through the crack, he saw with a shock that Señor Ong had removed the calendar from its place on the wall, and laid it on the table. He had a hammer and a chisel and he was pounding and scratching the bottom of the niche. Occasionally he would scoop out the resulting plaster and dust with his fat little hands, and dump it in a neat pile on the table. Nicho waited for a long time without daring to move. Even when the wind blew a little harder and chilled his naked back he did not stir, for fear of seeing Señor Ong turn around and look with his narrow eyes toward the door, the hammer in one hand, the chisel in the other. Besides, it was important to know what he was doing. But Señor Ong seemed to be in no hurry. Almost an hour went by, and still tirelessly he kept up his methodical work, pausing regularly to take out the debris and pile it on the table. At last Nicho began to feel like sneezing; in a frenzy he turned and ran through the patio to his room, scratching his chest against the branches on the way. The emotion engendered by his flight had taken away his desire to sneeze, but he lay down anyway for fear it might return if he went back to the door. In the midst of wondering about Señor Ong he fell asleep.

The next morning when he went into the *sala* the pretty Chinese girl covered the niche as usual. He stood still listening: his aunt and Señor Ong were talking in the next room. Quickly he pulled out the thumbtack in the lower left-hand corner of the calendar and reached in. He could feel nothing there. Disappointed, he fastened it back and went out into the garden. In the tree his treasure was undisturbed, but now that he suspected Señor Ong of having a treasure too, the little can of sand seemed scarcely worth his interest.

He went to the bridge and waited for Luz. When she came they

125

walked to the river below the garden and sat beside the water. Nicho's mind was full of the image of Señor Ong bending over the niche with his tools, and his fancy was occupied with speculation as to what exactly he had been doing. He was uncertain whether or not to share his secret with Luz. He hoped she would not talk about her silver this morning; to forestall inquiries about it he mentioned curtly that he had looked at it only a half hour ago and that it was intact. Luz sat regarding him perplexedly; he seemed scarcely the same person as yesterday. Finally she said, as he continued to fix his gaze on the black pebbles at his feet: "What's the matter with you today?"

"Nothing." He grasped her arm to belie his word; the gesture betrayed him into beginning the confidence. "Listen. In my house there's a lot of gold hidden." He told her everything: Señor Ong's arrival, his own dislike of him, the visits of the town's rich shopkeepers to the house, and finally the suspicious behavior of Señor Ong in the *sala* the night before. She listened, blinking rapidly all the while. And when he had finished she agreed with him that it was probably gold hidden there in the niche, only she was inclined to think that it belonged to his aunt, and that Señor Ong had stolen it from her. This idea had not occurred to Nicho, and he did not really believe it. Nevertheless, it pleased him. "I'll get it and give it back to her," he declared. "Of course," said Luz solemnly, as if there were no alternative. They sat awhile without speaking. Up in the garden all the cockatoos were screaming at once. The prospect of stealing back the gold in order to return it to his aunt excited him. But there were dangers. He began to describe the hideousness of Señor Ong's person and character, extemporaneously adding details. Luz shivered and looked apprehensively toward the shadowy path. *"Hay que tener mucho cuidado,"* she murmured. Then suddenly she wanted to go home.

Now there was only one thing to wait for: Señor Ong's absence from the house. In Tlaltepec there lived a Chinese man whom he usually visited each week, going on the early bus in the morning and returning in time for the midday meal. Three days went by. People came to the house and went away again, but Señor Ong sat quietly in the *sala* without once going into the street. Each day Nicho and Luz met on the bridge and sat by the river discussing the treasure with an excitement that steadily grew. *"Ay, qué maravilla!"* she would exclaim, holding her hands far apart. "This much gold!" Nicho would nod in agreement; all the same he had a feeling that when he saw the treasure he would be disappointed.

Finally the morning came when Señor Ong kissed Nicho's aunt on the cheek and went out of the house carrying a newspaper under his arm. "Where is he going?" Nicho asked innocently.

"Tlaltepec." His aunt was scrubbing the floor of the *sala*.

He went into the patio and watched a hummingbird buzz from one to another of the *huele-de-noche*'s white flowers. When his aunt had finished in the *sala* she shut the door and started on the floor of the bedroom. In agitation he tiptoed into the room and over to the calendar, whose two lower corners he unfastened from the wall. Again the niche was empty. Its floor consisted of four large flower-decorated tiles. Without touching them he could tell which was the loose one. He lifted it up and felt underneath. It was a paper packet, not very large, and, which was worse, soft to the touch. He pulled out a fat manila envelope, replaced the tile and the calendar, and walked softly out through the patio, into the garden to his tree.

In the large envelope were a lot of little envelopes, and in some of the little envelopes there was a small quantity of odorless white powder. The other little envelopes were empty, held together by a rubber band. That was all there was. Nicho had expected a disappointment, but scarcely so complete a one as this. He was furious: Señor Ong had played a joke on him, had replaced the gold with this worthless dust, just out of deviltry. But when he thought about it, he decided that Señor Ong could not have guessed that he knew about the niche, so that after all this powder must be the real treasure. Also he felt it unlikely that it belonged to his aunt, in which case Señor Ong would be even more angry to find it gone. He took out two of the small empty envelopes, and from each of the others he poured a tiny bit of powder, until these two also contained about the same amount. Then he replaced both empty and full envelopes in the larger folder, and seeing that his aunt was in the kitchen, went back to the *sala* with it. Señor Ong would never notice the two missing envelopes or the powder that Nicho had poured into them. Once back in the garden he hid the two tiny packets under the tin can full of sand, and wandered down to the bridge.

It was too early to expect Luz. A thin gray curtain of rain came drifting up the valley. In another few minutes it would have arrived. The green mountainside at the end of the street glared in the half light. Don

Anastasio came walking jauntily down the main street, and turned in at the side street where Nicho's house was. Obeying a blind impulse, he called to him: *"Muy buenos, Don Anastasio!"* The old man wheeled about; he seemed none too pleased to see Nicho. "Good-day," he replied, and then he hurried on. Nicho ran from the bridge and stood at the entrance of the street watching him. Sure enough, he was about to go into Nicho's house.

"Don Anastasio!" he shouted, beginning to run toward him.

Don Anastasio stopped walking and stood still, his face screwed up in annoyance. Nicho arrived out of breath. "You wanted to see Señor Ong? He's gone out."

Don Anastasio did not look happy now, either. "Where?" he said heavily.

"I think to Mapastenango, perhaps," said Nicho, trying to sound vague, and wondering if that could be counted as a lie.

"Qué malo!" grunted Don Anastasio. "He won't be back today, then."

"I don't know."

There was a silence.

"Can I do anything for you?" faltered Nicho.

"No, no," said Don Anastasio hastily; then he stared down at him. During the week when Nicho had been working at his store, he had had occasion to notice that the boy was unusually quick. "That is," he added slowly, "I don't suppose—did Señor Ong . . . ?"

"Just a minute," said Nicho, feeling that he was about to discover the secret and at the same time become master of the situation. "Wait here," he added firmly. At the moment Don Anastasio showed no inclination to do anything else. He stood watching Nicho disappear around the corner of the house.

In a minute the boy returned panting, and smiled at Don Anastasio. "Shall we go to the bridge?" he said.

Again Don Anastasio acquiesced, looking furtively up and down the long street as they came out into it. They stood on the bridge leaning over the water below, and Nicho brought one of the little envelopes out of his pocket, glancing up at Don Anastasio's face at the same time. Yes! He had been right! He saw the features fixed in an expression of relief, pleasure and greedy anticipation. But only for an instant. By the time he was handing over the packet to Don Anastasio, the old man's face looked the same as always.

"*Muy bien, muy bien,*" he grumbled. The first small drops of rain alighted softly on their heads, but neither noticed them. "Do I pay you or Señor Ong?" said Don Anastasio, pocketing the envelope.

Nicho's heart beat harder for a few seconds: Señor Ong must not know of this. But he could not ask Don Anastasio not to tell him. He cleared his throat and said: "Me." But his voice sounded feeble.

"Aha!" said Don Anastasio, smiling a little; and he ruffled Nicho's hair in paternal fashion. Finding it wet, he looked up vacantly at the sky. "It's raining," he commented, a note of surprise in his voice.

"*Sí, señor,*" assented Nicho weakly.

"How much?" said Don Anastasio, looking at him very hard. In the valley the thunder groaned faintly.

Nicho felt he must answer immediately, but he had no idea what to say. "Is a peso all right?"

Don Anastasio stared at him even harder; he felt that the old man's eyes would cut through him in another instant. Then Don Anastasio's countenance changed suddenly, and he said: "A peso. Good." And he handed him a silver coin. "Next week you come to my store with another envelope. I'll give you an extra twenty centavos for making the trip. And—sssst!" He put his fingers to his lips, rolling his eyes upward. "Ssst!" He patted Nicho on the shoulder, looking very pleased, and went up the street.

Señor Ong came back earlier than usual, wet through, and in rather a bad humor. Nicho never had paid any attention to the conversations that passed between his aunt and Señor Ong. Now from the kitchen he listened, and heard him say: "I have no confidence in Ha. They tell me he was in town here two days ago. Of course he swears he was in Tlaltepec all the time."

"Three thousand pesos thrown into the street!" declared his aunt savagely. "I told you so then. I told you he would go on selling here as well as in Tlaltepec. *Yo te lo dije, hombre!*"

"I am not sure yet," said Señor Ong, and Nicho could imagine his soft smile as he said the words. Now that he had stolen from him he disliked him more than ever; in a sense he almost wished Señor Ong might

129

discover the theft and accuse him, thereby creating the opportunity for him to say: "Yes, I stole from you, and I hate you." But he knew that he himself would do nothing to hasten such a moment. He went out through the rain to his tree. The earth's dark breath rose all around him, hung in the wet air. He took out the can of sand and dropped the peso into it.

It rained all day and through the night; Nicho did not see Luz until the following day. Then he adopted a mysterious, baffled air and conducted her to the tree.

"Look!" he cried, showing her the tin can. "The silver has made a peso!"

Luz was convinced and delighted, but she did not seem really surprised. *"Qué bueno!"* she murmured.

"Do you want to take it?" He held up the coin. But he was careful to keep his hand over the envelope in the tree's hollow.

"No, no! Leave it! Maybe it will make more. Put it back! Put it back!"

He was a little crestfallen to find that she took his miracle so nearly for granted. They stamped their feet to knock off the ants that were beginning to climb up their legs.

"And the gold?" she whispered. "Did you get it back for your aunt? Was it heavy? What did Señor Ong say?"

"There was nothing there at all," said Nicho, feeling uncomfortable without knowing why.

"Oh." She was disappointed.

They took a long walk down the river, and came upon an enormous iguana sunning himself on a rock above a pool. Nicho threw a stone, and the monster lumbered away into the leaves. Luz clutched his arm tightly as it disappeared from sight; there was the heavy sound of its body dragging through the underbrush. All at once Nicho shook himself free, pulled off his shirt and trousers, and gave a running leap into the pool. He splashed about, beating wildly at the water with his arms and legs, yelling loudly all the while. With an uncertain gait Luz approached the edge, where she sat down and watched him. Presently she said: "Find some more silver." She did not seem at all shocked by his nudity. He sank to the bottom and scrabbled about, touching only rock. Up again, he shouted: "There isn't any!" Her white head followed his movements as he cavorted around the pool. When he came out, he sat on the opposite side, letting the sun dry him. Behind the hill the machine-gun practice was again in progress.

"In San Lucas do you think they'd throw stones at me?" he shouted.

"Why?" she called. "No, no! *Claro que nó!* For boys it's all right."

The next few days were sunny, and they came each afternoon to the pool.

One morning, the other little envelope in his pocket, Nicho went into the center of town to Don Anastasio's shop. The old man seemed very glad to see him. He opened the envelope behind the counter and looked carefully at its contents. Then he handed Nicho a peso and a half.

"I have no change," said Nicho.

"The *tostón* is for you," said Don Anastasio gruffly. "There's a cinema tonight. Come back next week. Don't forget."

Nicho ran down the street, wondering when he would have the chance to fill another envelope for Don Anastasio. It was about time for Señor Ong to make a trip to Tlaltepec.

A moment before he got to the bridge a tall woman stepped out of a shop and confronted him. She had very large eyes and a rather frightening face.

"*Hola, chico!*"

"*Sí, señora.*" He stood still and stared at her.

"Have you got something for me?"

"Something for you?" he repeated blankly.

"A little envelope?" She held out two pesos. Nicho looked at them and said: "*No, señora.*"

Her face became more frightening. "Yes. Yes. You have," she insisted, moving toward him. He glanced up and down the street: there was no one. The shop seemed to be empty. It was the hot hour of the day. He was suddenly terrified by her face. "Tomorrow," he cried, ducking to one side in order to dart past her. But she caught hold of his neck. "Today," she said roughly; her long fingernails were pushing into his skin. "*Sí, señora.*" He did not dare look up at her. "On the bridge," she grated. "This afternoon."

"*Sí, señora.*"

She let go and he walked on, sobbing a little with anger and shame for having been afraid.

In the *sala* Señor Ong and his aunt were talking excitedly. He did not

131

go in, but climbed into a hammock in the patio and listened. Don Anastasio's name was mentioned. Nicho's heart skipped ahead: something had happened!

"Now I am almost sure," Señor Ong said slowly. "It is two weeks since he has been here, and Saenz tells me he is perfectly happy. That means only one thing: Ha must be supplying him directly."

"Of course," said his aunt bitterly. "You needn't have waited two weeks to know that. Three thousand pesos dropped into the river. What a waste! *Qué idiota, tú!*"

Señor Ong paid no attention to her. "There's also the Fernandez woman," he mused. "She should have been around a few days ago. I know she has no money, but so far she has always managed to scrape together something."

"That old hag!" said his aunt contemptuously. "With her face now, she'll be lucky if she can raise twenty, not to speak of fifty."

"She can raise it," said Señor Ong with confidence in his voice. "The question is, has Ha already found her and is he giving it to her for less?"

"Don't ask *me* all these questions!" cried his aunt with impatience. "Go to Tlaltepec and ask the old man himself!"

"When I go there," said Señor Ong in a quiet, deadly voice, "it will not be to ask him anything."

At that moment a knock came at the front door; his aunt immediately left the room, shutting the door behind her, and went through the patio into the kitchen. For a few minutes Nicho could hear only the confused sound of low voices talking in the *sala*. Presently someone closed the front door. The visitor was gone.

Before the midday meal Nicho went out into the garden and tossed the two silver coins Don Anastasio had given him into the can of sand. It gave him pleasure to think of showing them to Luz; her credulity made him feel clever and superior. He determined never to tell her about the powder. All through lunch he thought about the tall woman he was to meet on the bridge. When the meal was over, Señor Ong did something unusual: he took up his hat and said: "I am going to see Saenz and have a talk with him." And he went out. Nicho watched him disappear into the main street; then he went into the house and saw his aunt shut herself into the bedroom for her siesta. Without hesitating he walked straight to the niche in the *sala* and took out the big yellow envelope. He knew he was doing a dangerous thing, but he was determined to do it anyway. Quickly he slipped two fat little envelopes into his pocket. He left one in his tree, and with the other he went out and stood on the bridge to wait for the woman. She was not long in spotting him from the shop. As she came toward him, her haggard face seemed to darken the afternoon. He held the little white envelope out to her even as she approached, as if to keep her at a certain distance from him. Frowning mightily, she reached for it, snatched it from his fingers like a furious bird, and violently pushed it inside her bodice. With the other hand she put two pesos into his still outstretched palm; and then she strode away without saying a word. He decided to remain on the bridge, hoping that Luz would appear presently.

When she came, he suddenly did not want to take her to the tree, or even to the river. Instead, grasping her hand, he said: "I have an idea." This was not true: as yet he had no idea, but he felt the need of doing something new, important.

"What idea?"

"Let's take a trip!"

"A trip! Where to?"

They started up the street hand in hand.

"We can take a bus," he said.

"But where?"

"No importa adonde."

Luz was not convinced the idea was sound; her mind was encumbered with visions of her older sister's stern face when she returned. Nevertheless he could see that she would go. As they came to where the houses and shops began, he let go of her hand for fear of meeting one of his friends. He had never walked on the street with her. The sun's light was intense, but a gigantic white cloud was rising slowly up from behind the mountains in front of them. He turned to look at her pale shining head. Her eyes were painful, squinting slits in her face. Surely no one else in the world had such beautiful hair. Glancing at the cloud he whispered to her: "The sun will go in soon."

At the central plaza there was a bus half full of people. From time to time the driver, who stood leaning against its red tin body, shouted: "Tlaltepec! Tlaltepec!" No sooner had they got aboard and taken seats near the back alongside the windows than Luz, in an access of apprehensiveness, asked to get out. But he held her arm and said, hurriedly inventing: *"Oye,* I wanted to go to Tlaltepec because we have something very important to do there. We have to save somebody's life." She listened attentively to his story: the monstrous Señor Ong was going to kill old Señor Ha for not having kept his promise to stay in Tlaltepec. As he recounted the tale, and recalled the wording of Señor Ong's threat, he began to believe the story himself. "When I go there it will not be to ask him anything." The old man would be given no opportunity to explain, no chance to defend himself. As the bus moved out of the plaza, he was as convinced as Luz that they were off to Tlaltepec on an heroic mission.

Tlaltepec was below, in a closed valley with mountains on all sides. The great white cloud, its brilliant edges billowing outward, climbed higher into the sky; as into a cave, the bus entered the precinct of its shadow. Here suddenly everything was green. Scraps of birdsong came in through the open windows, sharp above the rattling of the ancient vehicle.

"Ay, el pobrecito!" sighed Luz from time to time.

They came into Tlaltepec, stopped in the plaza. The passengers got out and quickly dispersed in different directions. The village was very quiet. Bright green grass grew in the middle of the streets. A few silent Indians sat around the plaza against the walls. Nicho and Luz walked up the main street, awed by the hush which enveloped the village. The cloud had covered the sky; now it was slowly pulled down like a curtain over the other side of the valley. A sad little church bell began to ring behind them in the plaza. They turned into a small shop marked FARMACIA MODERNA. The man sitting inside knew Señor Ha: he was the only Chinese in the village. "He lives opposite the convent, in the last house." In Tlaltepec everything was nearby. The bell was still tolling from the plaza. In front of the ruined convent was an open square of sward; basketball posts had been put up at each end, but now they were broken. Before the last house stood a large tree laden with thousands of lavender flowers. In the still air they fell without cease, like silent tears, onto the damp earth beneath.

Nicho knocked on the door. A servant girl came and looked at the two children indifferently, went away. In a moment Señor Ha appeared. He was not quite so old as they had expected; his angular face was expressionless, but he looked closely at both of them. Nicho had hoped he would ask them into the house: he wanted to see if Señor Ha had a calendar like the one at home in the *sala,* but no such hospitality was forthcoming. Luz sat down on the stone step below them and picked up some of the blossoms that had fallen from the tree while Nicho told Señor Ha who he was and why he had come. Señor Ha stood quite still. Even when Nicho said: "And he is going to kill you," his hard little eyes remained in exactly the same position. Nothing in his face moved; he looked at Nicho as though he had not heard a word. For a moment Nicho thought that perhaps he understood nothing but Chinese, but then Señor Ha said, very clearly: "What lies!" And he shut the door.

They walked back to the plaza without saying anything, and sat down on an iron bench to wait for the bus. A warm, mistlike rain moved downward through the air, falling so softly that it was inaudible even in the stillness of the deserted plaza. At one point while they waited Nicho got up and went to the main street in search of some candy. As he came out of the shop, a little man carrying a briefcase walked quickly past and crossed the street. It was Señor Ha.

While they sat eating the candy a battered sedan came out of the main street and bumped across the plaza; on the edge of its back seat, leaning forward talking to the driver, was Señor Ha. They stared. The car turned into the road that led up the mountainside toward the town, and disappeared in the twilight.

"He's going to tell Señor Ong!" cried Nicho suddenly. He let his mouth stay open and fixed the ground.

Luz squeezed his arm. "You don't care," she declared. "They're only Chinamen. You're not afraid of them."

He looked blankly at her. Then with scorn he answered: "No!"

They talked very little on the ride up in the rain. It was night by the time they arrived in the town. Wet and hungry, they went down the street toward the bridge, still without speaking. As they crossed the river Nicho turned to her and said: "Come and have dinner at my house."

"My sister . . ."

But he pulled her roughly along with him. Even as he opened the front door and saw his aunt and Señor Ong sitting inside, he knew that Señor Ha had not been there.

"Why are you so late?" said his aunt. "You're wet." Then she saw Luz. "Shut the door, *niña,*" she said, looking pleased.

135

While they ate in the covered part of the patio, Señor Ong continued with what he apparently had been saying earlier in the evening . . . "She looked directly at me without saying a word."

"Who?" said his aunt, smiling at Luz.

"The Fernandez woman. This afternoon." Señor Ong's voice was edged with impatience. "For me that is proof enough. She's getting it somewhere else."

His aunt snorted. "Still you're looking for proof! *Niña*, take more meat." She piled extra food on Luz's plate.

"Yes, there's no doubt now," Señor Ong continued.

"What beautiful hair! *Ay, Dios!*" She smoothed the top of the girl's head. Nicho was ashamed: he knew that he had invited her to dinner because he had been afraid to come home alone, and he knew that his aunt was touching her hair only in order to bring herself good luck. He sighed miserably and glanced at Luz; she seemed perfectly content as she ate.

Suddenly there were several loud knocks on the front door. Señor Ong rose and went into the *sala*. There was a silence. A man's voice said: *"Usted se llama Narciso Ong?"* All at once there followed a great deal of noise; feet scuffled and funiture scraped on the tile floor. Nicho's aunt jumped up and ran into the kitchen where she began to pray very loudly. In the *sala* there was grunting and wheezing, and then as the racket grew less intense, a man said: *"Bueno,* I have it. A hundred grams, at least, right in his pocket. That's all we needed, my friend. *Vamonos."*

Nicho slid down from his chair and stood in the doorway. Two men in wet brown ponchos were pushing Señor Ong out the front door. But he did not seem to want to go. He twisted his head and saw Nicho, opened his mouth to speak to him. One of the men hit him in the side of the face with his fist. "Not in front of the boy," said Señor Ong, wriggling his jaw back and forth to see if it was all right. "Not in front of the boy," he said again thickly. The other man slammed the door shut. The *sala* was empty. There was no sound but his aunt's wailing voice in the kitchen, crying aloud to God. He turned to look at Luz, who was sitting perfectly still.

"Do you want to go home?" he said to her.

"Yes." She got up. His aunt came out of the kitchen wringing her

136

hands. Going over to Luz she laid her hand briefly on the white hair, still muttering a prayer.

"*Adiós, niña.* Come back tomorrow," she said.

There was still a light rain falling. A few insects sang from the wet leaves as the two silent children passed along the way to the house where Luz lived. When they rapped on the door it was opened immediately. A tall thin girl stood there. Without speaking she seized Luz with one arm and pulled her violently inside, closing the door with the other.

When Nicho got home and went into the *sala,* his first thought was that Señor Ong had returned, but the next instant he felt that he was in the middle of a bad dream. Señor Ha was sitting there talking with his aunt. She looked up tearfully. "Go to bed," she commanded.

Señor Ha reached out from his chair as Nicho passed and caught his arm—caught it very tightly. "*Ay!*" said Nicho in spite of himself. "One moment," said Señor Ha, still looking at Nicho's aunt, and never for a second relaxing his grip. "Perhaps this one knows." And without turning his face toward Nicho he said: "The police have taken Señor Ong to prison. He will not come back here. He hid something in this house. Where is it?"

It seemed as though the hard fingers would cut through his skin. His aunt looked up at him hopefully. He felt suddenly very important.

"There," he said, pointing to the calendar.

Señor Ha rose and yanked the pretty girl down from the wall. In an instant he had the yellow envelope in his hand. As he examined its contents, he said: "Is there any more?"

"No," said Nicho, thinking of the envelope lying in the safety of his tree out there in the rainy night. Señor Ha began to twist his arm, but the thought of his secret made him feel strong; his pain and his hatred flowed into that feeling of strength. He stood stiffly and let Señor Ha hurt him. A moment later Señor Ha let go of him and gave him a violent push that sent him halfway across the room. "Go to bed," he said.

When Nicho had gone out and closed the door, Señor Ha turned to the aunt. "Tomorrow I shall come back with my clothes," he said. "It is not good to have a boy around the house doing nothing; he gets into trouble. From now on he will deliver it; there will be no one coming to the house."

137

"But if the police catch him . . ." she objected.

"There will be no trouble with them. It is all arranged. Fortunately I had nearly three thousand pesos on hand." He picked up his briefcase and went to the door. She looked after him with frank admiration and sighed deeply. "You won't stay tonight?" She said the words timidly, and they sounded strangely coquettish.

"No. The car is outside waiting for me. Tomorrow." He opened the door. Rising, she went and took his hand, pressing it warmly between her two hands. "Tomorrow," he repeated.

When the car had driven away and she could no longer hear it, she closed the door, turned off the light, and went out into the patio, where she got into a hammock and lay swinging gently back and forth.

"An intelligent man," she said to herself. "What good luck!" She stopped swinging a moment. "Good luck! Of course! Dionisio must bring her to the house again one day very soon."

The town went on being prosperous, the Indians kept coming down from the heights with money, the thick jungle along the way to Mapastenango was hacked away, the trail widened and improved. Nicho bought a packet of little envelopes. Far down the river he found another hollow tree. Here he kept his slowly increasing store of treasure; during the very first month he picked up enough money on the side to buy Luz a lipstick and a pair of dark glasses with red and green jewels all around the rims.

THE FROZEN FIELDS

The train was late because the hotbox under one of the coaches had caught fire in the middle of a great flat field covered with snow. They had stayed there about an hour. After the noise and rushing of the train, the sudden silence and the embarrassed stirring of people in their seats induced a general restlessness. At one point another train had shot by on the next track with a roar worse than thunder; in the wake of that, the nervousness of the passengers increased, and they began to talk fretfully in low voices.

Donald had started to scratch pictures with his fingernail in the ice that covered the lower part of the windowpane by his seat. His father had said: "Stop that." He knew better than to ask "Why?" but he thought it; he could not see what harm it would do, and he felt a little resentful toward his mother for not intervening. He could have arranged for her to object to the senseless prohibition, but experience had taught him that she could be counted on to come to his defense only a limited number of times during any given day, and it was imprudent to squander her reserve of goodwill.

The snow had been cleared from the station platform when they got out. It was bitter cold; a fat plume of steam trailed downward from the locomotive, partially enveloping the first coach. Donald's feet ached with the cold.

"There's Uncle Greg and Uncle Willis!" he cried, and he jumped up and down several times.

"You don't have to shout," said his father. "We see them. And stand still. Pick up your bag."

Uncle Willis wore a black bearskin coat that almost touched the ground. He put his hands under Donald's arms and lifted him up so that

139

his head was at a level with his own, and kissed him hard on the mouth. Then he swung him over into Uncle Greg's arms, and Uncle Greg did the same thing. "How's the man, hey?" cried Uncle Greg as he set him down.

"Fine," said Donald, conscious of a feeling of triumph because his father did not like to see boys being kissed. "Men shake hands," he had told him. "They don't kiss each other."

The sky was crystal clear, and although it was already turning lavender with the passing of afternoon, it still shone with an intense light, like the sky in one scene at the Russian Ballet. His mother had taken him a few weeks earlier because she wanted to see Pavlova; it was not the dancing that had excited him, but the sudden direct contact with the world of magic. This was a magic sky above him now, nothing like the one he was used to seeing above the streets of New York. Everything connected with the farm was imbued with magic. The house was the nucleus of an enchanted world more real than the world that other people knew about. During the long green summers he had spent there with his mother and the members of her family he had discovered that world and explored it, and none of them had ever noticed that he was living in it. But his father's presence here would constitute a grave danger because it was next to impossible to conceal anything from him, and once aware of the existence of the other world he would spare no pains to destroy it. Donald was not yet sure whether all the entrances were safely guarded or effectively camouflaged.

They sat in the back of the sleigh with a brown buffalo robe tucked around them. The two big gray horses were breathing out steam through their wide nostrils. Silently the white countryside moved past, its frozen trees pink in the late light. Uncle Greg held the reins, and Uncle Willis, sitting beside him, was turned sideways in his seat, talking to Donald's mother.

"My feet hurt," said Donald.

"Well, God Almighty, boy!" cried Uncle Willis. "Haven't you got 'em on the bricks? There are five hot bricks down there. That's what they're there for." He bent over and lifted up part of the heavy lap robe. The bricks were wrapped in newspaper.

"*My* feet are like blocks of ice, too," said Donald's mother. "Here, take your shoes off and put your feet on these." She pushed two of the bricks toward Donald.

"He just wants attention," said Donald's father. But he did not forbid him to have the bricks.

"Is that better?" Uncle Willis asked a moment later.

"It feels good. How many miles is it to the farm?"

"Seven miles to The Corner, and a mile and a half from there."

"Oh, I know it's a mile and a half from The Corner," said Donald. He had walked it many times in the summer, and he knew the names of the farms along the road. "First you come to the Elders, then the Landons, then the Madisons——"

His father pushed him hard in the ribs with his elbow. "Just keep quiet for a while."

Uncle Willis pretended not to have heard this. "Well, well. You certainly have a good memory. How old are you now?"

Donald's throat had constricted; it was a familiar occurrence which did not at all mean that he was going to cry—merely that he felt like crying. He coughed and said in a stifled voice: "Six." Then he coughed again; ashamed, and fearful that Uncle Willis might have noticed something amiss, he added: "But I'll be seven the day after New Year's."

They were all silent after that; there were only the muffled rhythm of the horses' trot and the soft, sliding sound of the runners on the packed snow. The sky was now a little darker than the white meadows, and the woods on the hillside beyond, with their millions of bare branches, began to look frightening. Donald was glad to be sitting in the middle. He knew there were no wolves out there, and yet, could anybody be really certain? There had been wolves at one time—and bears as well—and simply because nobody had seen one in many years, they now said there weren't any. But that was no proof.

They came to The Corner, where the road to the farm turned off from the main road. Seven rusty mailboxes stood there in a crooked row, one for each house on the road.

"R.F.D. Number One," said Uncle Willis facetiously. This had always been a kind of joke among them, ever since they had bought the farm, because they were townspeople and thought the real farmers were very funny.

Now Donald felt he was on home ground, and it gave him the confidence to say: "Rural Free Delivery." He said the words carefully, since the first one sometimes gave him difficulty. But he pronounced it all right, and Uncle Greg, without turning round, shouted: "That's right! You go to school now?"

"Yes." He did not feel like saying more because he was following the curves in the road, which he knew by heart. But everything looked so different from the way he remembered it that he found it hard to believe it was the same place. The land had lost its intimacy, become bare and unprotected. Even in the oncoming night he could see right through the leafless bushes that should have hidden the empty fields beyond. His feet were all right now, but his hands in their woolen mittens under the buffalo skin were numb with cold.

The farm came into view; in each downstairs window there was a lighted candle and a holly wreath. He bent over and put his shoes on. It was hard because his fingers ached. When he sat up again the sleigh had stopped. The kitchen door had opened; someone was coming out. Everyone was shouting "Hello!" and "Merry Christmas!" Between the sleigh and the kitchen he was aware only of being kissed and patted, lifted up and set down, and told that he had grown. His grandfather helped him take off his shoes again and removed a lid from the top of the stove so he could warm his hands over the flames. The kitchen smelled, as in summer, of woodsmoke, sour milk and kerosene.

It was always very exciting to be in the midst of many people. Each one was an added protection against the constant watchfulness of his mother and father. At home there were only he and they, so that mealtimes were periods of torture. Tonight there were eight at the supper table. They put an enormous old leather-bound dictionary in a chair so he would be high enough, and he sat between his grandmother and Aunt Emilie. She had dark brown eyes and was very pretty. Uncle Greg had married her a year ago, and Donald knew from many overheard conversations that none of the others really liked her.

Gramma was saying: "Louisa and Ivor couldn't get down till tomorrow. Mr. Gordon's driving them down as far as Portersville in his car. They'll all stay in the hotel tonight, and we've got to go in first thing in the morning and bring them out."

"Mr. Gordon, too, I suppose," said his mother.

"Oh, probably," Uncle Greg said. "He won't want to stay alone Christmas Day."

His mother looked annoyed. "It seems sort of unnecessary," she said. "Christmas is *a family* day, after all."

"Well, he's part of the family now," said Uncle Willis with a crooked smile.

His mother replied with great feeling: "I think it's terrible."

"He's pretty bad these days," put in Grampa, shaking his head.

"Still on the old firewater?" asked his father.

Uncle Greg raised his eyebrows. "That and worse. You know. . . . And Ivor too."

Donald knew they were being mysterious because of him. He pretended not to be listening, and busied himself making marks on the tablecloth with his napkin ring.

His father's mouth had fallen open with astonishment. "Where do they get it?" he demanded.

"Prescription," said Uncle Willis lightly. "Some crooked Polack doctor up there."

"Oh, honestly," cried his mother. "I don't see how Louisa *stands* it."

Aunt Emilie, who had been quiet until now, suddenly spoke. "Oh, I don't know," she said speculatively. "They're both very good to her. I think Mr. Gordon's very generous. *He* pays the rent on her apartment, you know, and gives her the use of the car and chauffeur most afternoons."

"You don't know anything about it," said Uncle Greg in a gruff, unpleasant voice which was meant to stop her from talking. But she went on, a bit shrilly, and even Donald could hear that they were in the habit of arguing.

"I *do* happen to know that Ivor's perfectly willing to give her a divorce any time she wants it, because she told me so herself."

There was silence at the table; Donald was certain that if he had not been there they would all have begun to talk at that point. Aunt Emilie had said something he was not supposed to hear.

"Well," said Uncle Willis heartily, "how about another piece of cake, Donald, old man?"

"How about bed, you mean," said his father. "It's time he went to bed."

His mother said nothing, helped him from his chair and took him upstairs.

The little panes of his bedroom window were completely covered with ice. Opening his mouth, he breathed on one pane until a round hole had been melted through and he could see blackness outside. "Don't do that, dear," said his mother. "Gramma'll have to clean the window. Now come on; into bed with you. There's a nice hot brick under the covers so your feet won't get cold." She tucked the blankets around him, kissed him, and took the lamp from the table. His father's voice, annoyed, came up from the foot of the stairs. "Hey, Laura! What's going on up there? Come on."

"Won't there be any light in my room at all?" Donald asked her.

"I'm coming," she called. She looked down at Donald. "You never have a light at home."

"I know, but home I can turn it on if I need it."

"Well, you're not going to need it tonight. Your father would have a fit if I left the lamp. You know that. Now just go to sleep."

"But I won't be able to sleep," he said miserably.

"Laura!" shouted his father.

"Just a *minute!*" she cried, vexed.

"Please, Mother . . . ?"

Her voice was adamant. "This cold air will put you to sleep in two shakes of a lamb's tail. Now go to sleep." She went to the doorway, the lamp in her hand, and disappeared through it, closing the door behind her.

There was a little china clock on the table that ticked very loud and fast. At infrequent intervals from below came a muffled burst of laughter which immediately subsided. His mother had said: "I'll open this window about an inch; that'll be enough." The room was growing colder by the minute. He pushed the sole of one foot against the heated brick in the middle of the bed, and heard the crackle of the newspaper that enfolded it. There was nothing left to do but go to sleep. On his way through the borderlands of consciousness he had a fantasy. From the mountain behind the farm, running silently over the icy crust of the snow, leaping over the rocks and bushes, came a wolf. He was running toward the farm. When he got there he would look through the windows until he found the dining room where the grown-ups were sitting around the big table. Donald shuddered when he saw his eyes in the dark through the glass. And now, calculating every movement perfectly, the wolf sprang, smashing the panes, and seized Donald's father by the throat. In an instant, before anyone could move or cry out, he was gone again with his prey still between his jaws, his head turned sideways as he dragged the limp form swiftly over the surface of the snow.

The white light of dawn was in the room when he opened his eyes. Already there were bumpings in the bowels of the house: people were stirring. He heard a window slammed shut, and then the regular sound of someone splitting wood with a hatchet. Presently there were nearer noises, and he knew that his parents in the next room had gotten up. Then his door was flung open and his mother came in, wearing a thick brown flannel bathrobe, and with her hair falling loose down her back. "Merry Christmas!" she cried, holding up a gigantic red mesh stocking crammed with fruit and small packages. "Look what I found hanging by the fireplace!" He was disappointed because he had hoped to go and get his stocking himself. "I brought it up to you because the house is as cold as a barn," she told him. "You stay put right here in bed till it's warmed up a little."

"When'll we have the tree?" The important ritual was the tree: the most interesting presents were piled under it.

"You just hold your horses," she told him. "You've got your stocking. We can't have the tree till Aunt Louisa gets here. You wouldn't want her to miss it, would you?"

"Where's my present for Aunt Louisa and Uncle Ivor? Uncle Ivor's coming, too, isn't he?"

"Of course he's coming," she replied, with that faintly different way of speaking she used when she mentioned Uncle Ivor. "I've already put it under the tree with the other things. Now you just stay where you are, all covered up, and look at your stocking. I'm going to get dressed." She shivered and hurried back into her room.

The only person he had to thank at breakfast was his grandfather, for a box of colored pencils which had been jammed into the foot of the stocking. The other gifts had been tagged: "For Donald from Santa." Uncle Willis and Uncle Greg had eaten an early breakfast and gone in the sleigh to the hotel in Portersville to fetch Aunt Louisa and Uncle Ivor. When they got back, Donald ran to the window and saw that Mr. Gordon had come. Everyone had talked so mysteriously about Mr. Gordon that he was very eager to see him. But at that moment his mother called him upstairs to help her make the beds. "We all have to do as much

145

as we can for Gramma," she told him. "Lord knows she's got all she can manage with the kitchen work."

But eventually he heard Aunt Louisa calling up the staircase. They went down: he was smothered in kisses, and Aunt Louisa asked him: "How's my boy? You're *my* boy, aren't you?" Then Uncle Ivor kissed him, and he shook hands with Mr. Gordon, who was already sitting in Grampa's armchair, where nobody else ever sat. He was plump and pale, and he wore two big diamond rings on one hand and an even bigger sapphire on the other. As he breathed he wheezed slightly; now and then he pulled an enormous yellow silk handkerchief out of his breast pocket and wiped his forehead with it. Donald sat down on the other side of the room and turned the pages of a magazine, from time to time looking up to observe him. He had called Donald "my lad," which sounded very strange, like someone talking in a book. At one point he noticed Donald's attention, and beckoned to him. Donald went and stood beside the armchair while Mr. Gordon reached into his pocket and pulled out a fat watch with a little button, and tiny chimes struck inside the watch. A few minutes later he signaled to him afresh; Donald bounded over to him and pressed the button again. The next time, his mother told him to stop bothering Mr. Gordon.

"But he *asked* me to," objected Donald.

"Sit down right there. We're all going in and have our tree in a little while. Uncle Ivor's going to be Santa Claus."

Presently Uncle Willis came into the room. "Well, everybody," he said, rubbing his hands together, "I think the parlor's warm enough now. How about our tree?"

"It's about time," said Aunt Emilie. She was wearing a red taffeta dress which Donald had heard his mother discussing with his father earlier. "*Most* inappropriate," she had said. "The girl doesn't seem to realize she's living on a farm." Aunt Emilie reached down and took Donald's hand. "Would you care to accompany me, sir?" she said. They walked into the parlor holding hands. The fire in the fireplace roared and crackled.

"Where's Ivor?" said Uncle Greg. "Has everybody got a seat?"

"Here he is," said Uncle Ivor, coming in from the hallway. He had put on an old red knitted skullcap and a red dressing gown, and he had a wreath of green fluted paper around his neck. "This is all Santa Claus could find," he announced.

Aunt Louisa began to laugh. "Look at your Uncle Ivor," she told Donald. "I am," said Donald. But he was really looking at the tree. It was a tall hemlock that reached to the ceiling, and underneath it was piled the most enormous assortment of packages he had ever seen. "Look at that!" they all cried.

"What *do* you suppose is in them all?" said Aunt Louisa.

"I don't know," he replied.

Uncle Ivor sat down on the floor as near the tree as he could get, and lifting up a large crate he passed it to Uncle Greg, who stood in the middle of the room. "Let's get this out of the way first," he said. Then Uncle Greg intoned: "To Donald from the Folks at Rutland."

While Uncle Ivor went on passing out packages, Donald struggled with his box. He was vaguely aware of the little cries that were being uttered around him: "How lovely! But it's too much!" "Oh, you shouldn't have!" "Why did you do it?" as the others opened their gifts, but he was too preoccupied to notice that most of the exclamations were being addressed to Mr. Gordon, who sat in the window looking very pleased.

It was too good to believe: a fire engine three feet long, with rubber tires and a bell and a siren and three ladders that shot upward automatically when it stopped. Donald looked at it, and for a moment was almost frightened by the power he knew it had to change his world.

"Oh . . . isn't . . . that . . . lovely!" said his mother, her annoyance giving a sharp edge to each word. "Louisa, why did you do it?" Donald glanced up quickly and saw Aunt Louisa indicate Mr. Gordon with a jerk of her head, as if she were saying: "Everything is his fault."

His mother moved along the floor toward the crate and fished out the greeting card. "I want you to keep each card in with the present it came with," she told Donald, "because you'll have a lot of thank-you notes to write tomorrow, and you don't want to get them mixed up. But you can thank Aunt Louisa and Uncle Ivor right now."

He hated to be told to thank a person in that person's presence, as though he were a baby. But he said the words bravely, facing Mr. Gordon: "Thank you so much for the beautiful fire engine."

"There's more there, my lad," beamed Mr. Gordon; the diamonds flashed in the sunlight.

Aunt Emilie was holding out her arm in front of her, looking at her new wristwatch. Grampa had put on a black silk dressing gown and was smoking a cigar. He looked perfectly content as he turned to Mr. Gordon and said: "Well, you've spoiled us all." But Donald's mother interpreted his phrase as a reproach, and added in explanation: "We're not used to getting such *elaborate* gifts, Mr. Gordon."

Mr. Gordon laughed, and turning to Donald, told him: "You've barely started, my lad. Tell your Uncle Ivor to get on with it."

Now it seemed as though nearly every package was for Donald. He opened them as fast as he could, and was freshly bewildered by the apparition of each new marvel. There were, of course, the handkerchiefs and books and mufflers from the family, but there was also a Swiss music box with little metal records that could be changed; there were roller skates, a large set of lead soldiers, a real accordion and a toy village with a streetcar system that ran on a battery. As Donald opened each package, the little cries of admiration made by his parents came closer to sounding like groans. Finally his father said, in a voice loud enough for Mr. Gordon to hear him above the general conversation: "It's bad business for one kid to get so much."

Mr. Gordon had heard him. "You were young once yourself," he said airily.

Aunt Emilie was trying on a fur jacket that Uncle Greg had given her. Her face was flushed with excitement; she had just planted a big kiss on Uncle Greg's cheek.

"The little Astor baby got five thousand dollars' worth of toys on its last birthday," she said to Donald's father, running her hand back and forth along the fur.

Donald's father looked at her with narrowed eyes. "That," he said, enunciating very clearly, "is what might be called an *asinine* remark."

Save for the crackling of the fire there was silence for a moment in the room. Those who had not heard knew that something had happened. Uncle Greg looked quickly at Donald's father, and then at Aunt Emilie. Maybe there would be a quarrel, thought Donald, with everyone against his father. The idea delighted him; at the same time he felt guilty, as though it were his doing.

Uncle Ivor was handing him a package. Automatically he untied the ribbon, and pulled out a tan cashmere sweater. "That's Mother's and Daddy's present to you," his mother said quietly. "It's a little big for you now, but I got it big purposely so you could grow into it." The small crisis had passed; they all began to talk again. Donald was relieved and disappointed. "How about christening that bottle of brandy?" cried Uncle Willis.

"You menfolk sit here," Gramma told them. "We've got to get out into the kitchen."

"I'll bring yours out to you," said Uncle Ivor to Aunt Louisa as she got up.

On her way out of the room Donald's mother bent over and touched his shoulder. "I want you to put every present back into its box just the way it was. After that you carry them all up into your room and stack them carefully in the corner under the window. You hear me?"

She went out. Donald sat a moment; then he jumped up and ran after her to ask if he might save out just one thing—the fire engine, perhaps. She was saying to Gramma: ". . . quite uncalled for. Besides, I don't know how we're *ever* going to get it all back to New York. Owen can take the big things at least with him tomorrow, I suppose."

He stopped running, and felt peace descend upon him. His father was leaving the farm. Then let him take everything with him, fire engine and all; it would not matter. He turned and went back into the parlor, where he meticulously packed the toys into their boxes, put the covers on, and tied them up with lengths of ribbon and string.

"What's all this?" exclaimed Mr. Gordon suddenly, noticing him. "What are you doing?"

"I have to take everything upstairs," said Donald.

His father joined the conversation. "I don't want to find those boxes lying all over the place up there, either. See that you pile 'em neatly. Understand?"

Donald continued to work without looking up.

After a moment Mr. Gordon said under his breath: "Well, I'll be damned." Then to Donald's father: "I've seen some well-behaved kids in my time, but I don't mind telling you I never saw one like *that*. Never."

"Discipline begins in the cradle," said his father shortly.

"It's sinister," murmured Mr. Gordon to himself.

Donald glanced up and saw his father looking at Mr. Gordon with hatred.

In the kitchen his grandmother, his aunts and his mother were busy preparing dinner. Donald sat by the window mashing potatoes. The blue of the sky had disappeared behind one curtain of cloud, uniformly white. "We'll have more snow before night," said Gramma, looking out of the window above the sink.

"Want to smell something good?" Donald's mother asked him. He ran across to the stove and she opened the oven door: the aroma of onions mingled with that of the roasting turkey. "He's coming along beautifully," she announced. She shut the oven door with a bang and hung the potholders on their hooks. Then she went into the pantry. Donald followed her. It was very cold in here, and it smelled of pickles and spices. His mother was searching for something along the shelves, among the jars and tin boxes.

"Mother," he said.

"Hmm?" she replied distractedly, without looking down at him.

"Why does Mr. Gordon live at Uncle Ivor's?"

Now she did look at him, and with an intensity that startled him. "What was that?" she demanded sharply. Then, before he could repeat his question, she went on in a suddenly matter-of-fact voice: "Dear, don't you know that Uncle Ivor's what they call a male nurse? Like Miss Oliver, you remember, who took care of you when you had influenza? Only a man. A man nurse."

"Is Mr. Gordon sick?"

"Yes, he is," she said, lowering her voice to little more than a whisper. "He's a very sick man, but we don't talk about it."

"What's he got?" He was conscious of being purposely childish at the moment, in the hope of learning more. But his mother was already saying: "I don't know, dear. You go back into the kitchen now. It's too cold for you in here. Scoot! Out with you!" He giggled, ran back into the kitchen, satisfied for having definitely established the existence of a mystery.

During dinner his father looked across at him with the particular kind of sternness he reserved for remarks which he knew were unwelcome, and said: "You haven't been outside yet today, young man. We'll take a walk down the road later."

Aunt Louisa had brought a large glass of brandy to the table with her, and was sipping it along with her food. "It's too cold, Owen," she objected. "He'll catch his death o'cold." Donald knew she was trying to help him, but he wished she had kept quiet. If it became an issue, his father would certainly not forget about the walk.

"Too cold!" scoffed his father. "We have a few basic rules in *our* little family, and one of them is that he has to get some fresh air every day."

"Couldn't you make an exception for Christmas? Just for one day?" demanded Aunt Louisa.

Donald did not dare look up, for fear of seeing the expression on his father's face.

"Listen, Louisa," he said acidly. "I suggest you just stay on your side of the fence, and I'll stay on mine. We'll get along a lot better." Then as an afterthought he snapped: "That all right with you?"

Aunt Louisa leaned across Grampa's plate toward Donald's father and spoke very loud, so that everyone stopped eating. "No, it's not all right with me!" she cried. "All you do is pick on the child from morning till night. It's shameful! I won't sit by and watch my own flesh and blood plagued that way!"

Both Gramma and Donald's father began to speak at once. Gramma was saying, "Louisa," trying to soothe her. Donald's father shouted: "You've never *had* a kid. You don't know the first thing *about* raising kids."

"I know when a man's selfish and plain cussed," Aunt Louisa declared.

"Louisa!" cried Gramma in a tone of surprise and mild reproof. Donald continued to look at his plate.

"Have I ever come up to Rutland and stuck my nose in your affairs and criticized? Have I?" demanded Donald's father.

"Now come on," said Uncle Willis quickly. "Let's not spoil a beautiful Christmas."

"That's right," Grampa said. "We're all happy. Let's not say anything we'll be sorry for later."

But Aunt Louisa would not retreat. She took a fast gulp of brandy and almost choked on it. Then, still leaning toward Donald's father, she went on: "What do you mean, come to Rutland and criticize? What've you got to criticize in Rutland? Something wrong there?"

For an instant Donald's father did not reply. During that instant it was as though everyone felt the need to say something without being able to say it. The one who broke the short silence was Donald's father, using a peculiar, soft voice which Donald recognized immediately as a vicious imitation of Uncle Ivor. "Oh, *no!* There's nothing wrong in *Rut* land!"

Suddenly, with two simultaneous motions, Donald's mother slapped her napkin into her place and pushed her chair back violently. She rose and ran out of the room, slamming the door. No one said anything. Donald sat frozen, unable to look up, unable even to breathe. Then he realized that his father had got up, too, and was on his way out.

"Leave her alone, Owen," said Gramma.

"You keep out of this," his father said. His footsteps made the stairs creak as he went up. No one said anything until Gramma made as if to rise. "I'm going up," she declared.

"For God's sake, Abbie, sit still," Grampa told her. Gramma cleared her throat, but did not get up.

Aunt Louisa looked very red, and the muscles of her face were twitching. "Hateful," she said in a choked voice. "Just hateful."

"I felt like slapping his face," confided Aunt Emilie. "Did you hear what he said to me when we were having our presents?"

At a glance from Uncle Greg, Aunt Emilie stopped. "Why, Donald!" she exclaimed brightly, "you've scarcely touched your dinner! Aren't you hungry?"

In his mind's eye he was seeing the bedroom upstairs, where his father was twisting his mother's arm and shaking her to make her look at him. When she wouldn't, he punched her, knocking her down, and kicked her as hard as he could, all over her body. Donald looked up. "Not very," he said.

Without warning Mr. Gordon began to talk, holding his glass in front of him and examining it as he turned it this way and that. "Family quarrels," he sighed. "Same old thing. Reminds me of my boyhood. When I look back on it, it seems to me we never got through a meal without a fight, but I suppose we must have once in a while." He set the glass down. "Well, they're all dead now, thank God."

Donald looked quickly across at Mr. Gordon as if he were seeing him for the first time.

"It's snowing!" cried Gramma triumphantly. "Look, it's snowing again. I knew we'd have more snow before dark." She did not want Mr. Gordon to go on talking.

Aunt Louisa sobbed once, got up, and went out into the kitchen. Uncle Ivor followed her.

"Why, Donald! You've got the wishbone!" cried Aunt Emilie. "Eat the meat off it and we'll hang it up over the stove to dry, and tomorrow we'll wish on it. Wouldn't that be fun?"

He picked it up in his fingers and began to chew on the strips of white meat that clung to it. When he had carefully cleaned it, he got down and went out into the kitchen with it.

The room was very quiet; the tea kettle simmered on the stove. Outside the window the falling snowflakes looked dark against the whiteness beyond. Aunt Louisa was sitting on the high stool, doubled over, with a crumpled handkerchief in her hand, and Uncle Ivor was bending over her talking in a very low voice. Donald laid the wishbone on the sink shelf and started to tiptoe out, but Uncle Ivor saw him. "How'd you like to go up to the henhouse with me, Donald?" he said. "I've got to find us a dozen eggs to take back to Rutland."

"I'll get my coat," Donald told him, eager to go out before his father came back downstairs.

The path up the hill to the henhouse had been made not by clearing the snow away, but by tramping it down. The new snow was drifting over the track; in some places it already had covered it. When Uncle Ivor went into the henhouse Donald stood still, bending his head back to catch some snowflakes in his mouth. "Come on in and shut the door. You'll let all the heat out," Uncle Ivor told him.

"I'm coming," said Donald. He stepped through the doorway and closed the door. The smell inside was very strong. As Uncle Ivor approached the hens, they set up a low, distrustful murmur.

"Tell me, Donald," said Uncle Ivor as he explored the straw with his hands.

"What?" said Donald.

"Does your mother often run to her room and shut the door, the way she did just now?"

"Sometimes."

"Why? Is your father mean to her?"

"Oh," said Donald vaguely, "they have fights." He felt uncomfortable.

"Yes. Well, it's a great pity your father ever got married. It would have been better for everybody if he'd stayed single."

"But then I wouldn't have been born at all," cried Donald, uncertain whether Uncle Ivor was serious or not.

"At least, we *hope* not!" said Uncle Ivor, rolling his eyes and looking silly. Now Donald knew it was a kind of joke, and he laughed. The door was flung open. "Donald!" roared his father.

"What is it?" he said, his voice very feeble.

"Come out here!"

He stumbled toward the door; his father was peering inside uncertainly. "What are you doing in there?" he demanded.

"Helping Uncle Ivor look for eggs."

"Hmmph!" Donald stepped out and his father shut the door.

They started to walk along the road in the direction of the Smithson farm. Presently his father fell in behind him and prodded him in the back, saying: "Keep your head up. Chest out! D'you want to get round-shouldered? Before you know it you'll have curvature of the spine."

When they had got out of sight of the house, in a place where the tangle of small trees came to the edge of the road on both sides, his father stopped walking. He looked around, reached down, picked up a handful of the new snow, and rolled it into a hard ball. Then he threw it at a fairly large tree, some distance from the road. It broke, leaving a white mark on the dark trunk. "Let's see you hit it," he told Donald.

A wolf could be waiting here, somewhere back in the still gloom of the woods. It was very important not to make him angry. If his father wanted to take a chance and throw snowballs into the woods, he could, but Donald would not. Then perhaps the wolf would understand that he, at least, was his friend.

"Go on," said his father.

"No. I don't want to."

With mock astonishment his father said: "Oh, you don't?" Then his face became dangerous and his voice cracked like a whip. "Are you going to do what I told you?"

"No." It was the first time he had openly defied him. His father turned very red.

"Listen here, you young whippersnapper!" he cried, his voice tight with anger. "You think you're going to get away with this?" Before Donald knew what was happening, his father had seized him with one hand while he bent over and with the other scooped up as much snow as he could. "We'll settle this little matter right now," he said through his teeth. Suddenly he was rubbing the snow violently over Donald's face, and at the same time that Donald gasped and squirmed, he pushed what was left of it down his neck. As he felt the wet, icy mass sliding down his back, he doubled over. His eyes were squeezed shut; he was certain his father was trying to kill him. With a desperate lunge he bounded free and fell face-downward into the snow.

"Get up," his father said disgustedly. He did not move. If he held his breath long enough he might die.

His father yanked him to his feet. "I've had just about enough of your monkeyshines," he said. Clutching him tightly with both hands, he forced him to hobble ahead of him, back through the twilight to the house.

Donald moved forward, looking at the white road in front of him, his mind empty of thoughts. An unfamiliar feeling had come to him: he was not sorry for himself for being wet and cold, or even resentful at having been mistreated. He felt detached; it was an agreeable, almost voluptuous sensation which he accepted without understanding or questioning it.

As they advanced down the long alley of maple trees in the dusk his father said: "Now you can go and cry in your mother's lap."

"I'm not crying," said Donald loudly, without expression. His father did not answer.

Fortunately the kitchen was empty. He could tell from the sound of the voices in the parlor that Aunt Louisa, Uncle Ivor and Mr. Gordon were getting ready to leave. He ran upstairs to his room and changed his clothes completely. The hole he had breathed in the ice on the window-pane had frozen over thickly again, but the round mark was still visible. As he finished dressing his mother called him. It was completely dark outside. He went downstairs. She was standing in the hallway.

"Oh, you've changed your clothes," she said. "Come out and say good-bye to Aunt Louisa and Uncle Ivor. They're in the kitchen." He looked quickly at her face to see if there were signs of her recent tears: her eyes were slightly bloodshot.

Together they went into the kitchen. "Donald wants to say good-bye to you," she told Mr. Gordon, steering Donald to Aunt Louisa. "You've given him a wonderful Christmas"—her voice became reproachful—"but it was *much* too much."

The thick beaver collar of Mr. Gordon's overcoat was turned up over his ears, and he had on enormous fur gloves. He smiled and clapped his hands together expectantly; it made a cushioned sound. "Oh, it was a lot of fun," he said. "He reminds me a little of myself, you know, when I was his age. I was a sort of shy and quiet lad, too." Donald felt his mother's hand tighten on his shoulder as she pushed him toward Aunt Louisa. "Mm," she said. "Well, Auntie Louisa, here's somebody who wants to say good-bye to you."

Even in the excitement of watching Uncle Willis and Uncle Greg drive the others off in the sleigh, Donald did not miss the fact that his father had not appeared in the kitchen at all. When the sleigh had moved out of sight down the dark road, everyone went into the parlor and Grampa put another log on the fire.

"Where's Owen?" Gramma said in a low voice to Donald's mother.

"He must be upstairs. To tell the truth, I don't care very much where he is."

"Poor child," said Gramma. "Headache a little better?"

"A little." She sighed. "He certainly managed to take all the pleasure out of *my* Christmas."

"A mean shame," said Gramma.

"It was all I could do to look Ivor in the face just now. I meant it."

"I'm sure they all understood," said Gramma soothingly. "Just don't you fret about it. Anyway, Owen'll be gone tomorrow, and you can rest up."

Shortly after Uncle Willis and Uncle Greg got back, Donald's father came downstairs. Supper was eaten in almost complete silence; at no time did his father speak to him or pay him any attention. As soon as the meal was over his mother took him upstairs to bed.

When she had left him, he lay in the dark listening to the sound of the fine snow as the wind drove it against the panes. The wolf was out there in the night, running along paths that no one had ever seen, down the hill and across the meadow, stopping to drink at a deep place in the brook where the ice had not formed. The stiff hairs of his coat had caught the snow; he shook himself and climbed up the bank to where Donald sat waiting for him. Then he lay down beside him, putting his heavy head in Donald's lap. Donald leaned over and buried his face in the shaggy fur of his scruff. After a while they both got up and began to run together, faster and faster, across the fields.

HE OF THE ASSEMBLY

He salutes all parts of the sky and the earth where it is
bright. He thinks the color of the amethysts of Aguelmous
will be dark if it has rained in the valley of Zerekten. The
eye wants to sleep, he says, but the head is no mattress.
When it rained for three days and water covered the
flatlands outside the ramparts, he slept by the bamboo fence
at the Café of the Two Bridges.

It seems there was a man named Ben Tajah who went to Fez to visit his
cousin. The day he came back he was walking in the Djemaa el Fna, and
he saw a letter lying on the pavement. He picked it up and found that
his name was written on the envelope. He went to the Café of the Two
Bridges with the letter in his hand, sat down on a mat and opened the
envelope. Inside was a paper which read: "The sky trembles and the earth
is afraid, and the two eyes are not brothers." Ben Tajah did not understand, and he was very unhappy because his name was on the envelope.
It made him think that Satan was nearby. He of the Assembly was sitting
in the same part of the café. He was listening to the wind in the telephone
wires. The sky was almost empty of daytime light. "The eye wants to
sleep," he thought, "but the head is no mattress. I know what that is, but
I have forgotten it." Three days is a long time for rain to keep falling
on flat bare ground. "If I got up and ran down the street," he thought,
"a policeman would follow me and call to me to stop. I would run faster,
and he would run after me. When he shot at me, I'd duck around the
corners of houses." He felt the rough dried mud of the wall under his
fingertips. "And I'd be running through the streets looking for a place
to hide, but no door would be open, until finally I came to one door that
was open, and I'd go in through the rooms and courtyards until finally
I came to the kitchen. The old woman would be there." He stopped and
wondered for a moment why an old woman should be there alone in the

kitchen at that hour. She was stirring a big kettle of soup on the stove. "And I'd look for a place to hide there in the kitchen, and there'd be no place. And I'd be waiting to hear the policeman's footsteps, because he wouldn't miss the open door. And I'd look in the dark corner of the room where she kept the charcoal, but it wouldn't be dark enough. And the old woman would turn and look at me and say: 'If you're trying to get away, my boy, I can help you. Jump into the soup kettle.'" The wind sighed in the telephone wires. Men came into the Café of the Two Bridges with their garments flapping. Ben Tajah sat on his mat. He had put the letter away, but first he had stared at it a long time. He of the Assembly leaned back and looked at the sky. "The old woman," he said to himself. "What is she trying to do? The soup is hot. It may be a trap. I may find there's no way out, once I get down there." He wanted a pipe of kif, but he was afraid the policeman would run into the kitchen before he was able to smoke it. He said to the old woman: "How can I get in? Tell me." And it seemed to him that he heard footsteps in the street, or perhaps even in one of the rooms of the house. He leaned over the stove and looked down into the kettle. It was dark and very hot down in there. Steam was coming up in clouds, and there was a thick smell in the air that made it hard to breathe. "Quick!" said the old woman, and she unrolled a rope ladder and hung it over the edge of the kettle. He began to climb down, and she leaned over and looked after him. "Until the other world!" he shouted. And he climbed all the way down. There was a rowboat below. When he was in it he tugged on the ladder and the old woman began to pull it up. And at that instant the policeman ran in, and two more were with him, and the old woman had just the time to throw the ladder down into the soup. "Now they are going to take her to the commissariat," he thought, "and the poor woman only did me a favor." He rowed around in the dark for a few minutes, and it was very hot. Soon he took off his clothes. For a while he could see the round top of the kettle up above, like a porthole in the side of a ship, with the heads of the policemen looking down in, but then it grew smaller as he rowed, until it was only a light. Sometimes he could find it and sometimes he lost it, and finally it was gone. He was worried about the old woman, and he thought he must find a way to help her. No policeman can go into the Café of the Two Bridges because it belongs to the sultan's sister. This is why there is so much kif smoke inside that a *berrada* can't fall over even if it is pushed, and why most customers like to sit outside, and even there keep one hand on their money. As long as the thieves stay inside and their friends bring them food and kif, they are all right. One day police headquarters will forget to send a man to watch the café, or one man will leave five minutes before the other gets there to take his place. Outside everyone smokes kif too, but only for an hour or two—not all day and night like the ones inside. He of the Assembly had forgotten to light his *sebsi*. He was in a café where no policeman could come, and he wanted to go away to a kif world where the police were chasing him. "This is the way we are now," he thought. "We work backwards. If we have something good, we look for something bad instead." He lighted the *sebsi* and smoked it. Then he blew the hard ash out of the *chqaf.* It landed in the brook beside the second bridge. "The world is too good. We can only work forward if we make it bad again first." This made him sad, so he stopped thinking, and filled his *sebsi*. While he was smoking it, Ben Tajah looked in his direction, and although they were facing each other, He of the Assembly did not notice Ben Tajah until he got up and paid for his tea. Then he looked at him because he took such a long time getting up off the floor. He saw his face and he thought: "That man has no one in the world." The idea made him feel cold. He filled his *sebsi* again and lighted it. He saw the man as he was going to go out of the café and walk alone down the long road outside the ramparts. In a little while he himself would have to go out to the *souks* to try to borrow money for dinner. When he smoked a lot of kif he did not like his aunt to see him, and he did not want to see her. "Soup and bread. No one can want more than that. Will thirty francs be enough the fourth time? The *qaouaji* wasn't satisfied last night. But he took it. And he went away and let me sleep. A Moslem, even in the city, can't refuse his brother shelter." He was not convinced, because he had been born in the mountains, and so he kept thinking back and forth in this way. He smoked many *chqofa,* and when he got up to go out into the street he found that the world had changed.

Ben Tajah was not a rich man. He lived alone in a room near Bab Doukkala, and he had a stall in the bazaars where he sold coat hangers and chests. Often he did not open the shop because he was in bed with a liver attack. At such times he pounded on the floor from his bed, using a brass pestle, and the postman who lived downstairs brought him up some food. Sometimes he stayed in bed for a week at a time. Each morning and night the postman came in with a tray. The food was not very good because the postman's wife did not understand much about cooking. But he was glad to have it. Twice he had brought the postman a new chest to keep clothes and blankets in. One of the postman's wives a few years before had taken a chest with her when she had left him and gone back to her family in Kasba Tadla. Ben Tajah himself had tried having a wife for a while because he needed someone to get him regular meals and to wash his clothes, but the girl was from the mountains, and was wild. No matter how much he beat her she would not be tamed. Everything in the room got broken, and finally he had to put her out into the street. "No more women will get into my house," he told his friends in the bazaars, and they laughed. He took home many women, and one day he found that he had *en noua*. He knew that was a bad disease, because it stays in the blood and eats the nose from inside. "A man loses his nose only long after he has already lost his head." He asked a doctor for medicine. The doctor gave him a paper and told him to take it to the Pharmacie de l'Étoile. There he bought six vials of penicillin in a box. He took them home and tied each little bottle with a silk thread, stringing them so that they made a necklace. He wore this always around his neck, taking care that the glass vials touched his skin. He thought it likely that by now he was cured, but his cousin in Fez had just told him that he must go on wearing the medicine for another three months, or at least until the beginning of the moon of Chouwal. He had thought about this now and then on the way home, sitting in the bus for two days, and he had decided that his cousin was too cautious. He stood in the Djemaa el Fna a minute watching the trained monkeys, but the crowd pushed too much, so he walked on. When he got home he shut the door and put his hand in his pocket to pull out the envelope, because he wanted to look at it again inside his own room, and be sure that the name written on it was beyond a doubt his. But the letter was gone. He remembered the jostling in the Djemaa el Fna. Someone had reached into his pocket and imagined his hand was feeling money, and taken it. Yet Ben Tajah did not truly believe this. He was convinced that he would have known such a theft was happening. There had been a letter in his pocket. He was not even sure of that. He sat down on the cushions. "Two days in the bus," he thought. "Probably I'm tired. I found no letter." He searched in his pocket again, and it seemed to him he could still remember how the fold of the envelope had felt. "Why would it have my name on it? I never found any letter at all." Then he wondered if anyone had seen him in the café with the envelope in one hand and the sheet of paper in the other, looking at them both for such a long time. He stood up. He wanted to go back to the Café of the Two Bridges and ask the *qaouaji*: "Did you see me an hour ago? Was I looking at a letter?" If the *qaouaji* said, "Yes," then the letter was real. He repeated the words aloud: "The sky trembles and the earth is afraid, and the two eyes are not brothers." In the silence afterward the memory of the sound of the words frightened him. "If there was no letter, where are these words from?" And he shivered because the answer to that was: "From Satan." He was about to open the door when a new fear stopped him. The *qaouaji* might say, "No," and this would be still worse, because it would mean that the words had been put directly into his head by Satan, that Satan had chosen him to reveal Himself to. In that case He might appear at any moment. *"Ach haddou laillaha ill' Allah . . . ,"* he prayed, holding his two forefingers up, one on each side of him. He sat down again and did not move. In the street the children were crying. He did not want to hear the *qaouaji* say: "No. You had no letter." If he knew that Satan was coming to tempt him, he would have that much less power to keep Him away with his prayers, because he would be more afraid.

He of the Assembly stood. Behind him was a wall. In his hand was the *sebsi*. Over his head was the sky, which he felt was about to burst into light. He was leaning back looking at it. It was dark on the earth, but there was still light up there behind the stars. Ahead of him was the pissoir of the carpenters' souk which the French had put there. People said only Jews used it. It was made of tin, and there was a puddle in front of it that reflected the sky and the top of the pissoir. It looked like a boat in the water. Or like a pier where boats land. Without moving from where he stood, He of the Assembly saw it approaching slowly. He was going toward it. And he remembered he was naked, and put his hand over his sex. In a minute the rowboat would be bumping against the pier. He steadied himself on his legs and waited. But at that moment a large cat ran out of the shadow of the wall and stopped in the middle of the street to turn and look at him with an evil face. He saw its two eyes and for a while could not take his own eyes away. Then the cat ran across the street and was gone. He was not sure what had happened, and he stood very still looking at the ground. He looked back at the pissoir reflected in the puddle and thought: "It was a cat on the shore, nothing else." But the cat's eyes had frightened him. Instead of being like cats' eyes, they had looked like the eyes of a person who was interested in him. He made himself forget he had this thought. He was still waiting for the rowboat to touch the landing pier, but nothing had happened. It was going to stay where it was, that near the shore but not near enough to touch. He stood still a long time, waiting for something to happen. Then he began to walk very fast down the street toward the bazaars. He had just remembered that the old woman was in the police station. He wanted to help her, but first he had to find out where they had taken her. "I'll have to go to every police station in the Medina," he thought, and he was not hungry anymore. It was one thing to promise himself he would help her when he was far from land, and another when he was a few doors from a commissariat. He walked by the entrance. Two policemen stood in the doorway. He kept walking. The street curved and he was alone. "This night is going to be a jewel in my crown," he said, and he turned quickly to the left and went along a dark passageway. At the end he saw flames, and he knew that Mustapha would be there tending the fire of the bakery. He crawled into the mud hut where the oven was. "Ah, the jackal has come back from the forest!" said Mustapha. He of the Assembly shook his head. "This is a bad world," he told Mustapha. "I've got no money," Mustapha said. He of the Assembly did not understand. "Everything goes backwards," he said. "It's bad now, and we have to make it still worse if we want to go forwards." Mustapha saw that He of the Assembly was *mkiyif ma rassou* and was not interested in money. He looked at him in a more friendly way and said: "Secrets are not between friends. Talk." He of the Assembly told him that an old woman had done him a great favor, and because of that three policemen had arrested her and taken her to the police station. "You must go for me to the commissariat and ask them if they have an old woman there." He pulled out his *sebsi* and took a very long time filling it. When he finished it he smoked it himself and did not offer any to Mustapha, because Mustapha never offered him any of his. "You see how full of kif my head is," he said laughing. "I can't go." Mustapha laughed too and said it would not be a good idea, and that he would go for him.

"I was there, and I heard him going away for a long time, so long that he had to be gone, and yet he was still there, and his footsteps were still going away. He went away and there was nobody. There was the fire and I moved away from it. I wanted to hear a sound like a muezzin crying *Allah akbar!* or a French plane from the Pilot Base flying over the Medina, or news on the radio. It wasn't there. And when the wind came in the door it was made of dust high as a man. A night to be chased by dogs in the Mellah. I looked in the fire and I saw an eye in there, like the eye that's left when you burn *chibb* and you know there was a *djinn* in the house. I got up and stood. The fire was making a noise like a voice. I think it was talking. I went out and walked along the street. I walked a long time and I came to Bab el Khemiss. It was dark there and the wind was cold. I went to the wall where the camels were lying and stood there. Sometimes the men have fires and play songs on their *aouadas*. But they were asleep. All snoring. I walked again and went to the gate and looked out. The big trucks went by full of vegetables and I thought I would like to be on a truck and ride all night. Then in another city I would be a soldier and go to Algeria. Everything would be good if we had a war. I thought a long time. Then I was so cold I turned around and walked again. It was as cold as the belly of the oldest goat of Ijoukak. I thought I heard a muezzin and I stopped and listened. The only thing I heard was the water running in the *seguia* that carries the water out to the gardens. It was near the *mçid* of Moulay Boujemaa. I heard the water running by and I felt cold. Then I knew I was cold because I was afraid. In my head I was thinking: 'If something should happen that never happened before, what would I do?' You want to laugh? Hashish in your heart and wind in your head. You think it's like your grandmother's prayer mat. This is the truth. This isn't a dream brought back from another world past the customs like a teapot from Mecca. I heard the water and I was afraid. There were some trees by the path ahead of me. You know at night sometimes it's good to pull out the *sebsi* and smoke. I smoked and I started to walk. And then I heard something. Not a muezzin. Something that sounded like my name. But it came up from below, from the *seguia, Allah istir!* And I walked with my head down. I heard it again saying my name, a voice like water, like the wind moving the leaves in the trees, a woman. It was a woman calling me. The wind was in the trees and the water was running, but there was a woman too. You think it's kif. No, she was calling my name. Now and then, not very loud. When I was under the trees it was louder, and I heard that the voice was my mother's. I heard that the way I can hear you. Then I knew the cat was not a cat, and I knew that Aïcha Qandicha wanted me. I thought of other nights when perhaps she had been watching me from the eyes of a cat or a donkey. I knew she was not going to catch me. Nothing in the seven skies could make me turn around. But I was cold and afraid and when I licked my lips my tongue had no spit on it. I was under the *safsaf* trees and I thought: 'She's going to reach down and try to touch me. But she can't touch me from the front and I won't turn around, not even if I hear a pistol.' I remembered how the policeman had fired at me and how I'd found only one door open. I began to yell: 'You threw me the ladder and told me to climb down. You brought me here! The filthiest whore in the Mellah, with the pus coming out of her, is a thousand times cleaner than you, daughter of all the *padronas* and dogs in seven worlds.' I got past the trees and I began to run. I called up to the sky so she could hear my voice behind: 'I hope the police put a hose in your mouth and pump you full of salt water until you crack open!' I thought: 'Tomorrow I'm going to buy *fasoukh* and *tib* and *nidd* and *hasalouba* and *mska* and all the *bakhour* in the Djemaa, and put them in the *mijmah* and burn them, and walk back and forth over the *mijmah* ten times slowly, so the smoke can clean out all my clothes. Then I'll see if there's an eye in the ashes afterwards. If there is, I'll do it all over again right away. And every Thursday I'll buy the *bakhour* and every Friday I'll burn it. That will be strong enough to keep her away.' If I could find a window and look through and see what they're doing to the old woman! If only they could kill her! I kept running. There were a few people in the streets. I didn't look to see where I was going, but I went to the street near Mustapha's oven where the commissariat was. I stopped running before I got to the door. The one standing there saw me before that. He stepped out and raised his arm. He said to me: 'Come here.'"

He of the Assembly ran. He felt as though he were on horseback. He did not feel his legs moving. He saw the road coming toward him and the doors going by. The policeman had not shot at him yet, but it was worse than the other time because he was very close behind and he was blowing his whistle. "The policeman is old. At least thirty-five. I can run faster." But from any street others could come. It was dangerous and he did not want to think about danger. He of the Assembly let songs come into his head. When it rains in the valley of Zerekten the amethysts are darker in Aguelmous. The eye wants to sleep but the head is no mattress. It was a song. Ah, my brother, the ink on the paper is like smoke in the air. What words are there to tell how long a night can be? Drunk with love, I wander in the dark. He was running through the dye souk, and he splashed into a puddle. The whistle blew again behind him, like a crazy bird screaming. The sound made him feel like laughing, but that did not mean he was not afraid. He thought: "If I'm seventeen I can run faster. That has to be true." It was very dark ahead. He had to slow his running. There was no time for his eyes to get used to the dark. He nearly ran into the wall of the shop at the end of the street. He turned to the right and saw the narrow alley ahead of him. The police had tied the old woman naked to a table with her thin legs wide apart and were sliding electrodes up inside her. He ran ahead. He could see the course of the alley now even in the dark. Then he stopped dead, moved to the wall, and stood still. He heard the footsteps slowing down. "He's going to turn to the left." And he whispered aloud: "It ends that way." The footsteps stopped and there was silence. The policeman was looking into the silence and listening into the dark to the left and to the right. He of the Assembly could not see him or hear him, but he knew that was what he was doing. He did not move. When it rains in the valley of Zerekten. A hand seized his shoulder. He opened his mouth and swiftly turned, but the man had moved and was pushing him from the side. He felt the wool of the man's *djellaba* against the back of his hand. He had gone through a door and the man had shut it without making any noise. Now they both stood still in the dark, listening to the policeman walking quickly by outside the door. Then the man struck a match. He was facing the other way, and there was a flight of stairs ahead. The man did not turn around, but he said, "Come up," and they both climbed the stairs. At the top the man took out a key and opened a door. He of the Assembly stood in the doorway while the man lit a candle. He liked the room because it had many mattresses and cushions and a white sheepskin under the tea tray in the corner of the floor. The man turned around and said: "Sit down."

His face looked serious and kind and unhappy. He of the Assembly had never seen it before, but he knew it was not the face of a policeman. He of the Assembly pulled out his *sebsi*.

Ben Tajah looked at the boy and asked him: "What did you mean when you said down there: 'It ends that way'? I heard you say it." The boy was embarrassed. He smiled and looked at the floor. Ben Tajah felt happy to have him there. He had been standing outside the door down-stairs in the dark for a long time, trying to make himself go to the Café of the Two Bridges and talk to the *qaouaji*. In his mind it was almost as though he had already been there and spoken with him. He had heard the *qaouaji* telling him that he had seen no letter, and he had felt his own dismay. He had not wanted to believe that, but he would be willing to say yes, I made a mistake and there was no letter, if only he could find out where the words had come from. For the words were certainly in his head: ". . . and the two eyes are not brothers." That was like a footprint found in the garden the morning after a bad dream, the proof that there had been a reason for the dream, that something had been there after all. Ben Tajah had not been able to go or to stay. He had started and stopped so many times that now, although he did not know it, he was very tired. When a man is tired he mistakes the hopes of children for the knowledge of men. It seemed to him that He of the Assembly's words had a meaning all for him. Even though the boy might not know it, he could have been sent by Allah to help him at that minute. In a nearby street a police whistle blew. The boy looked at him. Ben Tajah did not care very much what the answer would be, but he said: "Why are they looking for you?" The boy held out his lighted *sebsi* and his *mottoui* fat with kif. He did not want to talk because he was listening. Ben Tajah smoked kif only when a friend offered it to him, but he understood that the police had begun once more to try to enforce their law against kif. Each year they arrested people for a few weeks, and then stopped arresting them. He looked at the boy, and decided that probably he smoked too much. With the *sebsi* in his hand he was sitting very still listening to the voices of some passersby in the street below. "I know who he is," one said. "I've got his name from Mustapha." "The baker?" "That's the one." They walked on. The boy's expression was so intense that Ben Tajah said to him: "It's nobody. Just people." He was feeling happy because he was certain that Satan would not appear before him as long as the boy was with him. He

166

said quietly: "Still you haven't told me why you said: 'It ends that way.' " The boy filled his *sebsi* slowly and smoked all the kif in it. "I meant," he said, "thanks to Allah. Praise the sky and the earth where it is bright. What else can you mean when something ends?" Ben Tajah nodded his head. Pious thoughts can be of as much use for keeping Satan at a distance as camphor or *bakhour* dropped onto hot coals. Each holy word is worth a high column of smoke, and the eyelids do not smart afterward. "He has a good heart," thought Ben Tajah, "even though he is probably a guide for the Nazarenes." And he asked himself why it would not be possible for the boy to have been sent to protect him from Satan. "Probably not. But it could be." The boy offered him the *sebsi*. He took it and smoked it. After that Ben Tajah began to think that he would like to go to the Café of the Two Bridges and speak to the *qaouaji* about the letter. He felt that if the boy went with him the *qaouaji* might say there had been a letter, and that even if the man could not remember, he would not mind so much because he would be less afraid. He waited until he thought the boy was not nervous about going into the street, and then he said: "Let's go out and get some tea." "Good," said the boy. He was not afraid of the police if he was with Ben Tajah. They went through the empty streets, crossed the Djemaa el Fna and the garden beyond. When they were near the café, Ben Tajah said to the boy: "Do you know the Café of the Two Bridges?" The boy said he always sat there, and Ben Tajah was not surprised. It seemed to him that perhaps he had even seen him there. He seized the boy's arm. "Were you there today?" he asked him. The boy said, "Yes," and turned to look at him. He let go of the arm. "Nothing," he said. "Did you ever see me there?" They came to the gate of the café and Ben Tajah stopped walking. "No," the boy said. They went across the first bridge and then the second bridge, and sat down in a corner. Not many people were left outside. Those inside were making a great noise. The *qaouaji* brought the tea and went away again. Ben Tajah did not say anything to him about the letter. He wanted to drink the tea quietly and leave trouble until later.

When the muezzin called from the minaret of the Koutoubia, He of the Assembly thought of being in the Agdal. The great mountains were ahead of him and the olive trees stood in rows on each side of him. Then he heard the trickle of water and he remembered the *seguia* that is there in the Agdal, and he swiftly came back to the Café of the Two Bridges.

Aïcha Qandicha can be only where there are trees by running water. "She comes only for single men by trees and fresh moving water. Her arms are gold and she calls in the voice of the most cherished one." Ben Tajah gave him the *sebsi*. He filled it and smoked it. "When a man sees her face he will never see another woman's face. He will make love with her all the night, and every night, and in the sunlight by the walls, before the eyes of children. Soon he will be an empty pod and he will leave this world for his home in Jehennem." The last carriage went by, taking the last tourists down the road beside the ramparts to their rooms in the Mamounia. He of the Assembly thought: "The eye wants to sleep. But this man is alone in the world. He wants to talk all night. He wants to tell me about his wife and how he beat her and how she broke everything. Why do I want to know all those things? He is a good man but he has no head." Ben Tajah was sad. He said: "What have I done? Why does Satan choose me?" Then at last he told the boy about the letter, about how he wondered if it had had his name on the envelope and how he was not even sure there had been a letter. When he finished he looked sadly at the boy. "And you didn't see me." He of the Assembly shut his eyes and kept them shut for a while. When he opened them again he said: "Are you alone in the world?" Ben Tajah stared at him and did not speak. The boy laughed. "I did see you," he said, "but you had no letter. I saw you when you were getting up and I thought you were old. Then I saw you were not old. That's all I saw." "No, it isn't," Ben Tajah said. "You saw I was alone." He of the Assembly shrugged. "Who knows?" He filled the *sebsi* and handed it to Ben Tajah. The kif was in Ben Tajah's head. His eyes were small. He of the Assembly listened to the wind in the telephone wires, took back the *sebsi* and filled it again. Then he said: "You think Satan is coming to make trouble for you because you're alone in the world. I see that. Get a wife or somebody to be with you always, and you won't think about it anymore. That's true. Because Satan doesn't come to men like you." He of the Assembly did not believe this himself. He knew that Father Satan can come for anyone in the world, but he hoped to live with Ben Tajah, so he would not have to borrow money in the souks to buy food. Ben Tajah drank some tea. He did not want the boy to see that his face was happy. He felt that the boy was right, and that there never had been a letter. "Two days on a bus is a long time. A man can get very tired," he said. Then he called the *qaouaji* and told

168

him to bring two more glasses of tea. He of the Assembly gave him the *sebsi*. He knew that Ben Tajah wanted to stay as long as possible in the Café of the Two Bridges. He put his finger into the *mottoui*. The kif was almost gone. "We can talk," he said. "Not much kif is in the *mottoui*." The *qaouaji* brought the tea. They talked for an hour or more. The *qaouaji* slept and snored. They talked about Satan and the bad thing it is to live alone, to wake up in the dark and know that there is no one else nearby. Many times He of the Assembly told Ben Tajah that he must not worry. The kif was all gone. He held his empty *mottoui* in his hand. He did not understand how he had got back to the town without climbing up out of the soup kettle. Once he said to Ben Tajah: "I never climbed back up." Ben Tajah looked at him and said he did not understand. He of the Assembly told him the story. Ben Tajah laughed. He said: "You smoke too much kif, brother." He of the Assembly put his *sebsi* into his pocket. "And you don't smoke and you're afraid of Satan," he told Ben Tajah. "No!" Ben Tajah shouted. "By Allah! No more! But one thing is in my head, and I can't put it out. The sky trembles and the earth is afraid, and the two eyes are not brothers. Did you ever hear those words? Where did they come from?" Ben Tajah looked hard at the boy. He of the Assembly understood that these had been the words on the paper, and he felt cold in the middle of his back because he had never heard them before and they sounded evil. He knew, too, that he must not let Ben Tajah know this. He began to laugh. Ben Tajah took hold of his knee and shook it. His face was troubled. "Did you ever hear them?" He of the Assembly went on laughing. Ben Tajah shook his leg so hard that he stopped and said: "Yes!" When Ben Tajah waited and he said nothing more, he saw the man's face growing angry, and so he said: "Yes, I've heard them. But will you tell me what happened to me and how I got out of the soup kettle if I tell you about those words?" Ben Tajah understood that the kif was going away from the boy's head. But he saw that it had not all gone, or he would not have been asking that question. And he said: "Wait a while for the answer to that question." He of the Assembly woke the *qaouaji* and Ben Tajah paid him, and they went out of the café. They did not talk while they walked. When they got to the Mouassine mosque, Ben Tajah held out his hand to say good-night, but He of the Assembly said: "I'm looking in my head for the place I heard your words. I'll walk to your door with you. Maybe I'll remember." Ben Tajah said: "May

Allah help you find it." And he took his arm and they walked to Ben Tajah's door while He of the Assembly said nothing. They stood outside the door in the dark. "Have you found it?" said Ben Tajah. "Almost," said He of the Assembly. Ben Tajah thought that perhaps when the kif had gone out of the boy's head he might be able to tell him about the words. He wanted to know how the boy's head was, and so he said: "Do you still want to know how you got out of the soup kettle?" He of the Assembly laughed. "You said you would tell me later," he told Ben Tajah. "I will," said Ben Tajah. "Come upstairs. Since we have to wait, we can sit down." Ben Tajah opened the door and they went upstairs. This time He of the Assembly sat down on Ben Tajah's bed. He yawned and stretched. It was a good bed. He was glad it was not the mat by the bamboo fence at the Café of the Two Bridges. "And so, tell me how I got out of the soup kettle," he said laughing. Ben Tajah said: "You're still asking me that? Have you thought of the words?" "I know the words," the boy said. "The sky trembles. . . ." Ben Tajah did not want him to say them again. "Where did you hear them? What are they? That's what I want to know." The boy shook his head. Then he sat up very straight and looked beyond Ben Tajah, beyond the wall of the room, beyond the streets of the Medina, beyond the gardens, toward the mountains where the people speak Tachelhait. He remembered being a little boy. "This night is a jewel in my crown," he thought. "It went this way." And he began to sing, making up a melody for the words Ben Tajah had told him. When he had finished ". . . and the two eyes are not brothers," he added a few more words of his own and stopped singing. "That's all I remember of the song," he said. Ben Tajah clapped his hands together hard. "A song!" he cried. "I must have heard it on the radio." He of the Assembly shrugged. "They play it sometimes," he said. "I've made him happy," he thought. "But I won't ever tell him another lie. That's the only one. What I'm going to do now is not the same as lying." He got up off the bed and went to the window. The muezzins were calling the *fjer*. "It's almost morning," he said to Ben Tajah. "I still have kif in my head." "Sit down," said Ben Tajah. He was sure now there had been no letter. He of the Assembly took off his *djellaba* and got into bed. Ben Tajah looked at him in surprise. Then he undressed and got into bed beside him. He left the candle burning on the floor beside the bed. He meant to stay awake, but he went to sleep because he was not used to smoking kif and the kif was in his head. He of the Assembly did not believe he was asleep. He lay for a long time without moving. He listened to the voices of the muezzins, and he thought that the man beside him would speak or move. When he saw that Ben Tajah was surely asleep, he was angry. "This is how he treats a friend who has made him happy. He forgets his trouble and his friend too." He thought about it more and he was angrier. The muezzins were still calling the *fjer*. "Before they stop, or he will hear." Very slowly he got out of the bed. He put on his *djellaba* and opened the door. Then he went back and took all the money out of Ben Tajah's pockets. In with the bank notes was an envelope that was folded. It had Ben Tajah's name written across it. He pulled out the piece of paper inside and held it near the candle, and then he looked at it as he would have looked at a snake. The words were written there. Ben Tajah's face was turned toward the wall and he was snoring. He of the Assembly held the paper above the flame and burned it, and then he burned the envelope. He blew the black paper ashes across the floor. Without making any noise he ran downstairs and let himself out into the street. He shut the door. The money was in his pocket and he walked fast to his aunt's house. His aunt awoke and was angry for a while. Finally he said: "It was raining. How could I come home? Let me sleep." He had a little kif hidden under his pillow. He smoked a pipe. Then he looked across his sleep to the morning and thought: "A pipe of kif before breakfast gives a man the strength of a hundred camels in the courtyard."

THE TIME OF FRIENDSHIP

The trouble had been growing bigger each year, ever since the end of the war. From the beginning, although aware of its existence, Fräulein Windling had determined to pay it no attention. At first there were only whispered reports of mass arrests. People said: "Many thousands of Moslems have been sent to prison in France." Soon some of her own friends had begun to disappear, like young Bachir and Omar ben Lakhdar, the postmaster of Timimoun, who suddenly one morning were gone, or so she was told, for when she returned the following winter they were not there, and she never had seen them since. The people simply made their faces blank when she tried to talk about it. After the hostilities had begun in earnest, even though the nationalists had derailed the trains and disrupted the trans-Saharan truck service on several occasions, still it was possible to get beyond the disturbed region to her oasis. There in the south the fighting was far away, and the long hours of empty desert that lay between made it seem much farther, almost as though it had been across the sea. If the men of her oasis should ever be infected by the virus of discontent from the far-off north—and this seemed to her almost inconceivable—then in spite of the fact that she was certain that war could bring them nothing but unhappiness, she would have no recourse but to hope for their victory. It was their own land they would be fighting for, their own lives they would be losing in order to win the fight. In the meantime people did not talk; life was hard but peaceful. Each one was aware of the war that was going on in the north, and each one was glad it was far away.

Summers, Fräulein Windling taught in the Freiluftschule in Bern, where she entertained her pupils with tales of the life led by the people

172

in the great desert in Africa. In the village where she lived, she told them, everything was made by the people themselves out of what the desert had to offer. They lived in a world of objects fashioned out of baked earth, woven grass, palmwood and animal skins. There was no metal. Although she did not admit it to the children, this was no longer wholly true, since recently the women had taken to using empty oil tins for carrying water, instead of the goathide bags of a few years before. She had tried to discourage her friends among the village women from this innovation, telling them that the tins could poison the water; they had agreed, and gone on using them. "They are lazy," she decided. "The oil tins are easier to carry."

When the sun went down and the cool air from the oasis below with its sting of woodsmoke rose to the level of the hotel, she would smell it inside her room and stop whatever she was doing. Then she would put on her burnoose and climb the stairs to the roof. The blanket she lay on while she sunbathed each morning would be there, and she would stretch out on it facing the western sky, and feel the departed sun's heat still strong underneath her body. It was one of the pleasures of the day, to watch the light changing in the oasis below, when dusk and the smoke from the evening fires slowly blotted out the valley. There always came a moment when all that was left was the faint outline, geometric and precise, of the mass of mud prisms that was the village, and a certain clump of high date palms that stood outside its entrance. The houses themselves were no longer there, and eventually the highest palm disappeared; and unless there was a moon all that remained to be seen was the dying sky, the sharp edges of the rocks on the hammada, and a blank expanse of mist that lay over the valley but did not reach as far up the cliffs as the hotel.

Perhaps twice each winter a group of the village women would invite Fräulein Windling to go with them up into the vast land of the dunes to look for firewood. The glare here was cruel. There was not even the trace of a twig or a stem anywhere on the sand, yet as they wandered along the crests barefoot the women could spot the places where roots lay buried beneath the surface, and then they would stoop, uncover them, and dig them up. "The wind leaves a sign," they told her, but she was never certain of being able to identify the sign, nor could she understand how there might be a connection between the invisible roots in the sand

and the wind in the air above. "What we have lost, they still possess," she thought.

Her first sight of the desert and its people had been a transfiguring experience; indeed, it seemed to her now that before coming here she had never been in touch with life at all. She believed firmly that each day she spent here increased the aggregate of her resistance. She coveted the rugged health of the natives, when her own was equally strong, but because she was white and educated, she was convinced that her body was intrinsically inferior.

All the work in the hotel was done by one quiet, sad-faced man named Boufelja. He had been there when she had first arrived many years ago; for Fräulein Windling he had come to be as much a part of the place as the cliffs across the valley. She often sat on at her table by the fireplace after lunch, playing cards by herself, until the logs no longer gave out heat. There were two very young French soldiers from the fort opposite, who ate in the hotel dining room. They drank a great amount of wine, and it annoyed her to see their faces slowly turning red as they sat there. At first the soldiers had tipped their caps to her as they went out, and they had stopped their laughing long enough to say, *"Bonjour, madame,"* to her, but now they no longer did. She was happy when they had left, and savored the moment before the fire burned out, while it still glowed under the gusts of wind that wandered down the wide chimney.

Almost always the wind sprang up early in the afternoon, a steady, powerful blowing that roared through the thousands of palms in the oasis below and howled under each door in the hotel, covering the more distant village sounds. This was the hour when she played solitaire, or merely sat, watching the burnt-out logs as they fell to pieces before her eyes. Later she would go along the terrace, a high, bright place like the deck of a great ship sailing through the desert afternoon, hurrying into her room for an instant to get her sweater and cane, and start out on a walk. Sometimes she went southward following the river valley, along the foot of the silent cliffs and through the crooked gorges, to an abandoned village built in a very hot place at a turn in the canyon. The sheer walls of rock behind it sent back the heat, so that the air burned her throat as she breathed it in. Or she went farther, to where the cliff dwellings were, with their animals and symbols incised in the rock.

Returning along the road that led to the village, deep in the green shade of the thickest part of the palm forest, she was regularly aware of the same group of boys sitting at the turn of the road, at a place just before it led up the hill to the shops and the village. They squatted on the sand behind the feathery branches of a giant tamarisk, quietly talking. When she came up to them she greeted them, and they always replied, remained silent a moment until she had passed by, and then resumed their conversation. As far as she could tell, there was never any reference to her by word, and yet this year it sometimes seemed to her that once she had gone by, their inflection had subtly altered, as though there had been a modulation into another key. Did their attitude border on derision? She did not know, but since this was the first time during all her years in the desert that the idea had ever suggested itself to her, she put it resolutely out of her mind. "A new generation requires a new technique if one is to establish contact," she thought. "It is for me to find it." Nevertheless she was sorry that there was no other way of getting into the village save along this main road where they invariably gathered. Even the slight tension caused by having to go past them marred the pleasure of her walks.

One day she realized with a slight shock of shame that she did not even know what the boys looked like. She had seen them only as a group from a distance; when she drew near enough to say good-day to them, she always had her head down, watching the road. The fact that she had been afraid to look at them was unacceptable; now, as she came up to them, she stared into the eyes of one after the other, carefully. Nodding gravely, she went on. Yes, they were insolent faces, she thought—not at all like the faces of their elders. The respectful attitudes into which they had been startled were the crudest sort of shamming. But the important thing to her was that she had won: she was no longer preoccupied with having to pass by them every day. Slowly she even grew to recognize each boy.

There was one, she noted, younger than the others, who always sat a little apart from them, and it was this shy one who stood talking to Boufelja in the hotel kitchen early one morning when she went in. She pretended not to notice him. "I am going to my room to work on the machine for about an hour," she told Boufelja. "You can come then to make up the room," and she turned to go out. As she went through the doorway she glanced at the boy's face. He was looking at her, and he did not turn away when his eyes met hers. "How are you?" she said. Perhaps half an hour later, when she was typing her second letter, she raised her head. The boy was standing on the terrace looking at her through the open door. He squinted, for the wind was strong; behind his head she saw the tops of the palms bending.

"If he wants to watch, let him watch," she said to herself, deciding to pay him no attention. After a while he went away. While Boufelja served her lunch, she questioned him about the boy. "Like an old man," said Boufelja. "Twelve years old but very serious. Like some old, old man." He smiled, then shrugged. "It's the way God wanted him to be."

"Of course," she said, remembering the boy's alert, unhappy face. "A young dog that everyone has kicked," she thought, "but he hasn't given up."

In the days that followed, he came often to the terrace and stood watching her while she typed. Sometimes she waved to him, or said: "Good morning." Without answering he would take a step backward, so that he was out of her range. Then he would continue to stand where he was. His behavior irked her, and one day when he had done this, she quickly got up and went to the door. "What is it?" she asked him, trying to smile as she spoke.

"I didn't do anything," he said, his eyes reproachful.

"I know," she answered. "Why don't you come in?"

The boy looked swiftly around the terrace as if for help; then he bowed his head and stepped inside the door. Here he stood waiting, his head down, looking miserable. From her luggage she brought out a bag of hard candy, and handed him a piece. Then she put a few simple questions to him, and found that his French was much better than she had expected. "Do the other boys know French as well as you?" she asked him.

"*Non, madame,*" he said, shaking his head slowly. "My father used to be a soldier. Soldiers speak good French."

She tried to keep her face from expressing the disapproval she felt, for she despised everything military. "I see," she said with some asperity, turning back to her table and shuffling the papers. "Now I must work," she told him, immediately adding in a warmer voice, "but you come back tomorrow, if you like." He waited an instant, looking at her with unchanged wistfulness. Then slowly he smiled, and laid the candy wrapper, folded into a tiny square, on the corner of her table. "*Au revoir, madame,*" he said, and went out of the door. In the silence she heard the scarcely audible thud of his bare heels on the earth floor of the terrace. "In this cold," she thought. "Poor child! If I ever buy anything for him it will be a pair of sandals."

Each day thereafter, when the sun was high enough to give substance to the still morning air, the boy would come stealthily along the terrace to her door, stand a few seconds, and then say in a lost voice that was all the smaller and more hushed for the great silence outside: *"Bonjour, madame."* She would tell him to come in, and they would shake hands gravely, he afterward raising the backs of his fingers to his lips, always with the same slow ceremoniousness. She sometimes tried to fathom his countenance as he went through this ritual, to see if by any chance she could detect a shade of mockery there; instead she saw an expression of devotion so convincing that it startled her, and she looked away quickly. She always kept a bit of bread or some biscuits in a drawer of the wardrobe; when she had brought the food out and he was eating it, she would ask him for news about the families in his quarter of the village. For discipline's sake she offered him a piece of candy only every other day. He sat on the floor by the doorway, on a torn old camel blanket, and he watched her constantly, never turning his head away from her.

She wanted to know what he was called, but she was aware of how secretive the inhabitants of the region were about names, seldom giving their true ones to strangers; this was a peculiarity she respected because she knew it had its roots in their own prehistoric religion. So she forbore asking him, sure that the time would come when he trusted her enough to give it of his own volition. And the moment happened one morning unexpectedly, when he had just recounted several legends involving the great Moslem king of long ago, whose name was Solomon. Suddenly he stopped, and forcing himself to gaze steadily at her without blinking, he said: "And my name too is Slimane, the same as the king."

She tried to teach him to read, but he did not seem able to learn. Often just as she felt he was about to connect two loose ends of ideas and perhaps at last make a contact which would enable him to understand the principle, a look of resignation and passivity would appear in his face, and he would willfully cut off the stream of effort from its source, and remain sitting, merely looking at her, shaking his head from side to side to show that it was useless. It was hard not to lose patience with him at such moments.

The following year she decided not to go on with the lessons, and to use Slimane instead as a guide, bearer and companion, a role which she immediately saw was more suited to his nature than that of pupil. He did not mind how far they went or how much equipment he had to carry; on the contrary, to him a long excursion was that much more of an event, and whatever she loaded onto him he bore with the air of one upon whom an honor is conferred. It was probably her happiest season in the desert, that winter of comradeship when together they made the countless pilgrimages down the valley. As the weeks passed the trips grew in scope, and the hour of departure was brought forward until it came directly after she had finished her breakfast. All day long, trudging in the open sun and in the occasional shade of the broken fringe of palms that skirted the riverbed, she conversed passionately with him. Sometimes she could see that he felt like telling her what was in his head, and she let him speak for as long as his enthusiasm lasted, often reviving it at the end with carefully chosen questions. But usually it was she who did the speaking as she walked behind him. Pounding the stony ground with her steel-tipped stick each time her right foot went down, she told him in great detail the story of the life of Hitler, showing why he was hated by the Christians. This she thought necessary since Slimane had been under a different impression, and indeed had imagined that the Europeans thought as highly of the vanished leader as did he and the rest of the people in the village. She talked a good deal about Switzerland, casually stressing the cleanliness, honesty and good health of her countrymen in short parables of daily life. She told him about Jesus, Martin Luther and Garibaldi, taking care to keep Jesus distinct from the Moslem prophet Sidna Aissa, since even for the sake of argument she could not agree for an instant with the Islamic doctrine according to which the Savior was a Moslem. Slimane's attitude of respect bordering on adoration with regard to her never altered unless she inadvertently tangled with the subject of Islam; then, no matter what she said (for at that point it seemed that automatically he was no longer within hearing) he would shake his head interminably and cry: "No, no, no, no! Nazarenes know nothing about Islam. Don't talk, madame, I beg you, because you don't know what you're saying. No, no, no!"

Long ago she had kept the initial promise to herself that she would buy him sandals; this purchase had been followed by others. At fairly regular intervals she had taken him to Benaissa's store to buy a shirt, a pair of baggy black cotton trousers of the kind worn by the Chaamba camel drivers and ultimately a new white burnoose, despite the fact that she knew the entire village would discuss the giving of so valuable an object. She also knew that it was only the frequent bestowing of such gifts that kept Slimane's father from forbidding him to spend his time with her. Even so, according to reports brought by Slimane, he sometimes objected. But Slimane himself, she was sure, wanted nothing, expected nothing.

It was each year when March was drawing to a close that the days began to be painfully hot and even the nights grew breathless; then, although it always required a strenuous effort of the will to make herself take the step which would bring about renewed contact with the outside world, she would devote two or three days to washing her clothing and preparing for the journey. When the week set for her departure had come, she went over to the fort and put in a call to the café at Kerzaz, asking the proprietor to tell the driver of the next northbound truck to take the detour that would enable her to catch him at a point only about three kilometers from the village.

She and Slimane had come back to the hotel on the afternoon of their last excursion down the valley; Fräulein Windling stood on the terrace looking out at the orange mountains of sand behind the fort. Slimane had taken the packs into the room and put them down. She turned and said: "Bring the big tin box." When he had pulled it out from under the bed he carried it to her, dusting it off with the sleeve of his shirt, and she led the way up the stairs to the roof. They sat down on the blanket; the glow of the vanished sun's furnace heated their faces. A few flies still hovered, now and then attacking their necks. Slimane handed her the biscuit tin and she gave him a fistful of chocolate-covered cakes. "So many all at once?"

"Yes," she said. "You know I'm going home in four days."

He looked down at the blanket a moment before replying. "I know," he murmured. He was silent again. Then he cried out aggrievedly: "Boufelja says it's hot here in the summer. It's not hot! In our house it's cool. It's like the oasis where the big pool is. You would never be hot there."

"I have to earn money. You know that. I want to come back next year."

179

He said sadly: "Next year, madame! Only Moulana knows how next year will be."

Some camels growled as they rolled in the sand at the foot of the fort; the light was receding swiftly. "Eat your biscuits," she told him, and she ate one herself. "Next year we'll go to Abadla with the caid, *incha' Allah.*"

He sighed deeply. "Ah, madame!" he said. She noted, at first with a pang of sympathy and then, reconsidering, with disapproval, the anguish that lent his voice its unaccustomed intensity. It was the quality she least liked in him, this faintly theatrical self-pity. "Next year you'll be a man," she told him firmly. Her voice grew less sure, assumed a hopeful tone. "You'll remember all the things we talked about?"

She sent him a postcard from Marseille, and showed her classes photographs they had taken of one another, and of the caid. The children were impressed by the caid's voluminous turban. "Is he a Bedouin?" asked one.

When she left the embassy office she knew that this was the last year she would be returning to the desert. There was not only the official's clearly expressed unfriendliness and suspicion: for the first time he had made her answer a list of questions which she found alarming. He wanted to know what subjects she taught in the Freiluftschule, whether she had ever been a journalist, and exactly where she proposed to be each day after arriving in the Sahara. She had almost retorted: I go where I feel like going. I don't make plans. But she had merely named the oasis. She knew that Frenchmen had no respect for elderly Swiss ladies who wore woolen stockings; this simply made them more contemptible in her eyes. However, it was they who controlled the Sahara.

The day the ship put into the African port it was raining. She knew the gray terraced ramps of the city were there in the gloom ahead, but they were invisible. The ragged European garments of the dockworkers were soaked with rain. Later, the whole rain-sodden city struck her as grim, and the people passing along the streets looked unhappy. The change, even from the preceding year, was enormous; it made her sad to sit in the big, cold café where she went for coffee after dinner, and so she returned to her hotel and slept. The next day she got on the train for Perrégaux. The rain fell most of the day. In Perrégaux she took a room in a hotel near the station, and stayed in it, listening to the rain rattle down the gutter by her window. "This place would be a convenient model for Hell," she wrote to a friend in Basel before going to sleep that night. "A full-blown example of the social degeneracy achieved by forced cultural hybridism. Populace debased and made hostile by generations of merciless exploitation. I take the southbound narrow-gauge train tomorrow morning for a happier land, and trust that my friend the sun will appear at some point during the day. *Seien Sie herzlich gegrüsst von Ihrer Maria.*"

As the train crawled southward, up over the high plateau land, the clouds were left behind and the sun took charge of the countryside. Fräulein Windling sat attentively by the smeared window, enveloped in an increasing sadness. As long as it had been raining, she had imagined the rain as the cause of her depression: the gray cloud light gave an unaccustomed meaning to the landscape by altering forms and distances. Now she understood that the more familiar and recognizable the contours of the desert were to become, the more conscious she would be of having no reason to be in it, because it was her last visit.

Two days later, when the truck stopped to let her out, Boufelja stood in the sun beside the boulders waving; one of the men of the village was with him to help carry the luggage. Once the truck had gone and its cloud of yellow dust had fled across the hammada, the silence was there; it seemed that no sound could be louder than the crunch of their shoes on the ground.

"How is Slimane?" she asked. Boufelja was noncommittal. "He's all right," he said. "They say he tried to run away. But he didn't get very far." The report might be true, or it might be false; in any case she determined not to allude to it unless Slimane himself mentioned it first.

She felt an absurd relief when they came to the edge of the cliffs and she saw the village across the valley. Not until she had made the rounds of the houses where her friends lived, discussed their troubles with them and left some pills here and some candy there, was she convinced that no important change had come to the oasis during her absence. She went to the house of Slimane's parents: he was not there. "Tell him to come and see me," she said to his father as she left the house.

On the third morning after her arrival Slimane appeared, and stood there in the doorway smiling. Once she had greeted him and made him sit down and have coffee with her, she plied him with questions about life in the village while she had been in Europe. Some of his friends had gone to become patriots, he said, and they were killing the French like

181

flies. Her heart sank, but she said nothing. As she watched him smiling she was able to exult in the reflection that Slimane had been reachable, after all; she had proved that it was possible to make true friends of the younger people. But even while she was saying, "How happy I am to see you, Slimane," she remembered that their time together was now limited, and an expression of pain passed over her face as she finished the phrase. "I shall not say a word to him about it," she decided. If he, at least, still had the illusion of unbounded time lying ahead, he would somehow retain his aura of purity and innocence, and she would feel less anguish during the time they spent together.

One day they went down the valley to see the caid, and discussed the long-planned trip to Abadla. Another day they started out at dawn to visit the tomb of Moulay Ali ben Said, where there was a spring of hot water. It was a tiny spot of oasis at the edge of a ridge of high dunes; perhaps fifty palms were there around the decayed shrine. In the shade of the rocks below the walls there was a ruined cistern into which the steaming water dribbled. They spread blankets on the sand nearby, at the foot of a small tamarisk, and took out their lunch. Before starting to eat, they drank handfuls of the water, which Slimane said was famed for its holiness. The palms rattled and hissed in the wind overhead.

"Allah has sent us the wind to make us cool while we eat," Slimane said when he had finished his bread and dates.

"The wind has always been here," she answered carelessly, "and it always will be here."

He sat up straight. "No, no!" he cried. "When Sidna Aissa has returned for forty days there will be no more Moslems and the world will end. Everything, the sky and the sun and the moon. And the wind too. Everything." He looked at her with an expression of such satisfaction that she felt one of her occasional surges of anger against him.

"I see," she said. "Stand over by the spring a minute. I want to take your picture." She had never understood why it was that the Moslems had conceded Jesus even this Pyrrhic victory, the coda to all creation: its inconsistency embarrassed her. Across the decayed tank she watched Slimane assume the traditional stiff attitude of a person about to be photographed, and an idea came into her head. For Christmas Eve, which would come within two weeks, she would make a crèche. She would

182

invite Slimane to eat with her by the fireplace, and when midnight came she would take him in to see it.

She finished photographing Slimane; they gathered up the equipment and set out against the hot afternoon wind for the village. The sand sometimes swept by, stinging their faces with its invisible fringe. Fräulein Windling led the way this time, and they walked fast. The image of the crèche, illumined by candles, occurred to her several times on the way back over the rocky erg; it made her feel inexpressibly sad, for she could not help connecting it with the fact that everything was ending. They came to the point north of the village where the empty erg was cut across by the wandering river valley. As they climbed slowly upward over the fine sand, she found herself whispering: "It's the right thing to do." " 'Right' is not the word," she thought, without being able to find a better one. She was going to make a crèche because she loved Christmas and wanted to share it with Slimane. They reached the hotel shortly after sunset, and she sent Slimane home in order to sit and plan her project on paper.

It was only when she began actually to put the crèche together that she realized how much work it was going to be. Early the next morning she asked Boufelja to find her an old wooden crate. Before she had been busy even a half hour, she heard Slimane talking in the kitchen. Quickly she pushed everything under the bed and went out onto the terrace.

"Slimane," she said. "I'm very busy. Come in the afternoon." And that afternoon she told him that since she was going to be working every morning until after the day of the Christ Child, they would not be making any more long trips during that time. He received the information glumly. "I know," he said. "You are getting ready for the holy day. I understand."

"When the holy day comes, we will have a feast," she assured him.

"If Allah wills."

"I'm sorry," she said, smiling.

He shrugged. "Good-bye," he told her.

Afternoons they still walked in the oasis or had tea on the roof, but her mornings she spent in her room sewing, hammering and sculpting. Once she had the platform constructed, she had to model the figures. She carried up a great mass of wet clay from the river to her room. It was

183

two days before she managed to make a Virgin whose form pleased her. From an old strip of muslin she fashioned a convincing tent to house the Mother and the Child in its nest of tiny white chicken feathers. Shredded tamarisk needles made a fine carpet for the interior of the tent. Outside she poured sand, and then pushed the clay camels' long legs deep into it; one animal walked behind the other over the dune, and a Wise Man sat straight on top of each, his white *djellaba* falling in long pointed folds to either side of the camel's flanks. The Wise Men would come carrying sacks of almonds and very small liqueur chocolates wrapped in colored tinfoil. When she had the crèche finished, she put it on the floor in the middle of the room and piled tangerines and dates in front of it. With a row of candles burning behind it, and one candle on each side in front, it would look like a Moslem religious chromolithograph. She hoped the scene would be recognizable to Slimane; he might then be more easily persuaded of its poetic truth. She wanted only to suggest to him that the god with whom he was on such intimate terms was the god worshiped by the Nazarenes. It was not an idea she would ever try to express in words.

An additional surprise for the evening would be the new flashbulb attachment to her camera, which Slimane had not yet seen. She intended to take a good many pictures of the crèche and of Slimane looking at it; these she would enlarge to show her pupils. She went and bought a new turban for Slimane; he had been wearing none for more than a year now. This was a man's turban, and very fine: ten meters of the softest Egyptian cotton.

The day before Christmas she overslept, duped by the heavy sky. Each winter the oasis had a few dark days; they were rare, but this was one of them. While she still lay there in bed, she heard the roar of the wind, and when she got up to look out the window she found no world outside—only a dim rose-gray fog that hid everything. The swirling sand sprayed ceaselessly against the glass; it had formed in long drifts on the floor of the terrace. When she went for breakfast, she wore her burnoose with the hood up around her face. The blast of the wind as she stepped out onto the terrace struck her with the impact of a solid object, and the sand gritted on the concrete floor under her shoes. In the dining room Boufelja had bolted the shutters; he greeted her enthusiastically from the gloom inside, glad of her presence.

"A very bad day for your festival, alas, mademoiselle!" he observed as he set her coffeepot on the table.

"Tomorrow's the festival," she said. "It begins tonight."

"I know. I know." He was impatient with Nazarene feasts because the hours of their beginnings and ends were observed in so slipshod a manner. Moslem feasts began precisely, either at sundown or an hour before sunup, or when the new moon was first visible in the western sky at twilight. But the Nazarenes began their feasts whenever they felt like it.

She spent the morning in her room writing letters. By noon the air outside was darker with still more sand; the wind shook the hotel atop its rock as if it would hurl it over the tips of the palms below into the riverbed. Several times she rose and went to the window to stare out at the pink emptiness beyond the terrace. Storms made her happy, although she wished this one could have come after Christmas. She had imagined a pure desert night—cold, alive with stars, and the dogs yapping from the oasis. It might yet be that; there was still time, she thought, as she slipped her burnoose over her head to go in to lunch.

With the wind, the fireplace was an unsure blessing: besides the heat it gave, it provided the only light in the dining room, but the smoke that belched from it burned her eyes and throat. The shutters at the windows rattled and pounded, covering the noise of the wind itself.

She got out of the dining room as soon as she had finished eating, and hurried back to her room to sit through the slowly darkening afternoon, as she continued with her letter-writing and waited for the total extinction of daylight. Slimane was coming at eight. There would be enough time to carry everything into the dining room before that, and to set the crèche up in the dark unused wing into which Boufelja was unlikely to go. But when she came to do it, she found that the wind's force was even greater than she had imagined. Again and again she made the trip between her room and the dining room, carrying each object carefully wrapped in her burnoose. Each time she passed in front of the kitchen door she expected Boufelja to open it and discover her. She did not want him there when she showed the crèche to Slimane; he could see it tomorrow at breakfast.

Protected by the noise of the gale she succeeded in transporting all the parts to the far dark corner of the dining room without alerting Boufelja. Long before dinnertime the crèche was in readiness, awaiting only the lighting of the candles to be brought alive. She left a box of matches on the table beside it, and hurried back to her room to arrange her hair and change her clothing. The sand had sifted through her garments and was now everywhere; it showered from her underwear and stuck like sugar to her skin. Her watch showed a few minutes after eight when she went out.

Only one place had been laid at table. She waited, while the blinds chattered and banged, until Boufelja appeared carrying the soup tureen. "What a bad night," he said.

"You forgot to prepare for Slimane," she told him. But he was not paying attention. "He's stupid!" he exclaimed, beginning to ladle out the soup.

"Wait!" she cried. "Slimane's coming. I mustn't eat until he comes."

Still Boufelja misunderstood. "He wanted to come into the dining room," he said. "And he knows it's forbidden at dinnertime."

"But I invited him!" She looked at the lone soup plate on the table. "Tell him to come in, and set another place."

Boufelja was silent. He put the ladle back into the tureen. "Where is he?" she demanded, and without waiting for him to reply she went on. "Didn't I tell you he was going to have dinner with me tonight?" For suddenly she suspected that in her desire for secrecy she might indeed have neglected to mention the invitation to Boufelja.

"You didn't say anything," he told her. "I didn't know. I sent him home. But he'll be back after dinner."

"Oh, Boufelja!" she cried. "You know Slimane never lies."

He looked down at her with reproach on his face. "I didn't know anything about mademoiselle's plans," he said aggrievedly. This made her think for a swift instant that he had discovered the crèche, but she decided that if he had he would have spoken of it.

"Yes, yes, I know. I should have told you. It's my fault."

"That's true, mademoiselle," he said. And he served the remaining courses observing a dignified silence which she, still feeling some displeasure with him, did not urge him to break. Only at the end of the meal, when she had pushed back her chair from the table and sat studying the pattern of the flames in the fireplace, did he decide to speak. "Mademoiselle will take coffee?"

"I do want some," she said, trying to bring a note of enthusiasm into her voice. *"Bien,"* murmured Boufelja, and he left her alone in the room. When he returned carrying the coffee, Slimane was with him, and they were laughing, she noted, quite as though there had been no misunderstanding about dinner. Slimane stood by the door an instant, stamping his feet and shaking the sand from his burnoose. As he came forward to take her hand, she cried: "Oh, Slimane, it's my fault! I forgot to tell Boufelja. It's terrible!"

"There is no fault, madame," he said gravely. "This is a festival."

"Yes, this is a festival," she echoed. "And the wind's still blowing. Listen!"

Slimane would not take coffee, but Boufelja, ceding to her pressure, let her pour him out a cup, which he drank standing by the fireplace. She suspected him of being secretly pleased that Slimane had not managed to eat with her. When he had finished his coffee, he wished them good-night and went off to bed in his little room next to the kitchen.

They sat a while watching the fire, without talking. The wind rushed past in the emptiness outside, the blinds hammered. Fräulein Windling was content. Even if the first part of the celebration had gone wrong, the rest of the evening could still be pleasant.

She waited until she was sure that Boufelja had really gone to bed, and then she reached into her bag and brought out a small plastic sack full of chocolate creams, which she placed on the table.

"Eat," she said carelessly, and she took a piece of candy herself. With some hesitation Slimane put out his hand to take the sack. When he had a chocolate in his mouth, she began to speak. She intended to tell him the story of the Nativity, a subject she already had touched upon many times during their excursions, but only in passing. This time she felt she should tell him the entire tale. She expected him to interrupt when he discovered that it was a religious story, but he merely kept his noncommittal eyes on her and chewed mechanically, showing that he followed her by occasionally nodding his head. She became engrossed in what she was saying, and began to use her arms in wide gestures. Slimane reached for another chocolate and went on listening.

She talked for an hour or more, aware as from a distance of her own eloquence. When she told him about Bethlehem she was really describing Slimane's own village, and the house of Joseph and Mary was the house down in the *ksar* where Slimane had been born. The night sky arched above the Oued Zousfana and its stars glared down upon the cold hammada. Across the erg on their camels came the Wise Men in their burnooses and turbans, pausing at the crest of the last great dune to look ahead at the valley where the dark village lay. When she had finished, she blew her nose.

Slimane appeared to be in a state bordering on trance. She glanced at him, expected him to speak, but as he did not, she looked more closely at him. His eyes had an obsessed, vacant expression, and although they were still fixed on her face, she would have said that he was seeing something much farther away than she. She sighed, not wanting to make the decision to rouse him. The possibility she would have liked to entertain, had she not been so conscious of its unlikelihood, was that the boy somehow had been captivated by the poetic truth of the story, and was reviewing it in his imagination. "Certainly it could not be the case," she decided; it was more likely that he had ceased some time back to listen to her words, and was merely sitting there, only vaguely aware that she had come to the end of her story.

Then he spoke. "You're right. He was the King of Men."

Fräulein Windling caught her breath and leaned forward, but he went on. "And later Satan sent a snake with two heads. And Jesus killed it. Satan was angry with Him. He said: 'Why did you kill my friend? Did it hurt you, perhaps?' And Jesus said: 'I knew where it came from.' And Satan put on a black burnoose. That's true," he added, as he saw the expression of what he took to be simple disbelief on her face.

She sat up very straight and said: "Slimane, what are you talking about? There are no such stories about Jesus. Nor about Sidna Aissa either." She was not sure of the accuracy of this last statement; it was possible, she supposed, that such legends did exist among these people. "You know those are just stories that have nothing to do with the truth."

He did not hear her because he had already begun to talk. "I'm not speaking of Sidna Aissa," he said firmly. "He was a Moslem prophet. I'm talking about Jesus, the prophet of the Nazarenes. Everyone knows that Satan sent Him a snake with two heads."

She listened to the wind for an instant. "Ah," she said, and took another chocolate; she did not intend to carry the argument further. Soon she dug into her bag again and pulled out the turban, wrapped in red and white tissue paper.

"A present for you," she said, holding it out to him. He seized it mechanically, placed it on his lap and remained staring down at it. "Aren't you going to open it?" she demanded.

He nodded his head twice and tore open the paper. When he saw the pile of white cotton he smiled. Seeing his face at last come to life, she jumped up. "Let's put it on you!" she exclaimed. He gave her one end, which she pulled taut by walking all the way to the door. Then with his hand holding the other end to his forehead, he turned slowly round and round, going toward her all the time, arranging the form of the turban as it wound itself about his head. "Magnificent!" she cried. He went over to the row of black windows to look at himself.

"Can you see?" she asked.

"Yes, I can see the sides of it," he told her. "It's very beautiful."

She walked back toward the center of the room. "I'd like to take your picture, Slimane," she said, seeing an immediate look of puzzlement appear in his face. "Would you do me a favor? Go to my room and get the camera."

"At night? You can take a picture at night?"

She nodded, smiling mysteriously. "And bring me the yellow box on the bed."

Keeping the turban on his head, he got into his burnoose, took her flashlight and went out, letting the wind slam the door. She hoped the sound had not wakened Boufelja; for an instant she listened while there was no sound but the roar of air rushing through the corridor outside. Then she ran to the dark wing of the room and struck a match. Quickly she lighted all the candles around the crèche, straightened a camel in the sand, and walked back around the corner to the fireplace. She would not have thought the candles could give so much light. The other end of the room was now brighter than the end where she stood. In a moment the door burst open and Slimane came back in, carrying the camera slung over his shoulder. He put it down carefully on the table. "There was no yellow box on the bed," he told her. Then his glance caught the further walls flickering with the unfamiliar light, and he began to walk toward the center of the room. She saw that this was the moment. "Come," she said, taking his arm and pulling him gently around the corner to where the crèche was finally visible, bright with its multiple shuddering points of light. Slimane said nothing; he stopped walking and stood completely

189

still. After a moment of silence, she plucked tentatively at his arm. "Come and see," she urged him. They continued to walk toward the crèche; as they came up to it she had the impression that if she had not been there he would have reached out his hand and touched it, perhaps would have lifted the tiny gold-clad infant Jesus out of His bed of feathers. But he stood quietly, looking at it. Finally he said: "You brought all that from Switzerland?"

"Of course not!" It was a little disappointing that he should not have recognized the presence of the desert in the picture, should not have sensed that the thing was of his place, and not an importation. "I made it all here," she said. She waited an instant. "Do you like it?"

"Ah, yes," he said with feeling. "It's beautiful. I thought it came from Switzerland."

To be certain that he understood the subject matter, she began to identify the figures one by one, her voice taking on such an unaccustomed inflection of respect that he glanced up at her once in surprise. It was almost as if she too were seeing it for the first time. "And the Wise Men are coming down out of the erg to see the child."

"Why did you put all those almonds there?" asked Slimane, touching some with his forefinger.

"They're gifts for the little Jesus."

"But what are you going to do with them?" he pursued.

"Eat them, probably, later," she said shortly. "Take one if you like. You say there was no yellow box on the bed?" She wanted to take the photographs while the candles were still of equal height.

"There was nothing but a sweater and some papers, madame."

She left him there by the crèche, crossed the room and put on her burnoose. The darkness in the corridor was complete; there was no sign that Boufelja had awakened. She knew her room was in great disorder, and she played the beam of the flashlight around the floor before entering. In the welter of displaced things that strewed the little room there seemed small chance of finding anything. The feeble ray illumined one by one the meaningless forms made by the piling of disparate objects one on the other; the light moved over the floor, along the bed, behind the flimsy curtain of the armoire. Suddenly she stopped and turned the beam under the bed. The box was in front of her face; she had put it with the crèche.

"I mustn't fall," she thought, running along the corridor. She forced herself to slow her pace to a walk, entered the dining room and shut the door after her carefully. Slimane was on his knees in the middle of the room, a small object of some sort in his hand. She noted with relief that he was amusing himself. "I'm sorry it took me so long," she exclaimed. "I'd forgotten where I'd put it." She was pulling her burnoose off over her head; now she hung it on a nail by the fireplace, and taking up the camera and the yellow box, she walked over to join him.

Perhaps a faint glimmer of guilt in his expression as he glanced up made her eyes stray along the floor toward another object lying nearby, similar to the one he held in his hand. It was one of the Wise Men, severed at the hips from his mount. The Wise Man in Slimane's hand was intact, but the camel had lost its head and most of its neck.

"Slimane! What are you doing?" she cried with undisguised anger. "What have you done to the crèche?" She advanced around the corner and looked in its direction. There was not really much more than a row of candles and a pile of sand that had been strewn with tangerine peel and date stones; here and there a carefully folded square of lavender or pink tinfoil had been planted in the sand. All three of the Wise Men had been enlisted in Slimane's battle on the floor, the tent ravaged in the campaign to extricate the almonds piled inside, and the treasure sacks looted of their chocolate liqueurs. There was no sign anywhere of the infant Jesus or his gold-lamé garment. She felt tears come into her eyes. Then she laughed shortly, and said: "Well, it's finished. Yes?"

"Yes, madame," he said calmly. "Are you going to make the photograph now?" He got to his feet and laid the broken camel on the platform in the sand with the other debris.

Fräulein Windling spoke evenly. "I wanted to take a picture of the crèche."

He waited an instant, as if he were listening to a distant sound. Then he said: "Should I put on my burnoose?"

"No." She began to take out the flashbulb attachment. When she had it ready, she took the picture before he had time to strike a pose. She saw his astonishment at the sudden bright light prolong itself into surprise that the thing was already done, and then become resentment at having been caught off his guard; but pretending to have seen nothing, she went on snapping covers shut. He watched her as she gathered up her things. "Is it finished?" he said, disappointed. "Yes," she replied. "It will be a very good picture."

"*Incha' Allah.*"

She did not echo his piety. "I hope you've enjoyed the festival," she told him.

Slimane smiled widely. "Ah, yes, madame. Very much. Thank you."

She let him out into the camel-square and turned the lock in the door. Quickly she went back into her room, wishing it were a clear night like other nights, when she could stand out on the terrace and look at the dunes and stars, or sit on the roof and hear the dogs, for in spite of the hour she was not sleepy. She cleared her bed of all the things that lay on top of it, and got in, certain that she was going to lie awake for a long time. For it had shaken her, the chaos Slimane had made in those few minutes of her absence. Across the seasons of their friendship she had come to think of him as being very nearly like herself, even though she knew he had not been that way when she first had met him. Now she saw the dangerous vanity at the core of that fantasy: she had assumed that somehow his association with her had automatically been for his ultimate good, that inevitably he had been undergoing a process of improvement as a result of knowing her. In her desire to see him change, she had begun to forget what Slimane was really like. "I shall never understand him," she thought helplessly, sure that just because she felt so close to him she would never be able to observe him dispassionately.

"This is the desert," she told herself. Here food is not an adornment; it is meant to be eaten. She had spread out food and he had eaten it. Any argument which attached blame to that could only be false. And so she lay there accusing herself. "It has been too much head and high ideals," she reflected, "and not enough heart." Finally she traveled on the sound of the wind into sleep.

At dawn when she awoke she saw that the day was going to be another dark one. The wind had dropped. She got up and shut the window. The early-morning sky was heavy with clouds. She sank back into bed and fell asleep. It was later than usual when she rose, dressed and went into the dining room. Boufelja's face was strangely expressionless as he wished her good morning. She supposed it was the memory of last night's misunderstanding, still with him—or possibly he was annoyed at having had to clean up the remains of the crèche. Once she had sat down and spread her napkin across her lap, he unbent sufficiently to say to her: "Happy festival."

"Thank you. Tell me, Boufelja," she went on, changing her inflection. "When you brought Slimane back in after dinner last night, do you know where he had been? Did he tell you?"

"He's a stupid boy," said Boufelja. "I told him to go home and eat and come back later. You think he did that? Never. He walked the whole time up and down in the courtyard here, outside the kitchen door, in the dark."

"I understand!" exclaimed Fräulein Windling triumphantly. "So he had no dinner at all."

"I had nothing to give him," he began, on the defensive.

"Of course not," she said sternly. "He should have gone home and eaten."

"Ah, you see?" grinned Boufelja. "That's what I told him to do."

In her mind she watched the whole story being enacted: Slimane aloofly informing his father that he would be eating at the hotel with the Swiss lady, the old man doubtless making some scornful reference to her, and Slimane going out. Unthinkable, once he had been refused admittance to the dining room, for him to go back and face the family's ridicule. "Poor boy," she murmured.

"The commandant wants to see you," said Boufelja, making one of his abrupt conversational changes. She was surprised, since from one year to the next the captain never gave any sign of being aware of her existence; the hotel and the fort were like two separate countries. "Perhaps for the festival," Boufelja suggested, his face a mask.

"Perhaps," she said uneasily.

When she had finished her breakfast, she walked across to the gates of the fort. The sentry seemed to be expecting her. One of the two young French soldiers was in the compound painting a chair. He greeted her, saying that the captain was in his office. She went up the long flight of stairs and paused an instant at the top, looking down at the valley in the unaccustomed gray light, noting how totally different it looked from its usual self, on this dim day.

A voice from inside called out: *"Entrez, s'il vous plaît!"* She opened the door and stepped in. The captain sat behind his desk; she had the unwelcome sensation of having played this same scene on another occasion, in another place. And she was suddenly convinced that she knew what he was going to say. She seized the back of the empty chair facing his desk. "Sit down, Mademoiselle Windling," he said, rising halfway out of his seat, waving his arm, and sitting again quickly.

There were several topographical maps on the wall behind him, marked with lavender and green chalk. The captain looked at his desk and then at her, and said in a clear voice: "It is an unfortunate stroke of chance that I should have to call you here on this holiday." Fräulein Windling sat down in the chair; leaning forward, she seemed about to rest her elbow on his desk, but instead crossed her legs and folded her arms tight.

"Yes?" she said, tense, waiting for the message. It came immediately, for which she was conscious, even then, of being grateful to him. He told her simply that the entire area had been closed to civilians; this order applied to French nationals as well as to foreigners, so she must not feel discriminated against. The last was said with a wry attempt at a smile.

"This means that you will have to take tomorrow morning's truck," he continued. "The driver has already been advised of your journey. Perhaps another year, when the disturbances are over . . . ." ("Why does he say that?" she thought, "when he knows it's the end, and the time of friendship is finished?") He rose and extended his hand.

She could not remember going out of the room and down the long stairway into the compound, but now she was standing outside the sentry gate beside the wall of the fort, with her hand on her forehead. "Already," she thought. "It came so soon." And it occurred to her that she was not going to be given the time to make amends to Slimane, so that it was really true she was never going to understand him. She walked up to the parapet to look down at the edge of the oasis for a moment, and then went back to her room to start packing. All day long she worked in her room, pulling out boxes, forcing herself to be aware only of the decisions she was making as to what was to be taken and what was to be left behind once and for all.

At lunchtime Boufelja hovered near her chair. "Ah, mademoiselle, how many years we have been together, and now it is finished!" "Yes," she thought, but there was nothing to do about it. His lamentations made her nervous and she was short with him.

Then she felt guilt-stricken and said slowly, looking directly at him:
"I am very sad, Boufelja."

He sighed. "Ay, mademoiselle, I know!"

By nightfall the pall of clouds had been blown away across the desert,
and the western sky was partly clear. Fräulein Windling had finished all
her packing. She went out onto the terrace, saw the dunes pink and
glowing, and climbed the steps to the roof to look at the sunset. Great
skeins of fiery stormcloud streaked the sky. Mechanically she let her gaze
follow the meanders of the river valley as it lost itself in the darkening
hammada to the south. "It is in the past," she reminded herself; this was
already the new era. The desert out there looked the same as it always
had looked. But the sky, ragged, red and black, was like a handbill that
had just been posted above it, announcing the arrival of war.

It was a betrayal, she was thinking, going back down the steep stairs,
running her hand along the familiar rough mud wall to steady herself,
and the French of course were the culprits. But beyond that she had the
irrational and disagreeable conviction that the countryside itself had
connived in the betrayal, that it was waiting to be transformed by the
struggle. She went into her room and lit the small oil lamp; sitting down,
she held her hands over it to warm them. At some point there had been
a change: the people no longer wanted to go on living in the world they
knew. The pressure of the past had become too great, and its shell had
broken.

In the afternoon she had sent Boufelja to tell Slimane the news, and
to ask him to be at the hotel at daybreak. During dinner she discussed
only the details of departure and travel; when Boufelja tried to pull the
talk in emotional directions, she did not reply. His commiseration was
intolerable; she was not used to giving voice to her despair. When she
got to her room she went directly to bed. The dogs barked half the night.

It was cold in the morning. Her hands ached as she gathered up the
wet objects from around the washbowl on the table, and somehow she
drove a sliver deep under the nail of her thumb. She picked some of it
out with a needle, but the greater part remained. Before breakfast she
stepped outside.

Standing in the wasteland between the hotel and the fort, she looked
down at the countryside's innocent face. The padlocked gasoline pump,
triumphant in fresh red and orange paint, caught the pure early sunlight.

For a moment it seemed the only living thing in the landscape. She turned around. Above the dark irregular mass of palm trees rose the terraced village, calm under its morning veil of woodsmoke. She shut her eyes for an instant, and then went into the hotel.

She could feel herself sitting stiffly in her chair while she drank her coffee, and she knew she was being distant and formal with Boufelja, but it was the only way she could be certain of being able to keep going. Once he came to tell her that Slimane had arrived bringing the donkey and its master for her luggage. She thanked him and set down her coffee cup. "More?" said Boufelja. "No," she answered. "Drink another, mademoiselle," he urged her. "It's good on a cold morning." He poured it out and she drank part of it. There was a knocking at the gate. One of the young soldiers had been sent with a jeep to carry her out to the truck stop on the trail.

"I can't!" she cried, thinking of Slimane and the donkey. The young soldier made it clear that he was not making an offer, but giving an order. Slimane stood beside the donkey outside the gate.

While she began to speak with him the soldier shouted: "Does he want to come, the *gosse?* He can come too, if he likes." Slimane ran to get the luggage and Fräulein Windling rushed inside to settle her bill. "Don't hurry," the soldier called after her. "There's plenty of time."

Boufelja stood in the kitchen doorway. Now for the first time it occurred to her to wonder what was going to become of him. With the hotel shut he would have no work. When she had settled her account and given him a tip which was much larger than she could afford, she took both his hands in hers and said: "*Mon cher* Boufelja, we shall see one another very soon."

"Ah, yes," he cried, trying to smile. "Very soon, mademoiselle."

She gave the donkey driver some money, and got into the jeep beside the soldier. Slimane had finished bringing out the luggage and stood behind the jeep, kicking the tires. "Have you got everything?" she called to him. "Everything?" She would have liked to see for herself, but she was loath to go back into the room. Boufelja had disappeared; now he came hurrying out, breathless, carrying a pile of old magazines. "It's all right," she said. "No, no! I don't want them." The jeep was already moving ahead down the hill. In what seemed to her an unreasonably short time they had reached the boulders. When Fräulein Windling tried to lift out her briefcase the pain of the sliver under her nail made the tears start to her eyes, and she let go with a cry. Slimane glanced at her, surprised. "I hurt my hand," she explained. "It's nothing."

The bags had been piled in the shade. Sitting on a rock near the jeep, the soldier faced Fräulein Windling; from time to time he scanned the horizon behind her for a sign of the truck. Slimane examined the jeep from all sides; eventually he came to sit nearby. They did not say very much to one another. She was not sure whether it was because of the soldier with them, or because her thumb ached so constantly, but she sat quietly waiting, not wanting to talk.

It was a long time before the far-off motor made itself heard. When the truck was still no more than a puff of dust between sky and earth, the soldier was on his feet watching; an instant later Slimane jumped up. "It is coming, madame," he said. Then he bent over, putting his face very close to hers. "I want to go with you to Colomb-Bechar," he whispered. When she did not respond, because she was seeing the whole story of their friendship unrolled before her, from the end back to its beginning, he said louder, with great urgency: "Please, madame."

Fräulein Windling hesitated only an instant. She raised her head and looked carefully at the smooth brown face that was so near. "Of course, Slimane," she said. It was clear that he had not expected to hear this; his delight was infectious, and she smiled as she watched him run to the pile of bags and begin carrying them out into the sunlight to align them in the dust beside the edge of the trail.

Later, when they were rattling along the hammada, she in front beside the driver and Slimane squatting in the back with a dozen men and a sheep, she considered her irresponsible action in allowing him to make this absurd trip with her all the way to Colomb-Bechar. Still, she knew she wanted to give this ending to their story. A few times she turned partially around in her seat to glance at him through the dirty glass. He sat there in the smoke and dust, laughing like the others, with the hood of his burnoose hiding most of his face.

It had been raining in Colomb-Bechar; the streets were great puddles to reflect the clouded sky. At the garage they found a surly Negro boy to help them carry the luggage to the railway station. Her thumb hurt a little less.

"It's a cold town," Slimane said to her as they went down the main street. At the station they checked the bags and then went outside to stand and watch a car being unloaded from an open freight train: the roof of the automobile was still white with snow from the high steppes. The day was dark, and the wind rippled the surface of the water in the flooded empty lots. Fräulein Windling's train would not be leaving until late in the afternoon. They went to a restaurant and ate a long lunch.

"You really will go back home tomorrow?" she asked him anxiously at one point, while they were having fruit. "You know we have done a very wicked thing to your father and mother. They will never forgive me." A curtain seemed to draw across Slimane's face.

"It doesn't matter," he said shortly.

After lunch they walked in the public garden and looked at the eagles in their cages. A fine rain had begun to be carried on the wind. The mud of the paths grew deeper. They went back to the center of the town and sat down on the terrace of a large, shabby modern café. The table at the end was partly sheltered from the wet wind; they faced an empty lot strewn with refuse. Nearby, spread out like the bones of a camel fallen on the trail, were the rusted remains of an ancient bus. A long, newly felled date palm lay diagonally across the greater part of the lot. Fräulein Windling turned to look at the wet orange fiber of the stump, and felt an idle pity for the tree. "I'm going to have a Coca-Cola," she declared. Slimane said he, too, would like one.

They sat there a long time. The fine rain slanted through the air outside the arcades and hit the ground silently. She had expected to be approached by beggars, but none arrived, and now that the time had come to leave the café and go to the station she was thankful to see that the day had passed so easily. She opened her pocketbook, took out three thousand francs, and handed them to Slimane, saying: "This will be enough for everything. But you must buy your ticket back home today. When you leave the railway station. Be very careful of it."

Slimane put the money inside his garments, rearranged his burnoose, and thanked her. "You understand, Slimane," she said, detaining him with her hand, for he seemed about to rise from the table. "I'm not giving you any money now, because I need what I have for my journey. But when I get to Switzerland I shall send you a little, now and then. Not much. A little."

His face was swept by panic; she was perplexed.

"You haven't got my address," he told her.

"No, but I shall send it to Boufelja's house," she said, thinking that would satisfy him. He leaned toward her, his eyes intense.

"No, madame," he said with finality. "No. I have your address, and I shall send you mine. Then you will have it, and you can write to me."

It did not seem worth arguing about. For most of the afternoon her thumb had not hurt too much; now, as the day waned, it had begun to ache again. She wanted to get up, find the waiter and pay him. The fine rain still blew; the station was fairly far. But she saw Slimane had something more to say. He leaned forward in his chair and looked down at the floor. "Madame," he began.

"Yes?" she said.

"When you are in your country and you think of me you will not be happy. It's true, no?"

"I shall be very sad," she answered, rising.

Slimane got slowly to his feet and was quiet for an instant before going on. "Sad because I ate the food out of the picture. That was very bad. Forgive me."

The shrill sound of her own voice exclaiming, "No!" startled her. "No!" she cried. "That was good!" She felt the muscles of her cheeks and lips twisting themselves into grimaces of weeping; fiercely she seized his arm and looked down into his face. *"Oh, mon pauvre petit!"* she sobbed, and then covered her face with both hands. She felt him gently touching her sleeve. A truck went by in the main street, shaking the floor.

With an effort she turned away and scratched in her bag for a handkerchief. "Come," she said, clearing her throat. "Call the waiter."

They arrived at the station cold and wet. The train was being assembled; passengers were not allowed to go out onto the platform and were sitting on the floor inside. While Fräulein Windling bought her ticket Slimane went to get the bags from the checkroom. He was gone for a long time. When he arrived he came with his burnoose thrown back over his shoulders, grinning triumphantly, with three valises piled on his head. A man in ragged European jacket and trousers followed behind carrying the rest. As he came nearer she saw that the man held a slip of paper between his teeth.

The ancient compartment smelled of varnish. Through the window she could see, above some remote western reach of wasteland, a few strips

199

of watery white sky. Slimane wanted to cover the seats with the luggage, so that no one would come into the compartment. "No," she said. "Put them in the racks." There were very few passengers in the coach. When everything was in place, the porter stood outside in the corridor and she noticed that he still held the slip of paper between his teeth. He counted the coins she gave him and pocketed them. Then quickly he handed the paper to Slimane, and was gone.

Fräulein Windling bent down a bit, to try and see her face in the narrow mirror that ran along the back of the seat. There was not enough light; the oil lantern above illumined only the ceiling, its base casting a leaden shadow over everything beneath. Suddenly the train jolted and made a series of crashing sounds. She took Slimane's head between her hands and kissed the middle of his forehead. "Please get down from the train," she told him. "We can talk here." She pointed to the window and began to pull on the torn leather strap that lowered it.

Slimane looked small on the dark platform, staring up at her as she leaned out. Then the train started to move. She thought surely it would go only a few feet and then stop, but it continued ahead, slowly. Slimane walked with it, keeping abreast of her window. In his hand was the paper the porter had given him. He held it up to her, crying: "Here is my address! Send it here!"

She took it, and kept waving as the train went faster, kept calling: "Good-bye!" He continued to walk quickly along beside the window, increasing his gait until he was running, until all at once there was no more platform. She leaned far out, looking backward, waving; straightway he was lost in the darkness and rain. A bonfire blazed orange by the track, and the smoke stung in her nostrils. She pulled up the window, glanced at the slip of paper she had in her hand and sat down. The train jolted her this way and that; she went on staring at the paper, although now it was in shadow; and she remembered the first day, long ago, when the child Slimane had stood outside the door watching her, stepping back out of her range of vision each time she turned to look at him. The words hastily printed for him on the scrap of paper by the porter were indeed an address, but the address was in Colomb-Bechar. "They said he tried to run away. But he didn't get very far." Each detail of his behavior as she went back over it clarified the pattern for her. "He's too young to

200

be a soldier," she told herself. "They won't take him." But she knew they would.

Her thumb was hot and swollen; sometimes it seemed almost that its throbbing accompanied the side-to-side jolting of the coach. She looked out at the few remaining patches of colorless light in the sky. Sooner or later, she argued, he would have done it.

"Another year, perhaps," the captain had said. She saw her own crooked, despairing smile in the dark window glass beside her face. Maybe Slimane would be among the fortunate ones, an early casualty. "If only death were absolutely certain in wartime," she thought wryly, "the waiting would not be so painful." Listing and groaning, the train began its long climb upward over the plateau.

201

MEJDOUB

A man who spent his nights sleeping in cafés or under the trees or wherever he happened to be at the time when he felt sleepy, wandered one morning through the streets of the town. He came to the marketplace, where an old mejdoub dressed in rags cavorted before the populace, screaming prophecies into the air. He stood watching until the old man had finished and gathered up the money the people offered him. It astonished him to see how much the madman had collected, and having nothing else to do, he decided to follow him.

Almost before he got out of the market he was aware that small boys were hurrying from under the arcades to run alongside the mejdoub, who merely strode forward, chanting and waving his sceptre, and from time to time threatening the children who came too close. Walking at some distance behind, he saw the old man go into several shops. He came out each time with a bank note in his hand, which he promptly gave to one of the small boys.

It occurred to him then that there was much he could learn from this mejdoub. He had only to study the old man's behavior and listen carefully to the words he uttered. Then with practice he himself could make the same gestures and shout the same words. He began to look each day for the mejdoub and to follow him wherever he went in the town. At the end of a month he decided that he was ready to put his knowledge to use.

He traveled south to another city where he had never gone before. Here he took a very cheap room by the slaughterhouse, far from the center of town. In the flea market he bought an old and tattered djellaba.

Then he went to the ironmongers and stood watching while they made him a long sceptre like the one the mejdoub had carried.

The next day, after practicing for a while, he went into the town and sat down in the street at the foot of the largest mosque. For a while he merely looked at the people going past. Slowly he began to raise his arms to the sky, and then to gesture with them. No one paid him any attention. This reassured him, as it meant that his disguise was successful. When he began to shout words the passersby looked toward him, but it was as if they could not see him, and were only waiting to hear what he had to say. For a time he shouted short quotations from the Koran. He moved his eyes in a circular motion and let his turban fall over his face. After crying the words "fire" and "blood" several times he lowered his arms and bent his head, and said no more. The people moved on, but not before many of them had tossed coins on the ground in front of him.

On succeeding days he tried other parts of the city. It did not seem to matter where he sat. The people were generous to him in one place the same as in another. He did not want to risk going into the shops and cafés until he was certain that the town had grown used to his presence. One day he stormed through the streets, shaking his sceptre to the sky and screaming: Sidi Rahal is here! Sidi Rahal tells you to prepare for the fire! This was in order to give himself a name for the townspeople to remember.

He began to stand in the doorways of shops. If he heard anyone refer to him as Sidi Rahal, he would step inside, glare at the proprietor, and without saying a word, hold out his hand. The man would give him money, and he would turn and walk out.

For some reason no children followed him. He would have been happier to have a group of them with him, like the old mejdoub, but as soon as he spoke to them, they were frightened and ran away. It's quieter like this, he told himself, but secretly it bothered him. Still, he was earning more money that he ever had thought possible. By the time the first rains arrived, he had saved up a large sum. Leaving his sceptre and ragged djellaba in his room by the slaughterhouse, he paid the landlord several months' rent in advance. He waited until night. Then he locked the door behind him and took a bus back to his own city.

First he bought a great variety of clothing. When he was richly dressed he went out and looked for a house. Soon he found one that suited him. It was small and he had enough money left to pay for it. He furnished two rooms and prepared to spend the winter eating and smoking kif with all his old friends.

When they asked him where he had been all summer, he spoke of the hospitality and generosity of his wealthy brother in Taza. Already he was impatient for the rains to stop. For there was no doubt that he truly enjoyed his new work.

The winter finally came to an end. He packed his bag and told his friends that he was going on a business trip. In the other town he walked to the room. His djellaba and sceptre were there.

This year many more people recognized him. He grew bolder and entered the shops without waiting in the doorways. The shopkeepers, eager to show their piety to the customers, always gave a good deal more than the passersby.

One day he decided to make a test. He hailed a taxi. As he got in he bellowed: I must go to Sidi Larbi's tomb! Fast! The driver, who knew he was not going to be paid, nevertheless agreed, and they rode out to a grove of olive trees on a hill far from the town.

He told the driver to wait, and jumped out of the taxi. Then he began the long climb up the hill to the tomb. The driver lost patience and drove off. On the way back to the town he missed a curve and hit a tree. When he was let out of the hospital he spread the word that Sidi Rahal had caused the car to go off the road. Men talked at length about it, recalling other holy maniacs who had put spells on motors and brakes. The name of Sidi Rahal was on everyone's lips, and people listened respectfully to his rantings.

That summer he amassed more money than the year before. He returned home and bought a larger house to live in, while he rented out the first one. Each year he bought more houses and lands, until finally it was clear that he had become a very prosperous man.

Always when the first rains fell he would announce to his friends that he was about to travel abroad. Then he would leave secretly, never allowing anyone to see him off. He was delighted with the pattern of his life, and with the good luck he had been granted in being able to continue it. He assumed that Allah did not mind if he pretended to be one of His holy maniacs. The money was merely his reward for providing men with an opportunity to exercise their charity.

One winter a new government came to power and announced that all beggars were to be taken off the streets. He talked about this with his friends, all of whom thought it an excellent thing. He agreed with them, but the news kept him from sleeping at night. To risk everything by going back, merely because that was what he wanted to do, was out of the question. Sadly he resigned himself to spending the summer at home.

It was not until the first few weeks of spring had gone by that he realized how close it had been to his heart, the starting out on a fine starry night to go in the bus to the other city, and what a relief it had been each time to be able to forget everything and live as Sidi Rahal. Now he began to understand that his life here at home had been a pleasure only because he had known that at a certain moment he was going to leave it for the other life.

As the hot weather came on he grew increasingly restless. He was bored and lost his appetite. His friends, noticing the change in him, advised him to travel, as he always had done. They said that men had been known to die as a result of breaking a habit. Again he lay awake at night worrying, and then secretly he determined to go back. As soon as he had made the decision he felt much better. It was as though until then he had been asleep, and suddenly had awakened. He announced to his friends that he was going abroad.

That very night he locked up his house and got onto a bus. The next day he strode joyously through the streets to sit in his favorite spot by the mosque. Passersby looked at him and remarked to one another: He's back again, after all. You see?

He sat there quietly all day, collecting money. At the end of the afternoon, since the weather was very hot, he walked down to the river outside the gates of the town, in order to bathe. As he was undressing behind some oleander bushes, he glanced up and saw three policemen coming down the bank toward him. Without waiting he seized his slippers, threw his djellaba over his shoulder, and began to run.

Sometimes he splashed into the water, and sometimes he slipped in the mud and fell. He could hear the men shouting after him. They did not chase him very far, for they were laughing. Not knowing this, he kept on running, following the river, until he was breathless and had to stop. He put on the djellaba and the slippers, thinking: I can't go back to the town, or to any other town, in these clothes.

He continued at a slower gait. When evening came he was hungry, but there were no people or houses in sight. He slept under a tree, with only the ragged djellaba to cover him.

The next morning his hunger had grown. He got up, bathed in the river, and set out again. All that day he walked under the hot sun. In the late afternoon he sat down to rest. He drank a little water from the river and looked around him at the countryside. On the hill behind him stood a partially ruined shrine.

When he was rested, he climbed up to the building. There was a tomb inside, in the center of the big domed room. He sat down and listened. Cocks crowed, and he heard the occasional barking of dogs. He imagined himself running to the village, crying to the first man he met: Give me a piece of bread, for the love of Moulay Abdelkader! He shut his eyes.

It was nearly twilight when he awoke. Outside the door stood a group of small boys, watching him. Seeing him awaken, they laughed and nudged one another. Then one boy tossed in a piece of dry bread, so that it fell beside him. Soon they were all chanting: He's eating bread! He's eating bread!

They played the game for a while, throwing in clods of earth and even uprooted plants along with the scraps of bread. In their faces he could read wonder, malice and contempt, and shining through these shifting emotions the steady gleam of ownership. He thought of the old mejdoub, and a shiver ran through him. Suddenly they had gone. He heard a few shrill cries in the distance as they raced back to the village.

The bread had given him a little nourishment. He slept where he was, and before it grew light he set out again along the river, giving thanks to Allah for having allowed him to get beyond the village without being seen. He understood that heretofore the children had run from him only because they knew that he was not ready for them, that they could not make him theirs. The more he thought about this, the more fervently he hoped never to know what it was like to be a true mejdoub.

That afternoon as he turned a bend in the river, he came suddenly upon a town. His desperate need for food led him straight to the market. Paying no heed to the people's stares, he went into a stall and ordered a bowl of soup. When he had finished it and paid, he entered another stall for a dish of stew. In a third place he ate skewered meat. Then he walked to the bread market for two loaves of bread to carry with him. While he was paying for these, a policeman tapped him on the shoulder and asked for his papers. He had none. There was nothing to say. At the police station they locked him into a small foul-smelling room in the cellar. Here in this closet he passed four days and nights of anguish. When at the end of that time they took him out and questioned him, he could not bring himself to tell them the truth. Instead he frowned, saying: I am Sidi Rahal.

They tied his hands and pushed him into the back of a truck. Later in the hospital they led him to a damp cell where the men stared and shivered and shrieked. He bore it for a week, and then he decided to give the officials his true name. But when he asked to be taken before them, the guards merely laughed. Sometimes they said: Next week, but usually they did not answer at all.

The months moved by. Through nights and days and nights he lived with the other madmen, and the time came when it scarcely mattered to him anymore, getting to the officials to tell them who he was. Finally he ceased thinking about it.

ALLAL

He was born in the hotel where his mother worked. The hotel had only three dark rooms which gave on a courtyard behind the bar. Beyond was another smaller patio with many doors. This was where the servants lived, and where Allal spent his childhood.

The Greek who owned the hotel had sent Allal's mother away. He was indignant because she, a girl of fourteen, had dared to give birth while she was working for him. She would not say who the father was, and it angered him to reflect that he himself had not taken advantage of the situation while he had had the chance. He gave the girl three months' wages and told her to go home to Marrakech. Since the cook and his wife liked the girl and offered to let her live with them for a while, he agreed that she might stay on until the baby was big enough to travel. She remained in the back patio for a few months with the cook and his wife, and then one day she disappeared, leaving the baby behind. No one heard of her again.

As soon as Allal was old enough to carry things, they set him to work. It was not long before he could fetch a pail of water from the well behind the hotel. The cook and his wife were childless, so that he played alone.

When he was somewhat older he began to wander over the empty tableland outside. There was nothing else up here but the barracks, and they were enclosed by a high blind wall of red adobe. Everything else was below in the valley: the town, the gardens, and the river winding southward among the thousands of palm trees. He could sit on a point of rock far above and look down at the people walking in the alleys of the town. It was only later that he visited the place and saw what the inhabitants were like. Because he had been left behind by his mother they called him a son of sin, and laughed when they looked at him. It seemed to him that in this way they hoped to make him into a shadow, in order not to have to think of him as real and alive. He awaited with dread the time when he would have to go each morning to the town and work. For the moment he helped in the kitchen and served the officers from the barracks, along with the few motorists who passed through the region. He got small tips in the restaurant, and free food and lodging in a cell of the servants' quarters, but the Greek gave him no wages. Eventually he reached an age when this situation seemed shameful, and he went of his own accord to the town below and began to work, along with other boys of his age, helping to make the mud bricks people used for building their houses.

Living in the town was much as he had imagined it would be. For two years he stayed in a room behind a blacksmith's shop, leading a life without quarrels, and saving whatever money he did not have to spend to keep himself alive. Far from making any friends during this time, he formed a thorough hatred for the people of the town, who never allowed him to forget that he was a son of sin, and therefore not like others, but *meskhot*—damned. Then he found a small house, not much more than a hut, in the palm groves outside the town. The rent was low and no one lived nearby. He went to live there, where the only sound was the wind in the trees, and avoided the people of the town when he could.

One hot summer evening shortly after sunset he was walking under the arcades that faced the town's main square. A few paces ahead of him an old man in a white turban was trying to shift a heavy sack from one shoulder to the other. Suddenly it fell to the ground, and Allal stared as two dark forms flowed out of it and disappeared into the shadows. The old man pounced upon the sack and fastened the top of it, at the same time beginning to shout: Look out for the snakes! Help me find my snakes!

Many people turned quickly around and walked back the way they had come. Others stood at some distance, watching. A few called to the old man: Find your snakes fast and get them out of here! Why are they here? We don't want snakes in this town!

Hopping up and down in his anxiety, the old man turned to Allal. Watch this for me a minute, my son. He pointed at the sack lying on the earth at his feet, and snatching up a basket he had been carrying, went swiftly around the corner into an alley. Allal stood where he was. No one passed by.

It was not long before the old man returned, panting with triumph. When the onlookers in the square saw him again, they began to call out, this time to Allal: Show that *berrani* the way out of the town! He has no right to carry those things in here. Out! Out!

Allal picked up the big sack and said to the old man: Come on.

They left the square and went through the alleys until they were at the edge of town. The old man looked up then, saw the palm trees black against the fading sky ahead, and turned to the boy beside him.

Come on, said Allal again, and he went to the left along the rough path that led to his house. The old man stood perplexed.

You can stay with me tonight, Allal told him.

And these? he said, pointing first at the sack and then at the basket. They have to be with me.

Allal grinned. They can come.

When they were sitting in the house Allal looked at the sack and the basket. I'm not like the rest of them here, he said.

It made him feel good to hear the words being spoken. He made a contemptuous gesture. Afraid to walk through the square because of a snake. You saw them.

The old man scratched his chin. Snakes are like people, he said. You have to get to know them. Then you can be their friends.

Allal hesitated before he asked: Do you ever let them out?

Always, the old man said with energy. It's bad for them to be inside like this. They've got to be healthy when they get to Taroudant, or the man there won't buy them.

He began a long story about his life as a hunter of snakes, explaining that each year he made a voyage to Taroudant to see a man who bought them for the Aissaoua snake charmers in Marrakech. Allal made tea while he listened, and brought out a bowl of kif paste to eat with the tea. Later, when they were sitting comfortably in the midst of the pipe smoke, the old man chuckled. Allal turned to look at him.

Shall I let them out?

Fine!

But you must sit and keep quiet. Move the lamp nearer.

He untied the sack, shook it a bit, and returned to where he had been

210

sitting. Then in silence Allal watched the long bodies move cautiously out into the light. Among the cobras were others with markings so delicate and perfect that they seemed to have been designed and painted by an artist. One reddish-gold serpent, which coiled itself lazily in the middle of the floor, he found particularly beautiful. As he stared at it, he felt a great desire to own it and have it always with him.

The old man was talking. I've spent my whole life with snakes, he said. I could tell you some things about them. Did you know that if you give them *majoun* you can make them do what you want, and without saying a word? I swear by Allah!

Allal's face assumed a doubtful air. He did not question the truth of the other's statement, but rather the likelihood of his being able to put the knowledge to use. For it was at that moment that the idea of actually taking the snake first came into his head. He was thinking that whatever he was to do must be done quickly, for the old man would be leaving in the morning. Suddenly he felt a great impatience.

Put them away so I can cook dinner, he whispered. Then he sat admiring the ease with which the old man picked up each one by its head and slipped it into the sack. Once again he dropped two of the snakes into the basket, and one of these, Allal noted, was the red one. He imagined he could see the shining of its scales through the lid of the basket.

As he set to work preparing the meal Allal tried to think of other things. Then, since the snake remained in his mind in spite of everything, he began to devise a way of getting it. While he squatted over the fire in a corner, he mixed some kif paste in a bowl of milk and set it aside.

The old man continued to talk. That was good luck, getting the two snakes back like that, in the middle of the town. You can never be sure what people are going to do when they find out you're carrying snakes. Once in El Kelaa they took all of them and killed them, one after the other, in front of me. A year's work. I had to go back home and start all over again.

Even as they ate, Allal saw that his guest was growing sleepy. How will things happen? he wondered. There was no way of knowing beforehand precisely what he was going to do, and the prospect of having to handle the snake worried him. It could kill me, he thought.

Once they had eaten, drunk tea and smoked a few pipes of kif, the old man lay back on the floor and said he was going to sleep. Allal sprang up. In here! he told him, and led him to his own mat in an alcove. The old man lay down and swiftly fell asleep.

Several times during the next half hour Allal went to the alcove and peered in, but neither the body in its burnoose nor the head in its turban had stirred.

First he got out his blanket, and after tying three of its corners together, spread it on the floor with the fourth corner facing the basket. Then he set the bowl of milk and kif paste on the blanket. As he loosened the strap from the cover of the basket the old man coughed. Allal stood immobile, waiting to hear the cracked voice speak. A small breeze had sprung up, making the palm branches rasp one against the other, but there was no further sound from the alcove. He crept to the far side of the room and squatted by the wall, his gaze fixed on the basket.

Several times he thought he saw the cover move slightly, but each time he decided he had been mistaken. Then he caught his breath. The shadow along the base of the basket was moving. One of the creatures had crept out from the far side. It waited for a while before continuing into the light, but when it did, Allal breathed a prayer of thanks. It was the red and gold one.

When finally it decided to go to the bowl, it made a complete tour around the edge, looking in from all sides, before lowering its head toward the milk. Allal watched, fearful that the foreign flavor of the kif paste might repel it. The snake remained there without moving.

He waited a half hour or more. The snake stayed where it was, its head in the bowl. From time to time Allal glanced at the basket, to be certain that the second snake was still in it. The breeze went on, rubbing the palm branches together. When he decided it was time, he rose slowly, and keeping an eye on the basket where apparently the other snake still slept, he reached over and gathered together the three tied corners of the blanket. Then he lifted the fourth corner, so that both the snake and the bowl slid to the bottom of the improvised sack. The snake moved slightly, but he did not think it was angry. He knew exactly where he would hide it: between some rocks in the dry riverbed.

Holding the blanket in front of him he opened the door and stepped out under the stars. It was not far up the road, to a group of high palms, and then to the left down into the oued. There was a space between the boulders where the bundle would be invisible. He pushed it in with care, and hurried back to the house. The old man was asleep.

There was no way of being sure that the other snake was still in the basket, so Allal picked up his burnoose and went outside. He shut the door and lay down on the ground to sleep.

Before the sun was in the sky the old man was awake, lying in the alcove coughing. Allal jumped up, went inside, and began to make a fire in the *mijmah*. A minute later he heard the other exclaim: They're loose again! Out of the basket! Stay where you are and I'll find them.

It was not long before the old man grunted with satisfaction. I have the black one! he cried. Allal did not look up from the corner where he crouched, and the old man came over, waving a cobra. Now I've got to find the other one.

He put the snake away and continued to search. When the fire was blazing, Allal turned and said: Do you want me to help you look for it?

No, no! Stay where you are.

Allal boiled the water and made the tea, and still the old man was crawling on his knees, lifting boxes and pushing sacks. His turban had slipped off and his face ran with sweat.

Come and have tea, Allal told him.

The old man did not seem to have heard him at first. Then he rose and went into the alcove, where he rewound his turban. When he came out he sat down with Allal, and they had breakfast.

Snakes are very clever, the old man said. They can get into places that don't exist. I've moved everything in this house.

After they had finished eating, they went outside and looked for the snake between the close-growing trunks of the palms near the house. When the old man was convinced that it was gone, he went sadly back in.

That was a good snake, he said at last. And now I'm going to Taroudant.

They said good-bye, and the old man took his sack and basket and started up the road toward the highway.

All day long as he worked, Allal thought of the snake, but it was not until sunset that he was able to go to the rocks in the oued and pull out the blanket. He carried it back to the house in a high state of excitement.

Before he untied the blanket, he filled a wide dish with milk and kif paste, and set it on the floor. He ate three spoonfuls of the paste himself and sat back to watch, drumming on the low wooden tea table with his fingers. Everything happened just as he had hoped. The snake came slowly out of the blanket, and very soon had found the dish and was drinking the milk. As long as it drank he kept drumming; when it had finished and raised its head to look at him, he stopped, and it crawled back inside the blanket.

Later that evening he put down more milk, and drummed again on the table. After a time the snake's head appeared, and finally all of it, and the entire pattern of action was repeated.

That night and every night thereafter, Allal sat with the snake, while with infinite patience he sought to make it his friend. He never attempted to touch it, but soon he was able to summon it, keep it in front of him for as long as he pleased, merely by tapping on the table, and dismiss it at will. For the first week or so he used the kif paste; then he tried the routine without it. In the end the results were the same. After that he fed it only milk and eggs.

Then one evening as his friend lay gracefully coiled in front of him, he began to think of the old man, and formed an idea that put all other things out of his mind. There had not been any kif paste in the house for several weeks, and he decided to make some. He bought the ingredients the following day, and after work he prepared the paste. When it was done, he mixed a large amount of it in a bowl with milk and set it down for the snake. Then he himself ate four spoonfuls, washing them down with tea.

He quickly undressed, and moving the table so that he could reach it, stretched out naked on a mat near the door. This time he continued to tap on the table, even after the snake had finished drinking the milk. It lay still, observing him, as if it were in doubt that the familiar drumming came from the brown body in front of it.

Seeing that even after a long time it remained where it was, staring at him with its stony yellow eyes, Allal began to say to it over and over: Come here. He knew it could not hear his voice, but he believed it could feel his mind as he urged it. You can make them do what you want, without saying a word, the old man had told him.

Although the snake did not move, he went on repeating his command, for by now he knew it was going to come. And after another long wait, all at once it lowered its head and began to move toward him. It reached his hip and slid along his leg. Then it climbed up his leg and lay for a time across his chest. Its body was heavy and tepid, its scales wonderfully smooth. After a time it came to rest, coiled in the space between his head and his shoulder.

By this time the kif paste had completely taken over Allal's mind. He lay in a state of pure delight, feeling the snake's head against his own, without a thought save that he and the snake were together. The patterns forming and melting behind his eyelids seemed to be the same ones that covered the snake's back. Now and then in a huge frenzied movement they all swirled up and shattered into fragments which swiftly became one great yellow eye, split through the middle by the narrow vertical pupil that pulsed with his own heartbeat. Then the eye would recede, through shifting shadow and sunlight, until only the designs of the scales were left, swarming with renewed insistence as they merged and separated. At last the eye returned, so huge this time that it had no edge around it, its pupil dilated to form an aperture almost wide enough for him to enter. As he stared at the blackness within, he understood that he was being slowly propelled toward the opening. He put out his hands to touch the polished surface of the eye on each side, and as he did this he felt the pull from within. He slid through the crack and was swallowed by darkness.

On awakening Allal felt that he had returned from somewhere far away. He opened his eyes and saw, very close to him, what looked like the flank of an enormous beast, covered with coarse stiff hair. There was a repeated vibration in the air, like distant thunder curling around the edges of the sky. He sighed, or imagined that he did, for his breath made no sound. Then he shifted his head a bit, to try and see beyond the mass of hair beside him. Next he saw the ear, and he knew he was looking at his own head from the outside. He had not expected this; he had hoped only that his friend would come in and share his mind with him. But it did not strike him as being at all strange; he merely said to himself that now he was seeing through the eyes of the snake, rather than through his own.

Now he understood why the serpent had been so wary of him: from here the boy was a monstrous creature, with all the bristles on his head and his breathing that vibrated inside him like a far-off storm.

He uncoiled himself and glided across the floor to the alcove. There was a break in the mud wall wide enough to let him out. When he had pushed himself through, he lay full length on the ground in the crystalline moonlight, staring at the strangeness of the landscape, where shadows were not shadows.

He crawled around the side of the house and started up the road toward the town, rejoicing in a sense of freedom different from any he had ever imagined. There was no feeling of having a body, for he was perfectly contained in the skin that covered him. It was beautiful to caress the earth with the length of his belly as he moved along the silent road, smelling the sharp veins of wormwood in the wind. When the voice of the muezzin floated out over the countryside from the mosque, he could not hear it, or know that within the hour the night would end.

On catching sight of a man ahead, he left the road and hid behind a rock until the danger had passed. But then as he approached the town there began to be more people, so that he let himself down into the *seguia*, the deep ditch that went along beside the road. Here the stones and clumps of dead plants impeded his progress. He was still struggling along the floor of the *seguia*, pushing himself around the rocks and through the dry tangles of matted stalks left by the water, when dawn began to break.

The coming of daylight made him anxious and unhappy. He clambered up the bank of the *seguia* and raised his head to examine the road. A man walking past saw him, stood quite still, and then turned and ran back. Allal did not wait; he wanted now to get home as fast as possible.

Once he felt the thud of a stone as it struck the ground somewhere behind him. Quickly he threw himself over the edge of the *seguia* and rolled squirming down the bank. He knew the terrain here: where the road crossed the oued, there were two culverts not far apart. A man stood at some distance ahead of him with a shovel, peering down into the *seguia*. Allal kept moving, aware that he would reach the first culvert before the man could get to him.

The floor of the tunnel under the road was ribbed with hard little waves of sand. The smell of the mountains was in the air that moved through. There were places in here where he could have hidden, but he kept moving, and soon reached the other end. Then he continued to the second culvert and went under the road in the other direction, emerging once again into the *seguia*. Behind him several men had gathered at the entrance to the first culvert. One of them was on his knees, his head and shoulders inside the opening.

He now set out for the house in a straight line across the open ground, keeping his eye on the clump of palms beside it. The sun had just come up, and the stones began to cast long bluish shadows. All at once a small boy appeared from behind some nearby palms, saw him, and opened his eyes and mouth wide with fear. He was so close that Allal went straight to him and bit him in the leg. The boy ran wildly toward the group of men in the *seguia*.

Allal hurried on to the house, looking back only as he reached the hole between the mud bricks. Several men were running among the trees toward him. Swiftly he glided through into the alcove. The brown body still lay near the door. But there was no time, and Allal needed time to get back to it, to lie close to its head and say: Come here.

As he stared out into the room at the body, there was a great pounding on the door. The boy was on his feet at the first blow, as if a spring had been released, and Allal saw with despair the expression of total terror in his face, and the eyes with no mind behind them. The boy stood panting, his fists clenched. The door opened and some of the men peered inside. Then with a roar the boy lowered his head and rushed through the doorway. One of the men reached out to seize him, but lost his balance and fell. An instant later all of them turned and began to run through the palm grove after the naked figure.

Even when, from time to time, they lost sight of him, they could hear the screams, and then they would see him, between the palm trunks, still running. Finally he stumbled and fell face downward. It was then that they caught him, bound him, covered his nakedness, and took him away, to be sent one day soon to the hospital at Berrechid.

That afternoon the same group of men came to the house to carry out the search they had meant to make earlier. Allal lay in the alcove, dozing. When he awoke, they were already inside. He turned and crept to the hole. He saw the man waiting out there, a club in his hand.

The rage always had been in his heart; now it burst forth. As if his body were a whip, he sprang out into the room. The men nearest him were on their hands and knees, and Allal had the joy of pushing his fangs into two of them before a third severed his head with an axe.

TAPIAMA

Just behind the hotel was the river. If it had come from very far inland it would have been wide and silent, but because it was really only a creek swollen by the rains, and its bed was full of boulders, it made a roaring noise which the photographer briefly mistook for more rain. The heat and the trip had tired him out; he had eaten the cold fried fish and the leathery omelet that oozed grease, the brown bean paste with rice and burned bananas, and had been overtaken suddenly by a sleepiness powerful as the effect of a drug. Staggering to his bed, he had ripped off his shirt and trousers, lifted the stiff mosquito net that reeked of dust, and dropped like a stone onto the mattress, only distantly noticing its hardness before he lost himself in sleep.

But in the night when he awoke he realized he had been in the false sleep of indigestion; staring into the blackness over his head he told himself that it was going to be hard to find the way back into oblivion. It was then that he had become aware of the night's changeless backdrop of sound, and had taken it for rain. Now and then, far above his head (how could the ceiling be that high?) a firefly's nervous little light flashed its indecipherable code for an instant or two. He was lying on his back; something small was crawling down his chest. He put his hand there; it was a slowly moving drop of sweat. The rough sheet under him was wet. He wanted to move, but if he did there would be no end to the shifting, and each new position would be more uncomfortable than the last. In the anonymous darkness of a nearby room someone coughed from time to time; he could not tell whether it was a man or a woman. The meal he had eaten lay like ten meals in his stomach. Slowly the memory of it was

218

suffused with a nebulous horror—particularly the heavy cold omelet shining with grease.

Lying there smelling the dust from the netting was like being tied up inside a burlap bag. To get out into the street and walk—that was what he wanted, but there were difficulties. The electricity went off at midnight; the old man who ran the hotel had told him that. Instead of putting the matches under his pillow he had left them in his trouser pocket, and the idea of stepping out onto the floor barefoot without a light did not appeal to him. Besides, he reminded himself, listening again to the wide, strangely distant clamor out there, it was raining. But to move along the dead streets even under the invisible rain would be a pleasure. . . . If he lay quite still, sleep might return. Finally, in desperation he yanked the net aside and sprang out of bed, across the room in the direction of the chair over which he had thrown his clothes.

He managed to get into his shirt and trousers in the space of three matches; his shoes he pounded on the concrete floor in the dark, to tumble out a possible centipede or scorpion. Then he struck a fourth match and opened the door into the *patio*. Here it was no longer pitch-black. The huge potted plants were visible in the night's lead-colored light, but the sky, stifled by a cloud that no starlight could pierce, seemed not to be there at all. It was not raining. "The river must be very close," he thought.

He walked along the covered *corredor,* grazing the tentacles of orchids that hung in baskets and jars from the eaves, bumping into the pieces of wicker furniture, and found the entrance door, closed and doubly bolted. Carefully he slid back the metal bars and opened the door, pulling it shut after him. The gloom of the street was as profound as that of the *patio* and the air as still as it had been under the mosquito net. But it had an indefinite vegetable scent—a sweet odor of both fulfillment and exhaustion.

He turned to the left: the long empty main street, lined with one-story buildings, led straight down to the *paseo* along the sea. As he walked, the unmoving hothouse air became veined with the fresher smell of seaweed on the beach. At each intersecting street he had to go down six steps to the road level, cross, and climb up again to the sidewalk. In the rainy season, the *proprietario* of the hotel had told him, there was a rowboat at each corner to ferry the pedestrians across. Like the intermingling of the land and sea odors that he breathed, two opposing but entwined sensations took possession of him: a relief amounting almost to delight, and a faint feeling of nausea which he decided to combat because he felt that not to have been able to leave all suggestion of illness behind showed a lack of strength. He tried to put more springiness into his walk, but discovered almost immediately that it was too hot to make any more than a minimum of effort. He was sweating even more now than he had been in his bed. He lighted an Ovalado. The taste of the sweet tobacco was a part of the night.

The *paseo* bordering the seafront was about half a mile long. He had imagined there would be some slight stirring of the air here, but he could detect no difference. Still, now and then there was the soft intimate sound of a small wave breaking gently on the sand just below. He sat down on the balustrade and rested, in the hope of cooling off a little. The sea was invisible. He could have been sitting on the peak of a cloud-covered mountain—the gloom in front of him would have been that formless and all-embracing. Yet the sea's casual noises had no element of distance in them, as sea sounds have. It was as though they were taking place in a vast, closed courtyard. The concrete slabs on which he sat were damp, and a little cooler than his flesh. He smoked two cigarettes and strained his ears to hear some sound, made even indirectly, by human agency. But there was nothing more than the desultory slipping and sucking of the lazy water on the beach below. He glanced up and down the empty *paseo*. Far out along the shore to the west there was a light. It was orange, it flickered: a bonfire? He resumed walking, more slowly than before, ahead of him the distant blaze, the one point of light in the landscape.

A wide flight of steps led down onto the beach. Just beyond, he could see the flimsy structure of a pier that had been built out over the water. He stood still and listened. The fitful licking of small waves around the piles sounded as though it were happening in an echo chamber.

He ran lightly down the steps and passed underneath the pier. It was definitely cooler walking along on the sand than it had been up on the *paseo*. He felt wide awake now, and decided to see how much nearer to the light down the shore fifteen minutes would put him. Night-colored crabs hurried along the sand just ahead of his moving feet, completely soundless and almost invisible. A little beyond the end of the *paseo* the sand gave place to a hard coral surface which was easier to walk on. Out of prudence he kept as near to the water's edge as possible.

There was a difference between this walk and innumerable other midnight jaunts he had made, and he was inclined to wonder what made it so pleasant. Perhaps he was enjoying it simply because the fabric here was of pure freedom. He was not looking for anything; all the cameras were back in the hotel room.

Occasionally he lifted his eyes from the dim brainlike configurations of coral beneath his feet and looked inland, to see whether he could make out any signs of habitation. It seemed to him that there might be sand dunes a few hundred feet back, but in the absence of light it was impossible to be certain of even that much. The sweat trickled down his spine and over his coccyx, sliding in between his buttocks. Maybe the best idea would be to undress completely. But then there would be the bother of carrying his clothing, and he wanted his hands free, even at the risk of chafing.

The question of freedom was governed by the law of diminishing returns, he said to himself, walking faster. If you went beyond a certain point of intensity in your consciousness of desiring it, you furnished yourself with a guarantee of not achieving it. In any case, he thought, what is freedom in the last analysis, other than the state of being totally, instead of only partially, subject to the tyranny of chance?

There was no doubt that this walk was dispelling the miasma of indigestion that had lain within him. Three minutes to go, said the bright minute hand of his watch; the orange light ahead seemed smaller than it had from the town. Why an arbitrary fifteen minutes? He smiled at the precise urban pattern in which his mind had automatically moved. If he lifted his arm he could touch the sky, and it would be moist, tepid and voluptuously soft.

And now in the distance ahead, on the landward side, he heard sounds which he quickly identified as the voices of hundreds of young frogs. The light, now that he studied it, was moving in a strange fashion: slightly up and down, and sideways as well, but without appearing to alter its position. All at once it became a huge flame belching upward, an instant later scattering cascades of red sparks, and he understood that he had arrived. The bonfire burned on the floor of a gently swaying craft not a hundred feet ahead of him. A naked man stood above it, tossing it palm branches. The photographer stopped walking and listened for the sound of human voices, but the happy chorus of frogs filled the air.

He stepped ahead several paces and decided to call out. *"Hola!"* The man wheeled about, jumped over the nearer side of the boat (the water was extremely shallow) and came running up to him.

Without greeting him, taking him perhaps for someone else, the man said: *"Tapiama? Vas a Tapiama?"* The photographer, never having heard of Tapiama, stuttered a bit and finally said, *"Sí,"* whereupon the other seized his arm and pulled him along to the edge of the water. "The tide's all the way out. We'll start in a minute."

He could see two other people in the craft, lying flat on the floor, one on each side of the fire, as far from its heat as possible. The photographer squatted down and removed his shoes and socks, then waded to the boat. When he stood in the center of it (the fire was still crackling brightly) he turned and watched the naked man loosening the rope that held the craft in place.

"The whole thing is absurd." He could only distrust the very natural-ness with which all this was coming about—the indifference to his unexpected arrival on the part of the two passengers, and perhaps even more, the highly suspect readiness of the boatman to take off the moment he had appeared. He told himself, "Things don't happen this way," but since beyond a doubt they were doing so, any questioning of the process could lead only in the direction of paranoia. He dropped to the floor of the boat and pulled out his packet of Ovalados. The naked boatman, the coil of dripping rope around his black forearm like a bracelet, sprang aboard, and with his big toe nudged one of the supine passengers who stirred, rose to his knees, and glanced about with annoyance. "Where is it?" he demanded. Without replying, the boatman handed him the shorter of two poles that had lain along the gunwale. Together they began to propel the punt along the invisible surface of the water. The frogs' canticle and the fire's flare filled the night.

Having answered *"Sí,"* to the Tapiama question, the photographer felt he could scarcely take the retrogressive step of asking "What is Tapiama?" or "Where is Tapiama?" And so, much as he would have liked to know, he decided to wait. This shallow body of water beneath them—estuary, lagoon? River more likely, since the boatman had said the tide was out.

But not the stream whose troubled passage among the boulders he had heard from his bed.

They pushed on, now and then passing beneath clumps of high vegetation where the frogs' song was briefly covered by another sound, inexplicable and brutal, like the sudden tearing of a vast sheet of strong linen. From time to time something solid and heavy splashed nearby, as if a man had fallen into the water. And occasionally the recumbent man raised himself on one elbow and without too much effort managed to revive the dying fire with another dry palm leaf.

Probably it was less than an hour before they came to a landing in the mud. The two passengers leapt out and hurried away into the darkness. The boatman, after carefully donning a pair of short underpants, tapped the photographer on the arm and asked him for sixty centavos. He gave him seventy-five and clambered out into the soft mud, his shoes in his hand.

"Wait a minute," said the man. "I'll go with you." The photographer was pleased. When the boatman, looking blacker now in his white shorts, had secured the punt to an upright log driven into the mud, he led the way upward through a tangle of undergrowth, saying casually at one point: "Are you going across tomorrow?"

"Across? No."

"Aren't you here for the company?" The voice implied that to be here otherwise than for the company laid one open to unnameable suspicion.

The time had come to be truthful, he feared, although he did not relish the position he knew it would put him in. "I never heard of the company," he said. "I just arrived in Rio Martillo tonight. What sort of company?"

"Sugar," said the other. Then he stood still in the dark and spoke slowly: "*Entonces*—why have you come to Tapiama? They don't like *millonarios* here, you know." Understanding that this was the contemptuous coastal term for Americans, the photographer quickly lied. "I'm Danish," he said, but feeling that his voice lacked conviction he immediately added: "Do we go through any more mud, or can I put my shoes on?"

The man had started up again. "Wash your feet at the *cantina,* if you like," he told him over his shoulder. In another minute they were there: all in the dimness an open space, a dozen or so palm-leaf huts at one end of it, at the other a platform which must be a loading dock, the empty night and openness of water behind it; and halfway between the dock and the cluster of dwellings, the *cantina,* itself only a very large hut without a front wall.

A faint light came from within; there was no sound but the frogs on all sides, and the occasional tearing rasp in the branches high overhead. "Why is the place open at this hour?" demanded the photographer. The boatman stopped in the middle of the clearing and adjusted his shorts briefly. "Don Octavio runs it from six in the morning until six at night. His brother runs it from six at night until six in the morning. The company lets the men off from work at different hours. They come here with their *pago* and spend it. They like it better here than at home. Not so many mosquitoes." It could have been the photographer's imagination that made the man's voice sound bitter as he spoke the last words. They continued across the clearing and stepped into the *cantina.*

There was no floor; the ground was covered with white sand. A counter of boards had been built diagonally across a far corner. Here an oil lamp smoldered and two men stood drinking. Wooden packing cases were scattered here and there, some standing on end with empty beer bottles on them, and others on their sides, to be used as seats. *"Muy triste,"* commented the boatman, glancing around. Then he went behind the bar and disappeared through a small door in the wall there. Apart from the two at the bar, who had ceased their conversation and now stood staring at the photographer, there was no one else in the place. "When in doubt, speak," he told himself, advancing toward them, although it occurred to him that he might just as well have made it, "When in doubt, keep quiet," even as he opened his mouth to say, *"Buenas noches,"* for their expressions did not alter in any manner that he could detect. For a full three seconds they continued to gaze at him before they replied, which they then did more or less simultaneously. These two had nothing in common, he noted: one was a soldier in uniform, an Indian boy of perhaps eighteen, the other a tired-looking mulatto civilian of indeterminate age. Or perhaps—the idea came to him as he put his elbow on the bar with a show of casualness—they did have at least a common antagonism, now that he had entered the *cantina.* "Oh, well, I'm barefoot and my shoes are covered with mud," he thought.

"Hay alguien?" he said aloud to the palm-leaf wall behind the bar. The two neither resumed their conversation nor spoke further with him, and

he did not turn his head again toward them. Presently the small door opened and a fat man pushed through. He stood with his hands outspread on the bar, his eyebrows raised in anticipation. "I'll have a *cumbiamba*," said the photographer, remembering the name of the coastal region's favorite drink, an herbal concoction famous for its treacherous effects.

It was foul-tasting but strong. The second one seemed less objectionable. He walked across to the open side of the *cantina* and sat down on a packing case, looking out at the formless night. The two at the bar were talking again in low tones. It was not long before five men appeared from the platform end of the clearing; they straggled in and stood at the bar, laughing as they waited for their drinks. All of them were black, and wore only underpants, like the boatman. Now a mulatto girl with gold teeth came through the little door behind the bar and joined them. Almost immediately, however, she became aware of the photographer sitting by himself, and with her hands on her hips, half dancing, she made her way across the open space toward him. When she arrived, she squatted down beside him grinning and with one thin yellow hand reached out to unfasten his fly. His reaction was instantaneous and automatic: he drew back his leg and kicked her full in the breast, so that she toppled over backward in silence onto the sand. The noise of the resulting laughter at the bar was not sufficient to cover her thin voice, made sharp by rage: *"Qué bruto, tú! Pendejo!"* Hands on hips again, she retreated to the bar and was given a beer by one of the workmen. Although the photographer had not meant to kick her, he felt no regret at the turn the incident had taken. The *cumbiambas* seemed to be having their effect; he was beginning to feel very well. He sat still a while, tapping rhythms on the side of his empty glass. Soon more Negro workmen came in and joined the others at the bar. One carried a guitar on which he set to work strumming a syncopated chordal accompaniment for a melody which failed to appear. However, it was music of a sort, and everyone was pleased with it. Perhaps awakened by the sound, the dogs of the village had now started an angry chorus of barking; this was particularly audible to the photographer, who sat at the entrance, and it bothered him. He rose and moved over to an empty crate alongside the opposite wall, resting his head against a rough-hewn pole that was one of the supports of the roof. A foot or so above his head there was a strange object dangling from a nail. Now and then he rolled his eyes upward and studied it.

All at once he jumped up and began violently to brush the back of his neck and head. The pole behind him was swarming with tiny ants, thousands upon thousands of them: someone had hung a small crushed coral snake over the nail, and they had come to eat the flesh. It took him a good while not to feel any more of the insects running over his back; during that time two other individuals had come into the *cantina* (whether from the outside or through the door behind the counter, he had not noticed), and now sat between him and the bar in such a fashion that both of them faced him. The old man looked Nordic, the innocent-looking one-legged boy with him could be Spanish; the old man was telling the boy a humorous story, leaning toward him with great interest, occasionally poking his arm with a forefinger to drive home a point, but the boy was distractedly making designs in the sand with the tip of his crutch.

The photographer stood up; he had never before had such an effect from two drinks. "A very peculiar sensation," he said to himself. "Very peculiar," he repeated aloud under his breath as he started toward the bar to order another. It was not that he felt drunk so much as that he had become someone who was not he, someone for whom the act of living was a thing so different from what he had imagined it could be, that he was left stranded in a region of sensation far from any he had heretofore known. It was not unpleasant: it was merely indefinable. *"Dispénseme,"* he said to a tall Negro in pink-and-white striped BVD's, and he handed his empty glass to the fat man. He wanted to see what went into a *cumbiamba,* but the barman did everything quickly beneath the counter and handed him back the glass, brimming with the slightly frothy mixture. He took a good swallow of it and set it down, turning a little to his right as he did so. Standing beside him was the Indian soldier, his cap at an angle atop a pre-Columbian face. "Why does the army put such big visors on them?" he wondered.

He saw that the soldier was about to speak. "Whatever he says is going to turn out to be an insult," he warned himself, in the hope that this would help him to avoid possible anger later.

"Do you like this place?" the soldier said; his voice was silken.

"Es simpático. Yes, I like it."

"Why?" The dogs outside had come nearer; he could hear their yapping now above the laughter.

"Can you tell me why they hung that dead snake on the wall there?" he found himself asking, and supposed it was to change the subject. But the soldier was going to be even more boring than he had feared. "I asked you why you like this *cantina*," he insisted.

"And I told you it was *simpático*. Isn't that enough?"

The soldier tilted his head back and looked down his nose.

"Far from being enough," he replied, his manner pedantic, his expression infuriating.

The photographer returned to his drink, picked it up, slowly finished it off. Then he pulled out his cigarettes and offered one to the other. With exaggerated deliberateness the soldier reached for the cigarette, took it, and began to tap it on the counter. The man playing the guitar at last had started to sing in a small falsetto voice along with it, but most of the words were in a dialect the photographer could not understand. When the cigarettes were lighted, he found himself wondering who had lighted them—he or the soldier.

"Just where did you come from?" asked the soldier.

He was not bothering to answer, but the soldier misunderstood even this. "I can see you're inventing something," he said, "and I don't want to hear it."

The photographer, disgusted, exclaimed, "Aaah!" and ordered another *cumbiamba*. This most recent one had done something extraordinary to him: he felt that he had become very precise, thin and hard, an object made of enamel or some similar material, something other than a living being, but intensely conscious all the same. "Four ought to do the trick," he thought.

The empty glass was in his hand, the fat barman was staring at him, and at that point he had not the slightest idea whether he had already drunk the fourth one or whether it was still the moment just after he had ordered it. He felt himself laughing, but he could not hear whether any sound was coming out or not. The mangled snake, seething with ants, had upset him a little; recognizing it, he had then been made aware of its smell, which he was not sure he had escaped even now. Here at the bar the kerosene lamp smoked heavily; its strong fumes choked him. *"Gracias a Dios,"* he confided to the barman, handing him the glass.

The old man who had been sitting on the crate behind them rose and came vaguely toward the bar. "Where did this come from?" said the photographer, laughing apologetically, looking at the full glass in his hand. The frenzied dogs out in the clearing yapped and howled, an exasperating sound. *"Qué tienen esos perros?"* he demanded of the soldier.

The old man had stopped beside them. "Say, Jack, I don't mean to butt in or anything," he began. He was bald, sunburned; he wore a fishnet shirt. The furrows between his ribs showed as parallel shadows, and irregular tufts of gray hair waved out from his chest between the meshes of the shirt. He stretched his lips in a smile, showing naked white gums. The soldier's stance became over-nonchalant; he stared at the newcomer, open hatred suddenly in his eyes, and gently blew the smoke from his cigarette into the old man's face.

"You from Milwaukee? Siddown."

"In a little while, thanks," said the photographer.

"A little while?" the old man echoed incredulously, running his hand over the top of his head. Then he called out in Spanish to the one-legged boy. The photographer was thinking: "This is not going to work out right, at all. It's just not going to work out." He wished the Negro would stop singing and the dogs would stop barking. He looked at the glass in his hand, full of what looked like soapsuds. Someone tapped him on the shoulder. "Say, bud, lemme give you a little advice." The old man again. "There's money in this country if you know where to look. But the guy that finds it is the guy that sticks to his own kind, if you know what I mean." He put his face nearer and lowered his voice. Three skeletal fingers touched the photographer's arm. "You take it from me, from one white man to another. I'm tellin' you!" The three fingers, dark with tobacco stain, lifted themselves, trembled, and dropped back. "These guys all mean trouble from the word go."

The boy, having both gathered up his crutch and managed to rise from where he had been sitting, had now arrived at the bar. "Take a look at this, Jack," the old man said. "Show him," he told the boy in Spanish, and the boy, leaning on his crutch, bent over and rolled up the right leg of his ragged khaki shorts until he had exposed the stump of his amputated leg. It was not far below the groin; the scar tissue had puckered and wrinkled curiously in countless tiny convolutions. "See?" cried the old man. "Two hundred and sixty tons of bananas went over that. Feel it."

"You feel it," said the photographer, wondering how it was possible for him to go on standing and talking exactly as if he were a person like the rest of them. (Could it be that what had happened to him did not show?) He turned his head and looked toward the entrance. The mulatto girl was vomiting just outside. With a cry the barman rushed across and furiously pushed her farther away, out into the clearing. When he came back in he was theatrically holding his nose. "That prostitute ape!" he yelled. "In another minute we'd have had the dogs inside here."

The boy was still looking expectantly at the old man, to see if it was time to lower his trouser leg. "You think he got a centavo from them?" said the old man sadly. "Hah!"

The photographer had begun to suspect that something had gone very wrong inside him. He felt sick, but since he was no longer a living creature he could not conceive it in those terms. He had shut his eyes and put his hand over his face. "It's going around backward," he said. The undrunk *cumbiamba* was in his other hand.

Saying the sentence had made it more true. It was definitely going around backward. The important thing was to remember that he was alone here and that this was a real place with real people in it. He could feel how dangerously easy it would be to go along with the messages given him by his senses, and dismiss the whole thing as a nightmare in the secret belief that when the breaking point came he could somehow manage to escape by waking himself up. A little unsteadily he set his drink down on the counter. An argument which had arisen a while ago between the Indian soldier and his sad companion had now reached its noisy stage, with the companion attempting to drag the soldier away from the bar against his will, and the soldier, his two booted legs firmly apart, breathing rapidly, noisily in his resistance. Suddenly there was a small, shining knife in his right hand, and his face assumed the look of a little boy about to burst into tears. The old man quickly moved around to the photographer's other side. "That guy's bad news in any language," he muttered, gesturing nervously to the boy with the crutch as he bade him move out of the way.

The photographer was saying to himself: "If I can hold out. If I can only hold out." The whole place was slipping away from him, downward and outward; the guitar strummed and the dogs barked, the soldier flashed his knife and pouted, the old American talked about caves with buried emeralds only six days up the Tupurú, the lamp grew redder and more

229

smoke came out of it. He understood nothing except that he must stay there and suffer; to try to escape would be fatal. The soldier's face was very near his own now, breathing black tobacco smoke at him. Languorously, with an insane natural coquetry, he made his long lashes tremble as he asked: "Why have you not offered me a *copita*? All night I have been waiting for you to invite me." The hand holding the knife hung listlessly at his side; the photographer thought of a sleeping baby still clutching its rattle.

"*Sí quieres. . . . Qué tomas?*" he murmured, reflecting that his shoes should be in his hand and were not; then where were they? Someone had brought a large spider monkey into the *cantina* and was forcing it to dance to the guitar's syncopations, making it stand upright by holding its two front paws. With an air of distraught gravity it stepped about, peering this way and that, grimacing nervously at the loud peals of laughter that came from those at the bar watching its antics. The dogs, having noticed its arrival, had rushed to the very entrance of the *cantina*, where they braced themselves to shriek and snap with determined fury.

The soldier's drink had been bought and paid for, but he was not drinking it. He was leaning far back against the bar, reclining on his elbow almost as though he were in bed, his eyes simple black slits, whispering: "You don't like it here. You want to go, *verdad*? But you are afraid to go."

In spite of the constant sliding away, everything had remained just as it was. It would have been better if he could have sat down. "Oh, God," he asked himself. "Am I going to be able to stand this?"

"Why are you afraid to go?" pursued the other tenderly, smiling so that the photographer could admire his small, perfect teeth. The photographer laughed silently, did not reply.

The face of the soldier, ovoid, honey-colored, so near to his, moved now with consummate smoothness into another face, that of a general. ("*Sí, mi general,*" with stiff *bigotes* sprouting from beneath the nostrils, almond eyes, black, deadly with a delicate lust, the uniform svelte, plaited steel riding crop in hand, sharpened spurs shining by the anklebone. "*Bien, mi general.*" Lying on the hot barrack mattress, *tarde tras tarde,* the soldier had dreamed of being the general. Which mountain village had he said he was from? How long had he been talking?)

". . . and that day alone they killed forty-one pigs before my eyes.

There in the corral. *Me bizo algo; no sé. . . ."* His smile was apologetic, intimate; he lowered his eyes imperceptibly, made the effort and raised them again to look at the photographer in such a way that, since they were wider than before, they glistened. "I never forgot it; I don't know why."

Between them the gold-toothed girl came sliding, her hands wriggling over her head, her hips circling, her thin voice shouting: *"Abii! Abii! El fandango de la Guajira."* The soldier must have pushed her, for all at once she slapped him. But it was happening very slowly. How could it take the soldier so long to bring up his knife, and as he raised his hand, how could the stupid girl wait that way before screaming and ducking aside? Even so, the blade caught her only on the arm; she was in the middle of the floor, kneeling on the sand, moaning: "He cut me! Oh God! He cut me!" And because the man who had been dancing with the spider monkey let go of it to get as quickly as all the others to the bar, the beast toddled over to the girl and distractedly wrapped one long hairy arm around her neck. But then the photographer was being roughly jostled, his bare feet were being stepped on as everyone tried to get at the soldier and disarm him. (A demon mask shiny with venom, a voice of barbed wire that rasped: *"Os mato a todos! A todos!"*)

It was exactly nineteen steps from the place where he had stood to the trunk of a small papaya tree in front of the entrance. The tree was not very strong; it swayed slightly as he leaned against it. The dogs were yelping now from inside the *cantina*. Here the air was sweet and almost cool; the faintest glimmer of morning was in the sky and water behind the landing. "I must start to walk," he told himself; it seemed important to believe it. The shouts and screams inside the *cantina* were growing in volume, and people were beginning to call to one another from the doors of their huts. The landing platform was empty—just boards and no railing. Shuffling along with great care because he was not used to going barefoot, he followed what he thought was the path he had taken earlier, through the undergrowth back down to the river's edge, and there was the punt, mud-beached in the mangroves.

It was easy to get in, easy to untie the rope, and easy (for the level of the water had risen considerably since the craft had been left) to pry it loose from the shelf of mud where it rested. But once he was floating among the now nearly visible trunks and branches, bumping against them

231

and being spun to face first the dark chaotic riverbank and then the wide whitening emptiness of open sky and water, he understood dimly that it was not going to be possible to pole his way back to the beach whence he had come, since the tide was still coming in. It was a comforting thought, he decided, because it meant that everything was going ahead instead of backward. A minute later he was floating quietly by the base of the landing: people were running around the clearing. Quickly he lay down flat on the bottom of the punt, and there he stayed, looking straight up at the gray sky, hoping in this way to remain invisible until he had been carried out of sight, beyond Tapiama.

It was going to be one of those stillborn tropical days, when there would be no sun, no wind, no clouds—because the entire sky was enfolded in one vast suffocating blanket of cloud—when nothing at all would happen save that hourly it would grow hotter until an approximate dusk came along. Already the eastern side of the sky was the hot side, arching above the flatness of the swampland. The punt scarcely moved now, the channel having broadened into this wide marshy lake. The photographer lay still and groaned. Little by little the fear that someone might see him gave way to the hope that what current there was would propel the craft in the direction of the shore rather than out toward the wilderness of water and tiny islands; sometimes, even though suffering be implicit in it, contact with others is preferable to the terror of solitude and the unknown. He laid an arm over his eyes to shield them from the corrosive gray light that beat down upon him from the spaces above. The other hand lay in the ashes of last night's fire. And he floated in utter silence on the calm bosom of the lagoon, not stirring as the morning hours moved along, but growing increasingly conscious of the infernal seething of the *cumbiambas* in his brain, a seething which expressed itself as a senseless nightmare imposed from without, in the face of which he could only be totally passive. It was an invisible spectacle whose painful logic he followed with the entire fiber of his being, without, however, once being given a clear vision of what agonizing destinies were at stake.

Some time toward mid-morning the punt grazed a submerged root and was swung into an eddyless pool in the shelter of the vegetation near the shore. Here fierce flies stung him, and from among the leaves high above, a talking bird remarked casually, over and over again: *"Idigaraga. Idigaraga. Idigaraga."*

It was no particular consolation to him, so intent was he on the obscure drama being enacted within him, to hear human voices presently, or to feel the craft seized by the hands of someone splashing in the water alongside. Only when several people had climbed in and crouched chattering around him did he move his arm and squint up at them. Five young men, all of whom looked remarkably alike, surrounded him. Water dripped down upon him from their naked bodies. He shut his eyes again: it was too unlikely a scene. During this time one of them dived overboard, was gone a short while, and returned with a green coconut whose top he had sliced off. He began to let the water dribble into the photographer's face, whereupon the photographer partially sat up and drank the rest of it. In minute he looked around at them again, and said: "Are you brothers?"

"Sí sí," they chorused. This was for some reason a consolation.

"Hermanos," he sighed, sliding down into the ashes again. Then he added desperately, hoping they could still hear him: "Please take me to Rio Martillo."

It had been a brief interlude of clarity. Now they poled the punt back out under the hot sky, letting him lie there and moan as he liked. At one point he felt he must try to explain that he would give them each seventy-five centavos for their trouble, but they giggled and pushed him back down.

"My shoes!" he cried. "There are no shoes," they told him. "Lie still."

"And when we get to the beach," he panted, seizing a brown ankle beside his face, "how will you get me to Rio Martillo?"

"We are not going to any beach," they replied. "We go through the swamp and the canal."

He lay still a while, trying to disassociate himself from the irrational ideas boiling up in his head. "Is this the way to Rio Martillo?" he demanded, thrusting himself up a little and gasping, trying to see beyond the enclosing thicket of brown legs and arms, and feeling a deep unreasoned shame at having once again accepted defeat. They laughed, pushed him gently down to the floor, and went on rhythmically poling the craft eastward. "The factory chimney," they said to one another, pointing into the distance. His mind took him back to the quiet region by the riverbank where the small bird had spoken, high up in the trees, and he heard again the conversational tone. *"Idigaraga,"* he said aloud, imitating perfectly its voice and intonation. There was an explosion of mirth around him. One of the youths took his arm, shook it lightly.

"You know that bird?" he said. "It is a very comic bird. It goes to the nests of other birds and wants to sit there, and when the other birds fight with it and drive it away, it sits down in the same tree there and says: *'Idigaraga.'* That means: *'Iri garagua, nadie me quiere,* nobody likes me.' And it says it over and over, until they make it go farther away so they can't hear it anymore. You said it just right. Say it again."

"Sí, sí," the others agreed, *"otra vez!"*

The photographer had no intention of saying it again. His shame at having accepted defeat already troubled him less. It was hard in his present condition to fit the bird correctly into the pattern, but he knew it had to be done.

When the Compañía Azucarera Riomartillense blew a long blast on its whistle to announce the advent of noon, the sound hovered for an instant over the empty swampland like an invisible trail of smoke. *"Las doce,"* said one of the brothers. A great black and gold dragonfly came skimming across the water and lighted on the photographer's bare foot. After raising and lowering its wings twice, it was again on its crooked course, curving and swooping over the lagoon toward Tapiama.

"Say it again," the brothers begged him.

THE LITTLE HOUSE

The little house had been built sixty or seventy years ago on the main street of what had been a village several miles outside the town; now the town had crept up on all sides. Originally there had been only the ground floor, but at some point an extra room had been added above the kitchen. In clear weather from one window of the upstairs room it was still possible to see the line of distant mountains to the southwest. It was here that Lalla Aïcha liked to sit, running her fingers over the beads of her chaplet while she considered how greatly her life had changed since her son had brought her to the town to stay with him. Somewhere behind the mountains was the valley where she had passed her life. She did not expect to see it again.

At first she had felt that moving to the town was a great triumph for her, but now she was not certain. It was true that the food was better, and there was plenty of it, but the house was very small, and she felt cramped living in it. Privately she was sorry that Sadek had not found a better wife than Fatoma, even though Fatoma's parents owned a large house not far away. It seemed to her that in return for having married their useless daughter, Sadek might have been offered a part of their house to live in. They all could have lived there easily, without getting in each other's way. But when she mentioned it to Sadek, he merely laughed.

The young people had been married for more than a year, and there was no sign of a child, a circumstance which Lalla Aïcha blamed on the girl, unaware that the couple had agreed to start a family only when they had some money set aside for the purpose.

As for Fatoma, she had been nervous and unhappy since the day Lalla Aïcha had moved in with them. The old woman was particular about her

235

food, and found constant fault with Fatoma's method of keeping house. Whatever the girl happened to be doing, Lalla Aïcha would stand watching her closely, then shake her head and say: That's not the way we did it in my day, when Moulay Youssef was alive. She felt that Fatoma was too casual about serving Sadek's dinner to him when he came in from work.

Why should he have to wait half an hour before he can eat? she demanded. Why don't you have everything ready so you can bring in the *taifor* as soon as you hear him come in? He's too good to you, that's the trouble, and you take advantage of his easy nature.

Then Lalla Aïcha would get Sadek aside and tell him how much Fatoma disliked her and how insultingly she treated her. She won't take me out for a walk, and she won't let me go to market with her. I like to get out once in a while, but I can't go by myself. And the other day when she took me to the doctor's, she went so fast I couldn't catch my breath. I know, she wishes I were dead, that's all.

Sadek laughed and said: You're crazy.

Ever since the older woman had moved in with them, Fatoma had been trying to persuade her to discard her haik and wear a djellaba like other women of the town, but Lalla Aïcha disapproved strongly of djellabas on women, saying that Moulay Youssef would surely have forbidden such a shameless custom. For Fatoma the haik was an emblem of rusticity; above all she did not want to be taken for a girl from the country. It filled her with shame to walk in the street beside a tottering old woman in a haik.

Each time she could slip it into the conversation, Fatoma reminded Lalla Aïcha that she had been given the best room in the house. They both knew this was not the case. True, it had more windows and better light than the room where the married couple slept. But it was upstairs, and with each heavy rain the roof sprang new leaks, while Sadek and Fatoma were snug in a room near the kitchen.

Neither of them was sure enough of her position in the household to risk a show of open hostility; each had the fear that Sadek might unaccountably side with the other. Thus they were quiet in his presence, and life in the house continued with relative tranquillity.

For a long time Lalla Aïcha had been aware that a fleshy growth was developing in the middle of her spine, although she had mentioned it to no one. One day as he helped her rise from the floor where she had been sitting, Sadek felt the bulbous object beneath her clothing, and cried out in surprise. It was not an easy matter to persuade her to see a doctor, but Sadek was determined, and eventually had his way. The doctor advised prompt removal of the tumor, and set a date for the operation.

During the days immediately prior to her hospitalization the old woman fretted. She had heard that the anaesthetic was something to be dreaded, she was afraid she might bleed to death, and she made it very clear that she had no faith in Nazarene medicines.

It's all right, Sadek told her. You're going to be fine.

The night before she was to leave, Sadek and Fatoma sat in their room discussing the probable cost of the operation. Lalla Aïcha had gone upstairs and was getting her things together to be packed.

All the money I've saved trying to make cheap meals, Fatoma said with bitterness.

If it were your own mother you wouldn't feel that way, he told her.

She did not answer. There was a knock at the door. Lalla Halima, an elderly woman who lived across the street, had come to call on Lalla Aïcha and bid her good-bye.

She's upstairs, said Fatoma listlessly. Sighing and groaning, the woman mounted the staircase, and Sadek and Fatoma continued their unhappy discussion.

In the morning after Lalla Aïcha had gone to the hospital, and Sadek and Fatoma were having breakfast, Sadek looked around the room. It seems different, having her gone, doesn't it?

It's quiet, said Fatoma.

He turned quickly to her. I know you don't like having her here. I know she makes you nervous. But she's my mother.

Fatoma assumed an injured air. I only said it was quiet, and it is.

That afternoon when Sadek came home from work, Fatoma handed him a large basket. He lifted it. It's heavy, he said.

Take it to your mother in the hospital. It's a *tajine* with lemon, still hot.

It was his mother's favorite dish. By Allah, she's going to be very happy! he said, and he kissed Fatoma, happy that she should have gone to such trouble.

When he got to the hospital the doors were locked. He tapped on the glass. A guard came who told him that visiting hours were over, and that in any case no food from outside could be taken in. Sadek cajoled, pleaded, threatened, but it had no result. The guard shut the door, leaving him on the steps with the basket.

Both he and Fatoma heartily disliked *tajine* with lemon, so that he saw no purpose in carrying it back home. It would be a sin to waste it; someone must eat it while it was hot. Then he thought of Fatoma's parents, who lived just down the street from the hospital. They liked the old-fashioned dishes, and would surely appreciate being brought a fresh *tajine*.

He found Fatoma's mother in the kitchen, greeted her, and took the pot out of the basket. Here's a *tajine* Fatoma just made, he told her.

She burst into smiles. Si Mohammed's going to be very happy when he sees what we're going to eat tonight, she said.

Early the following morning, before Sadek had eaten his breakfast, there was a great banging on the door. The two police officers who stood outside seized him and without allowing him to say good-bye to Fatoma, forced him into a jeep.

His mystification did not last long. At the *comisaría* they confronted him with the basket and the pot, which still had a good amount of the *tajine* in it. He was made to understand that the food was full of poison, and that his mother-in-law was dead. Si Mohammed, who lay in the hospital, had accused him of her murder.

At that point only one thought occupied Sadek's mind: Fatoma had tried to kill his mother. Confused by the lengthy questioning, he muttered aloud some of his inward preoccupations; these scraps caught the attention of the police.

Allah has punished her! She meant to kill mine, and she killed her own.

They soon learned that he was talking about his wife, but placed no credence in his account until the hospital guard had been called in and had verified it. The man remembered Sadek very distinctly, he said, because he had been so annoyingly insistent upon getting the food delivered to his mother.

They sent for Fatoma. She was overcome by the news of her mother's death, and stunned by Sadek's sudden arrest. Her replies were inarticulate beyond her admission that she had given Sadek the basket with the pot of *tajine* in it, and told him to take it to the hospital. She was locked into a cell.

Several weeks passed before the trial was held. Lalla Aïcha had been discharged from the hospital and gone home to find the empty house. She received the bad news about Sadek and Fatoma with no show of emotion, save that she shook her head and murmured: It was written.

She doesn't understand what has happened, they whispered behind her back. It's too much for her, poor thing.

They brought her food each day so she would not have to go to the market. Instead of climbing up to her room to sleep, Lalla Aïcha installed herself downstairs in the matrimonial bedroom, explaining to the neighbors that by the time Sadek and Fatoma came home she would be entirely recovered from her operation, and could then climb the stairs with more ease.

She still doesn't realize, they told one another.

At the trial Fatoma testified that she had given Sadek the basket with the food in it, but that she knew nothing about any poison.

Yet you admit that the *tajine* came from your kitchen.

Of course, said Fatoma. I was there while the old woman was making it. The afternoon before she went to the hospital she put everything together the way she likes her *tajine*. She told me to cook it the next day and have Sadek take it to her in the hospital.

This struck the court as an unlikely tale. It was decided to adjourn and call in Lalla Aïcha at the next session.

The old woman arrived on the witness stand entirely covered in her haik. She was asked to remove it from around her head so they could hear what she was saying. Then they were startled to hear her declare with a note of pride in her voice that indeed she had made the *tajine* with her own hands. Yes, yes, she said. I like to use lots of marinated lemons.

And what else did you put into it? the qadi asked in a deceptively gentle voice.

Lalla Aïcha began the recital of a list of ingredients. Then she stopped and said: Do you want the whole recipe?

Everyone laughed. The qadi called for silence, and fixing her with a baleful stare, said: I see. We have a humorist with us. Sit down. We'll come back to you later.

Lalla Aïcha sat and looked into her lap, murmuring as she told the beads on her chaplet. The qadi glared at her from time to time, incensed by her unconcern. He was waiting for a report from some special police who had been left behind in Sadek's house when Lalla Aïcha had been brought in. It came soon enough. Upstairs in her closet among her clothes they had come across a half-empty container of the same rat killer that had been found in the *tajine*.

The qadi's expression was triumphant when he next called Lalla Aïcha to the stand. In his left hand he held a tin box which he shook in front of her face. Have you ever seen this box? he demanded.

Lalla Aïcha did not hesitate. Of course I've seen it. It belongs to me. That's what I used in the *tajine*.

The sound of whispering moved through the chamber: the spectators had decided that the old woman was feeble-minded. For an instant the qadi's eyes and mouth opened wide. Then he frowned.

Ah, you admit that it was you who put the poison into the *tajine?*

Lalla Aïcha sighed. I asked you if you wanted the recipe, and you didn't. I put half a kilo of lemons in. It covers up the taste of the powder.

Go on, said the qadi, looking fixedly at her.

That was special food for me, she continued, a note of indignation in her voice. Not for anybody else. It was medicine. You don't think I was going to eat it, do you? I wanted to let the poison in the *tajine* draw out the poison in my body.

I don't know what you're talking about, the qadi told her.

You put it into your mouth and spit it out. Then you put more in and spit it out, and keep doing it, and you wash your mouth out with water in between. That's an old medicine from my *tchar*. It gets rid of all the poison.

Don't you know you killed a woman with your nonsense?

Lalla Aïcha shook her head. No, no. It was written, that's all.

From another part of the chamber came Fatoma's shrill voice: Lies! It's not true! She knew they weren't going to let the food in! She knew before she went to the hospital!

Fatoma was silenced. The qadi, nevertheless, made a note, and the following day when she was called to the witness stand, he asked her to elaborate. As a result of Fatoma's tale, they next called in Lalla Halima, the neighbor from across the street. She too had to be asked to loosen her haik, which she did with visible distaste.

Two, maybe three days before Lalla Aïcha was going to leave for the hospital, I went to see her. I wanted to be good to her, so I said: I'm going to have my daughter make some *cabrozel*s and maybe some *mrozeiya,* and take them around to you in the hospital. She said: That's very kind of you, but it's no use. They have a new law, so the doctor told me, and they don't let anything in from the outside. So I had my daughter make some *cabrozel*s anyway, and I took them to her myself the night before she went. I thought maybe she could wrap her clothes around them and put them into her bag, and they wouldn't see them.

That's all, said the qadi, making a gesture of dismissal. His eyes glittered as he said to Lalla Aïcha: And now what are you going to tell me?

I've told you everything, she said calmly. I was very busy trying to get my medicine made, and I forgot they wouldn't let it in. I'm an old woman. It went out of my head.

There was a commotion in one corner of the hall as Fatoma screamed: She didn't forget! She knew Sadek would leave it at my mother's!

Fatoma was hustled out of the court, still shouting and struggling. Lalla Aïcha stood quietly, waiting to be addressed. The qadi merely looked at her, an expression of doubt on his face.

Finally he said with exasperation: You're a stupid, ignorant woman. Who ever heard of poison in the mouth absorbing poison in the blood? Do you think anyone believes that nonsense?

Lalla Aïcha was unmoved. Yes, she said patiently. Everybody knows that Nazarene medicine works better if you take Moslem medicine at the same time. The power of Allah is very great.

In despair the qadi dismissed the case and sent the three defendants home, after warning Sadek that he would be held responsible for any further trouble caused by his mother, since she was clearly not responsible for her actions.

That night, when Lalla Aïcha was asleep in her room upstairs, Fatoma presented Sadek with an ultimatum. Either he sent his mother away, or she would leave him and go to live with her father.

She killed my mother. I won't stay in the house with her.

Sadek was wise enough to accept this; he offered no objection. In the light of what she had done, he himself had come to the conclusion that it would be better to take his mother back to the country to live with the rest of her family.

She received the news quietly; indeed, she seemed to have been expecting it. In the hope of persuading her that he was not being arbitrary, was not merely getting rid of her, he added: You see what your foolishness has done.

Then she faced him and looked into his eyes. You have no right to blame me for anything, she told him. It's not my fault if you're still living in this little house.

At the time the remark meant nothing to him; it was merely a senile non sequitur. Later, when he had returned from the *tchar* in the valley and was living quietly with Fatoma, he recalled it. After that, he often thought about it.

HERE TO LEARN

I

Malika needed no one to tell her she was pretty. From the beginning of her memory people had murmured about her beauty, for even when she was a baby girl the symmetry of her head, neck and shoulders was remarkable. Before she was old enough to go to the spring to fetch water she knew she had eyes like a gazelle and that her head was like a lily on its stalk. At least, these were the things older people said about her.

On a hill above the town stood a large building with palm-shaded walks leading up to it. This belonged to the Hermanas Adoratrices. Certain of these nuns, upon catching sight of Malika, had gone to her father, offering to take her in charge and teach her to speak Spanish and to embroider. Enthusiastically he had agreed. Allah has sent us here to learn, he would say. Malika's mother, who disapproved of her daughter's spending her time with Nazarenes, did her utmost to make him change his mind. Nevertheless Malika stayed with the sisters for five years, until her father died.

Malika's grandmother was fond of saying that when she had been Malika's age she had looked exactly like her, and that if it were possible for her to become a little girl again and stand beside Malika, no one would be able to tell them apart. At first Malika found this impossible to believe; she studied the old woman's ravaged face and straightway rejected the idea. After her grandmother had died, she began to understand what the old woman had meant when she said: Only Allah remains the same. One day she would no longer be pretty, but now she was. Thus, when she was able to go by herself to the spring and carry back two full

243

pails of water, it meant nothing to her if the older boys and the young men called to her and tried to speak with her. They would do better, she thought, to say all those flattering things to girls who needed such reassurance.

A barracks full of soldiers stood just outside the town. The men were rough and brutal. When she caught sight of one of them, even in the distance, Malika would hide until he had disappeared. Fortunately the soldiers seldom strayed into the arroyo that lay between her house and the spring; they preferred to saunter in groups up and down the main road leading through the town.

There came a day when her mother insisted that she go to sell a hen at the market on the main highway. Her older sister always had done this, but she was at a neighbor's house helping prepare for a wedding. Malika begged her mother to lend her her haik so she could cover her face.

Your sister's been a thousand times. She never wears a haik.

Malika knew this was because no one paid any attention to her sister, but she could not say it to her mother. I'm afraid, she said, and burst into tears. Her mother had no patience with the silly behavior of girls, and refused to let her take the haik. As Malika ran out of the house, holding the hen by its legs, she snatched up a soiled bath towel. As soon as she was out of sight, she wrapped it loosely around her head, so that when she got to the highway she could pull it down and cover at least a part of her face.

Several dozen women lined one side of the road, each sitting on the ground with her wares spread out around her. Malika went to the end of the row, which was opposite a small park where the soldiers sat on benches. People wandered past and picked up the hen to squeeze it and shake it, so that it constantly squawked and fluttered. She had pulled the towel down so far over her eyes that she could see only the earth at her feet.

After an hour or so had gone by, a woman came along who began to discuss the price of the hen with her. Eventually she bought it, and Malika, once she had tied the coins up in a piece of cloth, jumped to her feet. The towel slipped over her face and fell to the ground. She picked it up and started to hurry along the highway.

II

The town was derelict; it smelled of the poverty in which its people were accustomed to live. Nor was there any indication that in some past era something more had existed. The wind from the sea raised the dust of the streets high into the air and showered it angrily over the countryside. Even the leaves of the fig trees were coated white. The hot sand flying stung the skin on the backs of her legs as she turned the corner of the side street that led to the lower end of the gully. She draped the towel over her head and held onto it with one hand. It had never occurred to her to hate the town, for she assumed that anywhere else would be more or less the same.

The street was scarcely more than an alley, with walls on either side. All at once she heard the sound of heavy boots pounding the earth behind her. She did not turn around. Then a hard hand seized her arm and pushed her roughly against the wall. It was a soldier, and he was smiling. He braced his arms against the wall on each side of her so she could not escape.

Malika said nothing. The man stood gazing at her. He was breathing deeply, as though he had been running. Finally he said: How old are you?

She looked directly into his eyes. Fifteen.

He smelt of wine, tobacco and sweat.

Let me go, she said, and she tried desperately to duck under the barricade. The pain she felt as he twisted her arm made her open her eyes very wide, but she did not cry out. Two men in djellabas were approaching from the direction of the gully, and she fixed her eyes on them. The soldier turned, saw them, and began to walk quickly back toward the highway.

When she got home, she tossed the bit of cloth with the money in it onto the *taifor,* and indignantly showed her mother the marks on her arm.

What's that?

A soldier grabbed me.

Her mother dealt her a stinging blow across the face. Malika had never seen her in such a rage.

You young bitch! she screamed. That's all you're good for!

Malika ran out of the house and down into the gully, where she sat on a rock in the shade, wondering if her mother might be going mad.

245

The unexpectedness and injustice of the sudden blow had removed all thought of the soldier from her mind. She felt that she must find an explanation of her mother's behavior; otherwise she would hate her.

That night at dinner things were not much better; her mother would not look at her, and directed all her remarks to her other daughter. This proved to be the pattern for the days that followed. It was as if she had decided that Malika no longer existed.

Good, thought Malika. If I'm not here, then she's not here. She's not my mother and I do hate her.

This silent war between them did not mean that Malika was exempt from having to continue to go to the market. Nearly every week she would be sent off to sell a hen or a basket of vegetables and eggs. She had no further trouble with the soldiers, perhaps because she now stopped on her way down the gully each time and smeared a little mud over her face. It was always dry by the time she reached the highway, and although the women there sometimes stared at her with surprise, the men paid her no attention. On her way home, going up the gully, she would wash her face.

There was always suspicion in her mother's glance now when she returned to the house. If you get into trouble, she said, I swear I'll kill you with my own hands. Malika sniffed and left the room. She knew what her mother meant, but it astonished her to see how little she knew about her own daughter.

III

One day as Malika sat in the front row of women and girls in the market on the highway, a long yellow car without a top drove up silently and stopped. There was only one man in it, and he was a Nazarene. The women began to murmur and cry out, for the man held a camera in his hands and was pointing it at them. A girl sitting next to Malika turned to her and said: You speak Spanish. Tell him to go away.

Malika ran over to the car. The man lowered his camera and stared at her.

Señor, you musn't take pictures here, she said, looking at him gravely. She pointed back at the row of indignant women.

The Nazarene was big, with light-colored hair. He understood and smiled. *Muy bien, muy bien,* he said good-naturedly, still looking fixedly at her. She was suddenly conscious of the dirt on her face. Without thinking she rubbed her cheek with the back of her hand. The man's smile became broader.

Will you let me take your picture?

Malika's heart began to beat painfully. No! No! she cried, aghast. Then by way of explanation she added: I have to go and sell my eggs.

The Nazarene looked more pleased than ever. You have eggs for sale? Bring them over.

Malika went and fetched the little packet of eggs, tied in a cloth. A group of boys had caught sight of the dazzling yellow car, and now they surrounded it, demanding money. The Nazarene, trying to wave them away, opened the door for Malika and pointed to the empty seat. She laid the bundle on the leather cushion and bent to undo the knot, but the arms of the boys kept pushing in front of her and jostling her. The Nazarene shouted angrily at the urchins in a foreign language, but this deterred them only for an instant. Finally, in a rage, he said to Malika: Get in. She lifted the eggs and obeyed, seating herself with the bundle on her lap. The man reached in front of her and slammed the door shut. Then he raised the window. But two beggars now had joined the boys, and they were able to reach over the top of the window.

Without warning the Nazarene started up the motor with a great roar. The car shot forward. Startled, Malika turned to see some of the boys sprawling in the road. When she looked again, they were almost out of the town. The Nazarene still seemed to be very angry. She decided not to ask him how far he was going before he stopped and bought the eggs. Her emotions hovered between delight at being in the fine car and anxiety about walking back to the town.

The trees were going by very fast. It seemed to her that she had always known something strange like this would happen to her one day. It was a comforting thought, and it kept her from feeling actual fear.

IV

Soon they turned onto a dirt road that burrowed deep into a eucalyptus grove. Here in the dubious shade the Nazarene shut off the motor and turned to Malika with a smile. He took the bundle of eggs from her lap and put it into the back of the car. From a basket behind her seat he brought out a bottle of mineral water and a napkin. He poured a little water onto the napkin and with one hand on her shoulder set to work wiping the streaks of mud from her cheeks. She let him rub, and she let him remove the towel wrapped around her head, so that her hair fell to her shoulders. Why shouldn't he see me? she thought. He's a good man. She had already noticed that he did not smell at all, and his gentleness with her gave her a pleasant sensation.

Now shall I take your picture?

She nodded. There was no one to witness the shameful act. He made her sit lower in the seat, and held the camera above her. It clicked so many times, and he looked so peculiar with the big black apparatus in front of his face, that she began to laugh. She thought he might stop then, but he seemed even more pleased, and went on clicking the camera until it would click no more. Then he spread a blanket on the ground and set a basket of food in the center of it. They sat with the basket between them and ate chicken, cheese and olives. Malika was hungry, and she thought this great fun.

When they had finished, he asked her if she wanted him to take her back to the market. It was as if darkness had fallen over the world. She thought of the women there, and of what they would say when they saw her. She shook her head vigorously. The present moment was real; she would not help it to end. No, not yet, she said lightly.

He looked at his watch. Shall we go to Tétouan?

Her eyes brightened. It was less than an hour's ride from her town, but she had only heard about it. The trees sped by again. Here a stiff breeze blew in from the Mediterranean, and Malika was chilly. The man took out a soft camel's hair cape and put it around her shoulders.

Tétouan was very exciting with all its traffic. The guards in scarlet and white stood at attention in front of the Khalifa's palace. But she would not get out of the car and walk with him in the street. They were parked there in the Feddane, where the hot afternoon sun beat down on them.

Finally the man shrugged and said: Well, if I'm going to get to Tangier tonight, I'd better take you back home.

Malika made a strange sound. She seemed to have become very small inside the cape.

What's the matter?

I can't!

The man stared at her. But you've got to go back home.

Malika began to wail. No, no! she cried. The man glanced nervously at the passersby, and tried to comfort her with words. But a possibility had just revealed itself to her, and at that moment the idea was powerful enough to occupy her totally. Seeing her too immersed in inner turmoil even to hear him, he started the car and slowly made his way through the throng of people to the other side of the plaza. Then he drove along the principal street to the outskirts of the city, stopped the car by the side of the road, and lighted a cigarette.

He turned to her. One would almost have said that on the seat beside him there was nothing but the cape. He tugged at it, and heard a sob. Gently slipping his hand inside, he smoothed her hair for a moment. Finally she began to push herself upward into a sitting position, and her head appeared.

I'm going to take you with me to Tangier, he said. She made no reply to this, nor did she look at him.

They sped westward, the late afternoon sun in front of them. Malika was conscious of having made an irrevocable choice. The results, already determined by destiny, would be disclosed to her one by one, in the course of events. It was only slowly that she became aware of the landscape around her and of the summer air rushing past.

They came to a tiny café, alone on the mountainside, and stopped. Come in and we'll have some tea, he said. Malika shook her head, pulling the cape more tightly around her.

The man went inside and ordered two glasses of tea. A quarter of an hour later a boy carried them to the car on a tray. The tea was very hot, and it took them a while to drink it. Even when the boy had come and taken away the tray, they went on sitting there. Eventually the man switched on the headlights, and they started down the mountainside.

V

Malika was frightened by the elevator, but she relaxed somewhat when the man had shown her into the apartment and shut the door behind them. There were thick rugs and soft couches piled with pillows, and lights that could be turned on and off by pushing a button. Most important of all, the Nazarene lived there by himself.

That night he showed her to a room, telling her it was to be hers. Before he said good-night he took her head in his hands and kissed her on the forehead. When he had gone she wandered into the bathroom and amused herself for a long time turning the hot and cold taps on and off, to see if sooner or later one of them would make a mistake. Finally she undressed, put on the muslin gandoura the man had left for her, and got into the bed.

A pile of magazines lay on the table beside her, and she began to look at the pictures. There was one photograph which caught her attention and held it. The picture showed a luxurious room, with a beautiful woman lying back in a chaise longue. A wide collar of diamonds flashed from her neck, and in her hand she held a book. The book was open but she was not looking at it. Her head was raised, as though someone had just come into the room and found her reading. Malika studied the photograph, glanced at others, and returned to it. To her it illustrated the perfect pose to adopt when receiving guests, and she resolved to practice it by herself, so that when the time came she could put it to use. It would be a good idea to be able to read, too, she thought. One day she would ask the man to show her how.

They had breakfast on the terrace in the morning sun. The building overlooked a spacious Moslem cemetery. Beyond it was the water. Malika told him it was not good to live so near to a graveyard. Later, she looked over the railing, saw the elaborate domed mausoleum of Sidi Bou Araqia, and nodded her head in approval. As they sat over their coffee, he answered more of her questions. His name was Tim, he was twenty-eight years old, but he had no wife and no children. He did not live in Tangier all the time. Sometimes he was in Cairo and sometimes in London. In each of these places he had a small flat, but he kept his car in Tangier because that was where he came when he was not working.

As they sat there Malika heard sounds inside the apartment. Presently a fat black woman in a yellow *zigdoun* came onto the terrace. *Bonjour,* she said, and she began to carry out the dishes. Each time she appeared Malika sat very straight, looking fixedly out across the water at the mountains in Spain.

Someone would be coming in a little while, Tim said, an Italian woman who was going to take her measurements and make some clothes for her.

Malika frowned. What kind of clothes?

When he said: Whatever you want, she jumped up and went to her room, returning with a copy of *The New Yorker,* which she opened at a page showing a girl in a knit sports suit standing by a set of matched luggage. Like this one, she said. An hour or so later the Italian woman came in, very businesslike, tickled Malika with her tape measure for a while, and left, notebook in hand.

VI

Late that afternoon when the black woman had gone, Tim took Malika into her bedroom, pulled the curtains across the windows, and very gently gave her her first lesson in love. Malika did not really want this to happen then, but she had always known it would sooner or later. The slight pain was negligible, but the shame of being naked in front of the man was almost more than she could bear. It never had occurred to her that a body could be considered beautiful, and she did not believe him when he told her she was perfect in every part. She knew only that men used women in order to make children, and this preoccupied her, as she had no desire for a child. The man assured her that he was not hoping for children either, and that if she did as he told her there was no danger of having any. She accepted this as she accepted everything else he said. She was there in order to learn, and she intended to learn as much as possible.

When, during the next few weeks, she finally consented to go with him to the houses of his friends, he did not guess that she agreed to appear in public only because she had studied herself in the new clothes, and had found them sufficiently convincing to act as a disguise. The European garments made it possible for her to go into the streets with a Nazarene and not be reviled by other Moroccans.

251

After taking Malika to a photographer's studio and making several lengthy visits to the authorities, Tim returned triumphant one day, waving a passport at her. This is yours, he said. Don't lose it.

Nearly every day there were parties on the Mountain or picnics on the beach. Malika particularly loved the night picnics around a fire, with the sound of the waves breaking on the sand. Sometimes there were musicians, and everyone danced barefoot. One evening eight or ten of the guests jumped up and ran shouting toward the breakers to swim naked in the moonlight. Since the moon was very bright, and there were men and women together, Malika gasped and hid her face. Tim thought this amusing, but the incident caused her to question the fitness of the people in Tangier to be her models for the elegance she hoped to attain.

One morning Tim greeted her with a sad face. In a few days, he told her, he had to go to London. Seeing her expression of chagrin, he quickly added that in two weeks he would be back, and that she would go on living in the flat just as though he were there.

But how can I? she cried. You won't be here! I'll be all alone.

No, no. You'll have friends. You'll like them.

That evening he brought two young men to the apartment. They were handsome and well-dressed, and very talkative. When Malika heard Tim address one of them as Bobby, she burst into laughter.

Only dogs are called Bobby, she explained. It's not a man's name.

She's priceless, said Bobby. A teenage Nefertiti.

Absolute heaven, agreed his friend Peter.

After they had gone, Tim explained that they were going to keep Malika company while he was in England. They would live in the apartment with her. On hearing this, she was silent for a moment.

I want to go with you, she said, as if anything else were inconceivable.

He shook his head. *Ni hablar.*

But I don't want love with them.

He kissed her. They don't make love with girls. That's why I asked them. They'll take good care of you.

Ah, she said, partially reassured, and at the same time thinking how clever Tim was to have been able to find two such presentable eunuchs with so little apparent effort.

As Tim had promised, Bobby and Peter kept her amused. Instead of taking her out to parties they invited their friends in to meet her. Soon she realized that there were a good many more eunuchs in Tangier than she had suspected. Since, according to Bobby and Peter, these tea parties and cocktail hours were given expressly for Malika, she insisted on knowing exactly when the guests would be coming, so she could receive them in the correct position, lying back on the cushions of the divan with a book in her hand. When the new arrivals were shown in, she would raise her head slowly until its noble proportions were fully evident, fix her gaze on a point far behind anything in the room, and let the beginning of a smile tremble briefly on her lips before it vanished.

She could see that this impressed them. They told her they loved her. They played games and danced with each other and with her. They tickled her, nuzzled her, took her on their laps and fussed with her hair. She found them more fun to be with than Tim's friends, even though she was aware that the things they said had no meaning. To them everything was a game; there was nothing to learn from them.

VII

Tim had been gone for more than a week when they first brought Tony to the flat. He was a tall, noisy Irishman for whom the others of the group seemed to have a certain respect. At first Malika assumed that this was because he was not a eunuch like them, but quickly she discovered that it was only because he had far more money to spend than they did. Tony's clothing always smelled delicious, and his car, a green Maserati, attracted even more attention than Tim's. One day he came by at noon, while Bobby and Peter were still at the market. The black woman had received orders from Bobby to let no one in under any circumstances, but Tony was an expert in getting around such things. Malika had been playing a record of Abdelwahab's; now she quickly silenced it and gave all her attention to Tony. In the course of their dialogue, he remarked casually that her clothes were pretty. Malika smoothed her skirt.

But I'd like to see you in some other clothes, he went on.

Where are they?

Not here. In Madrid.

They heard the door slam, and knew that Bobby and Peter had returned. The two had quarreled and were communicating only in acid monosyllables. Malika saw that the game of dominoes they had promised to play with her when they got back would not take place. She sat and sulked for a while, turning the pages of one of Tim's financial magazines. Eunuchs were extremely childish, she reflected.

Bobby came into the room and stood at the other end, arranging books on the bookshelves in silence. Soon the black woman appeared in the doorway and announced to him in French that Monsieur Tim had telephoned from London and would not be in Tangier until the eighteenth.

When Tony had translated the information into Spanish, Malika merely sat staring at him, an expression of despair on her face.

Bobby hurried out of the room. Ill at ease, Tony stood up and followed him. A moment later Bobby's sharp voice cried: No, she can't go out to eat with you. She can't go out at all, anywhere, unless we go along. One of Tim's rules. If you want to eat here, you can.

Very little was said at lunch. In the middle of the meal Peter flung down his napkin and left the room. Afterward the black woman served coffee on the terrace. Bobby and Peter were arguing farther back in the flat, but their shrill voices were strangely audible.

For a while Malika sipped her coffee and said nothing. When she spoke to Tony, it was as if there had been no interruption to their earlier conversation. Can we go to Madrid? she said.

You'd like that? He grinned. But you see how they are. And he pointed behind him.

A mí me da igual cómo son. I only promised to stay with them for two weeks.

The next morning, while Bobby and Peter were at the market buying food, Tony and Malika put some valises into the Maserati and drove to the port to catch the ferry to Spain. Tony had left a short note for Bobby, saying that he had borrowed Malika for a few days, and would see to it that she telephoned.

VIII

They slept in Córdoba the first night. Before setting out for Madrid in the morning, Tony stopped at the cathedral to show it to her. When they walked up to the door, Malika hesitated. She peered inside and saw an endless corridor of arches extending into the gloom.

Go on in, said Tony.

She shook her head. You go. I'll wait here.

Driving out of the city, he scolded her a bit. You should look at things when you have the chance, he told her. That was a famous mosque.

I saw it, she said firmly.

The first day in Madrid they spent at Balenciaga's, morning and afternoon. You were right, Malika said to Tony when they were back in the hotel. The clothes here are much better.

They had to wait several days for the first items to be ready. The Prado was almost next door to the hotel, but Tony decided against making the attempt to entice Malika into it. He suggested a bullfight.

Only Moslems know how to kill animals, she declared.

They had been in Madrid for more than a week. One evening as they sat in the bar downstairs at the Ritz, Tony turned to her and said: Have you called Tangier? No, you haven't. Come.

Malika did not want to think of Tangier. Sighing, she rose and went with Tony up to his room, where he put in the call.

When finally he heard Bobby at the other end of the wire, he gestured and handed the telephone to Malika.

At the sound of her voice, Bobby immediately began to reproach her. She interrupted him to ask for Tim.

Tim can't get back to Tangier quite yet, he said, and the pitch of his voice rose as he added: But he wants *you* to come back right now!

Malika was silent.

Did you hear what I said? yelled Bobby. *Oíste?*

Yes, I heard. I'll let you know. She hung up quickly so as not to hear the sounds of outraged protest at the other end.

They went several more times to Balenciaga for fittings. Malika was impressed by Madrid, but she missed the comforting presence of Tim, particularly at night when she lay alone in her bed. While it was pleasant to be with Tony because he paid so much attention to her and constantly bought her gifts, she knew he did this only because he enjoyed dressing her the way he wanted her to look when they went out together, and not because he cared about her.

Although the deliveries continued to be made, and the gowns and ensembles were perfect, Malika's pleasure was somewhat lessened by her discovery that the only places where people really looked at what she was wearing were two restaurants and the bar downstairs. When she remarked about this to Tony, he laughed.

Ah! What you want is Paris. I can see that.

Malika brightened. Can we go there?

When the last garment had arrived, Tony and Malika ate a final dinner at Horcher, and started early the next morning for Paris. They spent the night in Biarritz, where the streets were rainswept and empty.

IX

Paris was far too big. She was frightened of it even before they arrived at the hotel, and she determined not to let Tony out of her sight unless she was safe in her room. At the Hôtel de la Trémoaille she watched him lying back on his bed, making one telephone call after the other while he joked, shouted, waved his legs, and screamed with laughter. When he was through telephoning he turned to her.

Tomorrow night I'm going to take you to a party, he said. And I know just what you'll wear. The oyster-colored satin number.

Malika was excited by the sumptuous house and the guests in evening clothes. Here at last, she was certain, she had reached a place where the people were of the ultimate degree of refinement. When she found that they looked at her with approval, she was filled with a sense of triumph.

Soon Tony led her up to a tall, pretty girl with flashing black eyes. This is my sister Dinah, he announced. She speaks better Spanish than I do.

Indicating Malika, he added: And this is the new Antinea. He left the two together and disappeared into another room.

Dinah's manner with her made her feel that they had been friends for a long time. When they had chatted for a few minutes, she led her over to a group of South Americans. The women were covered with jewels and some of them carried the pelts of animals over their shoulders. Even the men wore huge diamonds on their fingers. Malika suspected that Tim would disapprove of these people, but then it occurred to her that perhaps he could not be relied upon as an arbiter of taste in a city like this.

Paris es muy grande, she said to a man who smiled at her invitingly. I never saw it until yesterday. I'm afraid to go out. Why did they make it so big?

The man, smiling more broadly, said he was at her service, and would be delighted to go with her wherever she wished, whenever it suited her.

Oh, she said, looking pensive. That would be nice.

Mañana?

Somehow Dinah had caught the end of their dialogue. Not tomorrow, I'm afraid, she said briskly, taking Malika's arm. As she led her away she whispered furiously: His wife was standing there watching you.

Malika stole a frightened glance over her shoulder. The man was still smiling after her.

During the next few days Dinah, who lived nearby in the Avenue Montaigne, came regularly to the hotel. She and Tony had long discussions while Malika listened to Radio Cairo. One afternoon when Tony had gone out and Malika was bored, she asked Dinah to put in a call to Bobby in Tangier. A half hour later the telephone rang, and she heard Bobby's voice.

Hola, Bobby!

Malika! His voice was already shrill. You can't do this to me! Why are you in Paris? You've got to come back to Tangier.

Malika was silent.

We're waiting for you. What will Tim say if you're not here?

Tim! she said with scorn. Where is Tim?

He's coming back next week. I want to speak to Tony.

Tony's gone out.

Listen to me! Bobby shouted. What hotel are you in?

I don't know its name, she said. It's in Paris. It's a nice hotel. *Adiós.*

One morning not long afterward Tony announced abruptly that he was leaving for London in an hour. Dinah came in shortly before he set out. They seemed to be involved in a dispute, which ended only when he kissed each of them good-bye. After he had gone, Malika nodded her head sagely. London, she mused. He won't come back.

X

The day after Malika moved into Dinah's flat the weather turned rainy and cold. Dinah often went out, leaving her alone with the housemaid and cook. She was just as glad to stay indoors where it was warm. Her wardrobe, impressive as it was, failed to include any kind of covering for cold weather. Dinah had told her that the cold was just beginning, and that it would not be warm again for many months. It seemed to Malika that somewhere in Paris there must be a *joteya,* where she could take two or three evening gowns and exchange them for a coat, but Dinah shook her head when she asked her about it.

The apartment was spacious, and there were plenty of magazines to study. Malika spent her time curled up on a divan, examining the details in the fashion photographs.

Tony called from London, postponing his return for a few days. When Dinah gave her the news, Malika smiled and said: *Claro.*

I'm having lunch today with a friend. She has mountains of clothes, said Dinah. I'll see if I can't get a coat for you.

What she brought back that afternoon was a mink coat badly in need of repairs. Malika gazed at the rips with visible distaste.

You haven't any idea of how lucky you are, Dinah told her. She shrugged.

When the garment had been fitted at the furrier's and the skins resewn, it looked completely new, as if it had just been made for Malika. She ran her fingers over its glistening surface and examined herself in the mirror, and quickly decided that it was a very fine coat after all.

Dinah's friend came to lunch. Her name was Daphne. She was not very pretty and she tried to speak Italian with Malika. During the course of the meal she invited them both to a house party at Cortina d'Ampezzo.

Dinah was enthusiastic. She brought out an album of photographs after Daphne had left, and spread it in Malika's lap. Malika saw that the ground was white and the people, whose clothing was not at all elegant, wore long boards on their feet. She was doubtful, but the strange white landscape and the groups of festive people intrigued her. It might be more interesting than Paris, which in the end had turned out to be rather dull.

They went to the office to book plane passage. Have you any money at all? Dinah asked her as they waited.

Malika was suddenly very much ashamed. Tony never gave me any. It's all right, Dinah told her.

Before they left there was a lively argument between them as to whether Malika should take all her valises with her on the plane to Milano.

But you won't need all those clothes there, Dinah objected. And besides, it would cost so much.

I have to take everything, Malika said.

All of her belongings went with them on the plane. They had bad weather on the way to Milano, where Daphne's car met them. She was already in Cortina.

Malika had not enjoyed the plane ride. She did not understand why people with cars took planes. There was nothing to see but clouds, and the rocking of the plane made some of the passengers sick, so that by the end of the flight everyone seemed to be nervous and unhappy. For a while as they sped along the autostrada Malika thought she was back in Spain.

According to the driver, there were already so many friends staying at Daphne's chalet that no place was left for them. Daphne was putting them up in a hotel. Dinah received this news in silence; presumably she was displeased. Malika, when she understood the situation, secretly rejoiced. There would be many more people in the hotel than in the house.

XI

It was cold in Cortina. At first Malika would not go out of the hotel. The air is like poison, she complained. Then she began to experiment a bit, finally discovering that it was an agreeable kind of cold.

She would sit with the others on the terrace of the hotel in the brilliant sunshine, wearing her warm coat, sipping hot chocolate while they had their cocktails. The red-cheeked jollity of the people around her was a new experience, and the snow never ceased to fascinate her. Each morning when Daphne and her guests came to fetch Dinah, Malika would watch the noisy group rush out toward the ski fields. Then she would wander through the public rooms. The employees were polite, and often smiled at her. There was a shop in the hotel that sold skis and the clothes that had to be worn when using them. The window displays were changed daily, so that Malika was often to be seen standing outside the door, inspecting the merchandise through the glass.

Twice a tall young man had sauntered up to the shop windows as she stood there, giving the impression that he was about to speak to her. Both times she had turned away and resumed her aimless meandering. Tony and Dinah had warned her repeatedly against entering into conversation with strangers, and she thought it better to observe the etiquette they considered so important. She had discovered that Otto the barman spoke Spanish, and in the morning when the bar was often empty she would go in and talk with him. One morning he asked her why she never went out to ski with her friends.

I can't, she said in a muffled voice.

At that moment, in the mirror behind the bar, she saw the tall young man come into the room and remain standing by the door, as if he were listening to their conversation. She hoped Otto would not continue it, but he did. That's no reason, he said. Take lessons. There are plenty of good skiing professors in Cortina.

Malika shook her head slowly several times.

The young man stepped to the bar, saying, in Spanish: He's right, our friend Otto. That's what Cortina's for. Everybody skis here.

Now he leaned on the bar and faced Malika. I spend a lot of time south of the border myself, he said as though in confidence. I have a little hacienda down in Durango.

Malika stared at him. He was speaking in Spanish, but she had no idea of what he was talking about. He misunderstood her expression and frowned. What's the matter. Don't you like Durango?

She looked at Otto and back at the tall young man. Then she burst into laughter, and the sound filled the bar agreeably. The tall young man's face seemed to melt as he heard it.

She slid down from the bar stool, smiled at him, and said: I don't understand. *Hasta luego,* Otto. While the young man was still making a visible effort to collect his thoughts, she turned and walked out of the bar.

This marked the beginning of a new friendship, one which grew to substantial proportions later that same day. At the end of the afternoon Malika and the young man, who said his name was Tex, went for a walk along the road outside the hotel, where the snow had been packed down. The peaks of the mountains around them were turning pink. She sniffed the air with enthusiasm.

I like it here, she said, as though the subject had been under discussion.

You'd like it more if you learned to ski, he told her.

No, no!

She hesitated, then went on quickly: I can't pay for lessons. I haven't any money. They don't give me any.

Who's they?

She walked on beside him without answering, and he took her arm. By the time they got back to the hotel she had agreed to let Tex pay for lessons, skis and clothes, on condition that the clothes be bought at a shop in the town and not at the hotel.

Once she had been fitted out, the lessons were begun, Tex being always present. Dinah did not like the idea at all. She said it was unheard of, and she asked Malika to point Tex out to her.

Malika, who had felt no resentment at being left each day to her own devices, could not understand Dinah's objections. She was delighted with her new friend, and arranged for Dinah to meet him in the bar, where she sat for a half hour listening to them speak in English. Later that night Dinah told her Tex was uncivilized. Malika did not understand.

He's an idiot! Dinah cried.

Malika laughed, for she took this to mean that Dinah also liked him. He has a good heart, she replied calmly.

Yes, yes. You'll see that good heart soon enough, Dinah told her with a crooked smile.

Having observed that Tex's interest in her was due in part to the mystery with which she seemed to be surrounded, Malika offered him as little information about herself as possible. He was still under the impression that she was Mexican and a member of Dinah's family, and that for one reason or another Dinah was in charge of her. His misconception amused Malika, and she did nothing to correct it. She knew Dinah and Daphne were persuaded that she and Tex were having an affair, and this pleased her, too, since it was not true.

Sometimes, in spite of Malika's efforts to restrain him, Tex drank too much whiskey. This generally happened in the bar after dinner. At such moments his face often took on an expression that made her think of a fish dragged up onto the beach. His eyes bulging, his jaw slack, he would take one of her hands in both of his, and groan: Oh, Honey! To Malika this was an expression of momentary despair. She would sigh and shake her head, and try to comfort him by saying that he would feel better in a little while.

The lessons were going very well; Malika spent most of the daylight hours on the snow with Tex. She would have eaten at his table, too, if Dinah had not indignantly forbidden it.

One day at lunch Dinah lit a cigarette and said: You're going to have your last skiing lesson tomorrow. We're leaving for Paris on Thursday.

Malika saw that she was watching her closely to observe the effect of her announcement. She decided to look slightly crestfallen, but not enough to give Dinah any satisfaction.

It's been a marvelous holiday, Dinah went on, and we've all had a fine time, but now it's over.

Así es la vida, murmured Malika with lowered head.

XII

That afternoon when the lesson was over, Malika and Tex sat side by side in the snow, looking out across the valley in the fading light. All at once she found that she was sobbing. Tex stared at her in consternation, then drew her to him, trying to comfort her. Through her sobs, she repeated what Dinah had told her at lunch.

When she felt his arms around her, she knew that the only reason for her unhappiness was that she did not want to leave him. She leaned her head on his chest and sobbed: *Me quiero quedar contigo, Tex, contigo.*

These words transformed him. He began to glow. While he soothed her with gestures, he told her he would do anything in the world for her. If she wanted him to, he would take her away that very night. She stopped weeping and listened.

Before they rose from the snowbank, they had agreed upon the following morning for their departure, while Dinah would be out skiing. Tex was determined to have no further meeting with Dinah, but Malika made him leave a note behind for her, which she dictated.

Dinah, I don't want to go to Paris now. Thank you and thank Daphne. I loved Cortina. Now I'm going to learn to ski. I'll be in Switzerland for a while. Good luck, Malika.

Tex had made arrangements to have a chauffeur-driven car large enough to hold Malika's many valises pick them up at the hotel at half past nine in the morning. Everything went off smoothly. Malika handed the note for Dinah to the receptionist. He did not mention the subject of her bill, which she had feared he might do, but merely nodded gravely.

As they left Cortina behind them, Malika said: Dinah's going to be very angry.

I'm thinking of that, said Tex. Will she make trouble?

She can't do anything. She never saw my passport. She doesn't even know my name.

Tex appeared to be stunned by this information, and began to put a whole series of questions to her, but she, being happy to see the beautiful white landscape outside, replied without answering them, seized his hand now and then to draw his attention to a detail in the landscape, and, by taking gentle command, succeeded in putting him off without his being aware of it.

They had lunch at a small restaurant in Mezzolombardo. The waiter brought a bottle of wine and poured out two glasses. No, said Malika, pushing it away.

Your friend Dinah's not here now, Tex reminded her. You can do whatever you like.

Dinah! she scoffed. What's Dinah beside the words of God?

He stared at her, mystified, without pursuing the matter further, and drank the bottle of wine by himself, so that he was in a happy and relaxed state when they got back into the car. As they rolled southward on the autostrada he devoted himself to crushing her hand in his, nuzzling her neck with his lips, and finally kissing her feverishly on the lips. Malika could not have hoped for more.

XIII

At dinner that night in Milano she watched him drink two bottles of wine. Later in the bar he had several whiskeys. At Cortina she would have begged him to stop, but this night she affected not to notice that he was resolutely sliding into a drunken state. Instead, she began to tell him a complicated story she had known since her childhood, about a female ghoul that lived in a cave and unearthed newly buried corpses to extract their livers. Seeing his expression of total bewilderment, she stopped halfway through the tale.

He shook his head. What an imagination! he said.

I want to learn how to speak English, Malika went on, leaving the ghoul behind. That's what I'm going to do in Switzerland.

Tex was drunk by the time they went upstairs. She regretted this, for she liked him much better when he was sober. But she suspected that he was going to want to sleep with her and she thought it wiser for their first time together that he be in a state of befuddlement. It was imperative that he believe himself to be the first to have had her.

In the morning when he awoke staring, trying to remember, she confided that it had not been as painful as she had expected. Tex was contrite; he nearly wept as he begged her forgiveness. She smiled and covered him with kisses.

Having won this much, she pressed on, not with any specific purpose in mind, but simply to gain a stronger foothold. While he was still in the slough of early-morning remorse, she made him promise to abjure whiskey.

At the Grand Saint Bernard, as the police handed back their passports, Malika saw Tex stare at hers briefly with astonishment. When they were in the car, he asked to see the passport again. The Arabic characters seemed to cause him great excitement. He began to ask her questions about Morocco which she could not have answered even if she had been in the mood for such conversation. She assured him it was like any other country. Now I'm looking at Switzerland, she said.

They arrived in Lausanne at sunset and took rooms in a large hotel by the lake, at Ouchy. It was far grander than the hospice at Cortina, and the people living there, not being dressed for skiing, seemed to Malika much more elegant.

I like it here, she said to Tex that night at dinner. How long can we stay?

The next morning, at Malika's insistence, they went together to the Berlitz School for intensive language courses: she in English and he in French. She saw that Tex imagined she would soon tire of the strict schedule, but she was determined not to leave Lausanne before she could converse in English. They spent each morning in their respective classes, had lunch together, and returned to the school at three for further tutoring.

Every Friday afternoon Tex would rent a car, and they would drive to Gstaad, stopping to have dinner on the way. Saturdays and Sundays if no snow fell, they skied at Wasserngrat or Eggli. Sometimes he would insist on staying over until Monday, even though it meant missing their morning classes. Malika could see that if she had let him have his way he always would have done this, and very likely would have extended the weekends further and further. He approved of Malika's learning English, but he could not fathom her obsessive preoccupation with it. Nor, had he asked her, could she have explained it to him. She knew only that unless she kept on learning she was lost.

XIV

During the winter there in Lausanne they made no friends, being entirely satisfied with each other's company. One day as they were coming out of the Schweizerische Kreditanstalt, where Tex had opened an account for Malika, he turned to her and apropos of nothing asked her if she had ever thought of being married.

She looked at him wonderingly. I think of it all the time, she said. You know it makes me happy to be married to you.

He stared at her as if he had understood nothing she had said. After a moment he seized her arm and pulled her to him. It makes me happy, too, he told her. She could see, however, that something was on his mind. Later when they were alone, he said that of course it was true that they were married, but that what he had been speaking of was marriage with papers.

With papers or not with papers! It's the same thing, isn't it? If two people love each other, what have papers got to do with it?

It's the governments, he explained. They like married people to have papers.

Of course, she agreed. In Morocco, too. Many people are married with papers.

She was about to add that papers were important if you expected to produce children, but she checked herself in time, sensing that the observation bordered on dangerous ground. Already, from certain questions he had put to her, she suspected that he had begun to wonder if she were pregnant. His questions amused her, based as they were on the supposition that there had been no Tim before Tex, to show her how always to be safe.

One morning in early spring when she complained of feeling tired, he asked her outright.

You think Moroccan women don't know anything? she cried. If they want to make children they make them. If they don't, they don't make them.

He nodded dubiously. Those home remedies don't always work.

She saw that she was safe. He knew nothing about Morocco. Mine does, she said.

If she never mentioned America to him or asked about his family, it was because she could not envisage his life there with enough clarity to be curious about it. For his part, he spoke of America with increasing frequency. Never before had he stayed away for so long, he said. Malika interpreted these remarks as warnings that he had had enough of his present life and was contemplating a change. The thought struck terror to her heart, but she would not let him perceive this.

From time to time she would catch him in the act of staring at her, an expression of utter incomprehension on his face. By now, at Malika's insistence, they often spoke together in English. She thought it suited him much better than Spanish; he seemed to have an altogether different voice.

Would you like to be married? With papers, I mean.

Yes, if you want to.

And you? he insisted.

Of course I want to, if you want to.

They were married in the rectory office of a Protestant minister, who remarked in an aside to Tex that personally he was not in favor of marriage where the bride was as young as Malika. In my experience, he said, very few such unions prove to be permanent.

To Malika the episode was a bit of nonsense of the sort that Nazarenes appear so much to enjoy. Nevertheless she saw clearly that it was a matter of great importance to Tex. Indeed, his character seemed to have undergone a subtle metamorphosis since the ceremony, in that he was now more self-assertive. She liked him rather better this way, and concluded that secretly he was a very devout man. The papers were obviously a requirement of the Nazarene religion; now that he had them he felt more secure.

It was only a fortnight later that Tex, after drinking a little more wine than was his habit, announced to her that they were going home. Malika received the news with a sinking sensation. She could see that he was glad to be leaving the world of hotels and restaurants, and she suspected that life in a house would be very different and not nearly so much fun.

Once again she saw nothing from the plane, but this time the journey went on for such a long time that she grew worried. Tex was sleepy; nevertheless she disturbed him several times to ask: Where are we?

Twice he answered jovially: In the air. The next time he said: Somewhere over the ocean, I suppose. And he stole a glance at her.

We're not moving, she told him. We're standing still. The plane is stuck.

He only laughed, but in such a way that she realized she had made a mistake of some sort. I don't like this plane, she said.

Go to sleep, Tex advised her.

She shut her eyes and sat quietly, feeling that she had gone much too far away—so far that now she was nowhere. Outside the world, she whispered to herself in Arabic, and shivered.

XV

Being in Los Angeles persuaded Malika that she was right, that she had left behind everything that was comprehensible, and was now in a totally different place whose laws she could not know. They went from the airport to the top of the mountain, where a house was hidden in the woods. Tex had told her about it, but she had imagined something very different, like the Mountain in Tangier, where the villas had big gardens around them. This house was buried among the trees; she could not see the rest of it even when they went up to the door.

In the middle of the forest, she said wonderingly.

An ugly little Filipino in a white jacket opened the door for them. He bowed low and made a short formal speech of welcome to Malika. She knew he was speaking English, but it was not the English she had been taught in Lausanne. At the end she thanked him gravely.

Later she asked Tex what the little man had been saying.

He was hoping you'd be happy here in your new house, that's all.

My house? But it's your house, not mine!

Of course it's yours! You're my wife, aren't you?

Malika nodded. She knew, no matter what anyone pretended, that when men grew tired of their wives they put them out, and took new ones. She loved Tex and trusted him, but she did not expect him to be different from other men. When the time came, she knew he would find a pretext to rid himself of her. The important point was to know how to fight off the fatal moment, to make it come as late as possible. She nodded again and said with a smile: I like this house, Tex.

The rooms had irregular shapes, with unexpected alcoves and niches where there were soft couches with piles of cushions. As she inspected the house she noted with satisfaction that the windows were barred with iron grillwork. She had already seen the massive front door with its heavy bolts.

That night as they sat in front of the fireplace they heard the yapping of coyotes.

Jackals, murmured Malika, turning her head to listen. Very bad.

She found it incomprehensible that anyone should waste money building such a pretty house in a place so far from everything. Above all she could not understand why the trees had been left growing so close to the house. Silently she determined never to go outside unless Tex accompanied her, and never under any circumstances to remain in the house without him.

The next morning, when Tex was about to drive down into the city, Malika began to run from room to room, crying: Wait! I'm going with you.

268

You'd be bored, he told her. I've got to go to a lawyer's office. You stay here with Salvador.

She could not let Tex know that she was afraid to stay in the house; it would be an unforgivable affront. No, no, no. I want to see the town, she said.

He kissed her and they set out for the city. It was a bigger car than the one he had rented at the airport the day before.

I always want to go with you no matter where you go, she confided, hoping that this declaration would aid in establishing a precedent.

During these weeks, when she watched the life in the streets, she could find no pattern to it. The people were always on their way somewhere else, and they were in a hurry. She knew better than to imagine that they were all alike; still, she had no way of knowing who was who. In Morocco, in Europe, there had been people who were busy doing things, and there had been others watching. Always, no matter where one was or what one was doing, there were watchers. She had the impression that in America everyone was going some-where and no one sat watching. This disturbed her. She felt herself to be far, far away from everything she had ever known. The freeways inspired her with dread, for she could not rid herself of the idea that some unnameable catastrophe had occurred, and that the cars were full of refugees fleeing from the scene. She had ample opportunity to ob-serve the miles of small houses set side by side, and compare these simple dwellings with the house on the mountain. As a result it occur-red to her that perhaps she was fortunate to live where she did. One day as they drove into the city she turned to Tex and said: Do you have more money than these people?

What people?

She moved her hand. The ones who live in these houses.

I don't know about other people's money, he said. I know I never have enough of my own.

She looked out at the rows of frail wooden houses with their dusty shrubbery, and could not believe him. You *do* have more money, she declared. Why don't you want to say it?

This made him laugh. Whatever I have, I made myself. The day I was twenty-one my father handed me a check and said: Here. Let's see what you can do with this. In three years I changed it into four-and-a-half times as much. Is that what you meant, Dad? I asked him. That's what I meant, son, he said.

Malika thought a moment, saying finally: And now when he needs money you give it to him.

Tex looked sideways at her and said gravely: Of course.

She wanted to ask him if he had no friends in Los Angeles. Since their arrival she had not met anyone, and she thought this strange. It could be a custom here for recently married couples to keep strictly to themselves during a specified period. Or perhaps Tex's friends here were all girls, which would automatically preclude her knowing them. When she asked him, he said he seldom came to Los Angeles. I'm generally with my family in Texas, he said, or down at the hacienda.

There was a studio upstairs with a wide sundeck that was not hidden by trees in the middle of the day. Malika did not feel entirely at ease sitting out there, with nothing between her and the dark forest. She suspected that the trees harbored dangerous birds. Sometimes she and Tex sat up here between dips in the pool, which, being below inside the closed patio, she considered safe. Tex would observe her as she lay stretched on a mattress, and assure her she was more beautiful than ever. She had noticed this herself, but she was pleased to know that he too had seen it.

XVI

One day Tex told her that a man named F. T. was coming to dinner. F. T. was an old friend of his father's, who managed his financial affairs for him. Malika was interested to hear what such work entailed, so Tex made an effort to explain the mechanics of investment. She was quiet for a while. But then you can't make money unless you already have it, she said.

That's about it, Tex agreed.

F. T. was middle-aged and well-dressed, with a small gray mustache. He was delighted with Malika, and called her Little Lady. This struck her as vaguely insulting, but since she could see that he was a pleasant and well-behaved man otherwise, she made no objections. Besides, Tex had told her: Remember. If you should ever need anything, anything at all, just call F. T.'s number. He's like my father.

During dinner she decided that she really liked F. T., even though he seemed not to take her very seriously. Afterward he and Tex talked together for a long time. The words went on for so long that Malika fell asleep on a divan and awoke only after F. T. had gone. She was apologetic for having been rude, but she blamed Tex for allowing it to happen.

He threw himself down beside her. F. T. thought you were great. He says you're beyond a doubt the most beautiful girl he's ever seen.

He's a nice man, she murmured.

Ever since her arrival in California, her life had seemed static. When she thought back about it, she decided that it had stopped moving when she had left the Berlitz School. Innocently, she asked Tex if she might continue the lessons here. To her astonishment he ridiculed the suggestion, claiming that all she needed was practice in conversation. Because he was not in the habit of refusing her anything, she did not take him at his word, and continued to dwell on her desire for further instruction. All at once she saw that he was going to be firm; he seemed to consider her dissatisfaction a criticism of him. Finally she realized that he was angry.

You don't understand! she cried. I have to study English more before I can study anything else.

Study!

Of course, she said calmly. I'm always going to study. You think I want to stay like this?

I hope you do, Honey, for my sake. You're perfect.

He took hold of her, but she wriggled free.

That evening Tex said to her: I'm going to get an extra woman in the kitchen and let Salvador give you lessons in cooking. That's something you should learn, don't you think?

Malika was silent. Do you want me to learn? You know I want to make you happy.

She began to spend several hours each day in the kitchen with Salvador and Concha, a Mexican girl of whose work the little Filipino was scornful. It was a pleasant enough room, but the number of strange machines and the little bells that kept sounding as Salvador rushed from one spot to another awed and confused her. She was even a bit afraid of Salvador, because his face never changed its fixed expression—that of a meaningless grin. It seemed to her that when he was annoyed the grin became even wider. She took care to pay strict attention to everything

271

he told her. Soon he had her making simple dishes which they ate at lunch. If the recipe called for a béchamel or a chasseur, he made it himself and incorporated it, since the timing was more than Malika could manage. It gratified her to see that Tex thought her food good enough to be served at table. She continued to spend two hours in the kitchen each morning, and another hour or so before dinner in the evening. Sometimes she helped Salvador and Concha prepare a picnic hamper, and they went to the beach. She would have liked to tell Tex about the picnics on the beach at Tangier, but there was no way of doing that.

XVII

Occasionally, despite Malika's entreaties, Tex would take advantage of her morning session in the kitchen to drive the small car into the city on an errand. She would be uneasy until he returned, but he was always back in time for lunch. One morning he failed to appear at the usual hour. The telephone rang. Salvador wiped his hands and stepped into the butler's pantry to answer it, while Malika and Concha went on chatting together in Spanish. In a moment Salvador reappeared in the doorway, and with a radiant smile told Malika the police had called to say that Mister Tex had met with an accident and was in a hospital in Westwood.

Malika rushed at the little man and seized him by the shoulders. Telephone to F. T.!

She hopped up and down while he searched for the number and dialed it. As soon as she saw that he was speaking to F. T., she snatched the telephone from his hand.

F. T.! Come and get me! I want to see Tex.

She heard F. T.'s voice, calm and reassuring. Yes. Now you just wait quietly for me. I'll be there as soon as I can. Don't you worry. Let me speak to Salvador again.

She left Salvador talking into the telephone and rushed upstairs to the studio, where she began to walk back and forth. If Tex was in the hospital, he probably would not be home to sleep that night, and she would not stay in the house without him. She went out onto the sundeck and stared at the trees. Tex is dead, she thought.

It was mid-afternoon before F. T.'s car drew up at the door. He found her in the studio lying facedown on a couch. When she heard his voice she sprang up, wide-eyed, and ran to him.

That night Malika slept at F. T.'s house. He had insisted upon taking her home with him and leaving her in the care of his wife. For it was true that Tex was dead; he had succumbed not long after reaching the hospital.

F. T. and his wife did not commiserate with Malika. Mrs. F. T. said a show of sympathy could induce hysteria. Malika merely talked on and on, weeping intermittently. Sometimes she forgot that her listeners did not know Arabic or Spanish, until at their prompting she would go back into English. She had sworn to accompany Tex whenever he went out, and she had not done so, therefore he had been killed, he was the only being in the world she loved, and she was far from home, and what was going to become of her here alone?

That night as she lay in the dark listening to the occasional passing wail of a police siren, she was assailed afresh by the sensation she had felt on the plane—that of having gone too far for the possibility of return. Being with Tex had made it possible to accept the strangeness of the place; now she saw herself as someone shipwrecked on an unknown shore peopled by creatures whose intentions were unfathomable. And no one could come to rescue her, for no one knew she was there.

She slept at F. T.'s house for several nights. During the days she visited supermarkets and other points of interest with Mrs. F. T. You've got to keep busy, her hostess told her. We can't have you brooding.

There was no way, however, of preventing Malika from worrying about what was to become of her, stranded in this unlikely land without a peseta to buy herself bread, and only the caprice of F. T. and his wife between her and starvation.

XVIII

One morning F. T. himself drove Malika to his office. Out of respect for him she had dressed with great care in a severe gray silk suit from Balenciaga. Her entrance into the office with F. T. caused a stir of interest. When she sat facing him across his desk in a small inner room, he pulled a sheaf of papers from a drawer. As he leafed through them he began to talk.

Betty tells me you're worried about money.

Seeing Malika nod, he went on. I take it you haven't any at all. Is that right?

She felt in her handbag and pulled out a crumpled twenty-dollar bill that Tex had given her one day when they were shopping.

Only this, she said, showing him.

F. T. cleared his throat.

Well, I want you to stop worrying. As soon as we get everything cleared up you'll have a regular income. In the meantime I've opened a checking account for you at the bank downstairs in this building.

He saw anxiety flitting across her face, and added hastily: It's your money. You're his sole beneficiary. After taxes and all the rest, you'll still have a substantial capital. And if you're wise, you'll leave it all just where it is, in certificates of deposit and treasury notes. So stop worrying.

Yes, she said, understanding nothing.

I never let Tex play with stocks, F. T. went on. He had no head for business.

She was shocked to hear F. T. denigrate poor Tex in this way, but she said: I see.

When we get everything straight and running smoothly, you ought to have around fifty thousand a month. Possibly a little more.

Malika stared at F. T. Is that enough? she asked cautiously.

He shot a quick glance at her over his spectacles. I think you'll find it's enough.

I hope so, she said with fervor. You see, I don't understand money. I never bought anything myself. How much does a thing cost? I don't know. Only in my own country.

Of course. F. T. pushed a checkbook along the top of the desk toward her. You understand, this is a temporary account for you to draw on now, until all the legal work is finished. I hope you won't overdraw. But I'm sure you won't.

He smiled encouragingly at her. Remember, he went on. There are only twenty-five thousand dollars there. So be a good girl and keep track of your checks.

But I can't do what you tell me! she exclaimed. Please do it for me.

F. T. sighed. Can you write your name? he asked very quietly.

Tex showed me in Lausanne, but I've forgotten.

In spite of himself, F. T. raised his arms. But my dear lady, how do you expect to live? You can't go on this way.

No, she said miserably.

F. T. pushed back his chair and stood up. Well, he said jovially, what you don't know you can always learn. Why don't you come up here every morning and study with Miss Galper? She's as smart as a whip. She'll teach you everything you need to know. That's my suggestion for you.

He was not prepared for her vehement response. She jumped up and hugged him. Oh, F. T.! That's what I want! That's what I want!

XIX

The following day Malika moved her luggage into a hotel in Beverly Hills. Under F. T.'s advice she kept Salvador on, living in the house, but now functioning solely as chauffeur. Each morning he called at the hotel for her and drove her to F. T.'s office. She found this routine stimulating. Miss Galper, a pleasant young woman with glasses, would spend the forenoon working with her, after which they generally went to lunch together. There had not been much glamor in Miss Galper's life, and she was fascinated by Malika's accounts of Europe and Morocco. There remained a basic mystery in her story, nevertheless, since she never explained how she came to be living at Tim's flat in Tangier. In her version, she might have come into being during a picnic on the beach at Sidi Qacem.

When after two months F. T. saw that Malika was, if anything, even more serious and determined about pursuing her practical education, he suggested that the lessons continue at the hotel. Now it was Miss Galper whom Salvador drove to and from Beverly Hills. Occasionally they went shopping—small expeditions to Westwood that delighted Malika because for the first time she was aware of prices, and could gauge the buying power of her money. F. T. had told her that with what Tex had left for her she would be able to live better than most people. At the time she had supposed this was a part of his attempt to comfort her, but now that she understood the prices she realized that he had been stating a fact. She said nothing to Miss Galper of her surprise at finding the cost of goods so low. Instead, she overwhelmed her with a constant flow of small gifts.

You've got to stop this, Malika, Miss Galper told her.

The first month they had done nothing but arithmetic. After that there was the telling of time, the names of the days and the months. With some difficulty Miss Galper taught her to sign the two forms of her name: *Malika Hapgood* and *Mrs. Charles G. Hapgood*. By the time the lessons were moved to the hotel, Malika had begun to practice writing out in words complicated sums given her in figures. They went back to dates, and she had to learn to write them correctly.

You can leave everything else to a secretary, Miss Galper told her. But you've got to take care of your money yourself.

To this end she gave Malika a course in reading bank statements, and another in spacing the purchase of securities to assure regular turnover.

As the months went by and Malika's insight into the functioning of the world around her grew, she began to understand the true extent of her ignorance, and she conceived a passionate desire to be able to read the texts of newspapers and magazines.

I'm not an English teacher, Miss Galper told her. F. T. doesn't pay me for that. We can get you a good professor whenever you want.

Malika, being persuaded that she could learn only from Miss Galper, consulted F. T. about it. After a certain amount of deliberation, he devised a plan which delighted Malika and pleased Miss Galper as well. He would give Miss Galper a year's holiday with salary if Malika wanted to take her on as a paid companion during that time. In this way, he implied to Malika, she would be able to get the reading lessons she wanted. He added that he did not think Miss Galper was the person to give them, but since Malika had her heart set on being taught by her, this seemed to him a viable strategy.

It was Miss Galper's idea to make a tour of Europe. F. T. suggested they buy a big car, put it on a freighter, and take Salvador along with them to pick it up over there and drive it. When Malika heard this, she asked why they could not all go on the ship with the car. It might be possible, F. T. told her.

Eventually F. T. had arranged to get Malika a new passport, had even helped Miss Galper and Salvador expedite theirs, and, accompanied by Mrs. F. T., had bidden them a lengthy farewell at the dock in San Pedro. It was a comfortable Norwegian freighter bound for Panama and eventually for Europe.

The ship was already in tropical waters. Malika said she had imagined it could be this hot only in the Sahara, and certainly not on the sea. She had nothing to do all day. Salvador spent most of his time sleeping. Miss Galper sat in a deck chair reading. She had refused to give Malika any kind of lessons while they were on the ship. It would make me seasick, she assured her. But she noticed Malika's boredom, and talked with her for long periods of time.

XX

Malika could not sit, as Miss Galper could, looking at the sea. The flat horizon on all sides gave her much the same sensation of unreality she had experienced on the plane with Tex. Panama came as a relief, making it clear that the ship had not been static during all those days, and that they had reached a very different part of the world.

It took all day to go through the canal. Malika stood on deck in the sun, waving back to the men working along the locks. But from Panama on, her restlessness increased daily. She was reduced to playing endless games of checkers with a yawning Salvador each afternoon in the narrow passengers' lounge. They never spoke during these sessions. From the beginning of the voyage the captain had urged Malika to visit the bridge. At some point Miss Galper had mentioned that he had the power to seize anyone on the ship and have him locked into a dark cell somewhere below. When Malika finally accepted his invitation she took Miss Galper along.

Standing at the prow, Malika stared ahead at the white buildings of Cádiz. As the ship moved into the port, the combination of the light in the air, the color of the walls and the odors on the wind told her that she was back in her part of the world and close to home. For a long time she had refused to think about the little house above the gully. Now that it no longer frightened her, she was able to imagine it almost with affection.

It was her duty to go and visit her mother, however hostile a reception she might get from her. She would try to give her money, which she was certain she would refuse to take. But Malika was ready with a ruse. If her mother spurned the money, she would tell her she was leaving it next door with Mina Glagga. Once Malika was out of the way, her mother would lose no time in going to claim it.

Miss Galper had hoped to spend the night in Cádiz, but Malika insisted on driving straight to Algeciras. Now that she was so near home, she wanted to get there as soon as she could. I must see my mother, she said. I must see her first.

Of course, said Miss Galper. But you haven't seen her in two years or more and she isn't expecting you. One day sooner or later?

We can come back. Now I have to go and see my mother.

In Algeciras at the hotel that night they saw Salvador eating at the other end of the long dining room. He had changed from his uniform into a gray flannel suit. Malika observed him carefully, and said: He's drinking wine.

He'll be all right tomorrow, Miss Galper told her. They always drink, Filipinos.

He was at the door grinning when they came out of the hotel in the morning to be driven to the dock. Most of the passengers going to Tangier were Moroccans. Malika had forgotten the shameless intensity with which her countrymen stare at women. Now she was back among her own kind. The realization startled her; she felt both excitement and apprehension.

XXI

After they had settled into their quarters at the hotel, Malika went down to the desk. She hoped to visit her mother in the evening, when she was sure to be in the house, and when there would be a valid excuse for not staying too long. She intended to reserve two rooms in Tétouan for the night, one for Salvador and one for herself, and return to Tangier in the morning. In the lobby they told her of a new hotel on the beach only a mile or so from her town. She asked them to telephone for reservations.

Miss Galper's room was down the corridor from hers. Malika knocked on her door and told her she would be leaving about five o'clock, in order to get to the hotel before dark.

Miss Galper looked at her searchingly. I'm glad you're doing it now and getting it over with, she said.

You can have a good time, Malika told her. There are bars where you can go.

No, thank you. The men here give me the creeps. They all try to talk to you.

Malika shrugged. What difference does it make? You can't understand what they're saying.

This was fortunate, she thought. The brutally obscene remarks made by the men to women passing in the street disgusted and infuriated her. Miss Galper was lucky not to know any Arabic.

She said a lame good-bye and hurried to her room. The prospect of seeing her mother had unsettled her. Mechanically she put a few articles of clothing into an overnight bag. On the way out she cashed some traveler's checks at the office, and soon she and Salvador were on the road to Tétouan.

The mountains had scarves of white cloud trailing outward from their summits. Salvador criticized the narrow highway. Malika scarcely heard his complaints. Her heart was beating unusually fast. It was true that she was going back to help her mother; she was going because it was included in the pattern. Since the day she had run away, the vision of the triumphant return had been with her, when she would be the living proof that her mother had been mistaken, that she was not like the other girls of the town. Now that the moment was drawing near, she suspected that the visit was foredoomed to failure. Her mother would feel no pleasure at seeing her—only rancor and bitterness at the thought that she had been with Nazarenes.

Salvador said: In Pilipinas we got better roads than this one.

Don't go fast, she told him.

They skirted Tétouan and turned to the left along the road that led to her town. The sea wind rushed through the car. *Bismil'lah,* she murmured under her breath, for now she was entering the crucial part of the journey.

She did not even know they had reached the town until they were in the main street. It looked completely different. There were big new buildings and bright lights. The idea that the town might change during her absence had not occurred to her; she herself would change, but the town would remain an unmoving backdrop which would help her define and measure her transformation.

A moment later they had arrived at the new hotel, spread out along the beach in a glare of green floodlights.

XXII

Malika soon discovered that it was not a real hotel. There was no room service, and in the dining room they served only snack-bar food. Before eating, she changed into blue jeans, bought in Los Angeles at Miss Galper's suggestion. She wore a sweater and wrapped a silk kerchief tightly around her head. In this costume she felt wholly anonymous.

Salvador was already eating at the counter in the *comedor*. She sat on a stool near him and ordered *pinchitos*. Her stomach rebelled at the thought of eating, but she chewed and swallowed the meat because she had learned that to feel well she must eat regularly. Through the rasping of a transistor radio at the end of the counter she heard the dull, repeated sound of the waves breaking over the sand below. If her mother flew into a rage and began to beat her, she would go directly to Mina Glagga and give her the money, and that would finish it. She signed the chit and went out into the wind to the car.

The town's new aspect confused her. They had moved the market; she could not see it anywhere, and she felt a wave of indignation at this betrayal. Salvador parked the car at the service station and they set out on foot up the narrow street that led to the house. There were streetlights only part of the way; beyond, it would have been dark had it not been for the moon. Salvador glanced ahead and said it would be better to turn around and come again in the morning.

You wait here, she said firmly. I'll come back as soon as I can. I know the way. And she quickly went on, before he could argue about it.

She made her way up along the empty moonlit street until she came to a small open square from which, in the daytime at least, her mother's house was visible ahead, at the edge of the barranca. Now as she looked, the moon's light did not seem to strike it at all; she could see no sign of it. She hurried on, already assailed by a nightmarish premonition, and then she stopped, her mouth open in disbelief. The house was not there. Even the land where it had stood was gone. Mina Glagga's and all the houses bordering on the gully had disappeared. Bulldozers had made a new landscape of emptiness, a great embankment of earth, ashes and refuse that stretched downward to the bottom of the ravine. The little house with its garden had been just below where she now stood. She felt her throat tighten painfully as she told herself that it no longer existed.

Ceasing finally to stare at the meaningless terrain, she turned and went back to the square, where she knocked at the door of one of the houses. The woman who opened the door was a friend of her mother's whose name she had forgotten. She eyed Malika's blue jeans with distaste and did not ask her inside. They talked standing in the doorway. In an expressionless voice the woman told her that her mother had died more than a year earlier, during Ramadan. It was fortunate, she added, that she had not lived to see them destroy her house in order to build the new road. She thought Malika's sister had gone to Casablanca, but she was not certain.

By now the woman had pushed the door so that it was nearly shut. Malika thanked her and said good-night.

She went over and stood at the edge of the landfill, staring down at the uniform surface of the hillside, unreal even in the careful light dropped over it by the moon. She had to force her eyes shut to clear them of the tears that kept forming, and she found it strange, for she had not felt tenderness for her mother. Then she saw more clearly. It was not for her mother that she felt like weeping; it was for herself. There was no longer any reason to do anything.

She let her gaze wander over the dim expanse toward the mountains beyond. It would be good to perish here in the place where she had lived, to be buried along with the house under the hateful mass. She pounded the edge of it with her heel, lost her footing, and slid downward some distance through mounds of ashes and decayed food. In that instant she was certain it was happening, as a punishment for having wished to be dead a moment ago; her weight had started a landslide that would roll her to the bottom, leaving her under tons of refuse. Terrified, she lay still, listening. There were faint stirrings and clinks around her, but they quickly died away into silence. She scrambled up to the roadbed.

A cloud had begun to move across the moon. She hurried down the hill toward the streetlight where Salvador waited.

RUMOR AND A LADDER

I

Alone in Paris, Monsieur Ducros sat in his spacious hotel room, preparing to write a letter to his daughter in Kuala Lumpur. He frowned at the hotel stationery, which now was merely printed, instead of being embossed as it had been on his last visit. A symbol of the times, he thought automatically. The slow encroachment of poverty on all sides. Then he glanced down at the cast encasing his leg, smiled briefly at it, and started to write.

> My dear Clotilde:
>
> I hope my unwonted silence hasn't disturbed you. Ordinarily I'm a good correspondent; admit it. I can't believe Kuala Lumpur has altered much since 1965. As you know, it was my last post. I was pleased to hear that Abd er Rahman and his wife are still there; one never knows. I passed my eighty-fifth birthday quietly in Tangier. In a moment you will see what I mean by "quietly."
>
> The incredible irony of certain situations in which life insists upon involving us! What was I doing, standing at the top of a stepladder in the library on a Sunday morning? You may well ask. I also asked myself that, but a good deal too late.
>
> When I felt the ladder tilting (for this is the way it all began) and knew I was going to fall, I was aware of several things simultaneously: that everything was unfinished; that I had been an idiot to climb up there; that people would believe I had been drunk or the victim of an assault (suppositions equally damaging to one's posthumous reputation in that vicious city where, as you're aware, no one thinks well of anyone); and above all the

conviction that everything would go wrong, with the result that you and Pierrot somehow would not be able to inherit El Hafa. Because, my girl, I was certain that it was the end. Then the leg got involved with the ladder as we went down, there was a crash, and I lay there, my head pounding, and quite aware that my leg was broken above the knee. Fortunately the big Chichaoua rug was underneath, or I should have hit marble. I called endlessly for Annamaria. When she finally appeared, she claimed the wind was rattling the shutters so hard that she hadn't heard me at first. It's true that her room faces northeast, and there was a gale blowing outside. Still—

I had her send Abdeslam on foot to Dr. Rinaldi's clinic. (The telephone had been out of order for more than three weeks.) Rinaldi arrived. The femur was fractured. He saw the stepladder by the bookshelves, and looked at me reprovingly. Off I went to the clinic; in traction for what seemed an eternity. Actually it was something less than a month and a half. . . .

II

It's essential that I go to Paris, said Monsieur Ducros, surveying his leg, still in its cast. As you can see, I manage perfectly well now with the cane.

Dr. Rinaldi shrugged. Luck has been with you so far, he said. Why shouldn't we expect it to continue?

They sat sipping whiskey in the library where the accident had taken place. After a certain hesitation Dr. Rinaldi inquired if the rumor were true that his host planned to sell El Hafa.

Monsieur Ducros bristled. But what an idea! Certainly not! I haven't the slightest intention of selling. I know, that Saudi is interested, and the offer would be generous. I intend my daughter and her husband to have the property after my death. I've spent all my retired years in this house, and everything I own in the world is in it.

Dr. Rinaldi looked around the room approvingly. There are many treasures, yes. Astonishing how Japanese, Tibetan, Khmer and Persian can blend in a room.

Not really, if you think about it, said Monsieur Ducros, without elaborating. The point is, I don't want to give up anything. You understand. With my things around me, it's as though I were still out there in the Far East. I enjoy my little life, and I can assure you I have no intention of interrupting it by selling El Hafa.

There's one thing I'm curious about, Dr. Rinaldi said after a moment. Those paintings at the far end of the hall. I couldn't help noticing them.

Monsieur Ducros chuckled. Yes, it's a jarring note, I know. But they're not really much in evidence. I keep it fairly dark at that end, purposely. Madame Ducros bought those things shortly after the First World War. They say less than nothing to me, I confess. I've been told they have a certain value, but I don't take that too seriously. I've kept them because my wife was so fond of them.

A Moroccan in a white jacket announced that dinner was served. Dr. Rinaldi handed Monsieur Ducros his cane, and they rose from their chairs.

At the table Monsieur Ducros pointed to the carafes in the center, saying: The white is simply Valpierre. The red is a fairly good Bordeaux. You've taken Mademoiselle Herzler's tray up, Abdeslam?

When they were alone in the dining room, he spoke confidentially: My secretary insists upon eating by herself in her room. I think she's not entirely happy here. She objects very much to the wind. Swiss, he added, as if by way of explanation.

Dr. Rinaldi, busying himself with his sole meunière, did not reply. Presently he looked up and said with great seriousness: I suspect you of grossly underestimating the worth of those canvases. May I ask what you imagine they'd fetch on the market today?

Monsieur Ducros stopped eating, and thought for a moment. I have no idea, he said.

For the five Soutines alone I can get you two million French francs tomorrow. As he made the statement he stared fixedly at his host, as if to measure his reaction. He saw a flash of interest, followed immediately by disbelief.

Ridiculous. They're not Titians, after all.

I'm entirely serious.

Monsieur Ducros was quiet. Then he sighed. Even if your estimate is not dramatically exaggerated, and even if I wanted to dispose of them, what would be the point? The money would be of no use here, and it couldn't be taken out of Morocco.

Oh, come, said Dr. Rinaldi. There are ways.

No, thank you, Monsieur Ducros said firmly. The law is generally illogical and often unjust, but I'm not one to flout it.

My friend, you function according to the ethos of a bygone era. But I approve, I approve.

In my experience the rational man is the one who obeys the law.

But alas! sighed Dr. Rinaldi. How human it is to be irrational!

Monsieur Ducros glanced furtively at his guest: he suspected these last words to be a veiled reference to his accident. The doctor already had upbraided him severely for allowing the absurd thing to happen. What were servants for, if not to climb stepladders? He had not mentioned Monsieur Ducros's age, but this show of discretion counted for little because of the stern manner in which he had voiced his opinion. Monsieur Ducros recognized the minatory tone; since he had passed his eightieth birthday all his doctors had used it with him.

They spoke of other things. But later, over coffee and Armagnac in the den, Monsieur Ducros turned with a puzzled expression to his guest.

To return for a moment to the subject of those paintings. How would your buyer have arranged to get them out of the country? I'm curious.

The question wouldn't have arisen, the doctor told him. An American collector is building a house in Marrakech. Why? Are you tempted?

Monsieur Ducros shook his head. No, no! Not in the least.

III

Their next encounter, less than a week later, was unexpected and tempestuous. In the middle of a weekday afternoon Monsieur Ducros was brought by a taxi driver to Dr. Rinaldi's clinic in a state bordering on apoplexy. The cast on his leg had been split open, and tatters of gauze trailed out from inside it.

Seeing that Monsieur Ducros was not in a state to speak coherently, Dr. Rinaldi questioned the taxi driver. He was struck by a car?

The driver did not know. He had been summoned by an official at the airport and instructed to take the passenger home, but on the way the old man had demanded to be brought to the clinic.

Monsieur Ducros was put to bed and given an injection. Later that evening, after an enforced sleep of several hours, he was sufficiently rested to tell his tale to Dr. Rinaldi.

Abdeslam had driven him to the airport, given his luggage to a porter, and left. The plane for Paris arrived. As his passport was being examined, a man had appeared from nowhere, and asked him to go with him into an inner office, where he and two others had made him undress. Not content with that, they had refused to believe that his leg was broken, and had held him by force while they smashed open the cast and pulled the inside to pieces in their search for money.

It's that rumor! They had the effrontery to tell me they were acting on secret information that I'd sold El Hafa.

Dr. Rinaldi was deeply shocked. Unheard of! Herbier must be informed immediately at the consulate.

I shall sue for damages! Monsieur Ducros cried feebly.

My poor friend, that would produce an enormous zero. You've lived here long enough to realize that. All you can do is accept what has happened, be sure the leg is all right, put on a new cast, and start out again.

Monsieur Ducros shut his eyes for a moment, and opened them again. You can help me, he said.

Naturally. As your doctor I can attest to the authenticity of the fracture. Perhaps they'd like to see the X ray, too, he added acidly.

Monsieur Ducros did not seem to be listening. He was looking at the ceiling. Yes, you can help me, he repeated.

Dr. Rinaldi decided that the time had come for his patient to rest. You can count on me, he told him.

The next day he went into the sickroom and announced that he was ready to make a new cast. Monsieur Ducros waved him away. No, no. I don't want it.

But you must have a cast. You can't walk without one.

I shan't walk. I'll stay in my bed at home until you come to do it.

As you like, Dr. Rinaldi said shortly, feeling that he was being foolish to humor the caprice of an unreasonable old man.

Abdeslam can take me home this afternoon. Will you come by at five o'clock?

Fleetingly the idea occurred to the doctor that the experience at the airport might have caused a small cerebral lesion. In some subtle way Monsieur Ducros's personality seemed very slightly altered.

You must not use the leg, he said frowning. Not even to take a few steps in your room. Are we agreed?

IV

At El Hafa Dr. Rinaldi found his patient propped up in an enormous antique bed; the damask curtains that hung from the baldachin overhead nearly hid him from view.

I've obeyed you to the letter, he called out, even before the doctor and his assistant had got inside the room.

Dr. Rinaldi laughed. When do you plan your next escape attempt?

I haven't thought about it, said Monsieur Ducros. May I have a five-minute conversation with you in private?

Dr. Rinaldi spoke with the Moroccan, and he left the room. When they were alone, Monsieur Ducros leaned forward and beckoned to the other to approach.

I'll explain, he whispered. You see, I don't want you to put the cast on today. I merely wanted you to come by. And I've decided to sell those paintings, if you can get in touch with the American.

This inconsequential coupling of ideas confirmed Dr. Rinaldi's previous suspicions; he saw in it a clear instance of mental dysfunction. Come, he said, sitting down on the edge of the bed. One thing at a time. May I ask why you prefer to remain without the cast?

Because I must know whether or not the paintings can be sold. I should think that would be obvious.

I hadn't connected the two things, the doctor said dryly. But since what interests you most is evidently the sale of the paintings, I can say: yes, they definitely can be sold, and in short order, if you like. I myself will buy them and resell them.

At a reasonable profit, I hope, added Monsieur Ducros, smiling.

Very likely.

You said two million, as I recall.

Dr. Rinaldi laughed. If you want to throw in the Vlaminck, the Rouault and the Kokoschka, two and a quarter.

Monsieur Ducros threw up his hands. Kokoschka, indeed! I don't know one from the other. They're all equally inept. That would make

287

all eight of them, wouldn't it? I have some old Thai things I'll hang at that end of the hall. They'll be far more in keeping.

Dr. Rinaldi looked searchingly at his patient. This is serious? You really want my check now?

But not at all! The currency. In French francs.

Dr. Rinaldi opened his mouth. But, he began.

You don't agree?

It will take time. Perhaps by tomorrow evening.

Monsieur Ducros was waving his hands again. Just bring the francs here to me.

Shaking his head with disapproval, Dr. Rinaldi said: Far too much money to leave lying around the house.

This seemed to mystify Monsieur Ducros. Surely you've understood by now what I expect you to do with the bank notes? You'll build them into the cast. And what they imagined was happening the first time will actually happen this time.

After a long silence Dr. Rinaldi said slowly: You can scarcely expect me to be eager to risk my professional status simply to help you perpetrate a fraud.

Monsieur Ducros cried excitedly: Fraud! I've already been punished. Now I want to *deserve* that punishment!

The doctor stood up. I find it quite extraordinary, the total change in your views on morality.

Nothing has changed. What was a question of ethics has become a question of honor.

As Dr. Rinaldi moved around the room, following the patterns of the rug, he said: You realize how much more work it would mean for me, having to do it all without my assistant?

Monsieur Ducros, knowing he had won, pressed on. Herbier has been in touch with Rabat, no? He has a formal apology for the incident. There's absolutely no question of a repetition. The element of risk has been removed.

The doctor returned to the bed and placed his hands on the footboard. I retract what I said about you at dinner not too long ago. You are indeed a product of your times.

I don't see it that way at all, Monsieur Ducros said quickly. This little ploy of revenge in no way affects my point of view. We're playing a game of extralegal tit for tat, nothing more.

It's quite all right, said Dr. Rinaldi. You won't need any medical attestations if Herbier himself is accompanying you to the airport.

> ... And that is the bare outline of how your father took the first step along the pathway to crime. But criminals can be fiercely fond of their families, you know. So, go to the Hong Kong and Shanghai Bank in Kuala and ask for Mister Nigel Dawson. He will explain to you that you now have an account with them, and that it has seventy-five thousand British pounds in it at the moment. I'm sure there are many things for which it will be useful, including, I hope, a visit by you and Pierrot to Tangier before too long.
>
> I had the paintings thanks to your mother. And I think she would appreciate the ridiculous turn of events which made it possible for me to sell them for a small fortune. But luck is always absurd.
>
> I imagine you sitting in the dubious freshness of that air-conditioned apartment, looking down at the wet trees and traffic of *"Kuala l'impur,"* as Cocteau called it. But there are places far more impure!
>
> Know that I think of you, and, I beg you, let me have news soon.
>
> > *ton père qui t'aime*

289

IN THE RED ROOM

When I had a house in Sri Lanka, my parents came out one winter to
see me. Originally I had felt some qualms about encouraging their visit.
Any one of several things—the constant heat, the unaccustomed food and
drinking water, even the presence of a leprosy clinic a quarter of a mile
from the house—might easily have an adverse effect on them in one way
or another. But I had underestimated their resilience; they made a greater
show of adaptability than I had thought possible, and seemed entirely
content with everything. They claimed not to mind the lack of running
water in the bathrooms, and regularly praised the curries prepared by
Appuhamy, the resident cook. Both of them being in their seventies, they
were not tempted by the more distant or inaccessible points of interest.
It was enough for them to stay around the house reading, sleeping, taking
twilight dips in the ocean, and going on short trips along the coast by
hired car. If the driver stopped unexpectedly at a shrine to sacrifice a
coconut, they were delighted, and if they came upon a group of elephants
lumbering along the road, the car had to be parked some distance up
ahead, so that they could watch them approach and file past. They had
no interest in taking photographs, and this spared me what is perhaps the
most taxing duty of a cicerone: the repeated waits while the ritual
between man and machine is observed. They were ideal guests.

Colombo, where all the people I knew lived, was less than a hundred
miles away. Several times we went up for weekends, which I arranged
with friends by telephone beforehand. There we had tea on the wide
verandas of certain houses in Cinnamon Gardens, and sat at dinners with
professors from the University, Protestant ministers, and assorted members of the government. (Many of the Sinhalese found it strange that I

should call my parents by their first names, Dodd and Hannah; several of them inquired if I were actually their son or had been adopted.) These weekends in the city were hot and exhausting, and they were always happy to get back to the house, where they could change into comfortable clothing.

One Sunday not long before they were due to return to America, we decided to take in the horse races at Gintota, where there are also some botanical gardens that Hannah wanted to see. I engaged rooms at the New Oriental in Galle and we had lunch there before setting out.

As usual, the events were late in starting. It was the spectators, in any case, who were the focus of interest. The phalanx of women in their shot-silk saris moved Hannah to cries of delight. The races themselves were something of a disappointment. As we left the grounds, Dodd said with satisfaction: It'll be good to get back to the hotel and relax.

But we were going to the Botanical Gardens, Hannah reminded him. I'd like to have just a peek at them.

Dodd was not eager. Those places cover a lot of territory, you know, he said.

We'll just look inside and come out again, she promised.

The hired car took us to the entrance. Dodd was tired, and as a result was having a certain amount of difficulty in walking. The last year or so I find my legs aren't always doing exactly what I want 'em to do, he explained.

You two amble along, Hannah told us. I'll run up ahead and find out if there's anything to see.

We stopped to look up at a clove tree; its powerful odor filled the air like a gas. When we turned to continue our walk, Hannah was no longer in sight. We went on under the high vegetation, around a curve in the path, looked ahead, and still there was no sign of her.

What does your mother think she's doing? The first thing we know she'll be lost.

She's up ahead somewhere.

Soon, at the end of a short lane overhung by twisted lianas, we saw her, partially hidden by the gesticulating figure of a Sinhalese standing next to her.

What's going on? Dodd hastened his steps. Run over there, he told me, and I started ahead, walking fast. Then I saw Hannah's animated smile, and slowed my pace. She and the young man stood in front of a huge bank of brown spider orchids.

Ah! I thought we'd lost you, I said.

Look at these orchids. Aren't they incredible?

Dodd came up, nodded at the young man, and examined the display of flowers. They look to me like skunk cabbage, he declared.

The young man broke into wild laughter. Dodd stared at him.

This young man has been telling me the history of the garden, Hannah began hurriedly. About the opposition to it, and how it finally came to be planted. It's interesting.

The Sinhalese beamed triumphantly. He wore white flannels and a crimson blazer, and his sleek black hair gave off a metallic-blue glint in the sunlight.

Ordinarily I steer a determined course away from the anonymous person who tries to engage me in conversation. This time it was too late; encouraged by Hannah, the stranger strolled beside her, back to the main path. Dodd and I exchanged a glance, shrugged, and began to follow along behind.

Somewhere up at the end of the gardens a pavilion had been built under the high rain trees. It had a veranda where a few sarong-draped men reclined in long chairs. The young man stopped walking. Now I invite you to a cold ginger beer.

Oh, Hannah said, at a loss. Well, yes. That would be nice. I'd welcome a chance to sit down.

Dodd peered at his wristwatch. I'll pass up the beer, but I'll sit and watch you.

We sat and looked out at the lush greenness. The young man's conversation leapt from one subject to another; he seemed unable to follow any train of thought farther than its inception. I put this down as a bad sign, and tried to tell from the inflections of Hannah's voice whether she found him as disconcerting as I did.

Dodd was not listening. He found the heat of low-country Ceylon oppressive, and it was easy to see that he was tired. Thinking I might cover up the young man's chatter, I turned to Dodd and began to talk about whatever came into my head: the resurgence of mask making in Ambalangoda, devil dancing, the high incidence of crime among the fishermen converted to Catholicism. Dodd listened, but did no more than move his head now and then in response.

Suddenly I heard the young man saying to Hannah: I have just the house for you. A godsend to fill your requirements. Very quiet and protected.

She laughed. Mercy, no! We're not looking for a house. We're only going to be here a few weeks more.

I looked hard at her, hoping she would take my glance as a warning against going on and mentioning the place where she was staying. The young man was not paying attention, in any case. Quite all right. You are not buying houses. But you should see this house and tell your friends. A superior investment, no doubt about that. Shall I introduce myself, please? Justus Gonzag, called Sonny by friends.

His smile, which was not a smile at all, gave me an unpleasant physical sensation.

Come anyway. A five-minute walk, guaranteed. He looked searchingly at Hannah. I intend to give you a book of poems. My own. Autographed for you with your name. That will make me very happy.

Oh, Hannah said, a note of dismay in her voice. Then she braced herself and smiled. That would be lovely. But you understand, we can't stay more than a minute.

There was a silence. Dodd inquired plaintively: Can't we go in the car, at least?

Impossible, sir. We are having a very narrow road. Car can't get through. I am arranging in a jiffy. He called out. A waiter came up, and he addressed him in Sinhalese at some length. The man nodded and went inside. Your driver is now bringing your car to this gate. Very close by.

This was going a little too far. I asked him how he thought anyone was going to know which car was ours.

No problem. I was present when you were leaving the Pontiac. Your driver is called Wickramasinghe. Up-country resident, most reliable. Down here people are hopeless.

I disliked him more each time he spoke. You're not from around here? I asked him.

No, no! I'm a Colombo chap. These people are impossible scoundrels. Every one of the blighters has a knife in his belt, guaranteed.

When the waiter brought the check, he signed it with a rapid flourish and stood up. Shall we be going on to the house, then?

No one answered, but all three of us rose and reluctantly moved off with him in the direction of the exit gate. The hired car was there; Mr. Wickramasinghe saluted us from behind the wheel.

The afternoon heat had gone, leaving only a pocket here and there beneath the trees where the air was still. Originally the lane where we were walking had been wide enough to admit a bullock cart, but the vegetation encroaching on each side had narrowed it to little more than a footpath.

At the end of the lane were two concrete gateposts with no gate between them. We passed through, and went into a large compound bordered on two sides by ruined stables. With the exception of one small ell, the house was entirely hidden by high bushes and flowering trees. As we came to a doorway the young man stopped and turned to us, holding up one finger. No noises here, isn't it? Only birds.

It was the hour when the birds begin to awaken from their daytime lethargy. An indeterminate twittering came from the trees. He lowered his finger and turned back to the door. Mornings they are singing. Now not.

Oh, it's lovely, Hannah told him.

He led us through a series of dark empty rooms. Here the dhobi was washing the soiled clothing! This is the kitchen, you see? Ceylon style. Only the charcoal. My father was refusing paraffin and gas both. Even in Colombo.

We huddled in a short corridor while he opened a door, reached in, and flooded the space inside with blinding light. It was a small room, made to seem still smaller by having been given glistening crimson walls and ceiling. Almost all the space was filled by a big bed with a satin coverlet of a slightly darker red. A row of straight-backed chairs stood along one wall. Sit down and be comfy, our host advised us.

We sat, staring at the bed and at the three framed pictures on the wall above its brass-spoked headboard: on the left a girl, in the middle our host, and on the right another young man. The portraits had the imprecision of passport photographs that have been enlarged many times their original size.

Hannah coughed. She had nothing to say. The room gave off a cloying scent of ancient incense, as in a disused chapel. The feeling of absurdity I got from seeing us sitting there side by side, wedged in between the bed and the wall, was so powerful that it briefly paralyzed my mental processes. For once the young man was being silent; he sat stiffly, looking straight ahead, like someone at the theater.

Finally I had to say something. I turned to our host and asked him if he slept in this room. The question seemed to shock him. Here? he cried, as if the thing were inconceivable. No, no! This house is unoccupied. No one sleeping on the premises. Only a stout chap to watch out at night. Excuse me one moment.

He jumped up and hurried out of the room. We heard his footsteps echo in the corridor and then grow silent. From somewhere in the house there came the sonorous chiming of a grandfather's clock; its comfortable sound made the shiny blood-colored cubicle even more remote and unlikely.

Dodd stirred uncomfortably in his chair; the bed was too close for him to cross his legs. As soon as he comes back, we go, he muttered.

He's looking for the book, I imagine, said Hannah.

We waited a while. Then I said: Look. If he's not back in two minutes, I move we just get up and leave. We can find our way out all right.

Hannah objected, saying it would be unpardonable.

Again we sat in silence, Dodd now shielding his eyes from the glare. When Sonny Gonzag returned, he was carrying a glass of water which he drank standing in the doorway. His expression had altered: he now looked preoccupied, and he was breathing heavily.

We slowly got to our feet. Hannah still looking expectant.

We are going, then? Come. With the empty glass still in his hand he turned off the lights, shut the door behind us, opened another, and led us quickly through a sumptuous room furnished with large divans, Coromandel screens and bronze Buddhas. We had no time to do more than glance from side to side as we followed him. As we went out through the front door, he called one peremptory word back into the house, presumably to the caretaker.

There was a wide unkempt lawn on this side, where a few clumps of high areca palms were being slowly strangled by the sheaths of philodendron roots and leaves that encased their trunks. Creepers had spread themselves unpleasantly over the tops of shrubs like the meshes of gigantic cobwebs. I knew that Hannah was thinking of snakes. She kept her eyes on the ground, stepping carefully from flagstone to flagstone as we followed the exterior of the house around to the stables, and thence out into the lane.

The swift twilight had come down. No one seemed disposed to speak. When we reached the car Mr. Wickramasinghe stood beside it.

Cheery-bye, then, and tell your friends to look for Sonny Gonzag when they are coming to Gintota. He offered his hand to Dodd first, then me, finally to Hannah, and turned away.

They were both very quiet on the way back to Galle. The road was narrow and the blinding lights of oncoming cars made them nervous. During dinner we made no mention of the afternoon.

At breakfast, on the veranda swept by the morning breeze, we felt sufficiently removed from the experience to discuss it. Hannah said: I kept waking up in the night and seeing that awful bed.

Dodd groaned.

I said it was like watching television without the sound. You saw everything, but you didn't get what was going on.

The kid was completely non compos mentis. You could see that a mile away, Dodd declared.

Hannah was not listening. It must have been a maid's room. But why would he take us there? I don't know; there's something terribly depressing about the whole thing. It makes me feel a little sick just to think about it. And that bed!

Well, stop thinking about it, then! Dodd told her. I for one am going to put it right out of my mind. He waited. I feel better already. Isn't that the way the Buddhists do it?

The sunny holiday continued for a few weeks more, with longer trips now to the east, to Tissamaharama and the wild elephants in the Yala Preserve. We did not go to Colombo again until it was time for me to put them onto the plane.

The black weather of the monsoons was blowing in from the southwest as we drove up the coast. There was a violent downpour when we arrived in mid-afternoon at Mount Lavinia and checked into our rooms. The crashing of the waves outside my room was so loud that Dodd had to shut the windows in order to hear what we were saying.

I had taken advantage of the trip to Colombo to arrange a talk with my lawyer, a Telugu-speaking Indian. We were to meet in the bar at the Galleface, some miles up the coast. I'll be back at six, I told Hannah. The rain had abated somewhat when I started out.

Damp winds moved through the lobby of the Galleface, but the smoky air in the bar was stirred only by fans. As I entered, the first person I noticed was Weston of the Chartered Bank. The lawyer had not yet come in, so I stood at the bar with Weston and ordered a whiskey.

Didn't I see you in Gintota at the races last month? With an elderly couple?

I was there with my parents. I didn't notice you.

I couldn't tell. It was too far away. But I saw the same three people later with a local character. What did you think of Sonny Gonzag?

I laughed. He dragged us off to his house.

You know the story, I take it.

I shook my head.

The story, which he recounted with relish, began on the day after Gonzag's wedding, when he stepped into a servant's room and found his bride in bed with the friend who had been best man. How he happened to have a pistol with him was not explained, but he shot them both in the face, and later chopped their bodies into pieces. As Weston remarked: That sort of thing isn't too uncommon, of course. But it was the trial that caused the scandal. Gonzag spent a few weeks in a mental hospital, and was discharged.

You can imagine, said Weston. Political excitement. The poor go to jail for a handful of rice, but the rich can kill with impunity, and that sort of thing. You still see references to the case in the press now and then.

I was thinking of the crimson blazer and the Botanical Gardens. No. I never heard about it, I said.

He's mad as a hatter, but there he is, free to do whatever he feels like. And all he wants now is to get people into that house and show them the room where the great event took place. The more the merrier as far as he's concerned.

I saw the Indian come into the bar. It's unbelievable, but I believe it, I told Weston.

Then I turned to greet the lawyer, who immediately complained of the stale air in the bar. We sat and talked in the lounge.

I managed to get back to Mount Lavinia in time to bathe before dinner.

As I lay in the tepid water, I tried to imagine the reactions of Hannah and Dodd when I told them what I had heard. I myself felt a solid satisfaction at knowing the rest of the story. But being old, they might well brood over it, working it up into an episode so unpleasant in retrospect that it stained the memory of their holiday. I still had not decided whether to tell them or not, when I went to their room to take them down to dinner.

We sat as far away from the music as we could get. Hannah had dressed a little more elaborately than usual, and they both were speaking with more than their accustomed animation. I realized that they were happy to be returning to New York. Halfway through the meal they began to review what they considered the highlights of their visit. They mentioned the Temple of the Tooth, the pair of Bengal tiger cubs in Dehiwala which they had petted but regretfully declined to purchase, the Indonesian dinner on Mr. Bultjens's lawn, where the mynah bird had hopped over to Hannah and said: "Eat it up," the cobra under the couch at Mrs. de Sylva's tea party.

And that peculiar young man in the *strange* house, Hannah added meditatively.

Which one was that? asked Dodd, frowning as he tried to remember. Then it came to him. Oh, God, he muttered. Your special friend. He turned to me. Your mother certainly can pick 'em.

Outside, the ocean roared. Hannah seemed lost in thought. *I* know what it was like! she exclaimed suddenly. It was like being shown around one of the temples by a bhikku. Isn't that what they call them?

Dodd sniffed. Some temple! he chuckled.

No, I'm serious. That room had a particular meaning for him. It was like a sort of shrine.

I looked at her. She had got to the core without needing the details.

I felt that, too, I said. Of course, there's no way of knowing.

She smiled. Well, what you don't know won't hurt you.

I had heard her use the expression a hundred times without ever being able to understand what she meant by it, because it seemed so patently untrue. But for once it was apt. I nodded my head and said: That's right.

THE EYE

Ten or twelve years ago there came to live in Tangier a man who would have done better to stay away. What happened to him was in no way his fault, notwithstanding the whispered innuendos of the English-speaking residents. These people often have reactions similar to those of certain primitive groups: when misfortune overtakes one of their number, the others by mutual consent refrain from offering him aid, and merely sit back to watch, certain that he has called his suffering down upon himself. He has become taboo, and is incapable of receiving help. In the case of this particular man, I suppose no one could have been of much comfort; still, the tacit disapproval called forth by his bad luck must have made the last months of his life harder to bear.

His name was Duncan Marsh, and he was said to have come from Vancouver. I never saw him, nor do I know anyone who claims to have seen him. By the time his story reached the cocktail-party circuit he was dead, and the more irresponsible residents felt at liberty to indulge their taste for mythmaking.

He came alone to Tangier, rented a furnished house on the slopes of Djamaa el Mokra—they were easy enough to find in those days, and correspondingly inexpensive—and presently installed a teenage Moroccan on the premises to act as night watchman. The house provided a resident cook and gardener, but both of these were discharged from their duties, the cook being replaced by a woman brought in at the suggestion of the watchman. It was not long after this that Marsh felt the first symptoms of a digestive illness which over the months grew steadily worse. The doctors in Tangier advised him to go to London. Two months in hospital there helped him somewhat. No clear diagnosis was made,

299

however, and he returned here only to become bedridden. Eventually he was flown back to Canada on a stretcher, and succumbed there shortly after his arrival.

In all this there was nothing extraordinary; it was assumed that Marsh had been one more victim of slow poisoning by native employees. There have been several such cases during my five decades in Tangier. On each occasion it has been said that the European victim had only himself (or herself) to blame, having encouraged familiarity on the part of a servant. What strikes the outsider as strange is that no one ever takes the matter in hand and inaugurates a search for the culprit, but in the total absence of proof there is no point in attempting an investigation.

Two details complete the story. At some point during his illness Marsh told an acquaintance of the arrangements he had made to provide financial aid for his night watchman in the event that he himself should be obliged to leave Morocco; he had given him a notarized letter to that effect, but apparently the boy never tried to press his claim. The other report came from Dr. Halsey, the physician who arranged for Marsh's removal from the house to the airport. It was this last bit of information which, for me, at least, made the story take on life. According to the doctor, the soles of Marsh's feet had been systematically marked with deep incisions in the form of crude patterns; the cuts were recent, but there was some infection. Dr. Halsey called in the cook and the watchman: they showed astonishment and dismay at the sight of their employer's feet, but were unable to account for the mutilations. Within a few days after Marsh's departure, the original cook and gardener returned to take up residence, the other two having already left the house.

The slow poisoning was classical enough, particularly in the light of Marsh's remark about his provision for the boy's well-being, but the knife-drawn designs on the feet somehow got in the way of whatever combinations of motive one could invent. I thought about it. There could be little doubt that the boy was guilty. He had persuaded Marsh to get rid of the cook that came with the house, even though her wages had to continue to be paid, and to hire another woman (very likely from his own family) to do the cooking. The poisoning process lasts many months if it is to be undetectable, and no one is in a better position to take charge of it than the cook herself. Clearly she knew about the financial arrangement that had been made for the boy, and expected to share in it. At the same time the crosses and circles slashed in the feet were inexplicable. The slow poisoner is patient, careful, methodical; his principal concerns are to keep the dosage effective and to avoid leaving any visible marks. Bravado is unknown to him.

The time came when people no longer told the story of Duncan Marsh. I myself thought of it less often, having no more feasible hypotheses to supply. One evening perhaps five years ago, an American resident here came to me with the news that he had discovered a Moroccan who claimed to have been Marsh's night watchman. The man's name was Larbi; he was a waiter at Le Fin Bec, a small back-street restaurant. Apparently he spoke poor English, but understood it without difficulty. This information was handed me for what it was worth, said the American, in the event that I felt inclined to make use of it.

I turned it over in my mind, and one night a few weeks later I went down to the restaurant to see Larbi for myself. The place was dimly lit and full of Europeans. I studied the three waiters. They were interchangeable, with wide black mustaches, blue jeans and sport shirts. A menu was handed me; I could scarcely read it, even directly under the glow of the little table lamp. When the man who had brought it returned, I asked for Larbi.

He pulled the menu from my hand and left the table. A moment later another of the triumvirate came up beside me and handed me the menu he carried under his arm. I ordered in Spanish. When he brought the soup I murmured that I was surprised to find him working there. This brought him up short; I could see him trying to remember me.

"Why wouldn't I be working here?" His voice was level, without inflection.

"Of course! Why not? It was just that I thought by now you'd have a bazaar or some sort of shop."

His laugh was a snort. "Bazaar!"

When he arrived with the next course, I begged his pardon for meddling in his affairs. But I was interested, I said, because for several years I had been under the impression that he had received a legacy from an English gentleman.

"You mean Señor Marsh?" His eyes were at last wide open.

"Yes, that was his name. Didn't he give you a letter? He told his friends he had."

He looked over my head as he said: "He gave me a letter."

"Have you ever showed it to anyone?" This was tactless, but sometimes it is better to drive straight at the target.

"Why? What good is it? Señor Marsh is dead." He shook his head with an air of finality, and moved off to another table. By the time I had finished my crème caramel, most of the diners had left, and the place seemed even darker. He came over to the table to see if I wanted coffee. I asked for the check. When he brought it I told him I should like very much to see the letter if he still had it.

"You can come tomorrow night or any night, and I'll show it to you. I have it at home."

I thanked him and promised to return in two or three days. I was confused as I left the restaurant. It seemed clear that the waiter did not consider himself to be incriminated in Duncan Marsh's troubles. When, a few nights later, I saw the document, I no longer understood anything.

It was not a letter; it was a *papier timbré* of the kind on sale at tobacconists. It read, simply: *To Whom It May Concern: I, Duncan White-low Marsh, do hereby agree to deposit the sum of One Hundred Pounds to the account of Larbi Lairini, on the first of each month, for as long as I live.* It was signed and notarized in the presence of two Moroccan witnesses, and bore the date June 11, 1966. As I handed it back to him I said: "And it never did you any good."

He shrugged and slipped the paper into his wallet. "How was it going to? The man died."

"It's too bad."

"*Suerte.*" In the Moroccan usage of the word, it means "fate," rather than simple luck.

At that moment I could have pressed on, and asked him if he had any idea as to the cause of Marsh's illness, but I wanted time for considering what I had just learned. As I rose to leave I said: "I'm sorry it turned out that way. I'll be back in a few days." He held out his hand and I shook it. I had no intentions then. I might return soon or I might never go back.

For as long as I live. The phrase echoed in my mind for several weeks. Possibly Marsh had worded it that way so it would be readily understand-able to the *adoul* of Tangier who had affixed their florid signatures to the sheet; yet I could not help interpreting the words in a more melodramatic fashion. To me the document represented the officializing of a covenant already in existence between master and servant: Marsh wanted the watchman's help, and the watchman had agreed to give it. There was nothing upon which to base such an assumption, nevertheless I thought I was on the right track. Slowly I came to believe that if only I could talk to the watchman, in Arabic, and inside the house itself, I might be in a position to see things more clearly.

One evening I walked to Le Fin Bec and without taking a seat motioned to Larbi to step outside for a moment. There I asked him if he could find out whether the house Señor Marsh had lived in was occupied at the moment or not.

"There's nobody living there now." He paused and added: "It's empty. I know the guardian."

I had decided, in spite of my deficient Arabic, to speak to him in his own language, so I said: "Look. I'd like to go with you to the house and see where everything happened. I'll give you fifteen thousand francs for your trouble."

He was startled to hear the Arabic; then his expression shifted to one of satisfaction. "He's not supposed to let anyone in," he said.

I handed him three thousand francs. "You arrange that with him. And fifteen for you when we leave the house. Could we do it Thursday?"

The house had been built, I should say, in the fifties, when good construction was still possible. It was solidly embedded in the hillside, with the forest towering behind it. We had to climb three flights of stairs through the garden to get to the entrance. The guardian, a squinting Djibli in a brown djellaba, followed close on our footsteps, eyeing me with mistrust.

There was a wide terrace above, with a view to the southeast over the town and the mountains. Behind the terrace a shadowed lawn ended where the forest began. The living room was large and bright, with French doors giving onto the lawn. Odors of damp walls and mildew weighted the air. The absurd conviction that I was about to understand everything had taken possession of me; I noticed that I was breathing more quickly. We wandered into the dining room. There was a corridor beyond, and the room where Marsh had slept, shuttered and dark. A wide curving stairway led down to a level where there were two more bedrooms, and continued its spiral to the kitchen and servants' rooms below. The kitchen door opened onto a small flagstoned patio where high philodendrons covered the walls.

Larbi looked out and shook his head. "That's the place where all the trouble began," he said glumly.

I pushed through the doorway and sat down on a wrought-iron bench in the sun. "It's damp inside. Why don't we stay out here?"

The guardian left us and locked up the house. Larbi squatted comfortably on his heels near the bench.

There would have been no trouble at all, he said, if only Marsh had been satisfied with Yasmina, the cook whose wages were included in the rent. But she was a careless worker and the food was bad. He asked Larbi to find him another cook.

"I told him ahead of time that this woman Meriam had a little girl, and some days she could leave her with friends and some days she would have to bring her with her when she came to work. He said it didn't matter, but he wanted her to be quiet."

The woman was hired. Two or three days a week she came accompanied by the child, who would play in the patio where she could watch her. From the beginning Marsh complained that she was noisy. Repeatedly he sent messages down to Meriam, asking her to make the child be still. And one day he went quietly around the outside of the house and down to the patio. He got on all fours, put his face close to the little girl's face, and frowned at her so fiercely that she began to scream. When Meriam rushed out of the kitchen he stood up smiling and walked off. The little girl continued to scream and wail in a corner of the kitchen, until Meriam took her home. That night, still sobbing, she came down with a high fever. For several weeks she hovered between life and death, and when she was finally out of danger she could no longer walk.

Meriam, who was earning relatively high wages, consulted one *fqih* after another. They agreed that "the eye" had been put on the child; it was equally clear that the Nazarene for whom she worked had done it. What they told her she must do, Larbi explained, was to administer certain substances to Marsh which eventually would make it possible to counteract the spell. This was absolutely necessary, he said, staring at me gravely. Even if the señor had agreed to remove it (and of course she never would have mentioned it to him) he would not have been able to. What she gave him could not harm him; it was merely medicine to relax him so that when the time came to undo the spell he would not make any objections.

At some point Marsh confided to Larbi that he suspected Meriam of slipping soporifics into his food, and begged him to be vigilant. The provision for Larbi's well-being was signed as an inducement to enlisting his active support. Since to Larbi the mixtures Meriam was feeding her master were relatively harmless, he reassured him and let her continue to dose him with her concoctions.

Tired of squatting, Larbi suddenly stood up and began to walk back and forth, stepping carefully in the center of each flagstone. "When he had to go to the hospital in London, I told her: 'Now you've made him sick. Suppose he doesn't come back? You'll never break it.' She was worried about it. 'I've done what I could,' she said. 'It's in the hands of Allah.' "

When Marsh did return to Tangier, Larbi urged her to be quick about bringing things to a head, now that she had been fortunate enough to get him back. He was thinking, he said, that it might be better for the señor's health if her treatment were not continued for too long a time.

I asked no questions while he talked; I made a point of keeping my face entirely expressionless, thinking that if he noticed the least flicker of disapproval he might stop. The sun had gone behind the trees and the patio was chilly. I had a strong desire to get up and walk back and forth as he was doing, but I thought even that might interrupt him. Once stopped, the flow might not resume.

Soon Marsh was worse than ever, with racking pains in his abdomen and kidneys. He remained in bed then, and Larbi brought him his food. When Meriam saw that he was no longer able to leave the bed, even to go into the bathroom, she decided that the time had come to get rid of the spell. On the same night that a *fqih* held a ceremony at her house in the presence of the crippled child, four men from Meriam's family came up to Djamaa el Mokra.

"When I saw them coming, I got onto my motorcycle and went into the city. I didn't want to be here when they did it. It had nothing to do with me."

He stood still and rubbed his hands together. I heard the southwest wind beginning to sound in the trees; it was that time of afternoon. "Come. I'll show you something," he said.

We climbed steps around the back of the house and came out onto a terrace with a pergola over it. Beyond this lay the lawn and the wall of trees.

"He was very sick for the next two days. He kept asking me to telephone the English doctor."

"Didn't you do it?"

Larbi stopped walking and looked at me. "I had to clean everything up first. Meriam wouldn't touch him. It was during the rains. He had mud and blood all over him when I got back here and found him. The next day I gave him a bath and changed the sheets and blankets. And I cleaned the house, because they got mud everywhere when they brought him back in. Come on. You'll see where they had to take him."

We had crossed the lawn and were walking in the long grass that skirted the edge of the woods. A path led off to the right through the tangle of undergrowth, and we followed it, climbing across boulders and fallen tree trunks until we came to an old stone well. I leaned over the wall of rocks around it and saw the small circle of sky far below.

"They had to drag him all the way here, you see, and hold him steady right over the well while they made the signs on his feet, so the blood would fall into the water. It's no good if it falls on the side of the well. And they had to make the same signs the *fqih* drew on paper for the little girl. That's hard to do in the dark and in the rain. But they did it. I saw the cuts when I bathed him."

Cautiously I asked him if he saw any connection between all this and Marsh's death. He ceased staring into the well and turned around. We started to walk back toward the house.

"He died because his hour had come."

And had the spell been broken? I asked him. Could the child walk afterward? But he had never heard, for Meriam had gone to Kenitra not much later to live with her sister.

When we were in the car, driving back down to the city, I handed him the money. He stared at it for several seconds before slipping it into his pocket.

I let him off in town with a vague sense of disappointment, and I saw that I had not only expected, but actually hoped, to find someone on whom the guilt might be fixed. What constitutes a crime? There was no criminal intent—only a mother moving in the darkness of ancient ignorance. I thought about it on my way home in the taxi.

AN INOPPORTUNE VISIT

After several hundred years of traveling in space Santa Rosenda conceived a desire to return to Earth. Recently she had been homesick for her native land, and she had an unreasoning belief that feeling the Spanish earth beneath her feet once more would make her happy. She did not announce her arrival. If she were recognized, the attention she would attract would make the peace she sought an impossibility.

Yet for Santa Rosenda to feel entirely in touch with the Earth, it was necessary for her to materialize; only then could she be persuaded of the reality of what was around her. This of course made her visible—a drawback, partially because of her anachronistic clothing, and even more because the slight aura around her head bore the unmistakable form of a halo.

Her arrival was sudden: she simply appeared one afternoon from behind a clump of bushes in the public garden of a provincial Spanish city. A woman who taught chemistry at the nearby college was sitting on a bench. When she saw Santa Rosenda she sprang up in a panic and ran off. This did not augur well for a restful time on Earth, and Santa Rosenda realized then that she must avoid cities.

Accordingly she made a landing in a field outside a small village on the island of Menorca. She had chosen to come down in the field because the contours of the landscape pleased her, and she believed it to be deserted. But a village girl was crouched there gathering greens, and the sudden arrival of Santa Rosenda made her spring up in amazement. At this, Santa Rosenda quickly dematerialized, but it was too late. The girl rushed back to the village crying that she had witnessed a miracle. Her story was given complete credence. Several hundred people hurried to the field hoping for a glimpse of the saintly presence. Hovering above, Santa Rosenda observed them with distaste, and determined to transfer herself to the mainland. The problem was to find a pleasant spot where she could stay without fear of being seen.

Considering the various difficulties with which she had to contend, it is surprising that she did not renounce her project and return to space. She had no means of communicating with people, even if she had desired to do so, since she was without a voice. She could neither read nor write, for in her time literacy had not been considered necessary, even for saints.

These were not ideal conditions under which to return to her homeland, but she had no choice in the matter. If she wanted to be on Earth she must accept them. Such minor disadvantages, however, were more than outweighed by her having no need either to eat or to sleep, and above all by her ability to dematerialize at any moment if necessary, much as she disliked the sensation. In any case, she had not returned in order to converse with people; on the contrary, she hoped to avoid all contact with them.

Thus when she found an inviting cave in the side of a hill, she established herself not far from its entrance where she could gaze out at the sunlit landscape, and then close her eyes and meditate upon the differences which had come about since she had last left the earth. She knew that stasis did not exist on the planet, that everything was in a state of constant flux, thus she was not astonished by the extraordinary changes which she could sense had come about during her absence. Her clothing preoccupied her principally, for she realized that more than anything else it was the garments she wore which called attention to the disparity between her appearance and that of other women. She would not find the peace she sought until somehow she had managed to make herself indistinguishable from them. With this in mind, she wrapped her head in a rag she had found there in the cave. At least, she thought, the halo would not show.

One afternoon when she opened her eyes for a moment, she discovered two small boys playing not far from the entrance to the cave. They had seen her, she realized, but they appeared to take no particular notice of her. Reassured, she shut her eyes again. The next time she opened them, the boys were gone. They came nearly every day, always remaining at some distance from the cave.

What she did not know was that the boys had told their parents about the strange woman who was always seated there in the same spot, day after day. Since there was a military barracks with an airstrip on the other side of the hill, the public had been requested to report any suspicious-looking individuals in the vicinity.

The boys' father spoke to a civil guard about the continued presence of a woman in the cave, with the result that Santa Rosenda was visited by a group of soldiers, who obliged her to accompany them to a jeep waiting in the road on the other side of the woods. They plied her with questions which she heard and partially understood, but could not answer. Impelled largely by curiosity, she decided to acquiesce and go along with them; perhaps she could discover what they wanted of her. Besides, it seemed to her that there would be something highly indelicate about effecting a transformation and disappearing in front of them. She preferred to do that in private.

She was taken first to a police station, where she understood nothing of what was going on around her. From there they took her to a hospital, explaining to the nurse at the entrance that their charge was a deaf-mute. Another nurse led her to a small room and left her there by herself, locking the door. The doctor who was to examine her had caught a glimpse of her as she was brought into the building, and because of the outlandish clothing and the rag wrapped around her head, immediately suspected her of being a man in disguise. Hearing from the nurse that she could not speak merely strengthened his suspicion.

Vamos a ver, he said to himself as he opened the door of the room where she had been left. A moment earlier, Santa Rosenda, incensed at being shut into so tiny a room and wearied by the entire senseless procedure, had dematerialized. The room was empty. The doctor, in a fury, called the nurse and told her that her carelessness had allowed what was probably a dangerous criminal to escape. The nurse replied that the door had been locked, and that in any case, her opinion was that the woman was mentally deficient, nothing more. Nevertheless, the police were alerted and a search was inaugurated, beginning inside the hospital.

As the nurses and interns went through the building, looking in all the rooms, Santa Rosenda watched them, thinking that they were behaving like idiots. She could not imagine what they wanted of her, but she mistrusted their intentions. As she floated around the building, observing the turmoil she had caused, she came upon a cloakroom where the nurses left their street clothes before donning their uniforms. This was the stroke of good luck she had been hoping for. Dresses, sweaters and coats hung on hooks along the wall, and many of the lockers were open, disclosing more garments for her examination. It took her only about ten minutes to choose the pieces of clothing she wanted. There were shoes in which her feet were comfortable, and she discovered a large Italian silk kerchief to wind around her head in place of the rag. Now, it seemed to her, she could move through any street without attracting attention. To test her anonymity she walked out of the main entrance gate of the hospital, and passed unnoticed.

The city resembled no city she had ever seen. Its streets were thronged with people, and although they did not appear to be in a festive mood, she assumed they were celebrating a holiday of some sort. The automobiles (which she though of as wagons) all emitted an unpleasant smoke as they passed. A few minutes of contact with the crowd to persuade her that she was truly anonymous, and then she would leave for a quiet spot in the country, and would not set foot again in a city.

All at once, mixed with the smells of the street, she recognized the faint odor of resin burning in a censer. To her left a doorway opened into a church. Santa Rosenda turned and entered.

Immediately she knew that everything was wrong. The illumination within was almost like sunlight, and it did not come from candles. The music was not what it should have been. She listened until the priest began to speak. She could not understand the words. Suddenly she realized with horror that he was speaking, not in Latin, but in the language of the street.

Without a thought in her head save that of reaching the man and stemming the flow of sacrilege, Santa Rosenda began to run toward the altar. The few who noticed her did not try to stop her. Even when she was in front of the priest and he was staring into her face, he continued mechanically to intone the hateful words.

With both hands she pushed him in the chest, and for an instant they grappled, as people hurried in their direction. In the momentary struggle the silk kerchief was pulled from Santa Rosenda's head, and before the eyes of everyone the circle of light shone above her hair. She did not wait to see the reaction of the priest or the congregation, but resumed her normal state of invisibility. The degradation of the Mass was one metamorphosis she was not prepared to accept, and she no longer had any desire to be on Earth. In a few more centuries she might return; she hoped that by then matters would have been set straight.

IN ABSENTIA

(sent to Pamela Loeffler)

I'll try to keep this short so it won't take you too much time to read it. I know how women worry when they have to settle into a new house, with new servants to take charge of, and when they're faced with all those terrible decisions about how to place the furniture and where to store things.

This is a beautiful sunny day for a change. It's been raining on and off this past week, so that the sudden appearance of bright sunlight is a tonic. And the sun made me think of you, who have always loved it as much as I. Do you still sunbathe, out there where you are, or is it too hot? I gave up the practice years ago. Too many of my friends developed skin cancer from it.

So this morning I woke up thinking: I shall write to Pamela today. I know it's been a long time since we saw each other or communicated, but I've followed your activities from afar via what are admittedly unreliable sources: *Time* and the *International Herald Tribune.* And I can now congratulate you. (Nothing is sacred; everyone knows how much you got. But even that amount won't ruin old Loeffler, so don't ever feel guilt.) I can only remark that occasionally the scale tips in favor of justice, and I'm happy that you've been able to experience the phenomenon concretely.

I now have a vague concept of where you are: on the north shore of Maui. I've even found Kahului and Paukōkalo. As I studied the map I couldn't help noticing that the entire west coast of the island of Hawaii is decorated with lava flows, as you no doubt know. What amuses me

312

is that each one is named after the year the stuff slid down the mountainside, so that you get *Lava Flow of 1801, Lava Flow of 1859, Lava Flow of 1950.* It puts me in mind of the streets in Latin American countries, named after important dates. "He lives on the corner of the Fourth of April and the Nineteenth of October."

I remember, when people used to ask me what Pamela was doing, I'd reply: Oh, she's busy being beautiful. I remember, also, being taken to task for my flippant answer. But what's wrong with it? Isn't it true? You *are* beautiful (as we know) and you've remained beautiful thanks to your determination to do so. That requires concentration and effort. How otherwise would there have been a Loeffler?

Now I'm trying to imagine you in the un-American decor of our fiftieth state. Do you wear jodhpurs, like Karen Blixen in Kenya? When you have a moment, send a snapshot. I'll be waiting for it.

(sent to Pamela Loeffler)

No, a three-month silence is quite forgivable. I wonder you were able to find the time even when you did. Most of the matters I felt like asking you about in my last, but refrained from mentioning out of tact, seem to have been arranged more or less happily: plumbing, staff, provisions, neighbors. The last named would be rather important, I should think. Great that you should have discovered the Hollywood people only six miles up the road. I don't remember ever having seen his name. But then, he could have been the most famous director in the U.S. and I still wouldn't have heard of him. As you know, I was never a film enthusiast. Anyway, it's nice that they're there, and companionable to boot. They sound *echt* Beverly Hills, but that may be only because I'm relying on your description.

Above all I was happy to hear that a few old friends will be visiting you soon. If Florence actually arrives (does she ever know what she's doing?) give her my love. I can see her getting to San Francisco and deciding to go to Carmel instead of Honolulu, and then two months later suddenly arriving at your place without a word of warning, just when the house is *archicomplet.* I remember one winter when she kept the house in Turtle Bay open, with the housekeeper in residence, to take care of her cat while she was away (but for six months or more) because she believed that cats grow fond of places rather than people, and the cat would have been too unhappy if it had been taken away from the house. Then as soon as she got back home she gave the cat to somebody who lived in Connecticut.

Tell me—you ought to know this by now, being surrounded by exotic flora—is frangipani the same tree which is known in the Philippines as ylang-ylang, and in India as champak? I'm not trying to test you; I don't know myself, and there's no reason why I should expect you to. And yet it's just the sort of thing you might know. If you don't, perhaps one of your friends from Boston will. Bostonians often know the most unlikely things. At least, they used to. Or are there no true Bostonians left?

I see you understand the pleasure that can be got from writing letters. In other centuries this was taken for granted. Not any longer. Only a few people carry on true correspondences. No time, the rest tell you. Quicker to telephone. Like saying a photograph is more satisfying than a painting. There wasn't all that much time for writing letters in the past, either, but time was found, as it generally can be for whatever gives pleasure.

And when *you* find the time, send me a few recent snapshots of yourself and the place. I imagine they'll have to be Polaroids, since from what you write you haven't easy access to what we like to call the amenities of civilization. It sounds to me as though most of your supplies had to be flown over from Honolulu. That's all too reminiscent of the situation here. "We're waiting for a new shipment. Maybe in three or four months." Those are the honest *baqals;* the others say: "Next week, *in-cha'Allah,"* knowing it's untrue. You may, or you may never, get your saucepan or your powdered milk or your trowel or your broom or your Gruyère or your spatula. More likely you never will, for such things are not allowed entry into the country these days. *Tant pis et à bientôt.*

(sent to Pamela Loeffler)

Thank you for the year-old photo of the house-in-progress. Even without its finishing touches I can see how handsome it must be now. It's really very sumptuous, very grand. You must have room for a dozen visitors, in case you ever should feel afraid of succumbing to melancholia. But I see no sign of *you,* nor of anyone else. Incredibly fine vegetation.

What makes you think I should be able to interpret your dream? In the first place, I don't believe X can explain to Y what Y dreamed. How do I know what the act of running along a pier represents to you, or what your usual reaction to seaweed is? I don't understand my own dreams, much less those of others. I do notice that people have a tendency to recount dreams in which there is action, to such an extent that I often wonder if they don't unconsciously supply the action in the telling. Because I can't ever recall any narrative content in my own dreams. They're more like a succession of unrelated still photographs, rather than a film. But dream tellers go right on saying: "And then. And then." I'd like to know if it's really that way with them, or if they only feel that it should be that way.

And besides, why interpret a dream? If it's a warning from your unconscious mind, you'll get the message eventually in any case. Tell me, can you force a dream to recur? I can't. Anyway, good dreaming.

(sent to Pamela Loeffler)

Still at me about dreams? Why do you say that I "of all people" should know about them? I don't think about them in the way you do. For me they're a psychic barometer, useful only to the person who does the dreaming, in the way a clinical thermometer is useful to the one running a fever. It seems a mistake to attach particular importance to one image rather than another (no matter how significant it may seem at the time of dreaming) since the images themselves are only delegates for other, unformulated images. How can you expect anyone to give you the "meaning" of masses of red seaweed floating in the water? Seaweed means seaweed. You also claim that there was a total lack of affect connected with the sight of it. Then why in God's name are you interested in discovering its "meaning"? If it meant nothing to you in the dream, how can it mean anything in retrospect?

You ask if the Moslems here have a system for explaining dreams. They have, of course, as they have (theoretically) a system for everything, but it's divination using approved religious symbology. I can't see that it's in any sort of agreement with Freudian theory. (How could it be?) It all might have come out of a little book called *Ali Baba's Dream Almanac*. But they believe it, just as the Hindus believe in that idiotic zodiac with its twelve signs. (And not only the Hindus, alas.)

Dear Pamela, the value of a letter can't be measured quantitatively. If you haven't time to write what you call a "real" letter, then write a few lines. I don't expect anyone to compose long-winded epistles, as I sometimes do. I write letters because I enjoy doing it. It doesn't even matter too much whether the recipient takes pleasure in reading what I write; I've had my pleasure.

So don't decide not to write merely because you know it can be only a few lines. You could send me a note that read: "A muggy day and I'm depressed. I had baked ham and fruit salad for lunch." And I'd be delighted. But if you send nothing at all, you leave the field to the imagination, which is always ready with its angst. I want to hear how you feel about the house, as well as about the guests who are staying with you. You wouldn't need much time to tell me that, would you?

(sent to Pamela Loeffler)

I think Tangier is getting less and less livable. One of the principal reasons why I've continued to stay here has been the good air that we breathe. But the traffic has increased tenfold in the past five years, and with practically all the recent cars equipped with diesel engines, the streets are full of smoke. The buses and trucks constantly whoof out fat black columns of it. At home it doesn't bother me, because I live high up. It's walking in the street that's troublesome. Apart from the pollution, the sidewalks are crowded with obstacles: cars parked in the middle, groups of students sitting along the curb, and beggars installed against the walls. If you mention the beggars to a Moroccan, he'll tell you: Not one of them is from Tangier. They're all down from the mountains. Don't give them anything.

You underestimate the intelligence of the Moroccans at your peril. They know when you're lying and when you're only exaggerating, they know when you mean what you say and when you're only talking, and these things they know directly and not as a result of deduction. It's true that they sometimes scent deceit where there is none. I've argued with Moroccans who refuse to believe that anyone has been to the moon. "Just America advertising." Others, admitting the moonwalk, think the money should have been spent feeding hungry people. "What good did it do?" They're not fascinated or excited by the idea of exploring space, because they have no concept of historic movement or growth; for them time is an eternal stasis. Everything is as it always has been, and will remain thus forever. A comforting philosophy, if you can subscribe.

(sent to Pamela Loeffler)

Your letter about the Palmers very amusing, I thought. Surely you're not encouraging Dick to look for property in your vicinity? That would be catastrophic, wouldn't it? I agree that it's nice to have acquaintances living only fifteen or twenty miles away, if your first reaction each time you see them doesn't express itself as a sudden sinking sensation. It takes such a lot of energy to fight that. I've got to the point of preferring solitude to being under that sort of stress.

Of course Ruth was always a negative quantity, even before she married Dick. Collecting potsherds, pieces of quartz and crinoids, when I knew her. So the butterfly business is quite in line. It must be marvelous to see her bounding around as she wields the net! Hyperthyroid and graceless. Dick is merely obstinate and dictatorial; that's how I remember him. (I haven't seen him in fifteen years, more or less, but I feel pretty certain that he hasn't changed much. Perhaps extra years have decreased his energy, but it doesn't take much energy to be egotistical if that's one's nature.) When he had a flat here he was completely wrapped up in the Rolling Stones, who were friends he'd known in London. The name meant nothing to me, but Dick insisted they were the greatest rock group in existence. He got me out of bed one night at one o'clock, came pounding on my door, very excited. I must go with him to his flat because he had the Stones there. I, sleepy: "What stones?" He explained, and I went. A man named Jagger, dressed for a costume party, reclined on the bed, gnawing on a leg of lamb. A girl lay face down at his feet, and there were other people spread out asleep on the floor. It wasn't bright enough in the room for me to see their costumes in detail. Mr. Jagger said nothing. His muzzle was shiny with lamb fat. Dick saw my surprise at the sight of the inert bodies on the floor, and confided that everyone had taken a new drug which apparently induced a comatose state. It's strange: Dick has this air of breathless enthusiasm. It's a physical attribute which ought to be contagious, but isn't. Instead, it comes across as a sales talk, and creates next to no empathy.

After about an hour I thanked him and said I was off to bed. This didn't go down at all well. He took it as an offense, assuming, quite correctly, that I hadn't appreciated my great opportunity of meeting the Stones. I considered that I had been patient, but as I went out and turned to thank Dick again, he drew himself up and, pretending to be a very proper English governess, said: "Oh, urfty turfty wiffy bibben bibben, oh yes!" and slammed the door.

If the moment seems right, you may mention this episode to Dick, and see if he remembers it. What he's sure to remember is that they all went to Marrakech the next morning at seven o'clock, Dick included. That was in the pre-Ruth days.

I'm not surprised that Florence postponed her visit; in fact, I predicted it. What does strike me as strange is that you should have Dick and Ruth Palmer there, because I know they're not the ones you'd most like to have staying with you. But of course that's what happens when one has a large house in a remote place. Still, it's certainly better for you to have guests than to be alone. This next guest of yours, Fronda Farquhar, who is she and what is she? And that name, at the far end of credibility! You speak of her as if I should know who she is, but I don't. What does she do? Or is she another Ruth, searching for arrowheads and shells?

Well, it all sounds like fun.

(sent to Susan Choate)

Now what? Hippocrates strikes again. I wondered at your long silence, and now I understand. Hepatitis B is not so amusing. What astonishes me is that you got rid of it in a hospital, which I thought was a place where one contracted it rather than cured it. Do you think it's really gone? I must say I hope so. That hospital bill you enclosed is staggering. How can you be sure that I'll be able to pay it? Clearly I can't keep sending larger and larger amounts. All your expenses grow like weeds. I realize that you can't help it; money has less and less value, but that simply means that people like me can buy less and less. I'm not lecturing; I'm just bewailing this hospital bill. It's surprising they let you out of the institution without some sort of guarantee that it would be paid. Naturally you took it for granted that I could pay it, without considering the possibility that I might be short of funds. And I can pay it, yes, but not with pleasure. How did you ever get hepatitis? Did they have any theories as to the origin? I hope they gave you some pointers as to how to avoid it in the future.

Did you get the caftan? It should be ideal for dressy occasions in New York or Boston, if indeed there are any more such things. (Although I'm told that girls are becoming interested once more in clothes, and can conceive of wearing something besides those proletarian blue jeans they've been affecting for the past few decades.) Anyway, the caftan is a museum piece. That very heavy silk brocade is no longer woven—not even by Fortuny. I bought it from a Moroccan friend in whose family it had been since the turn of the century. I know you'll look superb in it, and I only hope you'll wear it. (Not in a hospital, however!) I hope to hear from you.

(sent to Susan Choate)

Glad to hear you've had no further trouble with your liver. But Good God, Suky, no wonder you came down with hepatitis. Haiti, of all insane places to go, even for a short holiday. I'm not surprised you didn't mention it to me. You must have known I'd do my best to discourage you. You seem to think it was all right because you were invited, so that it cost you nothing. But it did cost you six weeks of classes, not to mention that it cost me a fortune to pay for it.

You say Haiti was picturesque, and I'm sure it is. But it's precisely in this sort of poverty-induced picturesqueness that diseases are rampant. I myself have spent plenty of time enjoying the poverty of others in exotic places, and have paid for it with ailments and aches, as you know. But the point is that hepatitis is a serious disease, and you must take it

319

seriously, something I suspect you don't do, to judge by your flippant references to the experience. Remember that your great-grandmother Gray caught it on a trip to Mexico and died of it, and very quickly. So for God's sake stay put, there at Mount Holyoke, and don't add to my insomnia by going to places you know may be dangerous.

It's a help to know you don't drink. A heavy diet of cannabis can be almost as harmful to the liver, you know. (Likewise tobacco and coffee!) Your doctor must have told you all this, but that doesn't mean that you listened. Having withstood an attack doesn't make you immune; on the contrary, you're more vulnerable to another attack.

Forgive me if I lapse into pedantry, but you spoke of "convincing" the manager of the bookshop to extend credit. It's not possible to convince "to." If you're going to use *convince,* you need either "of" or "that." Otherwise use *persuade.* End of lecture, and until soon.

(sent to Pamela Loeffler)

There's no point in asking for news from here. News isn't generally made in this part of the world, or if something occurs here which becomes news in the rest of the world, we hear about it in foreign broadcasts. And the broadcasts of course are full of talk about terrorism. For most Europeans and Americans the word *terrorist* is unqualifiedly pejorative; while to the people here it suggests a patriot. Thus actions some consider criminal and contemptible are to others heroic. How can the two ever see eye to eye?

A theatrical agency in Sydney! I didn't know they had them. I understand her being called Fronda Farquhar if that's where she's from. You make the picnics sound like something out of Waugh or early Angus Wilson. How did you weather three of them, all with F. Farquhar as well as Ruth P.? My suspicion is that the reason Dick refused to go with you is that he was loath to get too far away from the source of supply: your refrigerator. He's always been a glutton. I shan't ask your opinion on that: you're too far away to put irrelevant questions to. But it must be something of a relief to have all of them gone, in spite of feeling alone and missing them. I can't believe you actually miss those three particular people, though. Isn't what you miss the presence of someone, anyone, to talk to now and then? That's not an irrelevant question, by the way, and

I do put it to you. Because it's occurred to me that Sue Choate, my father's sister's great-granddaughter, will be visiting a college friend in Honolulu, and might enjoy a visit with you. (I think I told you I was financing her education, so it's of great interest to me where she spends her vacations.) The last time she was out of the States she went to Haiti and caught hepatitis. One can't ask a seventeen-year-old to be circumspect in matters like that, of course. Haiti was there, she was invited, it sounded exciting, so she went.

Let me know about that. I think it might be pleasant for you both. She's charming, lively, and very attractive. Talkative, but intelligently so, and can be turned off with ease. (I'm describing her as she was at the age of fifteen; I haven't seen her since.)

If you have crowds of people scheduled to arrive, and Suky would be in the way, that's of course another story. But let me know when you can, so I can plan her summer.

What happened to those people from California who lived only six miles from you? Don't they like picnics?

See enclosed sheet with Sue's address and phone number at Mount Holyoke, in case.

(sent to Susan Choate)

It was good of you to write so soon, even if I wasn't exactly pleased to hear you'd sold the caftan. And without ever wearing it! I admit that you got an unbelievable price for it. Your friend Myra must be wallowing in dollars. But that wasn't why I sent it to you, so that you could sell it to have spending money. I was hoping it would be a very special item of your wardrobe. You say that one has to get used to doing without things when one becomes poor, and that you couldn't face asking me for money when I was paying for the hospital. All that I appreciate completely. Still, I'm sorry you didn't bring the subject up before getting rid of the garment. I'd have tried to dissuade you, even though I couldn't have sent you the twelve hundred you got for it—at least, not all at once, which is obviously the way you wanted it.

Have you thought of how you'll spend the summer? Much as I'd like to see you, I wouldn't advise your coming here. There's nothing much here to interest you, I'm afraid. Hotels are relatively inexpensive, yes, but not cheap enough for my purse. And the friends with guest houses where you might have stayed gratis have died or moved away.

It has occurred to me that you might like to visit Hawaii. I know the suggestion sounds absurd, coming directly after the song of poverty. But there I do know someone who might put you up, and probably would be delighted to do so. You've never met her, but you may have heard me speak of her when you were a child. More likely not. Your summer would cost me only the round-trip fare, and what's more, I shouldn't be worrying that you might have sneaked off to Mexico or Jamaica, or, God forbid, Haiti. You, of course, know what you want and how you feel like spending your vacation. This is just one suggestion; others may appear in the course of time.

I should add that I do appreciate your concern about money, and understand that you sold the caftan to help me, so I'm not too chagrined that you never wore it, and that I haven't a photo of you modeling it. The postal system, incidentally, is worse than ever.

(sent to Susan Choate)

I can't help wondering why you're so eager to know how much I paid for that caftan. It's clear that you hope it was very little, as if that would somehow justify your having sold it. But your logic is ailing. It's not a question of how much *I* paid for it; it's a question rather of how much *you* paid for it, and the answer is nothing. Therefore you cleared your twelve hundred and ought not to bother your head with what it cost me. I can see how your mind is working, and I suppose it shows family solidarity: that is, what's mine is ours. Since you write about practically nothing else in your short letter, I have to assume that it's important to you to know how much more your selling price was than my purchase price. You want to know how much "we" made on the deal. So in spite of your not seeming to be aware that it's unheard-of to inquire the price of a gift, I think you deserve an answer, since you made "us" a profit of an even thousand, minus the mailing charges. Does that please you?

You don't seem to take my suggestion about Hawaii very seriously.

I can see why, with all our talk about scarce money. Nevertheless I meant it in all seriousness, as a way of solving the vacation problem. I can see that you may not be eager to be the guest of a woman you don't know, or of anyone else, for that matter. But Pamela is what's called easygoing—tolerant and gregarious. She gives the impression of being twenty years younger than she really is. (She's in her late fifties, and may have had cosmetic surgery, but I somehow doubt it. That sort of thing she'd be secretive about.) Do I make her sound like someone to be avoided? I hope not, as I'd be delighted to see you established there for the summer. Besides solving the vacation problem, your sojourn there could prove advantageous in other ways.

Or perhaps I'm crazy, in which case nothing I've said makes sense. Anyway, let me hear.

(sent to Susan Choate)

Your friend McCall sounds like a real slob. Why would he drive you to Hartford knowing you were going to have to take the bus back, and not mention it to you beforehand? You didn't seem to find that unusual; I suppose this sort of irresponsible rudeness is part of today's etiquette. I don't find it appealing, but then, young people go out of their way to be as unattractive as possible, both in their persons and their behavior. So your date from Amherst is probably no worse than the rest.

I can see you're beginning to give the Hawaiian idea a little thought. You're wrong, however, to use the word *directive,* and to suggest that I've been "pressuring" you, as you put it. To issue a directive is one thing, and to request a favor is something else. Perhaps I didn't make myself clear in the last letter. Staying with Pamela out there you would be in a position, if you were clever enough, to receive financial assistance for the coming year. That wouldn't have occurred to you in your youthful innocence. But it occurred to me, and I see it as a distinct possibility. Pamela has more money than she can spend, and she's generous. She and I are old friends as you know, and if she took a fancy to you and offered to help you, she'd know she was also helping me. Obviously, once you were there it would be up to you to decide how to play it. A question

323

of choosing the right moment in which to be perfectly truthful. Clearly it's in my interest that you go (and even more in your own, I suspect).

Meditate some more, and when you come up with an answer, let me know. But don't wait too long.

(sent to Susan Choate)

Pamela has risen to the occasion. She's asked me to tell you that she'd be delighted to have you stay with her for as long as it suits you—the entire summer if you like. As soon as she knows what you've decided she'll be in touch directly with you. But if you make up your mind to go, wire or phone her immediately, even before you let me know. Because if you accept her invitation through me, it will take the rest of the spring. Massachusetts-Morocco, Morocco-Hawaii.

If I had access to a telephone I'd call you. And if sending a telegram didn't involve standing in line for an hour first, I'd wire you, and save that much more time. But I'm not up to that.

In any case, the machinery has been set in motion. Let me hear.

(sent to Susan Choate)

Your letter was the best sort of news. Thank God for Lucy Piper! Knowing that you had a friend who lived in Hawaii, I went out on a limb and lied a bit to Pamela, telling her that you'd been asked by this girl's family for a visit. I needed a pretext on which to hang my suggestion that Pamela invite you to Maui. (Since you were going to be in Hawaii, etc.) Now it turns out not to be a lie, after all. The two weeks in Honolulu ought to be fun, particularly if her parents aren't going to be there. The Pipers may be paragons of charm for all I know, but things are generally better when families are not around.

I'll have the New York bank send you fifteen hundred. With what you have, that should be enough for fare both ways. Send me a wire when you get to San Francisco before the Hawaii flight. I shan't write more now. I only wanted to let you know how delighted I am that you decided to go.

IN ABSENTIA

(sent to Susan Choate)

The wire Pamela sent you is essentially the same as the one she sent me. She'll pick you up at the Pipers' June twentieth and fly you on to Maui. It's an ideal solution. Providential. She wanted to be in Honolulu anyway that week, so she's not putting herself out for you. It just happened to fall right.

In spite of your trepidation, I'd say the possibility that Pamela will be bored by your presence is nil. You by her, who knows? But very unlikely.

What do you mean, "procedure" to follow with Pamela? Of course there is none. You simply play everything by ear. How can I advise you from here, or dictate a course of behavior? Or foresee the complex choreography of subterfuges and dissimulations which will make up your conversations? Women know how to handle each other, and need no man's advice.

Don't think about these things now. It will just interfere with your studying. Time enough for that later. Finish up your work and go with Lucy Piper. I hope she's fun to travel with.

Postscriptum: Destroy my letters once you've read them. There won't be all that many, in any case. The summer's too short.

(sent to Pamela Loeffler)

So everything meshed, *grace à Dieu.* And now Suky's with you. Could you gauge her immediate reaction to the new environment? I ask you because I don't expect her to tell me accurately in her letters, if she ever decides to write me. I'm a little surprised that she hasn't sent me even a few words. I suppose she thought a letter from you would be enough.

While we're still talking about Suky, I'm so glad you find her companionable. One never knows with the very young; their moods are mercurial. She's been alone far too much. Her parents both died when she was twelve, and I've seen her only once, and briefly, since then. She will have changed.

There never was such a thing as hashish in Morocco; it was the Americans who first manufactured it here. Kif is volatile, and they were

325

looking for a more compact and durable form of it, so they used a vise. This made an ersatz sort of hashish. The Moroccans, not knowing hashish, good or bad, followed suit, and found the product salable abroad. They've been pressing this inferior merchandise ever since, and are still making great fortunes exporting it. There's a direct relationship between the commerce in hashish and the prevalence of corruption. A huge sum can silence anyone. I take it the situation is very different where you are; do you know anything about it? That is, more than you can read in the press?

Suggest to Sue that she write me a note at least, if she can find the time between dates. Two boyfriends? Who are they? I imagined you as fairly isolated. Apparently you're not.

What makes you say I'm "obsessed" by the girl? If you've even suggested such an idea to her, inevitably she'll see it in a Freudian light. This would give her a perfect pretext for not writing. In what other way could she take it? And in what way did *you* mean it, for that matter? "Obsessed" is a word used too often.

(sent to Pamela Loeffler)

I can't help feeling some anxiety over not having had some word from Sue. I know you say she's fine, but I'm not convinced. If she were her usual self, she'd write. It's clear that something is troubling her that she shrinks from telling me, something more than this non-sense she's been feeding you about being "terrified" of me. She knows that's laughable. How can she speak of me as "authoritarian"? We haven't seen each other in several years, and no one can terrify by mail.

What's got into her? The difficulty is that you don't know her, so you can't notice any little changes that might have come over her recently. Have you tried to persuade her to sit down and scribble a few words?

It goes without saying that I don't expect you to choose her friends for her. I have no objection to her seeing a Japanese mechanic three nights a week, or every night, so you needn't feel uneasy on my account. Please understand that I don't consider you in any way responsible for her behavior. She's old enough to account for it herself. As she undoubtedly has told you, she's a partisan of feminine "liberation."

(sent to Susan Choate)

I saw something this morning that amused me. Two little boys about five years old were playing at bullfighting. The bull was a perambulator containing a strapped-in baby under blankets, and the one pushing the pram was making frantic attempts to gore the torero, who dodged and sidestepped the attacks. At one point the bull made an all-out desperate attempt and charged with such force that it banged into a telephone pole. Torero delighted. Baby jolted but impervious.

Do write a few lines about the place, about the general setup. Remember, I've never been there, and am curious. A few sentences in a personal report mean more than pages of a travel article. I'm not asking for an essay; you can tell it all in two paragraphs. One on the place and the other on Pamela. *Finis.*

(sent to Susan Choate)

And now you write me, when you're just about ready to leave, so that I can't even be sure this will reach you in time. At least you gave what is probably an honest reason for your silence: you were having too good a time. That is of course the best reason, and I'm glad it turned out that way. It would have been awful if you'd hated the place and been bored by Pamela. But what a peculiar creature you are, to keep me waiting all summer for a sheet of paper it would have taken five minutes to cover.

The last message I had from you was the wire you sent from San Francisco, so I have no idea of your present finances, or even whether you bought a round-trip passage. One can only worry so much, however; then one becomes philosophical. I suppose philosophy is merely sublimated worry. If this were a telephone conversation I could say: Let me speak to Pamela. So I shall speak to her, in a letter I'll write as soon as I get this one into its envelope. I'm very happy you've loved your vacation.

(sent to Pamela Loeffler)

I just finished a note to the culprit. As you probably know, she finally decided to write me before she returned to college. She describes everything and all in glowing terms—particularly you, about whom she made some highly astute observations, all favorable. I think she has seen the entire spectrum of your personality, complex though it is, and for that I give her good marks. I can see from your last letter that you loved having her there with you.

Does she seem at all preoccupied by the thought of money? If she's been sensible, she should have more than enough to get her back to Massachusetts. Nevertheless, if you get this in time, and think she should have a bit more, please let her have it. I'll repay you immediately.

I'll try to write an actual letter soon, which this is not. What I'd call a true letter ought to be an amalgam of personal conversation, diary (what happened) and journal (what one thinks about what happened). But anyway.

(sent to Pamela Loeffler)

Your letter was indeed bad news. Are you really satisfied with the doctor? I ask because I'm surprised that he didn't seem to be sure whether it was a return of the hepatitis she caught in Haiti, or simple dysentery (non-amoebic, I mean).

Poor Suky! Tell her to relax, and not to worry about being late in getting back to classes. She can make up the work easily.

I wonder if it occurred to your doctor that she might have sunstroke. You spoke of her long hours at the beach. Her symptoms sound a little like my own when I was struck by the sun in Cuba. It's at times like this that I wish I had a telephone. Wire me if there's any sudden change for the worse in her condition.

I saw something incredible in a French magazine last week. A friend of de Gaulle was being interviewed. One question: "Then de Gaulle was not anti-Semitic?" The reply: "Well, in 1940, I remember that André Maurois came and asked to speak to de Gaulle privately. The general turned to someone beside him and said: 'What's that kike doing here?'

But that was just his way of speaking. De Gaulle was never anti-Semitic."
Little things like that make life worth living.

The dog may be man's best friend, but only if he has a master who
feeds him. Here the dogs with no human ties are a menace. They hunt
in packs of fifteen or twenty, and have formed the habit of attacking
tethered donkeys when night comes. They crowd around the donkey's
head, trying to reach its neck. It backs up, and slowly winds its chain
tightly around the tree. When it can no longer move, it belongs to the
dogs, which devour it. In Tangier there used to be a dogcatcher, who
piled ownerless dogs into his little truck and took them to the pound.
Now there's neither catcher nor pound. The dogs are considered a natural
hazard, like wild boars and snakes.

I hope it doesn't make too much extra bother for you to have Suky
laid up in bed. I'm sorry I was instrumental in bringing this on you.
You're an angel, as always. Write me soon.

(sent to Pamela Loeffler)

You don't sound very sanguine about Sue's improvement. Of course she
hasn't written me, but I can scarcely expect her to if she feels miserable.
She knows you keep in touch.

So now Florence pays her visit, and unannounced. And naturally she
defends herself with the story of the letter she sent from Santa Barbara,
even though she saw that it hadn't arrived until three days after her own
arrival. And of course she appears just when you've got Suky in bed sick.
I know you say guests never bother you, but it always takes a lot of one's
time to care for a sick person. I hope by now that sick person is on her
feet. It's almost a month since she came down with whatever she has.

Still the doctor doesn't want to commit himself on what's wrong with
her? After all the laboratory tests? I find that unheard-of, but apparently
you don't, since you calmly quote him as though he were Pasteur. This
sort of thing strikes me as one of the disadvantages of living in Kahului.
You can see that I'm not at home with illness. I'd much rather be ill
myself than have to cope with a sufferer.

And you, are you all right? I'm sorry that Sue's holiday had to end
this way. I hope she's already on her way back to Mount Holyoke.

In any case, I'll be waiting to hear from you. And tell me more about Florence; she's always amused me. (At a distance.)

(sent to Pamela Loeffler)

You're as bad as Suky herself, if not worse, for as far as I know you're in good health, whereas I have to assume she's still in bed, having heard nothing to the contrary. How can you let an entire month go by without sending me some sort of word? I'm not berating you, but I'm curious and blessé at the same time. I get an indistinct impression that in spite of my being what you call "obsessed" by Suky, you think I don't care deeply about her.

It's true that I don't really know her; I've never had the opportunity. But that's beside the point. I've taken on the responsibility for her education and I want it to go well. Surely you can understand that.

As I was waking up this morning (a moment when things of the distant past can suddenly reappear in detail) I recalled the opening lines of two songs my mother used to sing when I was very young. They were both songs of rejection, I now realize. One went: "Take back your gold, for gold will never buy me," and the other, even more absurd: "I don't want to play in your yard; I don't love you any more." According to her, they were both very popular ditties. Have you ever heard of either?

I'm in a hurry to get this off, because I have a forlorn hope that in the event you haven't written, my pleas will make you decide to do so. Consider this note to be one long supplication. Let me hear about Sue!

(sent to Pamela Loeffler)

Your postcard from Fiji was a slap in the face. You think I'll be "amused" to see where you are, but I'm not. I'm astounded and exasperated that you should be dragging Sue off on a South Pacific trip when she should be in college. And I don't subscribe to your theory that such a voyage is a part of her convalescence. In fact, I think you don't believe it yourself. Obviously you imagine that old age makes people ingenuous. Or was that remark merely the first pretext that came to your mind? Do you find it incredible that having invested nervous energy, time and money in her education, I should want to see her complete it?

It goes without saying that this year is lost. It strikes me as an irresponsible act to gather the girl under your wing and fly off with her to God knows where and for God knows how long.

I suppose you won't receive this for many weeks. Tell S. that I'm disappointed to see how basically indifferent she is to her own well-being. Tell her I'm glad she's well (if indeed she ever was as ill as you gave me to believe) and tell her that when she gives a sign of life I'll reply. But she probably feels guilty and doesn't want to be in touch with me.

I'll get over my shock and indignation, but it won't be right away.

(sent to Pamela Loeffler)

In the past ten weeks I've had three postcards from you: from Fiji, Apia and Papeete, plus Sue's silly attempt at humor: "Having wonderful time. Glad you're not here." Tell her that message doesn't count. (Although it does show me it was only thanks to the security she felt in your presence that she was able to express her hostility toward me.) She'll have to write me a letter if she wants to hear from me.

If you've followed the schedule you outlined on your card from Papeete, you're back at home now. I'll expect to hear from you.

I'm still at a loss to understand why you went on that senseless trip. Perhaps when you're settled again you'll feel like explaining. Or perhaps you won't. It really doesn't matter. I think I perceive the general pattern.

(sent to Pamela Loeffler)

We seem to have arrived at an impasse: mutual misunderstandings due to I.P.I. (insufficient preliminary information). You take exception to whatever I say. You're unreasonable. I get the impression that you two are arrayed against me. I can also see that S. confided in you completely, and at my expense. I did tell her you were generous, which you always have been.

My mistake with her, I think, was in advising her to destroy my letters. It was foolish because there was nothing incriminating in them, as I'm sure you're aware, having read them. But it must have set her to thinking, so that she now imagines I used her as a "pawn" in my own "financial planning." It must be clear to you that this line of reasoning is unjustified. If it's not clear, there's nothing I can do about it, and it doesn't matter.

I had a brief note from Florence—the first in at least fifteen years. She wanted me to know what a fine time she'd had with you, and how much she liked Sue. Loved the climate, the landscape, the picnics and the bathing, and incidentally had not a word to say about anyone being sick in bed. According to her you all went everywhere together, and it was perfect. This deviates considerably from the official version.

(sent to Pamela Loeffler)

A few postmortem thoughts. You can tell S. that I've written her Aunt Emily West (who became her guardian when her parents died) informing her that her niece has left college and has an address in Hawaii where she can reach her. I've also been in touch with my lawyer in New York, explaining that my financial obligations to Susan Choate terminated with the end of her academic career, and asking him to cancel whatever future arrangements he had expected to make.

As to my writing S. herself, there doesn't seem to be any reason for it. She's made it very clear that she prefers not to hear from me. And what could I say at this point? "I hope you won't regret your decision"? As you tell me, she already suspects that I disapprove of that decision, so that anything I might say would change suspicion to conviction. It would be hard to get her to believe that I have no objection to what she's doing. She probably prefers to imagine me as being scandalized by her behavior; it would be more fun for her that way. She expects me to mind that things didn't work out in the way I thought they would. But that's only because she doesn't know me. What she must consider to be my archaic epistolary style has helped her to think of me as an opinionated and uncompromising old bastard.

Nevertheless, please believe me when I tell you that she can fall in love with a Japanese garage mechanic, sleep with you, and marry an orangutan, and it will all be the same to me. There's not enough time in life for recriminations.

TANGIER 1975

I first met her just after she'd bought the big villa overlooking the valley
Saudis have it now they've got most of the good properties I remember
she asked Anton and me to tea we hadn't been married very long then
she seemed very much interested in him she'd seen him dance years ago
in Paris before his accident and they talked about those days it was all
very correct she had delicious petits fours strange how that impressed
itself on my mind of course at that time you must remember we were
frightfully poor living on the cheapest sort of food fortunately Anton
was a fantastic cook or we should have starved he knew how to make
a meal out of nothing at all I assure you well it wasn't a fortnight later
that she invited us to lunch terribly formal a large staff everything perfect
and afterward I remember we were having coffee and liqueurs beside the
fireplace and she suddenly offered us this little house she had on the
property there were several extra cottages hidden around you know guest
houses but most of them were up above nearer the big house this one was
way down in the woods far from everything except a duck pond I was
absolutely stunned it was the last thing I should have expected of her then
she took us down to see it very simple but charming tastefully furnished
and a rather primitive kitchen and bath but there were heaps of flowers
growing outside and lovely views from the windows we were enchanted
of course you understand there was nothing to pay we were simply given
the use of the house for as long as we wished I admit it was a very kind
gesture for her to make although at the time I suspected that she had her
eye on Anton I was quite wrong as it happened in any case having the
house made an enormous difference to us it was a gift from the gods there
was as a matter of fact one drawback for me Anton didn't seem to mind

333

them but there were at least twenty peacocks in an enormous aviary in the woods not far away and some nights they'd scream you know how hair-raising the sound is especially in the middle of the night it took me weeks to get used to it lying there in the dark listening to those insane screams eventually I was able to sleep through it well once we'd moved in our hostess never came near us which was her privilege naturally but it did seem a bit peculiar at least she wasn't after Anton the months went by and we never caught sight of her you see we had a key to the gate at the bottom of the estate so we always used the lower road to come and go it was much easier than climbing up past the big house so of course in order for us to see her she'd have had to come down to our part of the property but she never ventured near us time went on then all at once we began to hear from various directions a strange rumor that whenever she spoke of us she referred to us as her squatters I was all for going up and having it out with her on the spot is that why you invited us here so you could ridicule us wherever you go but Anton said I'd got no proof it could simply be the typical sort of malicious gossip that seems to be everywhere in this place he said to wait until I heard it with my own ears well clearly she wasn't likely to say it in front of me then one morning I went to take a little walk in the woods and what should I see but several freshly painted signs that had been put up along the paths all saying DEFENSE DE TOUCHER AUX FLEURS obviously they'd been put there for us there was no one else isn't it extraordinary the way people's minds work we didn't want her beastly flowers we'd never touched them I don't like cut flowers I much prefer to see them growing Anton said best pay no attention if we have words she'll put us out and he was right of course but it was very hard to take at all events you know she had lovers always natives of course what can one expect that's all right I'm not so narrow-minded I'd begrudge her that dubious pleasure but there are ways and ways of doing things you'd expect a woman of her age and breeding to have a certain amount of discretion that is she'd make everything as unnoticeable as possible but no not at all in the first place she allowed them to live with her quite as if they were man and wife and that gave them command over the servants which is unthinkable but worse she positively flourished those wretched lovers of hers in the face of the entire town never went out without the current incumbent if people didn't include him she didn't accept the invitation she was the sort of woman one couldn't imagine ever having felt embarrassment but she could have managed to live here without alienating half the Europeans you know in those days people felt strongly about such things natives couldn't even enter the restaurants it wasn't that she had lovers or even that her lovers were natives but that she appeared with them in public that was a slap in the face for the European colony and they didn't forgive it but she couldn't be bothered to care what anybody felt what I'm leading up to is the party we never caught a glimpse of her from one month to the next you understand and suddenly one day she came to call on us friendly as you please she said she had a favor to ask of us she was giving this enormous party she'd sent out two hundred invitations that had to be surrendered at the gate she said there were always too many gate-crashers at her parties the tourists would pay the guides to get them in and this time nobody was to get in excepting the ones she'd invited what she wanted us to do was to stand in a booth she'd built just outside the gate it had a little window and a counter Anton was to examine the invitations and give a sign to one of the policemen stationed outside to admit the holder I had a big ledger with all the names alphabetically listed and as Anton passed me the invitation I was to make a red check opposite the name she wanted to be sure later who had come and who hadn't I've got ten servants she said and not one of them can read or write it's discouraging then I thought of you and decided to ask this great favor of you is everything all right in your little house do you enjoy living here so of course we said oh yes everything is lovely we'd be glad to help you what fools we were it won't take long she said two hours at most it's a costume party drinks dinner and dancing by moonlight in the lower garden the musicians begin to play at half past seven after she'd gone I said to Anton two hundred invitations indeed she hasn't got twenty friends in this entire city well the night of the party came and we were up there in our little sentry box working like coolies the sweat was pouring down my back sometimes a dozen people came all together half of them already drunk and they didn't at all like having to wait and be admitted one at a time they kept arriving on and on I thought they'd never stop coming at midnight we were still there finally I told Anton this is too much I don't care who comes I'm not going to stand here another minute and Anton said you're right and he spoke to the guard and said that's it no more people are coming don't let anybody else in and good night and so on and we went down to where the party was the costumes were very elaborate we stood for a few minutes at the end of the garden watching them dancing suddenly a tall man in robes with a false beard and a big turban came up to us I had no idea who he was but Anton claimed he recognized him at once anyway it was her lover if you please she'd sent him to tell us that if we were going to come to the party would we please go and put on our costumes as if we had any costumes to put on I was staggered after getting us to stand for almost five hours in a suffocating little box she has the infernal gall to ask us to leave yes and not even the common courtesy to come and speak to us herself no she sends her native lover to do it I was starved there was plenty of food on the buffet but it was a hundred feet away from us at the other end of the garden when we got back down to our house I told Anton I hate that woman I know it's wrong but I really hate her to make things worse the next day she came down to see us again not as you might think to thank us far from that on the contrary she'd come to complain that we'd let in people who had no invitations what do you mean I cried look at the cards and look at the book they tally what are you talking about and she said the Duchesse de Saint Somethingorother was missing her evening bag where she'd put her emerald earrings and I said just what has that got to do with us will you please tell me well she said we'd left our post our post she called it as though we were in the army and after we'd gone some other people had arrived and the police let them in Anton asked if they'd presented their invitations well she said she hadn't been able to get hold of that particular policeman so she didn't know but if we'd been there it wouldn't have happened my dear lady I said do you realize we were in that booth for five hours you told us it wouldn't take more than two I hope you're aware of that well it's most unfortunate she said I've had to call in the police that made me laugh *eh bien madame* I said since according to you it was the police who let the thief in it ought to be very simple I don't see that we have anything to do with it then she raised her voice all I can say is I'm sorry I was foolish enough to count on you I shall know better another time and she went out it was then that I said to Anton look we can't go on living in this woman's house we've got to find somewhere else he was earning a little at that time working in an export-import office practically nothing but enough to pay rent on a small cottage he thought we should hang on there and hope that things would return to normal but I began to go out by myself nearly every day to look for somewhere we could move to this turned out later to have been very useful at least I'd seen a good many houses and knew which ones were possible you see the party was only the prelude to the ghastly thing that happened less than a month afterward one night some teenage hoodlums got into the big house the lover had gone to Marrakech for the weekend so she was alone yes she made the servants sleep in cabins in the upper garden she was alone in the house and you know these people they're always convinced that Europeans must have vast sums of money hidden about the premises so they tortured her all night long trying to make her tell where it was she was beaten and burned and choked and cut and both her arms were broken she must have screamed I should think but maybe they covered her face with pillows at all events no one heard a thing the maids found her in the morning she was alive but she died in hospital that afternoon we knew nothing about it until the police suddenly arrived two days later and said the property was being padlocked and everybody had to leave immediately meaning the servants and gardeners and us so out we went with all our things it was terrible but as Anton said at least we lived for more than a year without paying rent he always insisted on seeing the positive side of things in a way that was helpful later when I heard the details I was frightfully upset because you see the police traced the hooligans through a gold cigarette case and some other things they'd taken the night they tortured her and then it was discovered that they also had the Duchess's evening bag one of the criminals had arrived late the night of the party and slipped in along with a group of Spaniards after Anton and I had left the gate and of course that gave him the opportunity of examining the house and grounds for the break-in later so I felt terribly guilty of course I knew it wasn't my fault but I couldn't keep myself from thinking that if we'd only stayed on a little longer she'd still have been alive I was certain at first that the lover had had some part in it you see he never left her side she wouldn't hear of it and all at once he goes off to Marrakech for a weekend no it seemed too pat it fitted too well but apparently he had nothing to do with it besides he'd had every chance to make off with whatever he wanted and never had touched a thing so he must have been fairly intelligent at least he knew better than to bite the hand that was feeding him except that in the end he got nothing for his good behavior poor wretch I've

tried to think back to that night and sometimes it seems to me that in
my sleep maybe I did hear screams but I'd heard those blasted peacocks
so many times that I paid no attention and now it makes my blood run
cold to think that perhaps I actually did hear her calling for help and
thought it was the birds except that the big house was so far away she'd
have had to be screaming from a window that looked over the valley so
I keep telling myself I couldn't possibly have heard her they wouldn't
have let her get near a window but it's upsetting all the same

UNWELCOME WORDS

I

I'm glad you replied to my letter from the blue, although sorry to see that you imagine I think of you as a captive audience merely because you're confined to your room. Or was that said simply to make me feel guilty for having remained mobile?

Of course prices began to rise here long before the international oil blackmail of the seventies. We watched them go up, always thinking: They can't go any higher. Everything's five times as expensive as it was ten years ago. Since 1965 importation has been forbidden. So instead of imported goods we had smuggled goods, which fetched whatever people were willing to pay for them. (I suppose one should remember that prices here were incredibly low in the thirties and forties, so that they could keep on rising more or less indefinitely before they were equal to those of Europe or America. Then came the oil inflation, so that they're still going up, and still lower than other countries.)

Five years or so after independence, Christopher was talking with an old Berber somewhere in the south. In the midst of a general conversation the old man leaned toward him and said confidentially: "Tell me. How long is this Independence going to go on?"

I remember in 1947 I sent to New York for a thousand dollars. (If you care to remember, that was enough to live on for three or four months in those days, at least here.) The bank where it was supposed to have been sent didn't have it, but they advised me to try all the other banks in town. There were more than forty of them here then. I'd try two or three a day; nobody knew anything. A month later I still didn't have my money. The American Legation suggested I go to the first bank and demand it, at the same time hinting that the American Minister would take steps if

339

they failed to produce it. Magic result: the clerk went straight to a filing cabinet and pulled out the check. But I've always wondered what they hoped to gain by holding it up for such a long time. (It seemed very long to me then, and I was indignant about it.) Now things are much worse. All foreign money coming into the country is thrown into a pool in Casablanca and kept there while interest is collected from those who borrow it, generally over a period of three months. Eventually the sum shows up on your bank statement, charged at whatever was the lowest rate during that period. It's perfectly understandable considering that the war goes on and is expensive, but that doesn't lessen the inconvenience. We're probably lucky not to have to pay a special war tax, and God knows, that may yet come. Sufficient unto the day.

You ask for news about me: my daily life, what I think about, my opinions on exterior events. All in good time, if I can do it. But what happens here in the city carries much more weight than what we hear from outside. There are plenty of crimes, but each year we seem to have one murder which interests everyone. The special interest lies in the victims having been non-Moslems. This fascinates Moslems as well as infidels, although doubtless for different reasons.

For instance, two years ago, while the workmen were still building the new mosque between here and the Place de France, an elderly woman used to appear from a building across the street, carrying pots of tea and coffee to the men. She'd come early in the morning, before sunrise, when the air was still cold, and the workmen looked forward to her arrival. One day she failed to appear, and later the same day they heard that she'd been murdered in her bed. Someone had managed to climb up to her window and get into her apartment, and before leaving he had prudently cut her throat. He'd expected to find hidden money (which, the woman being Jewish, he naturally assumed he'd unearth somewhere). But she lived in poverty; he found nothing but a blue plastic transistor radio, and he took it. After that, although the workmen got no more tea or coffee, they had music from the blue transistor, but only for a few days. A neighbor of the murdered woman noticed the radio there among the mounds of tiles, and was so certain she had recognized it that she mentioned it to a policeman in the street. So of course they caught the workman, who said he wouldn't have cut the old Jewess's throat if he'd known how poor she was!

Then there was the case, last year, of the two old Americans (I don't think you ever knew them) who lived in a small house high up on the Old Mountain, at the very end of the navigable road, where it turns into what's left of the Roman road. They were truly isolated there, without a telephone or another house in sight. So after several decades of living up there in peace, they were suddenly attacked. The husband was in the garden at the edge of the woods, filling a ditch with water. The attackers felled him and pushed his head into the ditch. The wife saw everything through the window before they went into the house and beat her up, trying to make her tell where "the money" was hidden. (These people were penniless, living on their Social Security checks.) There was no money, so after landing a few more kicks in the woman's face, the marauders went on their way. The husband died; the wife survived. The incident alarmed the Europeans living on the Old Mountain Road, all of whom have large properties and are already guarded by night watchmen; the muggers chose the old couple precisely because they were unprotected, and of course got nothing at all out of it. The grapevine claims that the criminals were caught about two months later. They were part of a gang that lived in a cave on the coast to the west. But who knows? These things are taken more seriously by the European residents than food riots and battles with the so-called Polisario in the Sahara. The bridge-table mentality, if you'll pardon the slur.

So anyway, that's that for now.

II

Good that we're back in touch.

You're wrong; I do remember the last time we saw each other. You were living in that crazy apartment on the roof of the castle, and there was a terrible wind coming from the harbor. You had a few people there for dinner, and I remember the door onto the roof being opened and the wind blowing through the entire flat, so that everyone was calling out: Shut the door! What the precise year was, I don't know, because the episode seems to have no context. The only other detail I recall is your remark that you couldn't read anything written after the eighteenth century. I accepted it as a personal idiosyncrasy; since then I've thought about it, wondering how healthy such a self-imposed stricture is for a twentieth-century author. Is it that you don't read contemporary writing any longer in order to escape from its possibly pernicious influence, or that any contact with present-day fiction is repugnant to you because it suggests the idea of competition? Of course your reasons for excluding the nineteenth century remain unexplained in any case. Although in music I could easily make a similar sweeping statement, relegating to oblivion all the music of the nineteenth century. But that kind of generalization is never fruitful, it seems to me, and I wonder how closely you adhere to your dictum.

Half the time I haven't even been sure where you were during these past fifteen years or so. Through others I heard you'd been living in Hong Kong, Tokyo and even Malaysia. (There was a town there which you were said to be fond of, but I can't remember its name. On the east coast, and fairly far north.) Once you'd got out of the habit of writing to me, you no longer knew where to write, which is understandable. The excuse applies even more strongly to me, since you had no fixed residence, whereas I always had a home base.

I needn't ask you if you remember Betty and Alec Howe, since they were your bridge and canasta partners, along with all the other residents I avoided knowing for years. Both of them died ten days or so ago; who knows of what? He first, and she a few days later. Smina is convinced that Betty did herself in so as not to have to go through Alec's funeral. She could be right; I never knew the Howes except at parties and in the market. I suspect you won't bemoan their passing.

And of course there's the incredible Valeska. She's been back here several times since you have, although not in the past five years or so. Abdelouahaïd conceived a strong dislike for her, mainly because she steadfastly refused to sit in the front seat of the Mustang, even though it was the only comfortable passenger's seat in the car. Her insistence upon riding in back rubbed him the wrong way, since he assumed, and probably quite correctly, that she wanted to make it clear to the public that he was the chauffeur. This basic antipathy made it easy for him to criticize other facets of her behavior. This he constantly did to me, but of course not to her. Then one day he found his chance and sprang. The result was so insane that I couldn't upbraid him afterwards as I should have.

On the days when I went to fetch Valeska at the hotel she always sat by a table in the courtyard, reading, doing crossword puzzles or whatever, but very busy. Abdelouahaïd would drive right up to the head of the stairs so she couldn't help seeing us, and she always glanced up once, so that it was certain she'd noticed. For some reason I couldn't fathom, she never budged until I got out of the car and went down into the courtyard and crossed it and stood within a foot of her table. This was a sacred rite. One day I stayed at home and sent Abdelouahaïd for her. When she saw him going down into the courtyard she jumped up and followed him up to the car, he said, asking again and again: "Where's Paul? Where's Paul?"

At this point Satan must have arrived and prompted Abdelouahaïd to look at the ground and say sadly: "Paul's dead." You'll be able to imagine the screeches and squawks that followed on this announcement. He helped her into the car and they set off for Itesa. As you know, he doesn't speak English, but he knew enough words to convey to her that I was lying on the floor, and that people were standing around looking at me.

He said that as they got to the Plaza del Kuweit, Valeska suddenly cried out: "Oh Christ! My camera's at the hotel. Never mind. Go on."

She was literally hysterical when she saw me, safe and sound, and I thought: This is too much, and saw myself taking her to Beni Makada to the psychiatrist. Then she wheeled and shrieked at Abdelouahaïd: "You son of a bitch!"

I don't think she's ever forgiven him for his joke, but he's still delighted by the memory of it. As I say, I couldn't bring myself to criticize him, since in a way he did it for me, thinking that she might change her behavior as a result. But naturally it changed nothing, she considering it merely an arbitrary action by a crazy Arab who was curious to see how she'd react.

They're building fancy villas all around me. They're well built but hideous, and look like old-fashioned juke boxes, their façades plastered with wrought iron and tile work. Each one is required by law to have a chimney, but in no case is the chimney connected with anything inside the house, being purely decorative. The builders are waiting for buyers who don't arrive. Will they ever? The prices seem very high: between $125,000 and $200,000, and there's no heat, of course—no furnace, no fireplaces—and often no space outside for a garden. Yet it's that space which determines whether they're to be considered officially villas, or merely houses (which don't have to have chimneys).

I hope all's well with you, and that you'll reply.

III

I've made it an objective to write you regularly if not frequently, to keep you in touch with this section of the outside world; it may help to aerate your morale. Clearly the only way to give you an idea of my life is for me to write whatever comes into my head. In the conscious selection of material to include, there is the possibility of imposing a point of view, a *parti pris*. I think my procedure will give you a more accurate picture of my daily life—at least, that part of it which goes on inside my head, by far the most important part.

I've often imagined being in your unenviable situation in the event of a fire or an earthquake. Not to be able to get out of your bed and try to run to safety. Or if you're in your wheelchair, not to be able to go anywhere in it save up and down the corridors. I think that would be my main preoccupation, but again, maybe it wouldn't, since one doesn't live in constant expectation of fires and earthquakes. But I can see myself lying awake at night imagining in detail what it would be like to be asphyxiated by smoke or suddenly flung to the floor with a girder on top of my legs and the dust of plaster choking me. I hope you don't do that, and I somehow doubt that you do. By now you must have become enough of a fatalist to be able to consider all objective phenomena as concomitants of your condition. If that's the case, it may be partially due to your having had to put up for eight years with an impossible wife—a kind of training for the ultimate attainment of a state of total acceptance. At the same time it has occurred to me that the constant presence of a woman like Pamela may easily have augmented the tension which led eventually to the stroke. You suffered unnecessarily for those eight years. Pamela was a racist. She felt she operated on a higher level than yours because she was aware that three hundred years ago her ancestors were living in Massachusetts, whereas yours were living in some benighted region of the Ukraine. "We were here first, so of course it's ours, but we love to have you here, because it makes life more interesting." Am

344

I wrong, or was Pamela like that? Weren't you always aware of a profound contradiction between what she said and the way she acted? At this great remove, I don't remember her very well. That is to say, her face escapes me; I can't project an image of it. I do remember her voice however. It was beautifully modulated and a pleasure to listen to, except when she was angry. This was to be expected: one purposely changes one's voice and delivery as a means of communicating one's emotion. Yet now I have to ask: was Pamela *ever* angry? When I replay the mental tape I have of the breakfast in Quito (in that crazy ice-cream parlor with the balcony where they served food) I hear those trenchant staccato phrases of hers not as expressions of annoyance but as orders being given to an inferior. They had the desired effect: you shrank into your shell and said no more. Everything was delightful as long as there was no resistance; then commands had to be issued.

The truth is that for two or three decades I haven't thought of her at all. I thought of her this morning only because I was trying, from what I knew of your life, to imagine possible causes of a cerebral lesion. I admit that after the fact it's of purely academic interest. The autopsy doesn't cure the patient.

After I woke up this morning I recalled a silly song I heard as a child, when it was sung to me by a woman named Ethel Robb. (I don't know who she was, but I seem to remember that she was a schoolteacher.) The words struck me as so strange that I learned them by heart.

> In der vintertime ven der valley's green
> And der vind blows along der vindowsill
> Den der vomen in der vaudeville
> Ride der velocipedes around der vestibule.

(The melody was a variant of "Ach, du lieber Augustin.") Surely you never heard the song. I wonder if anyone ever did, outside Miss Robb's circle of acquaintances.

The early twenties was the time for absurd lyrics: witness "Oh by Jingo," "The Ogo Pogo," "Lena was the Queen of Palestina," "Yes, We Have No Bananas," "Barney Google" and God knows what else. There was also a Fanny Brice song called "Second-Hand Rose," which got me into trouble with the mother of my hostess when I sang it at a party here in the sixties. She paid no attention to: "Even the piano in the parlor Papa bought for ten cents on the dollar." But when I got to "Even Abie Cohen, that's the boy I adore, had the nerve to tell me he'd been married before," the lady jumped up and ran across to the divan where I was sitting. She seized my face between her thumb and fingers and squeezed, crying: "Even you, Paul Bowles, even you?" It was all so sudden and dramatic that I felt I'd committed a major solecism. Fortunately there were other guests who knew the song, and they were able to convince her that I hadn't been extemporizing for the occasion, although she didn't seem completely mollified.

I think the most important characteristic you and I have in common (although you'd be within your rights in claiming that we have no points at all in common) is a conviction that the human world has entered into a terminal period of disintegration and destruction, and that this will end in a state of affairs so violent and chaotic as to make any attempts at maintaining government or order wholly ineffective. I've always found you excoriating the decay of civilization even more vehemently than I. This of course was when the worst we could imagine was destruction by nuclear warfare. But now we can imagine conditions under which sudden death by fire might be a welcome release from the inferno of life; we might long for a universal euthanasia. Can we *hope* for nuclear war—I mean ethically—or are we bound out of loyalty to wish for the continuation of the human species at no matter what costs in suffering? I used the word "ethical" because it seems to me that unethical desires are bound to engender false conclusions.

I suppose what is at the bottom of my mind in all this is that I'm curious to know whether being totally incapacitated has altered your point of view in any way. Has it left you angrier, more resigned, or entirely indifferent? (Although that you never were, under any circumstances, so that I doubt the likelihood of such a major alteration in personality.) I have a feeling that you may consider these things a purely private matter, and as a result may resent my prurient probing.

IV

I can see that you don't really remember the weekend you referred to earlier. There's nothing shameful about not having total recall: still, it seems doubly unfortunate that you should have been deprived of both external *and* internal mobility: I mean the freedom to wander in the past, to explore the closets of memory. I know, it was forty years ago and you say you don't remember, that all three of us were so drunk none of us could possibly recall the details of that absurd excursion. But neither you nor I was drunk when we arrived in the village (and had to get off the train because that was as far as they'd built the railroad). It was still daylight, and we crossed the river on that unfinished bridge to get to the so-called hotel. Surely you remember that there was nothing to drink but mescal; you kept saying that it smelled like furniture polish, which as I recall it did. Have you ever drunk any since? And what a night, with Bartolomé sitting there getting drunker and drunker and giggling his head off. And at one point (search well—you *must* remember this) the mosquito net over my bed collapsed onto my head so that I was swathed in folds of netting, and the dust made me sneeze, and Bartolomé in his chair pointed at me while I struggled, and cried: *Pareces al Niño Dios!* And you and he laughed interminably while I sneezed and flailed my arms, trying to find an opening in the net. By then there was nothing to do but send Bartolomé down for another bottle of Tehuacan and go on drinking our mescal. I think it was he who finally extricated me from the netting. I admit that you were more or less intoxicated, but certainly not enough so to have drawn a blank. All that was fun, and belongs on the credit side of the ledger. As usual, however, I was more conscious of the unpleasant details than of all the amusement. The next day was eternal. It was agony to be on that plunging rattletrap little train, and I looked with loathing at the miles of cactus on the parched hillsides. Each jolt of the train increased the pounding in my head. Bartolomé slept. You seemed to have no hangover, for which I felt some bitterness; but then, you were used to alcohol and I was not. But since you say you don't remember, I'm left alone with the memory; I might as well have dreamed it all.

Sometimes I suspect you of exaggerating your present deficiencies, not, certainly, to evoke pity, since that would be unlike you, and besides, the desire to exaggerate is probably unconscious in its origin. Nevertheless, you do emphasize your unfortunate situation, so that one can't help feeling sorry for you. The question is: Why do you italicize your misfortune? My feeling is that it's simply out of bitterness. I feel you thinking: Now I'm in a wheelchair. That's that, and that's what the world wanted. In other words, *they* have done it to you. If only you were religious you could blame it on God, or wouldn't that be any more satisfactory?

As I remember, you're not particularly fond of animals. I've always been an ailurophile myself as opposed to a dog-lover. It seemed to me there'd be time enough later to make friends with the canines. Here there's not much likelihood of that. At night they're out in packs, and sometimes attack passersby in the street. A sextet of them chased an American friend for a quarter of a mile one evening along the new road that goes from the foot of the Old Mountain to the new section of Dradeb. When one particular dog gets to be a continuous sleep-disturber I've twice resorted to drastic measures. It would be better to describe the drastic measures, I realize, than let you think that I poisoned the beasts. Naturally that was the first thing that occurred to me, but I decided against it because of the suffering it causes. Also, the symptoms of death from rat poison (the only lethal product I'd have been able to find here) are so classical that the owner of the animal would immediately suspect that his watchdog had been poisoned. My system with the first brute, which used to bark all night from the garden next door, was time-consuming but effective. It involved my staying up half the night for a week in my wait for a completely deserted street. About half past one I would go to the kitchen and prepare the half pound of raw hamburger. One night I would mix Melleril and Largactyl with the meat, the following night I would grind up several tablets of Anafranil. I continued the alternation until the dog's owner decided it was rabid, and had it shot. There was no more barking after the first night of treatment. This seemed the most humane way of getting rid of the animal.

Another year a bitch whelped in the garage, which is always open. The night watchman gave her a carton to lie in with her pups. When these had been given away, she remained in the garage, encouraged by an eccentric Ethiopian woman who sent her maid at all hours with food for

her. As soon as she felt thoroughly at home in the garage, she began to
engage in long-distance conversations with friends in Ain Hayani and
Dradeb. I complained about this to Abdelouahaïd; I thought he might
have a solution. He had a very simple one. He picked up the bitch and
put her into the boot of the car. We drove to the Forêt Diplomatique,
to the edge of the beach, where there's a restaurant run by a Moroccan
with a crew of dogs. Before letting her out of the boot, Abdelouahaïd
turned the Mustang around, to be able to start up quickly. She stood on
the beach for a second, bewildered; the other dogs saw her and came to
investigate. While they surrounded her Abdelouahaïd started up, and we
escaped, even though I saw her running behind the car for a good distance
as we drove through the woods. She wasn't stupid: as soon as she heard
the motor she pushed the other dogs aside and rushed toward the car.

Something has happened to the Moroccans. Fifty years ago dogs were
execrated. Only people living in the country owned them. Too dirty to
live in the city. Somehow they noticed that practically all French women
went into the street accompanied by dogs on leashes, and gradually began
to imitate them. At first it was boys leading curs by ropes which they
tied tightly around the animals' necks. French ladies passing by would be
indignant. *Mais ce pauvre chien! Tu vas l'étrangler!* Now every Moroccan
child in neighborhoods such as mine has a canine pet. Most are German
shepherds: fathers think they provide better protection.

The French are unpredictable. Last month a young photographer from
Paris was here taking pictures for *Libération.* The only thing which
moved him to exclamations of surprise was the size of a peanut-butter
jar full of birdseed. Is that authentic? he wanted to know. Do they really
sell such large jars of peanut butter? When I said yes, I'm not sure he
didn't suspect me of pulling his leg, as he went across the room and
examined it carefully. Merry Christmas.

V

Someone sent me a box of American chocolate creams last week. On the
cover are the words *Home Fashioned.* On another facet of the same cover
is a list of ingredients included in the home-fashioning. Among these are:
invert sugar, partially hydrogenated vegetable oils, sorbitol, lecithin,

butylated hydroxytoluene, butylated hydroxyanisole, propyl gallate, potassium sorbate, sulphur dioxide and benzoate of soda. Even the most modern home isn't likely to have all these delicacies in its kitchen. Although I haven't been in an American kitchen in many years, I know that they're inclined to look more and more like laboratories. Perhaps by now they have chemical cabinets stocked with everything from triethylene glycol to metoclopramide.

The kitchens in farmhouses at the time of the First World War were not too pleasant to be in either, as I remember, in spite of all the propaganda romanticizing them. There were mingled odors of sour milk, dill and iron from the well water. Spirals of flypaper hung from every convenient hook, and the flies still buzzed on all sides. If there were dogs, they smelled. If there were children, they smelled. It was unbelievable that serious people should want to live that way. What's the matter with them? Nothing. They just don't know any better, that's all. This answer never satisfied me. It implied a double standard that made it possible for my parents to overlook these people's shortcomings. But they never forgave *me* for not knowing something I ought to know, and the severity was applied precisely because I was not a farm boy. Seventy years ago there existed that class difference between those brought up in the city and those brought up on the farm. Now there seems to be very little distinction made. The concept of class has been carefully destroyed. Either you have money or you don't. The result of democracy, I suppose, when it's misunderstood to mean similarity rather than equality.

You couldn't have known the typical small, medium-priced hotel of Paris in the twenties. (By the time you got to Paris, after the Second World War, things had changed somewhat.) There were only three or four rooms per floor, the staircases and corridors were heavily carpeted and the windows were hidden by two sets of curtains. Normally there were two lights in the room, one hanging from the center of the ceiling and the other above the bed's headboard. Both were affixed to a system of pulleys, so that they could be propelled upward or downward according to the needs of the moment. The wallpaper was always dark with wide stripes in colors which might at one time have been garish, although there was no way of knowing, since the patina of age had long since darkened them. It was easy to feel encased and protected in those rooms, and I often dream about them even now. Such dreams however aren't pleasant, since I seem always to be on the point of having to leave in order to let someone else move in. No dream without at least subliminal anxiety.

Incidentally, you have no reason to upbraid me for not giving my specific reactions to your most recent tale of woe. Such reactions can only be emotional in content, and there's never any point in expressing emotions in words, it seems to me. I assure you, nevertheless, that I experienced a feeling of profound chagrin when I read your letter and realized that you were undergoing further torments, and I thought I'd conveyed that impression earlier.

You may remember (although probably not, since you never crack a book written in our century) a phrase used by the Castor in *La Nausée:* *"Je me survis."* (Ineptly translated in the American edition as "I outlive myself.") I understand the Castor's feeling of being her own survivor; it's not unlike my feeling, save that I'd express mine as: *"Ma vie est posthume."* Do you make sense of that?

I've often wished that someone would rewrite the end of *Huckleberry Finn,* delivering it from the farcical closing scenes which Twain, probably embarrassed by the lyrical sweep of the nearly completed book, decided were necessary if the work were to be appreciated by American readers. It's the great American novel, damaged beyond repair by its author's senseless sabotage. I'd be interested to have your opinion, or do you feel that the book isn't worth having an opinion about, since a botched masterpiece isn't a masterpiece at all? Yet to counterfeit the style successfully, so that the break would be seamless and the prose following it a convincing continuation of what came before—that seems an impossible task. So I shan't try it, myself.

I think a warning sign of creeping senility is the shortening of the attention span, which strikes me as a form of regression to childhood. We'll see.

VI

I haven't mentioned the mounting hostility I've noted in your letters because I've assumed that it was directed at the world in general, and not at me. Now I see how mistaken I was. First you tell me that my letters are self-indulgent. I let that pass: it was merely a criticism of my method. But I can't overlook the word "gloating." On seeing that, I realize that I'd have done better to limit my correspondence to one necessarily cruel *Get Well* card, and let it go at that.

It seems to me that for this final period of your life it might be profitable to stop encouraging your masochistic tendencies. I can see that you don't feel that way at all, and that on the contrary you intend to go on giving free rein to them. Too bad. There's obviously nothing I can do from here to help you, so I may as well let it rest. But as you sink into your self-imposed non-being, I hope you'll remember (you won't) that I made this small and futile attempt to help you remain human.

Hasta el otro mundo, as Rosa Lopez used to say.

BOOKS BY
PAUL BOWLES

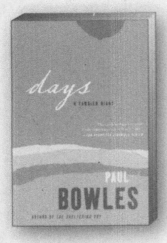

DAYS
A Tangier Diary
ISBN 0-06-113736-7
(paperback)

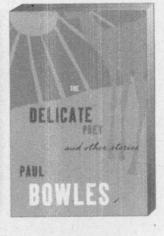

**THE DELICATE
PREY**
And Other Stories
ISBN 0-06-113734-0
(paperback)

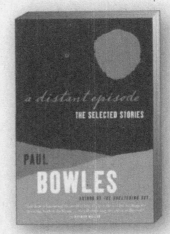

**A DISTANT
EPISODE**
The Selected Stories
ISBN 0-06-113738-3
(paperback)

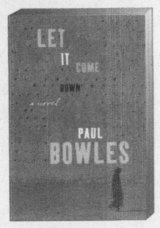

**LET IT COME
DOWN**
A Novel
ISBN 0-06-113739-1
(paperback)

POINTS IN TIME
Tales From Morocco
ISBN 0-06-113963-7
(paperback)

**THE SHELTERING
SKY**
A Novel
ISBN 0-06-083482-X
(paperback)